5

An author of more than ninety books for children and adults (seventy-five for Harlequin), **Janice Kay Johnson** writes about love and family—about the way generations connect and the power our earliest experiences have on us throughout life. A USA TODAY bestselling author and an eight-time finalist for a Romance Writers of America RITA® Award, she won a RITA® Award in 2008 for her Harlequin Superromance novel Snowbound. A former librarian, Janice raised two daughters in a small town north of Seattle, Washington.

Books by Janice Kay Johnson

Harlequin Superromance

Plain Refuge
A Mother's Claim

Brothers, Strangers

The Baby He Wanted
The Closer He Gets

Because of a Girl
The Baby Agenda
Bone Deep
Finding Her Dad
All That Remains
Making Her Way Home
No Matter What
A Hometown Boy
To Love a Cop

Two Daughters

Yesterday's Gone
In Hope's Shadow

Visit the Author Profile page
at Harlequin.com for more titles.

USA TODAY BESTSELLING AUTHOR

JANICE KAY JOHNSON

Amish Hideout and Her Amish Protectors

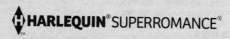

HARLEQUIN® SUPERROMANCE®

ISBN-13: 978-1-335-14503-1

Amish Hideout and Her Amish Protectors

Amish Hideout previously published as
Plain Refuge

Copyright © 2017 by Harlequin Books S.A.

Recycling programs
for this product may
not exist in your area.

The publisher acknowledges the copyright holder
of the individual works as follows:

Plain Refuge
Copyright © 2017 by Janice Kay Johnson

Her Amish Protectors
Copyright © 2017 by Janice Kay Johnson

CONTENTS

AMISH HIDEOUT

Dear Reader,

I confess: I'm a longtime fan of Marta Perry's and Karen Harper's romantic suspense novels set among the Amish. And then there's the movie *Witness*, with Harrison Ford dancing in the barn. Temptation came my way. I became even more intrigued once I started reading nonfiction about the Amish, notably Donald Kraybill's collaborations *The Amish* and *Amish Grace*. I found a whole lot to admire in beliefs that are very different from what we see in our typical lives. Forgiveness is not a concept we practice nearly often enough, for example. Their sense of community is extraordinary. Keeping their elderly close and caring for them through the end especially struck home with me, as I'm dealing with my mother's sharp decline into dementia.

Plus, I have always loved the clash of cultures. In this first book, both Daniel and Rebecca are steeped in Amish culture because of their childhoods, yet as adults are thoroughly modern Americans. Raised to turn his other cheek, Daniel now carries a gun. Talk about internal conflict! Yet, Rebecca's need to save her son drives her to do what she thinks she must, even if it betrays her deepest beliefs.

Janice

CHAPTER ONE

"DECIDED TO BOLT with your cut of the money, did you?" asked Detective Ray Estevez, his manner as insulting as his words.

Rebecca Gregory stared in disbelief at the man she had allowed into her apartment. Had he just accused her of being complicit in a crime? Thank goodness Matthew wasn't home! At five, her son was too young to understand the accusation, but he'd have picked up on the tone. Would Detective Estevez have bothered to restrain himself with a child in earshot?

"Or do you and Stowe plan to hook up once the investigation goes cold?" he continued, dark eyes flat and mouth curling in what she took for contempt.

Rebecca stiffened. What a creep. Steven Stowe, her former husband's business partner, had disappeared after embezzling millions of dollars from their construction firm. Why would this detective imagine for a minute that she had conspired with Steven, or had anything but the most distant relationship with him?

"I have never so much as had lunch with Steven Stowe without Tim present," she said icily.

"Yeah? Then why'd you leave your husband?"

Managing to meet his stare, she said, "That is between Tim and me." And, really, her marriage was irrelevant to any investigation, even though the separation had been precipitated by the tension surrounding the embezzlement.

In retrospect, she knew their marriage had already been in trouble when, several months ago, Tim's behavior changed. She knew now that he'd been hit by mysterious and crippling financial problems in the construction firm he had founded with Steven and another partner, Josh Griffen. Then, all she'd known was that the ridiculous hours he worked stretched even longer. He seldom bothered to spend time with his wife and son and brushed off her concern. Worried, frustrated, occasionally angry, he refused to even acknowledge there *was* a problem, not to her. In fact, he'd shut her out so completely it became obvious she held no meaningful role in his life. Increasingly, she saw that he had never really talked to her, not the way her parents had to each other.

Rebecca had taken her wedding vows seriously. She had sworn to stick with him through these troubles. So she'd kept quiet and made excuses to their five-year-old son when he asked why Daddy was mad or never home.

Except then one of the three partners vanished and it came out that he'd embezzled a great deal of money. Tim's reaction? Not grief at the betrayal committed by a friend. Oh, no. The day after the news of Steven's disappearance hit the *San Francisco Chronicle*, Tim had bounded into the house in a great mood, swung her in a circle and ebulliently told her they wouldn't have to worry about money ever again.

She had looked at him and thought, *I don't understand or know who you are, this man who is relieved, even joyous, because his partner and friend has fled with millions of dollars.* As if that solved all his problems.

She could no longer love a stranger whose ethics she doubted.

But she didn't *know* anything. And she couldn't understand what had precipitated the lead investigator to grill *her*.

"Funny timing to leave your husband," he shot back.

She had to say something. "Tim had been under stress for months while he and Josh and Steven tried to understand what was wrong. That…exacerbated our issues." Wonderful. She sounded like a marriage counselor or a self-help book.

Estevez tipped the chair back, letting her know not so subtly that he had settled in and would stay as long as he felt inclined. "When did he explain the problems at work?"

"The day after Steven disappeared."

He let out a bark of laughter. "You expect me to believe that? You were living with the guy!"

She had been, and it still hurt, remembering how unimportant she'd been to the man who was supposed to love her. Rebecca would be ashamed of herself for staying as long as she had with him, given the way he treated her, but she had been raised to believe marriage was forever. Despite the months of estrangement, if she had been sure he really loved her, she could have forgiven a lot.

Now, she raised her eyebrows. "Believe me or not, it's the truth."

"You're a cool one, aren't you?" He did not sound admiring.

Detective Estevez was of average height, but he was built like a bull, his neck thick, his shoulders powerful. He kept asking questions to which she had no answers.

His temper heated. He slammed the legs of the chair back on the floor and planted his forearms on the table so he could lean forward until his sneering face filled her field of vision. He shouted. He wondered aloud what would happen to her kid when she went to prison.

But she couldn't tell him what she didn't know. She didn't have the money; she had never felt close to either of Tim's partners, even though one or the other had dined at the house every few weeks until those last months, when she scarcely saw them.

"You're wasting your time," she said.

He snapped, "*I'll* decide that."

When he ran out of questions, he glared at her for what had to be a full minute. Rebecca laced her trembling fingers on her lap and stared back at him with the pretense of composure.

At last he shoved himself to his feet, eyes narrowed. After flinging a business card on the table, he said, "I'll be watching you."

She didn't respond—didn't move—until she heard the apartment door close behind him.

And then she hugged herself and tried to understand why Detective Estevez *had* wasted time on her when Steven Stowe was the embezzler.

FOUR MONTHS LATER, Rebecca let herself into this house for what she prayed would be the last time. Their house—Tim's house now. No, she'd be here to drop off Matthew for visits or pick him up, but that would be different.

And visits were all that Matthew's stays with his father would be. With resolve, she buried the whiff of fear that she would lose their custody battle.

Once she closed and locked the front door behind her, the silence was so complete that her footsteps on the marble floor of the foyer seemed to echo. Something about that silence gave her goose bumps, even though she had expected the house to be empty. Housekeeping staff had always been part-time.

As Rebecca walked from room to room, she marveled that she'd ever called this place home. Tim had been so excited about building it for them that she'd had to be careful about what she said. He'd ignored her gentle suggestions. An architectural magazine had run a feature on it because the design and function were cutting-edge. Naturally, the finest materials were used. It had just never come to feel homey to her. How could it, with six bedrooms, five bathrooms? To her, it felt like living in a hotel.

Would Tim have listened if she'd spoken out more strongly from the beginning? Rebecca smiled sadly. She could only imagine his expression if she'd said, *"For God resisteth the proud, and giveth grace to the humble."* She had strayed so far from her roots that she couldn't remember the whole quote, but knew there was something about clothing yourself in humility, too.

Pride, Tim understood. Humility wouldn't be a virtue in his eyes.

There was so much she hadn't let herself see when she'd foolishly fallen in love.

In the most recent meeting held at a law firm with both their attorneys present, Tim had told her to take anything from the house she wanted. Typical, she'd thought, feeling a mix of amusement and annoyance. He couldn't look stingy in front of the attorneys. Once he had understood really, truly, that reconciliation wasn't an option—something which had taken months—he'd been generous with financial settlements, as well as the small things.

His generosity had ended when it came to their son. Tim's father, Robert Gregory, was a cold man who too often expressed astonishment that his son had made anything of himself. Whatever had happened between Tim and her, she still detested her father-in-law for what his disdain had done to his own child. Unfortunately, Robert thought Tim had done one thing right— he'd sired a handsome, smart son to carry on the family name. *Divorce* wasn't a word Robert wanted to hear. He couldn't have a dynasty if he didn't have a firm grip on his grandson.

Rebecca had a very bad feeling that Tim's demand for joint custody was only the beginning. Her attorney supported her decision to fight for primary custody. No reasonable person could think a five-year-old boy should live half the time with a parent who routinely worked seventy- to eighty-hour weeks and rarely took a weekend off.

Her gut feeling was that Tim agreed, but he couldn't back down without facing his father's contempt. And so their current standoff continued.

Temporarily blocking her worries, she focused on her current task. She was here, so she should get this over with.

She walked quickly through the ground floor, surveying the ultramodern furniture, which had never been to her taste. Even though the apartment she had rented was still scantily furnished, she didn't want anything from here.

She did miss her exceptionally well-equipped kitchen,

so she might raid the cupboards. The fine china or crystal goblets and wineglasses had mostly been given as wedding gifts, and she couldn't imagine using any of them.

Cooking utensils were another matter. She selected a couple of favorite pans and tools and carried them to the box she had left in the foyer. She didn't bother with Tim's office, where she had rarely been invited. Thanks to staff, she hadn't even entered it to clean.

A quick scan of Matthew's bedroom assured her that she'd left only enough toys and books to allow him to feel at home during his weekends with his father. Everything important had already been packed up and brought to her new apartment.

The master bedroom was last. Rebecca was confident she had taken all her clothes and shoes. She had left behind most of the jewelry Tim had given her. She would never wear it again.

There was only one piece she would like to keep— the necklace that had been Tim's gift their first Christmas together. The pendant was simple and lovely, an eighteen-karat gold heart studded with sapphires. They were the color of her eyes, he had told her before gently kissing her. It wouldn't have been cheap, but neither was it extravagant and ostentatious like his later gifts. It would give her one memory to hold on to.

Tim had had a small safe built into his walk-in closet, hidden by stacked hemp storage boxes. Mostly, her jewelry had been kept in this safe rather than the larger one in his office. He'd always insisted on getting the jewelry out for her, but she had seen him dial the combination and remembered it. She doubted he would even notice that she had taken one necklace.

She moved a few boxes and dialed, and a moment later the safe door opened silently. She looked for the small blue box she kept the pendant in, but a surprising flash of red caught her eye. This was a ring, but massive and clearly masculine. Tim never wore rings. Stranger yet, a black leather wallet sat next to it.

Puzzled, she reached for the ring, lifting it out into better light.

Harvard University.

Steven Stowe, embezzler, had worn a ring just like this. An irritated Tim had claimed his partner wore it to flaunt his Ivy League education. Tim and the third partner, Josh Griffen, had graduated from a state university. She had thought they were being unfair. Steven didn't talk about his past much, but she'd heard enough to know he had grown up in lousy circumstances. Making it to Harvard had to have been hugely symbolic to him. The sad part was that his mother had walked out when he was only a kid, and his dad had died of cirrhosis of the liver something like ten years ago. With no siblings, there wasn't anyone left to be awed at his accomplishment.

Rebecca had wondered before whether his background explained why he'd been so desperate for wealth that he had been willing to betray his partners.

Her forehead crinkled as she set the ring back down.

What was she thinking? Of course this couldn't be Steven's! When he'd taken off with the money he'd stolen, he wouldn't have left his treasured class ring behind. And they knew he wasn't dead, because he'd been using his debit and credit cards on occasion, staying constantly on the move. Tim had told her the police hadn't blocked his accounts so that they could trace his movements.

But dread formed anyway, making Rebecca reluctant to pick up the slim billfold. Her hands had become blocks of wood and her chest felt compressed, as if there was something wrong with the air in here. *I don't want to open this.*

But the glow of the ruby was impossible to ignore. *Just do it,* she told herself, and flipped the wallet open.

Steven A. Stowe's face looked at her from his driver's license. His *current* driver's license. One by one, she pulled the debit card and four credit cards from their slots. None of them had passed their expiration dates, either.

But…he was *using* his cards. That was how the police knew—

A whimper escaped her before she could stifle it. Steven wasn't using them at all—Tim was. He traveled enough for business that it had never occurred to her to associate his trips with the times Steven had supposedly cropped up in Southern California. But maybe the investigators had.

Aghast, she thought about the huge risk Tim had been taking when he'd used someone else's credit card for cash advances and large purchases. Except… She gazed at the driver's-license photo. Tim and Steven did look a lot alike. People had always thought so. No one glancing at the awful driver's-license photo would have questioned his identity, especially not when the man presenting it dressed well and had a smile that said he was trustworthy. And, of course, he could present other ID.

Rebecca dropped the billfold onto a shelf as if the leather had singed her fingers.

Her almost ex-husband wouldn't have the wallet, credit cards and, most of all, that ring if Steven was still alive. So Tim knew he was dead...and had a stake in keeping the police chasing a man they believed to be alive and on the run.

And Tim was *happy* that Steven was dead. She couldn't forget that.

Panting, Rebecca ran head-on into a terrible dilemma. Did she ensure Matthew's father went to prison by giving these to that horrible detective? Tim might not have had anything to do with the death. *Knowing* Steven was dead wasn't the same thing. It could have been an accident. And his first instinct would be to protect the company.

She wished as she hadn't in years that she could talk to her mother. But she knew what *Mamm* would expect of her. *"Pray,"* she would have said. *"Ask God what the right course is for you to take."*

Only, Rebecca's faith had been worn down by life with a nonbeliever, by the modernity surrounding her. What her mother, raised Amish, really assumed was that prayer would open her heart, where God's will would be revealed to her.

She wasn't sure she'd recognize God's will if it appeared in letters of fire in front of her, not anymore.

What if she pretended she had never opened the safe? Tim would never know.

Billfold still in her hand, Rebecca was already shaking her head. At least if none of the cards were ever used again, the police would start looking harder at the possibility Steven was dead, wouldn't they? So, in a way, if she took these things she'd be doing the right thing while not betraying a man she'd once loved. Who *was* a good father, when he found time to spend with his son.

Heart hammering in her chest, Rebecca made her decision. She took the ring out of the safe again and replaced the hemp organizers. Then she rushed downstairs to stow the wallet and ring in her purse, and hurried for the front door.

Which opened just before she reached it.

"Shopping?" her husband said snidely.

A WEEK LATER, Tim arrived at the apartment to pick up Matthew. Playground and burgers, he'd promised.

The moment Rebecca let him in, she recoiled and took a couple of cautious steps back. He was waxen beneath his tan, his eyes wild and his forehead beaded with sweat.

"Dad!" Matthew yelled, and came galloping down the hall.

Taking a couple strides inside, Tim snarled at him. "I need to talk to your mother. Go to your room and shut the door."

Vibrating with shock, Matthew stared at his father. Then, with a muffled sob, he whirled and ran.

"Don't talk to him like that!"

Tim turned his turbulent glare on her. "Why did you have to go snooping?"

She opened her mouth to lie, but couldn't. "I wanted the sapphire necklace." Which, in the shock of what she'd found, she had forgotten to take. She no longer wanted it. Why cling to a memory of this man's tenderness?

"You don't understand what you stole."

Rebecca stared at him. "Really? I'm pretty sure I do." She searched his face. "Tim, tell me you wouldn't hurt anyone."

"Of course it wasn't me!" He turned away and, with a jerky motion, swung back. "Misleading the cops a little, that's not so awful. It was the only way to save the company. Don't you understand?" he begged. When she didn't respond, his face darkened. "You like your financial settlement, don't you? What if I couldn't keep paying child support? You might have to actually work for a living."

The scathing tone and flushed face pushed her over the edge. "It was your pride that kept me from working during our marriage, and you know it. As it happens, I have a job." Assisting in an elementary classroom would give her an in with the school district when she applied for a teacher's position starting in the fall.

He rocked back. "What?"

"You heard me. And here's something else you need to hear. I haven't gone to Detective Estevez. I know, whatever happened, you *think* you're doing the right thing. And, for better or worse, you're Matthew's father. I did hide the wallet and ring somewhere you'll never find them."

"You can't do this to me."

She crossed her arms. "What exactly am I doing to you?"

"You're holding them over my head." He shook his head, baffled. "Why? You're the one who left *me*. I loved you."

The fury she'd been suppressing swelled inside her. "So much so that I felt like a ghost in your house. One of the few times I tried to make you really see me, talk to me, you shoved me into the kitchen cabinet. I had to hide for days after that so nobody would see the bruises. But you weren't around to notice. You were never around."

"I told you I was sorry!" he yelled back.

"Sorry isn't good enough!" Rebecca struggled to calm herself. She had forgiven him, hadn't she? She wasn't acting like it. "Tim, whatever you believe, my taking Steven's wallet and ring had nothing to do with our history. I just…couldn't let you keep fooling the police. It's *wrong*. Whatever you did or didn't have to do with Steven's death—"

"I told you. I didn't have anything to do with it. And it was an accident, anyway. We just…" He swallowed. "Him dying would have complicated everything. He took the money, he ran. That's all anyone has to know."

Hating what was staring her in the face, Rebecca whispered, "Why?"

"You don't need to know. You need to quit interfering with something you don't understand!" Teeth showing, the muscles in his shoulders bunching, he leaned in. *"Give me back everything you took."*

Rebecca took a prudent step back. "No." Groping behind herself, she found the knob and opened the front door. "You need to leave. I'll make your excuses to Matthew."

He didn't move. "You're blackmailing me."

"No!"

"It's the custody issue, isn't it?" He gave an incredulous laugh. "You've got me over a barrel, and you know it. If I back off, you'll give me what I need."

The possibility had never crossed her mind. She

wasn't devious enough. But now that he'd laid it out...
heaven help her, she was tempted. Her pulse raced.
Matthew would stay with her, and he'd be safe from
his critical, domineering grandfather.

What she was contemplating was a lousy way to
protect her son, but she'd use anything or anyone for
him.

"No," she heard herself say. "I won't give it back.
But you have my promise that I'll keep quiet. No one
else will ever see what I found."

Her pulse raced as she waited. His eyes narrowed in
a way that told her he was thinking, and hard.

Finally he grunted, said a foul word and agreed.

THREE WEEKS LATER, she had her divorce and primary
custody of Matthew, subject to the usual visitation
schedule and swapping of holidays.

Detective Estevez might still be watching her, but,
thank heavens, he hadn't been back. She hated the idea
of lying to his face.

Rebecca already felt tainted enough by a decision
she knew wasn't morally defensible. She imagined her
mother shaking her head and chiding Rebecca with a
gentleness that could still sting.

Yet, her mother had never shed her discomfiture
regarding law enforcement. A fear of authority was
bred into any Amish man's or woman's very bones by
their heritage. Throughout their history, the Amish had
been driven out of one place after another by men in
uniforms. Burned at the stake, tortured, imprisoned.

To go to the police about a family member's behavior? No, *Mamm* would never have chosen that path.
She would help that person see the error of his ways,

guide him back to making godly choices. Punishing a wrongdoer wasn't the aim of the Amish, and they never willingly went to the law.

Rebecca shook her head.

Her mother wasn't here anymore. Rebecca was willing to live with a stain on her character if that was the only way to save Matthew from a life of being alternately shamed and molded by his grandfather.

THE DEAL HELD, although Matthew noticed the coolness between his parents. Worse, a couple of months after the divorce, he returned puffy eyed from a weekend with his father. Lower lip protruding, he stayed stiff when Tim hugged him.

Tim gave her an angry look, as if whatever had happened was her fault, then left. Rebecca followed Matthew to his bedroom and coaxed the story out of him.

Grandfather Gregory said some bad things about Mommy, and when Matthew objected, he had spanked him. Hard. And Daddy let him!

Furious, Rebecca hugged him. "Did he use his hand, or a belt, or…?"

Her little boy gaped at her. "A belt? Don't people always spank with their hand?"

Well, that was something. "Is your bottom sore?"

He wriggled on his bed. "Uh-huh."

She gave him another squeeze. "I'll talk to your dad. Sometimes I think he's a little afraid of your grandfather. He may have thought a spanking wasn't that terrible. Especially if you were rude."

"I wasn't rude!" he exclaimed. "I just said my mom wasn't a—" He sneaked a peek up at her. "He said a word you told me I can't."

She could imagine what Robert had called her. What she wondered was why. How much did he know about Tim's part in Steven's disappearance? And the leverage she held over Tim?

"Never mind," she said. "Remember, 'sticks and stones can break my bones, but words can never hurt me.'" Even so, he shouldn't *have* to listen to her being vilified.

Together, she and Matthew decided the best thing was for him to say with dignity, *Grandfather, I don't want to listen when you use bad words about my mom*, and then walk out of the room.

Forehead crinkling, Matthew repeated the line several times, then nodded firmly. "That's what I'll say."

As far as she knew, he wasn't spanked again. Perhaps Tim had confronted his father when Matthew wasn't there. She wanted to think so.

Two months after her confrontation with Tim over the ring, he attended Matthew's graduation ceremony from kindergarten. The three of them even went out afterward for pizza and had fun. At least, she thought they had, but when Tim drove them back to the apartment, he insisted on walking them up, where he asked Matthew to go to his bedroom.

He did it nicely enough, and Matthew shrugged and obeyed. Six now, he was growing like a weed and occasionally giving her glimpses of what he'd look like a few years down the road. That shrug was *almost* teenage. Rebecca wondered if he'd learned it from his fifteen-year-old babysitter.

She quit wondering when she glanced back at her ex-husband and saw the way his expression had tightened.

Feeling a little wary, she said, "What did you want to talk about?"

"Rebecca, you have to give me Steven's things." Tim kept his voice low, but urgency threaded every word. "Josh is angry about this arrangement. He feels threatened, too."

"Too?" she echoed.

"You don't know what it's like." Hostility darkened his eyes. "Josh is after me, and Dad is angry because I gave in and let you have my kid. Sometimes I feel like that guy in the movie. I'm walking a tightrope between two skyscrapers. The only way off is to fall. That's not a nice way to live."

He was right. It was.

"I'd…like to think I can trust you, but I don't trust your father," she admitted. "Or Josh. And I've kept my word. I haven't told anyone."

"You know Josh is my best friend."

She did know. Josh and Tim had met during orientation for their freshman year of college and had been roommates. Steven Stowe had been a much later addition, needed for his financial acumen. Because Josh had spent his summers working construction, he supervised the job sites. Tim's gift had been convincing clients to choose G, G & S over other contractors. It was because of Tim that half the architects in the city recommended G, G & S to *their* clients. And when the company needed financing, Tim worked his magic on bankers.

"He's leaning hard on me. You need to bend a little, Bec." He hadn't called her that in a long time. But then he said, "I don't know how long I can keep protecting you. Be smart and think about it."

She was speechless, and he departed without saying anything else. Rebecca almost lunged to flip the dead bolt on the door. Had he been telling her she needed to be *afraid*?

She tried to reason through the cloud of fear. Even if she returned the ring and the wallet and cards, she knew about them—about Steven. Even if she gave Tim the benefit of the doubt, what if *Josh* had killed Steven during an argument? Would he kill again to protect his secret? But there was the chance she'd given them to someone else as insurance.

Whatever he said to the contrary, keeping that proof might be the only way she could protect herself.

She put her back to the door and shuddered.

A COUPLE OF weeks later, Rebecca lay sprawled on the sidewalk, grit stinging her cheek. Dazed, she knew only that she was the near victim of a drive-by shooting, and that some man had tackled her to the pavement right after the first crack of gunfire.

I would have stood there frozen, like an idiot, she thought.

She groaned and pushed herself to a sitting position. People all around were babbling in excitement and alarm. The middle-aged man who had knocked her down was picking himself up, too. She heard an approaching siren.

Her phone rang and she groped in her handbag for it. She had to be sure someone from Matthew's day camp wasn't calling. Rattled, she stared at the strange number displayed on the screen. Even the area code was unfamiliar.

"Hello?"

A metallic voice said, "Call that a warning. You have something we need. Return it, or next time we won't miss. And if you go to the cops? Your son is dead."

Knowing the caller was gone, Rebecca began to shake.

CHAPTER TWO

DANIEL BYLER PULLED his squad car to the curb to let a bus pass. Having already noticed several buggies and horses lining the street, he assumed an Amish visitor was expected. Come to think of it, weren't Roy and Nancy Schwartz supposed to be arriving about now from Iowa?

Roy was a cousin of his, although Daniel had lost track of whether they were second cousins or first once removed or... It didn't matter. The Amish tended to have a lot of children, and family networks sprawled and frequently tangled. Daniel and Roy had played together as boys. Too much had passed for them to reconnect as friends, but he did hope his parents would invite him to dinner sometime during the visit so he could say hello.

The bus groaned to a stop in front of the general store. Daniel got out of his car, careful not to jostle the people exiting the bus. He didn't see anyone from his direct family among those waiting on the sidewalk. Apparently, this wasn't the day Roy and his wife and children would arrive. Emma and Samuel Graber, members of his parents' church district and their contemporaries in age, stood in front of this group. Leaning a shoulder against the brick building, Daniel exchanged nods with them.

As usual, it was the *Englisch* passengers who got off first. They had a way of assuming it was their right. That wasn't fair, Daniel realized, thinking of his good friends among the non-Amish in his county. There was no way around it, though—they had a different way of thinking.

And me? How do I think? he asked himself, as he did daily. Betwixt and between, that was him.

Finally a slender Amish woman wearing the usual black bonnet stepped off, reaching back to help a young boy down. Looking tired and shy, the boy pressed himself to his mother. The woman lifted her head to scan her surroundings, her gaze stopping on Daniel in what he thought was alarm.

He straightened on a jolt of anger, followed by curiosity. One side of her face was discolored and swollen. The eye on that side opened only a slit. Had she been in an accident? Or was she a victim of spousal abuse?

Her scan had been wary, and something about him triggered her fear. Was it because, like most Amish, she was unwilling to report the assault and thought he might press her to do so?

The driver unloaded the last piece of luggage from under the bus and got back on board. With a deep sigh, the bus started down the street. None of the buggy horses so much as flapped an ear. It took something much stranger than a noisy bus to bother them.

Daniel ambled forward, the picture of congeniality. After all, as county sheriff, he was an elected official. He greeted folks he knew and nodded at strangers while assessing them, until he reached the Grabers and a cluster of Yoders, all enveloping the two newcomers.

Looking him in the eye, Samuel Graber stepped away from the group.

Protecting the woman and child by distracting me? Daniel wondered.

"Sheriff." Samuel's greeting was pleasant, but he didn't smile. The Amish trusted Daniel as a person, but they were wary of everything he represented. Behind Samuel, his wife was hugging the woman from the bus, while the blond boy gripped her skirts. His summer straw hat fell to the sidewalk. One of the many relatives picked it up.

"Family?" Daniel asked easily.

"*Ja.*" Samuel cleared his throat as he made a mental switch to English from the Deitsch language the Amish used among themselves. "Rebecca is the daughter of one of my sisters. Here for a visit."

His gaze resting on the slim back clothed in a dark blue dress and apron, he said, "You know I'm only here to help."

"You saw she has been injured."

"I did."

"She was hit by a car and thrown over the hood of another. A miracle it is she was not hurt worse."

Daniel nodded. "I hope her little boy didn't see it happen. That would have been frightening."

"*Ja,* but I don't think he did. She will tell us more once we get her home." Without another word, Samuel returned to the group, his broad frame hiding the newcomers.

The message was not subtle: *this is none of your business.* But Daniel thought Samuel was wrong. The sight of a police uniform made many of the Amish wary, and accidents happened every day. But an accident did not leave a woman afraid of who might be waiting for her when she stepped off a bus.

Chances were that she was escaping trouble of one kind or another. In his experience, trouble had a way of following people, and the Amish were defenseless.

He often stopped to say hello to folks in his small county. He'd give the Grabers a day or two and then drive out to their farm, just to say he hoped their niece was recovering and enjoying her visit.

He was opening the door to the café, where he'd been headed for lunch, when he glanced back to catch Rebecca watching him, her expression now unreadable. With her high forehead, fine bones and sharp chin, she'd be a pretty woman once the swelling subsided. Between the bonnet and the prayer *kapp*, he couldn't tell what color hair she had, but she shared her son's blue eyes.

He smiled. She looked startled and quickly climbed into one of the buggies. Her *onkel* Samuel closed the door, and she was lost from Daniel's view. Thoughtful, he went into the café, taking a seat at the window.

As he watched the buggies drive away, he wondered how long the Grabers' guest intended to stay.

THE DRONE OF the metal wheels on the paved road, the sway of the buggy and the clip-clop of the horses' hooves would quickly make her drowsy, Rebecca feared. At least she didn't have to strain to understand Deitsch, often called Pennsylvania Dutch, which was actually a Germanic dialect. *Aenti* Emma and the others had spoken English from the moment she stepped off the bus. Or maybe they were doing so for Matthew's sake. Rebecca suspected the language

would come back to her quickly. She had been reasonably fluent once upon a time—as a child, she had spent
her summers with her Amish grandparents. She had
loved those visits until she became a snotty thirteen-
year-old with the same preoccupations as her other San
Francisco friends. Boys, the right clothes, boys, how
unfair their parents were, boys. The plain life had suddenly held no appeal. Her mother's disappointment in
her wasn't enough to combat peer pressure.

That, she thought now, was when her foolishness
had begun.

"Your *aenti* Mary gave you clothes, I see," *Aenti*
Emma said approvingly. Her round face was as cheerful as always, but she had become considerably stouter
since Rebecca had last seen her.

"Yes." Rebecca plucked at the fabric of her apron.
They had gone first to her *aenti* Mary and *onkel* Abe's
farm to confuse anyone trying to find them. "It feels
strange, I have to admit." She kissed the top of her
son's head. "Matthew doesn't know what to make of
the suspenders."

Sarah, the younger cousin she scarcely remembered,
chuckled. "They suit him fine! We are so pleased to
meet Matthew at last."

Matthew buried his face against Rebecca. His hat
fell off once again. The two other women laughed.
Onkel Samuel, in the driver's seat, either couldn't hear
or was ignoring the womenfolk.

Sarah said, "He will be less shy once he sees the
horses and cows and chickens, ain't so?"

Matthew sneaked a peek Sarah's way.

Rebecca would have smiled if it hadn't hurt. "He
was fascinated by *Onkel* Abe's horse. I don't think he's

ever been close enough to pet one before. He went to a birthday party this spring that included pony rides, but that's it."

Aenti Emma beamed at Matthew. "He will like our horses."

Rebecca let out a breath that seemed to drain her, mostly in a good way. She wouldn't be able to stay here forever, but for now she and Matthew were safe. She couldn't imagine Tim or Josh would think to look for her among the Amish, or succeed if they tried. She'd told Tim that her mother had grown up Amish, had mentioned summers with her grandparents, but would he remember? Would he know *Mamm's* maiden name? Or that those summers had been spent in Missouri? He'd rolled his eyes at the idea she had been happy even temporarily in what he considered a backward, restricted life, and she doubted he'd really listened when she talked about family. Because of his lack of interest, she hadn't mentioned her Amish roots in a very long time. And where the Amish were concerned, most people thought Pennsylvania or Ohio. An investigator could find her mother's maiden name on her marriage certificate, but no one from her family had attended the wedding or signed as a witness.

Graber wasn't quite as common a surname as some among the Amish, but there were Grabers in many settlements, so tracing her wouldn't be easy. In many ways, the Amish lived off the grid. They weren't in any phone directory unless their business was listed. They didn't need driver's licenses, and they didn't contribute to federal social security or draw from it. Living on a cash basis, none of the Amish Grabers would be found in a credit-agency search, either. They did have

Social Security numbers, or at least many of them did, because they paid federal income taxes and state and local taxes. Still, would a private investigator have access to income-tax records?

She had done her best to complicate any pursuit by initially flying to Chicago, then backtracking by bus to Des Moines, where she and Matthew had switched to various local buses, paying cash. They finally wended their way to Kalona, Iowa, where more of Rebecca's relatives lived. Having received a note from *Aenti* Emma, *Aenti* Mary and *Onkel* Abe Yoder had kept her arrival and departure as quiet as possible. Their bishop and some members of their church district knew that their niece and her child had fled something bad and needed help. If an outsider came asking questions, she had confidence they'd pretend ignorance. Staying reserved was their way even when they had nothing to hide.

The unquestioning generosity still shook her. Even though *Mamm* had jumped the fence—left her faith—to marry Dad, the family considered Rebecca and now her son their own. She'd never even met the Iowa relatives, and yet they'd welcomed her with open arms.

Once she and Matthew were appropriately garbed, another cousin had driven them several towns away, where they caught yet another bus. They had meandered south into Missouri, changing buses frequently. By this time, Rebecca's entire body ached until she could hardly pick out the new pains from the places that already hurt when they set out from San Francisco. But at last they were here.

Aenti Emma leaned forward and patted Rebecca's knee with her work-worn hand. "*Ach*, here we are, talking and talking, when I can see you close to collapsing! Lunch and some sleep is what you need."

"That sounds wonderful," she admitted. A glance told her Matthew was nodding off already.

She was grateful when her *aenti* and cousin lapsed into silence and let her do the same.

She found herself thinking about the cop who had talked to *Onkel* Samuel just before they left town. A sudden certainty that someone was watching her had felt like icy fingertips brushing her nape. She'd known she should keep her head down so as not to draw attention, but she hadn't been able to stop herself from looking around. If Tim was already here, waiting for her... But then she'd seen the uniformed police officer, instead, as broad-shouldered and strong as the farmers and woodworkers she knew among the Amish, men who labored hard. His face was too hard to be handsome, too inexpressive, his eyes too steely. His cold scrutiny reminded her of the way Detective Estevez had looked at her. She guessed this police officer to be older than she was, perhaps in his midthirties. His hair was a sun-streaked maple brown that probably darkened in the cold Missouri winters.

Rebecca looked down to see that her hands were clenched together hard enough to turn the tips of her fingers white. With an effort, she loosened her grip. Yes, that man made her anxious. Had he only been interested in her because he'd noticed the bruises? But why had he been leaning against the building watching people get off the bus in the first place? Did he check out new arrivals every time the bus stopped in Hadburg? Was that one of his duties? In this rural county, she wouldn't have thought the local police force would have the personnel to be so vigilant—unless they were watching for someone in particular. Could Detective Estevez have figured out where she'd gone already?

A bump in her pulse rate left her light-headed. She was being stupid. Estevez hadn't bothered her since their one interview. Tim shouldn't notice her disappearance until tomorrow, after he arrived to pick up Matthew for his scheduled visit. And violating the custody agreement wasn't an offense that would draw police attention, certainly not at first. Would Tim even dare file a missing-person's report on her or accuse her of custodial interference?

No, the last thing he wanted was to attract more attention from the police. That didn't mean he wouldn't hire a private investigator to find her, if he didn't set out to do so himself. She wondered what he'd tell his father. Tim wouldn't want the man to know his grandson was out of his reach.

And Josh. What would Tim tell the partner who'd been pressuring him? Would he try to protect her, as she was protecting him?

She feared not, given the results after she had gone to him about the shooting and the phone threat.

Aenti Emma swayed gently with the motion of the carriage, her gaze resting on Rebecca and Matthew.

"I saw *Onkel* Samuel talking to that police officer," Rebecca blurted, not sounding as casual as she wanted. "Does he know him?"

"We all know Sheriff Byler. His family moved here when he was, oh, sixteen or so, you see." An odd hint of discomfiture in her voice caught Rebecca's attention, but *Aenti* Emma continued, "He went away and nobody knew for a long time what he was up to, but he became a police officer, of all things! And in the big city." She shook her head, scandalized by the mere idea. *Aenti* Emma had probably never been as far as St. Joseph, let alone Kansas City. Why would a local boy want to leave placid Henness County for a place that was all concrete and towers of glass and steel and noise? Sirens and car horns and people shouting. So much noise.

"What city?" Rebecca asked, as if it made any difference.

"I heard he went to St. Louis. I guess he didn't like it, because he came back three years ago and got the *Englisch* to vote for him to be sheriff. That Gerald Warren, who was sheriff before, nobody liked him. He was lazy, and he looked down on the people."

The *Leit*, she meant. The Amish. Lazy Sheriff Warren wouldn't have been alone. Even tourists equated plain with simpleminded and gullible. Rebecca's mother used to talk about how much resentment was caused by the slow, horse-drawn buggies with metal wheels that wore ruts in roads, even though the Amish paid road taxes like everyone else.

"So you like this Sheriff Byler?"

"He's a good man," *Aenti* Emma said, although a hint of ambivalence remained. "He listens and understands why we won't go to the law most of the time."

Rebecca nodded her understanding. Would that "good man" poke his nose in her problems? Perhaps she should take advantage of the opportunity if he did. It wouldn't be a bad thing if he knew to watch for anyone asking about her. Even if she didn't tell him about the unholy bargain she'd made with Tim, if the sheriff thought she was running from her ex-husband because he was stalking her, he might form another line of protection.

But of course that would mean telling him she wasn't Amish. Almost instantly she shook her head. What if he went looking for police records concerning the alleged abuse? Or even searched online for information about Tim? It might be the modern equivalent of yelling, *Here she is.* No, it would be better to stay away from Sheriff Byler, however good his intentions were.

She had to grab the seat as the buggy turned sharply. The wheels made a crunching sound that told her they were no longer on a paved road. Peering out the small window, she saw fields of corn growing high in the August heat. Oh—and sunflowers, an entire field of them! A minute later, the crops were replaced in her view by grazing cattle. A sign for a produce stand caught her eye. This was all so familiar. Comforted, she sat back and gently stroked her now-sleeping son's hair.

Finally they turned into a narrow lane. Corn grew on one side, while to the other was pasture. Enormous, dappled silver horses grazed. Rebecca smiled. *Onkel* Samuel still bred and raised Percherons, as his father had before him. As a child, she'd been awed by the gentle giants with velvety lips and stiff whiskers and big brown eyes. They had seemed magical to her. She hoped they would to Matthew, too. He didn't understand why they were making this trip or who these people were, but she had confidence he'd enjoy himself as much here as she had as a girl.

Another bonus of staying here—she didn't have to worry about Matthew getting to a phone and calling his father. She had left her cell phone behind for fear it could be used to trace them, and Sarah was the last of *Aenti* Emma and *Onkel* Samuel's children left at home. Some Amish teenagers did have cell phones during their running-around time, but Sarah looked to be past that. Rebecca had no intention of telling Matthew about the phone in the shanty that used to be halfway between the Graber farm and the neighbors.

The buggy swayed to a stop and *Onkel* Samuel got down and came around to let them out. She carried her sleeping son in her arms, though he began to awaken with the movement.

The large farmhouse was just as she remembered it, painted a crisp white, the wide porch still holding a swing and several comfortable chairs. A small wing attached to one side of the house, the *grossdawdi haus* where her grandparents now lived, had its own porch. Two dogs raced toward them from the huge barn.

"Down, down," *Onkel* Samuel said, intercepting them. The dogs spun around in excitement, barking.

Matthew tightened his grip on her neck and lifted his feet out of reach. "Mom! Do they bite?"

Onkel Samuel set a gentle hand on his head and ruffled his hair. "No, they will be your best friends before you know it. Especially if you sneak them some treats."

His wife turned a look on him. "Don't suggest he waste my good cooking on dogs!"

He only laughed, his face creasing above the distinctive Amish beard that reached his chest. It was the clean-shaven upper lip that made it different from facial hair among the *Englisch*. "Boys will be boys," he declared. "I will bring your bags once I stable Molly," he added, and got back into the buggy. The dogs hesitated, then bolted after him as he drove toward the barn.

"It's so good to be here." Rebecca's eyes burned. She tried to smile. "Thank you for having us."

"You're family," *Aenti* Emma said simply.

Sarah hugged her.

"We can't know God's purpose," *Aenti* Emma murmured, "but the bad things that happened brought you and Matthew to us, which is reason to rejoice. *Grossmammi* especially has worried about you. Letters aren't the same."

"No. I wish…" Rebecca didn't finish the thought, and saw in the two women's kind faces that she didn't need to.

Just then the front door in the *grossdawdi haus* opened and her grandmother hurried across the lawn to envelop her in more hugs. Her grandfather followed more slowly, every breath a rasp. In the eighteen years since she'd seen them, they'd aged more than she had anticipated. Both had white hair now and looked frail. Guilt stabbed Rebecca. Why hadn't she managed to visit? Brought Matthew sooner for them to meet?

But her grandmother showed no hint of accusation. It would not be her way. "How often I have prayed to have you restored to us!" Her wide smile included Matthew. "And now to be able to get to know your son, as well! Such a blessing."

The entire family ushered her and Matthew into the house. In no time, Sarah had poured glasses of lemonade while Rebecca's *aenti* and grandmother set out home-baked bread, different cheeses and cold cuts, as well as a special peanut butter sweetened with marshmallow cream. There were at least two kinds of cookies and fudge besides. Matthew's eyes grew wide, while Rebecca knew this was a modest meal by her *aenti's* standards. There would be a much greater variety at dinner.

Matthew was initially suspicious, but he tried the strange peanut butter and grinned his approval, exposing the gaps where he'd lost baby teeth. Before she knew it, lunch was over and they were upstairs, ushered into a typically bare room with two twin beds. Sarah helped Rebecca out of her clothes, drew the curtains and left them to lay their aching bodies down to rest.

Safe, Rebecca thought, and then sleep claimed her.

DANIEL THOUGHT OF the strange woman on Sunday, and even drove by Reuben Gingerich's house where church was being held. The every-other-Sunday Amish services were held in homes or barns, the privilege of hosting it rotating among the families in each church district. A dozen or more buggies lined the fence at the top of the lane. The horses stood hipshot and lazy in the shade from a grove of old black walnut trees that Daniel suspected were quite profitable for Reuben.

Daniel usually attended a service at the Congregational Church in Hadburg, which he had joined on his return to Henness County. The occasional Sundays he missed were understood as part of his job. Sometimes that was even true. Sometimes, he parked out of sight and walked across a field to where he could hear the Amish singing hymns, so much a part of his childhood. He never went near enough to a barn or house to chance being seen or to hear the sermons, but the singing quieted something in him even as it reawakened his sense of loss.

It was very different from hymns sung in the Congregational and Baptist churches in town. All Amish hymns came from the *Ausbund*, a thick book passed down through many generations. It contained only the words, no musical scores. The singing was slow, often mournful, the voices blending together into one. An Amish would say, "One with God."

The familiar hymns sharpened Daniel's emotions. Sorrow seemed strongest—or perhaps *regret* was a better word to describe the jagged feeling in his chest. And yet…he wouldn't go back if he could. He still believed he had made the right decision. He was where he belonged, protecting his people but separate from them. Daniel only wished his choice hadn't left him alone, however many friends he made, belonging neither here nor there.

Annoyed with his self-pity, he shook his head and turned his back on the large red barn, where the multitude of voices had fallen silent. He walked back to his squad car and drove away. He always tried to be present when the fellowship meal broke up. Most locals were good about keeping watch for the slow buggies and Amish on foot, but despite all warnings tourists still drove too fast. They didn't understand how quickly a car could close in on a buggy pulled by a trotting horse. Car-and-buggy accidents were too often tragic. He and his deputies dreaded being called to the site of one.

Unfortunately, he couldn't be everywhere. Three separate church districts fell completely within this county, which meant services being held at three separate homes on any given Sunday. He had assigned two deputies to patrol today while he did the same, the best he could manage given limited resources. With fewer than ten thousand people in the county, Daniel's entire department consisted of himself, a sergeant and five deputies, as well as two administrative assistants who were also dispatchers.

The two largest cities in Henness County, including Byrum, the county seat, had their own police departments.

Amish businesses might be in town, but the people rarely lived within city limits, so they were, with few exceptions, in his care. A wry smile accompanied the thought. *They* believed they were in God's care, not his. He was careful not to mention his alternate opinion on the matter in the hearing of anyone Amish.

The cars he saw as he patrolled were likely driven by tourists. Amish businesses and roadside stands were closed on Sundays, but the idea was incomprehensible to the typical American who came to sightsee.

Daniel found himself thinking about the Grabers' guests, as he had more often than he should in the three days since their arrival. They would have been in the barn, the boy still young enough to sit beside his mother on a bench on the women's side. He wondered if Rebecca had been able to surrender herself wholeheartedly to God today, or whether she held some anger or fear in reserve. However good their intentions, Amish struggled with negative emotions like everyone else. Nonetheless, her feelings toward whoever had hurt her would be far more charitable than his, he could pretty well guarantee.

Tomorrow, he decided, wasn't too soon to stop by the Graber farm and ask after their visiting family.

He refused to question why he was so eager to do so.

CHAPTER THREE

"THEY'RE AWFULLY BIG," Matthew said, standing behind the board fence and well back from the row of Percheron horses.

Rebecca stroked the cheek of the nearest gelding, which whuffled a response that startled a giggle out of her, one that made her wince as her swollen cheek protested. "They're friendly," she said. "From birth, *Onkel* Samuel and cousin Mose groom them and feed them and pick up their feet, so they like being around people. Didn't you see these four pulling a plow yesterday? That was part of their training, to work as a team. I think they will be ready for a new home soon." The horse she was petting nudged her for more attention, and she added, "They can smell better than we can, so they know we have carrots."

"They really like carrots?" her son said dubiously. He didn't mind carrot sticks, but detested cooked carrots. His pickiness where food was concerned had already brought surprise from her family here, where children weren't indulged in the same way they were in the outside world.

"A carrot is like a cookie to a horse," Rebecca said firmly. "Watch."

She broke off a chunk and held it on the palm of her hand. The horse she'd been petting promptly lipped it up and crunched with such enthusiasm that saliva and flecks of carrot flew.

Matthew laughed.

She had just persuaded him to feed a piece of carrot to another of the horses when she heard a car engine followed by the sound of tires crunching on gravel. There were innocent reasons for a car to be driving down this quiet road, even if the homes on it were all Amish owned, but she couldn't control her spike of anxiety. She turned and saw the green-and-white SUV with a rack of lights on the roof slow and turn into the lane leading to her aunt and uncle's home. It would pass right by her and Matthew. Rebecca had no doubt who the driver was.

Turning her back on the police car, she cupped Matthew's hand and helped him hold it out. He squeaked in alarm when lips brushed his palm, then laughed in delight when the carrot vanished.

"It tickled!"

The police vehicle rolled to a stop right behind them. A door slammed, and she and Matthew both turned to face Daniel Byler, who strolled around the front bumper and joined them.

"These are beauties," he said in a voice that was just a little gravelly. "Your *onkel* raises the handsomest draft horses I've ever seen."

She smiled despite her tension. "Say that to him, and he would then tell you about three other Amish men he knows who raise horses just as fine. And he would also admonish you for admiring them for their looks, when it is strength and willingness and heart that truly matter."

His chuckle was a little rough, too. "You're right, he

would. Although I have no doubt he is willing to discuss desirable conformation with buyers."

"An entirely different thing from calling them beautiful," she said, trying to repress another smile.

"Why shouldn't they be beautiful?" Matt burst out. "Aren't horses s'posed to be—"

"Sheriff Byler is teasing," she said hastily, seeing his raised eyebrow. "And you know *Onkel* Samuel is right. These will be working horses. A horse pulling a plow could be mud brown and have a bump in the middle of his forehead and mismatched eyes, one blue and one brown—"

"Like that dog we saw!" he said excitedly.

"Yep." Uh-oh. *"Ja,"* she said hastily. "Remember how funny-looking he was? But if the horse was strong and did the job, no one would mind how he looks."

"Oh." Matthew frowned, then nodded. "Can I have another carrot?"

The sheriff stayed at their side as they proffered, piece by piece, all the carrots they'd brought. Rebecca was very careful to guide their minimal conversation so that Matthew wouldn't have a chance to say anything else so un-Amish.

Sheriff Byler offered them a ride up to the house, which she would have refused except for Matthew's excitement. She held him on her lap in the front seat. The sheriff showed him how to turn on the siren and flashing lights.

Matthew reached out. "Can we…?"

"No," she said quickly. "Think how it would frighten the horses."

"Oh." He subsided. "I guess it would."

He was happy when a voice came over the radio. A

deputy reported, using code that the sheriff translated, that he'd pulled over a motorist for speeding.

Byler's mouth was tight, and she knew why. Speeding was always dangerous, and particularly on narrow country roads shared by horse-and-buggy travelers.

At the house, she opened the door and let Matthew out first. Already used to the dogs, he giggled to find them waiting. "Go tell *Aenti* Emma or *Grossmammi* that Sheriff Byler is here. I'm sure he would like coffee or one of those sticky buns I saw going in the oven."

Accompanied by *Onkel* Samuel's dogs, Matthew raced for the house while the sheriff laughed. "You know your *aenti's* sticky buns are famous in these parts. She bakes enough so the café in Hadburg can sell them."

"*Ja*," Rebecca said, striving for the faint accent she heard in the speech of local Amish. "For sure, I know my cousin Sarah drove to town this morning to deliver some."

Matthew had wanted to go, but Rebecca wasn't ready to let him out of her sight. The plain clothing wasn't enough of a disguise. His hair was too short to resemble a typical Amish boy's bowl cut. His new, wide-brimmed straw hat didn't hide his face the way a bonnet did hers, and that was when he managed to keep it on his head. And if he saw his father…

Who couldn't possibly have found them yet, she kept reminding herself, for what good that did.

"You seem to move carefully," the sheriff said, before she could leave him. "Are you healing?" Turning toward her, he laid his forearm casually on the steering wheel.

"Yes, I am mostly sore."

"Mostly?"

Being this close to him unnerved her. She was too conscious of him in a short-sleeved uniform. His forearms were strong and tan, dusted with bronze hair tipped with gold. She could see the hint of darker stubble on an angular jaw and noticed the thick, short lashes and the wave in his hair. His eyes were a penetrating dark blue. To evade them, she lowered her gaze, which meant she was looking at powerful thighs. Not good.

"I have bruises," she admitted after a moment. "And two cracked ribs. They hurt the most."

He frowned. "You shouldn't lift your son."

"My middle—" she laid a hand over her stomach "—is wrapped for protection. Of course I must pick him up."

He made a grumbly sound she took for disagreement, but said, "What happened?"

Careful. "I stepped out in the street—" She cut herself off before she finished the sentence. The last thing she could admit was that she'd been about to get in her car. "I thought I had looked for traffic, but afterward I was confused, so I'm not sure. A car came fast and hit me. I think I was jumping out of the way, but it still lifted me in the air. I went over the hood and banged into a car coming the other way. That driver stopped to help me, but not the one who hit me."

"A hit-and-run."

"*Ja*, that's what the police called it. No one saw the license plate, so there was not much they could do."

As she had lain there waiting for an ambulance, she'd berated herself. She should have fled after the shooting. Instead, because Tim had sounded shocked about what had happened when she called him, she had given him a couple days to talk to "other people"—his vague reference. Make sure there was no repetition. Instead, he had called her back the next day to say tensely, "You've got to give those things back, Rebecca. You'll be okay if you do. I swear."

Not believing that for a second, she had packed and been ready to run as soon as she picked Matthew up at day care. That was where she'd been heading when she was hit.

This time, she hadn't been surprised when her phone rang. The message conveyed was even shorter: "Ignoring my last call, not so smart. Lucky for us, you have a weakness."

Matthew. All she could think to do was take him and hide.

Now Sheriff Byler watched her in a way that made her suspect he knew there was more to her story, but he only said, "I'm surprised you chose to travel when you were hurt."

"I wanted to go away," she said simply—and truthfully. "Here it is quiet. Not so busy."

"Where are you from?" he asked, as if making conversation. She knew better and had been prepared.

"Pennsylvania. There, we have so many tourists." She shook her head. "I was scared every time I crossed a street or heard a car coming up behind my buggy."

A twitch of his expressive eyebrows made her realize her mistake.

"You think I am not trusting in God."

He didn't say anything.

"I do in my head," she explained, "but my heart still races and my hands shake."

"Post-traumatic stress," he said quietly.

She pretended to look puzzled.

"Your body reacts without waiting for permission from you. It takes time for that kind of response to go away."

She shivered. "*Ja*."

He laid a big hand over hers. "You're cold."

Her fingers curled into her palms and she quickly withdrew from him. "My hands and feet are always cold."

A smile crinkled the skin beside his eyes. "Even in August here in Missouri? Teach me your trick."

She wanted to laugh. Instead, she said shyly, "There is no trick. It's fine in summer, not so good in winter."

"No." His gaze rested on her face a moment longer. Then he reached for his door handle. "We should go in. I see your *onkel* coming from the barn."

Oh, heavens—everyone in the house was probably peeking out the window by now.

"*Ja*, you are right." She leaped out faster than she ought to have and slammed the door. "I should have been helping to cook, not sitting here like a lump."

Walking beside her, the sheriff said, "I suspect your family wants you to rest until you don't hurt anymore before you dive into chores."

"That doesn't mean I have to listen to them. It is so kind of them to take us in."

Another mistake—he must know that visiting was a favorite pastime for the Amish, who loved having family even for extended stays.

But Sheriff Byler only glanced sidelong at her before remarking, as if at random, "It occurs to me your last name isn't Graber."

Her mind stuttered in panic. She couldn't admit to

being divorced. The Amish didn't divorce. Widowed. She would be widowed, except then she would have retained her husband's last name. And she'd never heard of anyone among the Amish with a last name of Gregory.

Lie? But Matthew might give her away. Oh, no—if he ever told anyone *his* last name was Gregory, they were in trouble.

"I... No," she said.

The front door opened just as *Onkel* Samuel reached them, his long strides eating up the ground. Amid the greetings, Rebecca was able to slip into the house and take Matthew to the bathroom to wash his hands. Heart still thudding, she realized how important it was that she avoid giving Sheriff Daniel Byler any more chances to corner her. She'd made too many slips already. He wasn't Amish, of course, but she suspected he knew the citizens of his county well enough to notice anomalies in her speech or behavior. And he was too interested in her.

Once back in the kitchen, she took a seat at the far end of the farmhouse table, staying silent as her *onkel* talked with the sheriff about local happenings, including an upcoming street fair and auction in Hadburg to raise money for the volunteer fire department. She tensed, knowing everyone would go. People would comment if she and Matthew didn't.

When Sheriff Byler finally rose to leave, her *onkel* politely standing to show him out, Rebecca only joined the others in murmuring "Goodbye."

She nudged her son, who said, "I liked looking at your police car," which was only polite. That was the moment when Rebecca realized in horror that they had

been speaking in English the entire time. Of course
they had been. But an Amish boy Matthew's age
shouldn't *be* fluent in English.

Frantically trying to think of an excuse if the sheriff
ever asked, Rebecca didn't let herself meet those dark
blue eyes, and she stayed seated until he was gone.
Once she heard the engine, she let Matthew run outside.

Onkel Samuel came back to sit across the table from
her. "Curious about you, he is."

She nodded. "I think that's why he came by this
morning."

"*Ja*, that is so." Lines in his forehead deepened. "I
didn't tell you, but after you got off the bus, he asked
about your face."

Her *aenti* Emma and *Grossmammi* bustled in the
background and didn't contribute to the conversation.

"I knew he'd seen my bruises," Rebecca said. "When
we were sitting in his car, he asked how it happened. I
made it sound like an accident, but told him the driver
didn't stop and the police hadn't been able to find him."

His face relaxed. "That is good. There was no need
to lie."

"No." *Onkel* Samuel wouldn't approve of lying,
but… "He asked what my last name is. You greeted
him then, so I didn't have to answer, but what if he
asks again?"

He pondered that. "Outsiders join us sometimes.
Someone named Holt could be one of them."

"Yes, but if he looked me up in his computers, he
might find me. And Matthew's name is different from
mine, besides." She hesitated. "I did lie to him. I said
I had come from Pennsylvania."

He frowned. "Perhaps we should tell him what you fear. Someone must set things right. I think he can be trusted." Still, he sounded reluctant.

Inexplicably, the idea of confiding in Sheriff Byler was appealing…as was he. And that triggered a new kind of alarm. Being attracted to him was a really bad idea. Plus, a physical attraction was absolutely the wrong reason to trust him. She could easily imagine him being cocky enough to think he could solve her problems, and arrogant enough to do what he thought best without asking her first. And that was assuming he didn't have more in common with Estevez than she wanted to believe.

"The fewer people who know I'm not Amish, the better," she said slowly. "What if he tells a friend, or one of his officers, who tells someone else? So fast, everyone could know."

"If you ask him to keep silent…"

"Why don't we wait and see what happens?" she said. "He came out here and saw that I'm doing fine. He may have satisfied his curiosity."

After a moment, he nodded. "*Ja*, that is so."

Rebecca hesitated. "You don't think I'm off in the head to think someone was trying to kill me?"

"*Wu schmoke is, is aa feier*," he said without hesitation.

That much of the language she remembered: where there is smoke, there is fire.

"God asks us to trust in Him, but He does not say to be a fool," her *onkel* added. "When a horse lifts a hoof and I see he will set it down on my toes, I move my foot *schnell*."

"*Denke*," she said, torn between humor and tears.

He only smiled and said, "I must get back to work." Clapping his straw hat onto his head, he departed.

It took her a moment to collect herself enough to rise and say, "Let me wash those dishes, *Aenti* Emma."

DANIEL DROVE AWAY from the Graber farm no more satisfied than before. He knew he didn't have Rebecca's whole story. She'd failed to offer her last name, which increased his suspicion that she was running from an abusive spouse.

He didn't much like that explanation for several reasons. At the forefront was the danger to Rebecca and her kid. In his experience, domestic violence was like dynamite, volatile and deadly.

What was most puzzling was the rarity of an Amish woman fleeing from her husband. They were a peaceful people, committed to nonviolence. Domestic abuse existed among them, but forgiveness was so ingrained that women rarely gave up on a husband. Or perhaps it was more that the women knew how few alternatives they had. If the abuse was bad enough, she might go to her bishop, who would chide the husband, maybe going so far as counseling him and demanding he confess and beg forgiveness from the entire congregation. But for the wife to take her child and run... Daniel had never heard of such a thing.

Even as he brooded, Daniel noted how well the corn seemed to be coming on, thriving in the heat. Many local farmers would plant a second crop once the corn was harvested—soybeans had become a success in the difficult northern Missouri climate, but many of the Amish chose a cover crop like forage turnips, which provided good grazing for livestock and kept down weeds. Even the Amish moved with the times, just with more deliberation than their neighbors.

He wasn't sure what more he could do to help Rebecca when she so clearly didn't *want* his help. Daniel fully understood the stubborn refusal of the Amish to turn to outsiders. Samuel Graber was a capable man, and he had extended family in the county. Yet he was ill equipped to counter violence. The best he could do was slow down an intruder to give Rebecca and Matthew time to hide in the barn or the woods at the back of the property. Samuel would let himself be shot rather than strike a blow.

And that was where Daniel had collided with the *Ordnung*, the rules directing the people that had once been his.

No, his decision to go out in the world had been more complicated than that, as nearly every life-altering decision was, but he knew his father or mother would say sadly, "Daniel could not forgive."

To them it was that simple.

He wished he thought any of the Grabers would call him if a dangerous man came seeking Rebecca.

"SLEEP TIGHT." REBECCA KISSED her son's forehead and stood. She lifted the kerosene lamp to light her way back downstairs. Thank goodness Matthew had never been afraid of the dark.

"Mommy?" he whispered.

She paused and turned back.

"Can Daddy come see us here?" Matthew asked. "I bet he'd like the horses, too."

He'd asked about his father when they first set out, but not since. After a moment, she returned to sit on the edge of his bed again. Smoothing his hair, she said, "You know how hard he works. He wouldn't be able to get away for days and days. This is our adventure."

"But...what about when it's *his* weekend?"

His weekend had just come and gone. She didn't like to think about how he'd reacted.

"We'll make up for it later," she said. "Just like we do if he has to travel for work and can't be home for his weekend."

Matthew was quiet. She knew he understood that much.

"I don't know when we'll go back," she said softly. Or *if.* "Aren't you having a good time?"

"*Aenti* Emma makes good cookies. And I liked fishing with Abram and his dad."

Mose, the son who farmed alongside Samuel, had his own house and a growing family on the far side of the cornfield. In his thirties, he already had four children, the oldest almost eleven. Like Matthew, Abram was six.

"Only, Abram doesn't talk that good."

"That *well.* And Abram talks just fine, but he's only starting to learn English. I actually thought he was doing pretty well with it for his age."

"But how come he doesn't speak English? *Everyone* does."

So she explained again how the Amish people spoke their own language, and that children weren't usually exposed to English until they began school at six years old. By the time they finished eighth grade, they would be able to speak two languages, which was more than you could say for the typical American student.

Matthew was quiet long enough that she hoped she

could slip out, but then he said, "Abram wants me to go to school with him. He says *Sarah* will be his teacher." He sounded astonished.

Rebecca smiled despite feeling a pang. When would she be able to have her own classroom again? She could hardly apply for jobs now. "It's true. Cousin Sarah is a teacher. Just like teachers and kids at home, she has the summer off. She told me that tomorrow she is going to the schoolhouse to start preparing for the new school year. I offered to help her clean. You can come with us, if you'd like."

"Can Abram come, too?" he asked, with eagerness that encouraged her.

"If his *mamm* and *daad* say he can. Now." She made her voice firm. "Sleep, and no argument."

"'Kay," he murmured. "But you'll come to bed real soon, too, won't you?"

"I will." Without electricity or television or smartphones, there was little temptation to stay up late. And on a farm, the work began early.

She kissed him once again and this time made her escape, taking old worries and new ones with her. What would she say if Matthew kept asking about his father? If he begged her to let him call Daddy? And how would he react when he found out he likely wouldn't be in Mrs. Chisholm's first-grade classroom this fall, but would instead be joining his cousin Abram and the other children in their church district in a one-room school?

He was young. He'd adapt.

But Rebecca knew she'd keep asking herself if this huge adjustment she expected of him was fair or even possible. And yet Tim had let her know he couldn't protect her or Matthew. Her priority had to be keeping herself and Matthew safe. If Tim truly loved their son, if he felt even a shadow of affection for her, he would understand what she'd done.

How long would they have to stay in hiding? Right now, all she could do was check the internet for any news about Steven, Josh, Tim or the construction company when she could make it to the library in Hadburg. If she found no news about an arrest or closing of the investigation, at some point, she had to talk to Tim again.

But not yet.

CHAPTER FOUR

A WEEK AFTER his visit to the Grabers', Daniel strolled down the middle of Grove Street, the main drag in Hadburg, closed today to motorized vehicles and horses and buggies for the three-block length of the business district. Instead of the usual traffic, stores had flung open their doors and spread out onto the sidewalks. Booths and tables offering crafts, fresh-picked produce, desserts and a bounty of home-canned goods lined both sides of the street. The quilt shop had attracted a crowd of locals and tourists with half a dozen tables covered with packets of coordinated fabrics and small quilts, mostly Amish made. Even the Amish Heritage Furniture store displayed small side tables and quilt racks on the sidewalk.

So far, so good. The cop in him leaned toward pessimism, but there was no reason to think there'd be any trouble. Support for the volunteer fire department was genuine hereabouts. People recognized its importance in their lives. Today's fair was part of an effort to buy a new tanker for the department. Naturally, the Amish were the big draw for outsiders. The tourists were thrilled because the street was thronged with Amish, buying and selling.

The impetus for the event had been the fire out at the Bontrager place in early July. The barn had not only burned to the ground, but sparks had caught on the roof of the house and they'd lost it, too. A tanker truck full of water might have made a difference. The drought had left the creek at the back of the property running too low to be any use.

Although Amish and *Englisch* neighbors alike had joined to rebuild, Eli Bontrager ran his harness business out of that barn. His tools, supplies and finished products had all been casualties, as had a young horse that pulled his daughter's open buggy.

Shaking off the memory of the horse's screams and the devastation on the faces of the entire family, Daniel ambled for another half block, exchanging greetings. He was glad to see so many people supporting the fire department. Their town didn't usually draw tourists the way the larger and better-known Jamestown did.

Today was hot as sin—a saying his father had particularly disliked. Had to be over a hundred in the shade. The stifling humidity didn't help. His summer-weight uniform already had wet circles beneath his arms. He could feel sweat running down his spine. Water stations up and down the street offered relief, and merchants and police alike knew to watch for the effects of heat on shoppers.

He'd have been happier if the plan hadn't included a beer garden, set up in the small park, which also boasted a bandstand and a bronze statue of a local Civil War hero, a major in the northern army. Some still muttered that there ought to be a statue representing the Confederate side, as well—or instead. Missouri had been torn in two by conflicting loyalties and an ugly guerrilla war between the Union army and the raiders with Confederate ties.

Food booths in the park were doing good business. His stomach rumbled at the smells emanating from grills. Seeing that Anna Ropp was selling her pierogi, Daniel veered in that direction.

But he detoured at a raised voice in the roped-off beer garden. He shook his head at the sight of an all-too-familiar face, flushed with anger and a beer or two too many. Billy Shaver. No surprise, his brother Damon was with him. Daniel had intended to make one of his every-couple-week stops at their run-down rural property in the next day or two, anyway. The two younger Shaver brothers had walked out of the penitentiary only four months ago after serving time for operating a meth lab in their barn. The oldest Shaver, Jethro, had another six months to go.

Stopping just outside the rope, Daniel caught their attention. "How you boys doing? Good you're out here supporting the fire department."

Billy, the hothead, opened his mouth but swallowed whatever he'd been about to say when Damon elbowed him.

"Just having a beer," Damon said. "Thinking about some lunch. Nothin' wrong with that."

"Not a thing," Daniel agreed, aware of their audience. "I was heading that way myself." He looked over the park. "Hadburg is doing itself proud today. Haven't been called for so much as a shoplifter."

Billy snickered. "Guess them weirdos think God would strike 'em dead if they stole a stick of gum."

Quelling his instinctive dislike for this weasel, Daniel only said easily, "Don't know that it's that extreme. They're raised to believe taking something they haven't earned is wrong. They don't lie, either."

"So that guy over there—" the little creep jerked his head toward a middle-aged Amish couple walking side by side "—tells his wife she's a fat cow before he climbs on top of her?"

"That's a good woman," Daniel said quietly. "She deserves respect." Figuring he'd about reached the end of his store of tact, he nodded and said, "Enjoy yourselves," and walked away.

As much as he disliked the Shaver brothers, he had to wonder how much of a chance any of them had ever had, being raised in that house. Their father had been even more notorious than they were. Once Daniel became sheriff, he had reviewed the domestic violence calls to that address, ending with Clara Shaver dying from a supposed fall down the stairs. Her husband had ultimately drunk himself to death, but not before he'd ruined his sons.

Behind him, a woman's voice rose above the hubbub. "Matthew! Matthew!"

He swung around to see a frantic Rebecca spinning in circles as she screamed her son's name. People hurried to her, trying to help, but she didn't even seem to see them.

Daniel reached her in a few strides. "Rebecca." More sharply, he repeated her name, and she finally focused on his face.

"When and where did you last see your boy?"

"I was buying carved wooden horses from Ike Schwartz, and when I turned around Matthew was gone." Wringing her hands, she cried, "He knows better! What if somebody—"

"I think I see him," he interrupted. Without conscious thought, he slid into Deitsch. "*Ja*, there is Mary

Yutzy, holding his hand. See?" He risked touching her, nudging her to face the woman who hurried toward them, holding the little boy's hand.

Her body quaked until she spotted her son, and then she sagged. Afraid she'd go down onto the concrete sidewalk, he supported her with his arm. But she sprang to life, leaping first to hug Matthew, then to scold him. She appeared to be unaware of the many people listening and probably wondering, as he did, that she spoke English. Did her boy not know Deitsch at all? Daniel speculated. How could that be?

Finally she wound down enough to thank Mary and him. Mary patted Rebecca a few times before hustling back to her table, where she sold honey from her hives.

"Have you two had lunch yet?" Daniel heard himself ask.

Her sky blue eyes widened. "I—"

Matthew shook his head. "Uh-uh. I'm hungry, Mom. Did you see those giant pretzels? I bet they're good. That's where I went. I woulda come right back, 'cept you weren't there." The accusatory tone suggested that if Mom hadn't panicked and started running around like a chicken with her head cut off, she'd have seen him right away. That she'd been afraid he was lost wasn't *his* fault.

Daniel didn't show it, but he thought if Matthew wasn't an all-American kid, he'd eat his hat. The one he rarely wore, of course. Speaking of which…

He ruffled the boy's blond hair. "Did you lose your hat?"

Matthew ducked his head guiltily. "I don't know where it is."

His mother rolled her eyes.

"Come on." Daniel smiled at her. "I'll buy you lunch."

That earned him another wide-eyed look of alarm. "Oh, you don't need—"

"I'd enjoy the company." He glanced at the boy. "Best get Matthew out of the sun."

"Oh!" she exclaimed. "I left my bag—"

While he waited with Matthew, Rebecca hurried back to Ike Schwartz's booth, returning with a woven-grass shopping basket that bulged with her purchases.

He set them moving across the lawn toward the food booths and tents that lined the north end of the park. The location had been chosen to take advantage of the big shady sycamore trees. A couple dozen plastic tables and chairs provided a place for folks to eat.

While mother and son looked at the vendors, Daniel radioed to let his officers know he was taking a break and where to find him. Matthew didn't seem to have ever seen a pierogi and went for a hot dog, while Rebecca chose chili and corn on the cob. Daniel bought giant snickerdoodles for all of them. Matthew decided they were *almost* as good as his *grossmammi's*.

Daniel grinned at him. "Even if they were better, a smart boy wouldn't say so, would he?"

"Uh-*uh*." He had a cute grin that gave him dimples and displayed missing teeth.

Rebecca's bruises had faded and the swelling had gone down, letting him see that she had a classic heart-shaped face, a high forehead framed by rich chestnut hair parted simply down the middle, in the Amish way, and a gauzy white prayer *kapp* with the ties loose. The lilac color of her dress and apron enhanced the blue of her eyes. He guessed her to be five foot six or seven, and curvy. Despite the modest dress with a hem at midcalf, he could tell that much.

Watching her smile at her son, he knew the tug he felt every time he saw her wasn't explained only by her looks. He liked that she wasn't good at hiding what she felt. It all showed on her face. This wasn't a woman used to lying or with any aptitude for it. Her fierce need to protect her son pleased him, too, as did her softness toward him.

Seemed his determination not to think about her this way hadn't lasted past setting eyes on her again.

Predictably, Matthew finished eating first and wanted to go watch the older boys playing a casual game of baseball in the nearby diamond. After making him promise to stay where she could see him, Rebecca let him go. The way her gaze followed him, Daniel could tell she wanted to keep the kid on a leash.

He'd have preferred not to add to her stress, but knew he might not get another chance to talk to her alone. So he asked right out, "Matthew was not raised plain?"

Those beautiful eyes met his, the color deepened by worry and inner conflict she wouldn't like to know she was betraying.

Her shoulders slumped. "I… No."

He raised his eyebrows.

"His father…"

She sneaked a desperate look at him. "We're running away."

No kidding.

Her gaze went to her son, then back to his face. "*Onkel* Samuel thought we should tell you. In case, well…" She hesitated.

"Your husband comes after you?"

Rebecca pressed her lips together. "Matthew's father, but not my husband." She swallowed. "Ex-husband."

Daniel didn't even blink as he stared at her, absorbing the words that changed everything.

SHE SAW HIS SHOCK, followed by understanding.

"He's not Amish. You jumped the fence," Daniel said.

Beyond the instinct that insisted he wasn't anything like the San Francisco detective, Rebecca didn't know why she was telling him anything. But she'd seen his expression as he'd gently teased Matthew and listened to him chattering away over lunch. He already knew. Not everything, but too much. They shouldn't have come today. She'd been foolish to let herself be persuaded by her *aenti*.

Now she had to make a quick decision. Still, there was no reason to lie about her background, given how much he had guessed.

"No," she said, staring across the grass to Matthew, whose fingers were wrapped in the chain link as he watched avidly. At home, he had been begging to play T-ball. "Not me. My mother. She fell in love with my father, who was a grad student here studying the language. He wanted to know how quickly it changed as the Amish migrated."

The sheriff nodded, although it was safe to say he didn't care how her parents had met.

"They were happy. He became a professor. They were, um, killed a few years ago. Matthew doesn't remember them."

Still not getting to the point.

"The thing is, Mom wasn't rejecting her faith or her

roots when she left. She hadn't been baptized yet, so she was able to stay in contact with her family." The Amish were not baptized until they fully committed to the church in their late teens or early twenties. "As a child, I spent summers here with my grandparents."

"The Grabers."

"Yes. I hadn't seen them in ages, but when I wrote asking for help, they didn't hesitate."

"They wouldn't," he said mildly.

"So…here I am." Was that enough to satisfy him?

"Did he hurt you?"

He was a cop. Of course he'd have questions. Probably lots of them.

Her gaze shied away. "No, it's not like that." Wait, she *wanted* him to believe her ex-husband was a stalker. Fumbling, she said, "At least, I…don't know for sure. He's been…threatening. And then, well, a couple things happened that really scared me." She nibbled on her bottom lip as she debated whether she needed to edit the next part. No. There was much she had to keep secret, but not this. "First, I was almost shot," Rebecca told him. "The police thought it was gang related and I just happened to be in the way." The phone threat… No, she couldn't tell him about that, not unless or until she had to admit to the entire story.

"What city?"

"Do you have to know?"

His eyebrows twitched. "We'll talk about that after you tell me the rest of what happened."

Wonderful. This was why it would have been better if she had been able to stay off his radar. But… *Onkel* Samuel was right. Sheriff Byler could be a first line of defense. She just had to convince him not to research any of what she'd told him.

She glanced at her son again before her eyes met his. She had a bad feeling she was baring too much of the pain and fear that filled her every time she thought about Tim. He had turned into a man she didn't like or respect, but she *knew* he'd never have said, *Sure, shoot my ex if you have to. And a threat against my son? Great idea.* He was being terrorized, too—she had to believe that.

Needing to answer the sheriff's question, she touched her cheek gingerly. "This. It happened only two days later. Like I told you, I was crossing the street to get to my own car, parked on the other side. I looked both ways, I swear I did. I'd almost made it when this dark SUV just came out of nowhere. I was flung into the air and came down on the hood of a car coming the other way. I was lucky. So lucky."

"You were," he agreed, his gaze lowering to her hands, clasped tightly together on the plastic tabletop. "Nobody saw the license plate?"

Rebecca shook her head, fluttering the white ribbons. The *kapp* still felt alien. She never wore hats. "Someone just coming out of an apartment building said the driver swerved and accelerated. The woman heard the tires squeal as he went around the next corner. She's the one who called 911."

"You didn't get a good look at the driver."

"Nooo." Uncertainty stretched the word. "I know it was a man, not my husband, but…" She half shrugged. "He could have hired someone." *Please forgive me for the lie*, she thought. But she couldn't tell this man that she didn't believe the real enemy was her ex-husband.

"He could have," Daniel said quietly, although she could tell he had his own thoughts about that. "Had he been stalking you?"

"Not…exactly." She'd intended to stick with the stalking ex-husband scenario, but Daniel—no, no, she had to keep thinking of him as the sheriff—had seen how extreme her panic had been when she lost sight of Matthew. He must have guessed Tim was focused on their son, too. "He wasn't happy about the divorce," she offered. When he didn't leap to fill the silence, she squirmed. "Our big conflict was over Matthew. My ex-husband works ten, twelve hour days at a minimum, but he demanded joint custody." She made a face. "Actually, I'm pretty sure the demands came from his father, who I suspect just wanted me out of the picture. Matthew is *his* grandson, and that's all he cared about." Letting this man hear her bitterness, she added, "I doubt he'd have been the slightest bit interested if Tim and I had had a daughter instead." Oops. She hadn't meant to use his name. But really, a first name didn't tell the sheriff much.

"Are you afraid of your ex-husband or your father-in-law?" he asked.

"I'd say my father-in-law, except… Tim has this *huge* need to impress his father. I wish I thought he was capable of saying no to him, but…" She trailed off.

Matthew turned away from the baseball game and started toward them. Following her gaze, Sheriff Byler said, "Rebecca, if I'm to be of any help, I need to know where you came from. And your ex-husband's full name." His mouth quirked. "Yours, too."

WELL, SHE'D TOLD him that much, if she hadn't lied. Which he was reasonably sure she had, even if not about her name.

Daniel had escorted her to her *aenti*, whose head had been turning until she spotted Rebecca.

"Do you want to stay longer?" Emma asked. "Samuel and I need to take Ephraim and Ruth home. Ephraim keeps saying he is fine, but he doesn't look so fine. We can come back later for you. Or Sarah says Katie and Paul Kurtz will bring her home. You and Matthew could ride along with them."

Ephraim and Ruth were Rebecca's grandparents. Ephraim's heart was failing, Daniel knew. He was surprised the old folks had decided to come out on such a hot day.

Naturally, Rebecca insisted she and Matthew were ready to go, too, which maybe they were. Was Matthew of an age to still take naps?

Daniel returned to his foot patrol after checking with his two deputies that there'd been no disturbances while he ate lunch. He caught a glimpse of a buggy briskly receding down the street in the direction of the Grabers' farm, the reflective orange triangle obvious on the back. Daniel was grateful that the church districts in his county embraced some modern safety standards. In Old Order settlements, every decision was made with a rigid belief that they must trust in God, not modern technology, to protect them. In some, the *Ordnung* did not allow for reflectors on the buggies, far less the battery-operated lights the more pragmatic local bishops permitted. Bishop Jonas had told Daniel their concern was not so much for themselves but for the *Englischers* who might be injured in an easily preventable accident.

Rebecca Holt. Daniel had committed the other names to memory, too. Timothy Gregory. Robert Gregory. Presumably, her kid was a Gregory, too.

He could find more information in a heartbeat now that he knew she'd come from San Francisco, not Pennsylvania. Except he'd made a promise.

"Please," she'd begged, keeping her voice low. "*Please.* Promise you won't contact San Francisco PD in *any* way. Tim's family is prominent enough, I'll bet they have an in at the police department. And that Tim has hired a PI by now. If you do anything, it will draw attention."

Matthew reached them at that inconvenient moment, leaning against his mother, his eyes fastened on Daniel.

"Not without talking to you again," he agreed. He hadn't had a chance to ask why she believed the man she'd been married to wouldn't know her grandparents' names or where they lived. Had her ex never met them?

Daniel had learned to swear casually when he went out in the world, part of the camouflage that had helped him blend into police culture even before his slight accent faded. Now he was trying to unlearn the words. His Amish constituents in particular would be shocked, and he found he didn't like that kind of language. But listening to her talk about the drive-by shooting, as well as being flung into the air by a speeding car, had strained his ability to maintain a professional demeanor. He'd had to bite back a few pungent words.

Even as he exchanged greetings with people, asked how sales were going, helped a frail older lady without the sense to get out of the sun before she collapsed, he kept mulling over what Rebecca had told him—and what she hadn't.

Taking her fears at face value left too many questions in his mind. If the Gregorys were so all-fired powerful!—which usually meant wealthy—why hadn't they challenged the custody agreement in court? Or fought harder for joint custody *before* the divorce was final? Murder was a pretty extreme solution for anyone but a mob figure.

And, while it was possible someone was trying to kill her, he had a lot of trouble believing it was a stalker ex-husband. Usually, domestic violence was up close and personal. Sure, there were instances when a person paid someone to knock off an inconvenient spouse. But those *were* the exception.

In Rebecca's case, she'd had two frightening experiences and, probably because they occurred so close together, leaped to the conclusion that somebody was trying to kill her. He could tell she didn't want to believe that somebody was her ex-husband. Better to blame the former father-in-law she so obviously disliked.

Coincidences bothered him, as they did most cops. But in this instance, he couldn't help thinking that the two near misses actually could have been coincidental. Cities did have more crime and crazier drivers than rural Missouri did. Had she checked to find out whether the drive-by shooting suspect had been arrested? By now, even the hit-and-run driver could have been charged. The police took things like that seriously, and they likely had a scrape of paint from the vehicle, which was a good start.

Had she ever sought a restraining order? He guessed

not. That especially bothered him now that he knew she wasn't Amish. What if the cops were after *her* for some reason?

Knowing how easily he could get some of his questions answered left him frustrated. Still, his promise didn't mean he couldn't do a general search for her ex and his father. He'd have to use his tablet—the police-department computers trawled the internet closer to the speed of a rowboat than a powerboat.

What kind of man had Rebecca Holt married? This need to know was more than curiosity. If it was an itch, it was the kind you got from poison ivy.

"DAD WOULDA HAD fun today, too," Matthew said wistfully, shortly after they left town.

Rebecca's grandmother was preoccupied by Ephraim, who kept irritably shaking off her concern even though they could all tell his breathing had worsened. If she heard Matthew at all, *Grossmammi* didn't react.

"Actually—" Rebecca injected amusement into her voice "—I think your dad would have hated it. He wouldn't have been interested in anything that was for sale." She smiled. "Maybe a straw hat. It is *hot*."

Her son's nose wrinkled. "Really hot. I wish it would get foggy."

She smoothed a hand over his hair. "I doubt we'll get that lucky."

He lapsed into silence again, and she couldn't tell if he was satisfied with their exchange or still thinking about his father. Her eyes caught her grandmother's, and Rebecca realized she'd been listening, after all.

"A nap will be good, *ja*?" she said. "This evening will be cooler. I'm thinking Mose might take you and

Abram fishing tonight or tomorrow. Fresh, fried cat-
fish, yum."

"Or sunfish," Rebecca said suddenly. "I remember
pulling in a few of those from the pond."

Matthew's eyes widened. "Would I have to kill
'em?"

"I think Mose would do that part," Rebecca said.
"He knows the fish you've eaten before came from the
grocery store."

"'Cept at Dad's," he argued. "Justina says she buys
fish at one of the piers, right off the boats. So it's fresh."

Tim had changed housekeepers right after the divorce. Justina was full-time and, according to Matthew,
prepared dinner for Tim as part of her duties. Matthew
liked her, and Rebecca had felt confident he was safe
with her. The meals she'd prepared were considerably
more gourmet than what Rebecca whipped together
after a day's work. The comparison might have annoyed her, except six-year-olds didn't generally appreciate gourmet. Matthew was happiest with fast food or
macaroni and cheese out of a box.

"Did you like the fish she prepared?" Rebecca
asked.

He wrinkled his nose. "It was okay, 'cept she always put gunk on it. Sometimes Dad got mad when I
scraped it off."

"Gunk?" *Grossmammi* queried.

"Sauce."

Matthew didn't like *any* sauce. He preferred his
foods carefully separated and undisguised.

"Ah," *Grossmammi* said, her face crinkling with
humor. "*Aenti* Emma, she won't put this *gunk* on any
fish you catch."

"Fishing might be fun," he decided. "I like Abram's *daad*. He helps us talk together."

"*Gut*," Rebecca said, teasing a bit, then intrigued to see that he didn't seem to notice she'd used Deitsch. She'd picked it up quickly her first summer here, when she was… She had to think. Six or seven. A new language was so much easier to learn at that age.

Matthew was silent for a couple of minutes. Then he mumbled, "I bet my *daad* would like fishing, too."

Rebecca smiled, but worry ratcheted up a notch. Back in San Francisco, Matthew had hardly mentioned his father between visits. So what was this really about?

CHAPTER FIVE

IT DIDN'T TAKE Daniel long to discover that Rebecca Holt was right about her former husband and father-in-law's status in San Francisco. The father lived on Nob Hill, while Tim Gregory had built a monstrosity of a house—featured in a local magazine as an architectural gem—in a neighborhood described as SoMa. Robert Allen Gregory was a venture capitalist, which meant he owned pieces of a lot of other businesses. Mostly high-tech, it appeared. Tim had grown up privileged, but one article mentioned in passing his degree from a state university. Given the younger Gregory's background, Daniel would have expected him to go to Stanford or someplace like that. Had he rebelled? Or had even Dad's influence failed to get him into a school with a fancy name?

Whatever his educational background, Tim had done well for himself, launching a construction business not long out of college with two partners. The senior Gregory's influence might have come to bear there, because they almost immediately made a name erecting ugly but enormous houses and condominiums for people made newly rich with tech start-ups.

Daniel studied a few G, G & S buildings and tried to imagine living in one. Why would anyone want a house big enough for five families when you didn't plan to fill it? As a boy, he had liked being able to hear the murmur of adult voices after he'd gone to bed. He would have been scared to be alone in a bedroom two floors away from the main living space. Apparently, these houses were "wired" to compensate for the great distances between rooms. A little boy could call for Mommy using his intercom.

He shook his head and went back to an article profiling the successful partners of G, G & S Construction. Tim Gregory and a second partner, Steven Stowe, were lean, handsome, tanned men with expensively cut blond hair and flashing smiles. In contrast, the third partner, Josh Griffen, had darker coloring and a bullish build. He came across as more blue-collar, which made sense since, in managing the job sites, he was the one who seemed to do the actual building. He hadn't bothered to summon a smile for the camera. Daniel found a photo of Tim and Rebecca. Its caption mentioned but didn't show Matthew. The other two men were described as "eligible bachelors," often seen on the city social scene.

Most interesting was the succession of articles in the *San Francisco Chronicle* and other newspapers about the shocking embezzlement of funds some ten months before from G, G & S by Steven Stowe, who had handled the money for the firm. The implication was that Griffen and Gregory had begun to suspect some malfeasance and perhaps confronted Stowe, who then disappeared with the money. The amount hadn't been disclosed, but the writer suggested it was "certainly" millions of dollars. Investigators were initially reported to be confident that they would find Stowe and be able to recover some, at least, of the stolen money.

Later articles became shorter and moved from the front page to inside sections. Stowe appeared to be staying on the move. Customs was on alert to prevent him from fleeing the country with his stolen wealth.

Days and weeks between articles followed. Daniel read an interview in a business magazine with Tim Gregory, who expressed heartfelt dismay that a friend could betray him and Griffen. At the same time, he was confident G, G & S would survive and continue to grow. He deftly directed attention to ongoing projects, including the new headquarters for a bank in the financial district.

Months later, that was where the situation remained, without Stowe having been dragged back to the city to stand trial, and with the construction firm seemingly bouncing back from the significant loss of operating capital. *A little help from Daddy?* Daniel wondered.

He was unable to determine when the divorce had happened without the kind of digging he'd promised not to do. The article that included the picture of Rebecca was dated eighteen months ago. She hadn't mentioned the embezzlement. Because she had already separated from her husband?

What were the odds this had nothing to do with her problems? The marriage might already have been history, or the separation and divorce happened later but had nothing to do with the uproar at her husband's company. Or it did, but only because stress exacerbated other problems.

He wasn't buying any of that.

He typed in a query about Robert Allen Gregory's wife and came up with an obituary dated sixteen years before. Quick calculations told Daniel that Tim would have been seventeen. Tim's looks must have come from her: Robert was undistinguished in appearance, except for a certain intensity the camera had captured. Like Josh Griffen, he never seemed to be smiling when the shutter clicked.

Daniel checked email and then turned off his tablet, disturbed. Instinct told him that Robert Gregory could be a dangerous enemy. With Tim, it was harder to determine—but Daniel had seen Rebecca's ambivalence where her husband was concerned. She didn't want to believe Tim was behind the assaults, which was dangerous in and of itself. If he found her, would she give him the benefit of the doubt for what could be a fatal instant?

After a minute, Daniel reached for his remote to turn on the TV.

Staring unseeing at the television screen, he tried to decide what, if anything, he could or should do about Rebecca Holt. Did she really need him?

The answer was very likely no. Given his uneasy feeling she still wasn't offering the entire truth, it might be best if he stayed away from her.

HER METAL BUCKET overflowing with weeds, Rebecca straightened with a groan, then was hit with a wave of light-headedness. Even midmorning, it was roasting hot out here.

The summers of her memory had always been hot, but not like this. *Onkel* Samuel and her cousin Mose weren't saying much—the weather was in God's hands and they wouldn't chafe against His decisions—but she'd seen worry on their faces nonetheless. There hadn't been so much as a thunderstorm since she'd arrived. The corn looked dry. If the cobs didn't mature in time, the entire crop would be a failure. Even the weeds she'd been pulling from the vegetable garden looked anemic, and at least this patch *was* being watered.

Laughter and shouts came from the back of the property. The creek there, while lower than she remembered it, still had enough water to entertain the children. Earlier, Sarah had taken Matthew, Abram and two of Abram's younger siblings to play in the water. Rebecca wanted to join them. Oh, to take off the stockings, hoist her skirt and dip her feet in chilly water! But she had resolutely shaken her head when they'd invited her. *Aenti* Emma had to spell *Grossmammi* in caring for *Grossdaadi*, who wasn't feeling well. He was irritable at the women hovering, but they were afraid to leave him alone. The least she could do was maintain the garden that supplied a good part of the family's food throughout the year.

She should count her blessings they weren't canning today. The hot stove would raise the temperature in the closed air of the kitchen unbearably.

The sound of a car engine came to her. Tensing, she made herself keep trudging to the compost bin. Even here, occasionally cars came and went. The near neighbors were Amish, but they had *Englisch* friends, or their teenage children did, or a sheriff's deputy patrolled, or...

Even if Tim drove up the lane right this minute, Matthew was out of sight and she could disappear by stepping into the cornfield. He would be greeted by puzzlement. Rebecca? *Ja*, they remembered her, she had visited when she was a *kind*, but here now? Why would he think such a thing? Was something wrong? They would pray for her well-being. They could imply much without actually lying.

But this car continued by and her shoulders relaxed.

Rebecca had learned something about herself in the past few weeks. She was very bad at waiting. And that was what this felt like: knowing the other shoe would inevitably drop, but when?

Almost more bothersome was the alternative. What if no one ever came looking for her and Matthew, or they simply never found them? What would she do? Become plain in truth? Raise her son Amish?

In her haste to find safety for herself and Matthew, she hadn't given any thought to a future beyond the coming days and weeks. Now the necessity was becoming unavoidable.

As increasingly comfortable as she was becoming in the Graber household, she knew that staying wasn't really an option. She might be able to give up her telephone and computer—although right now she'd have given a lot to go online to see if her disappearance had become public. But if she stayed and was baptized, Matthew would be limited to an eighth-grade education, and even though she understood and sympathized with the Amish reasons for limiting further education, she wanted something different for him.

Obedience would be a big problem for her, too. In the Grabers' hearing, she *said* the right things but knew that in her heart she was incapable—okay, *unwilling*— to yield herself to a higher authority completely. Rebecca remembered becoming impatient when she was a kid, annoyed at being forbidden to do something because the *Ordnung* said it wasn't allowed, and *Gross-*

mammi lecturing her on accepting the will of God and others better able to judge His will, such as the bishop. *Gelassenheit*, the Amish called this yielding. *Gross-mammi* claimed that it led to a calm spirit, in contrast to the seemingly eternal discontent of moderns.

Rebecca understood the Amish puzzlement with the frenetic way outsiders lived—always wanting more than they had, to get places faster whether there was any urgency or not, suffering boredom when life slowed down. But she didn't believe herself capable of giving up her independence or her right to make decisions for herself—and for her child.

No, like a turtle, eventually she would have to stick her head out of her shell to see whether danger had passed.

There had to be a way to find out who had made those threatening phone calls.

She smoothed damp strands of hair off her sweaty face, tucking them beneath the *kapp*, and carried her empty bucket back to the garden.

A bright flash of blue caught her eye. The bird settled for just an instant on a post at one end of a row of raspberries before taking flight again. Not big enough to be a blue jay. A long-ago memory surfaced. An indigo bunting. *Grossmammi* liked to identify birds and had had a book about them. Rebecca wondered if she still had that book. She'd seen half a dozen different birds today and had no idea what they were. Matthew might be interested, too.

She dropped to her knees and started on a row of green beans.

Another worry crept out of hiding. Had Sheriff Byler kept his word? She'd seen his skepticism and had expected him to appear with more questions, but four days had passed without him dropping by. She ought to be relieved, but for reasons she didn't understand, his absence left her…anxious.

DANIEL STEPPED OUT of the courtroom. He'd just testified in juvenile proceedings having to do with a teenager who had spray-painted obscenities all over two Amish barns. Daniel saw the Byrum police chief walking down the hall toward him.

"Ben."

Around Daniel's age, Benedict Slater had become the chief here in Byrum, the county's largest city and center of government, only a year ago, after the previous police chief suffered a heart attack. The ultimate outsider, Slater had come from Camden, New Jersey, right across the Delaware River from Philadelphia. Nobody seemed to quite know why he'd left a job in a major metropolitan area to take a job in Missouri. Daniel hadn't asked and didn't intend to. The two men were cautiously becoming friends and developing a level of trust, but they hadn't exchanged much that was personal.

Ben was tall and lean, with dark hair and eyes. He smiled and said, "Don't suppose it's anything good that brought you here."

Testifying wasn't Daniel's favorite way to kill half a day. Cops rarely enjoyed the experience of having defense attorneys trying to discredit them.

"Vandalism, believe it or not. And just a kid." He grimaced. "I let him slide the first couple times we caught him, but he won't let up, and he's targeting our Amish families."

"Doing?" When Daniel told him, Ben grunted. "I'd have lost patience, too." He raised his brows. "Do you have time for lunch?"

Ten minutes later, they had taken a booth in the back corner of a Mexican restaurant. After ordering, they exchanged news about ongoing investigations and problems.

Ben had just fired an officer for stealing money and drugs that should have been safely locked in Evidence.

"I'm having trouble holding on to the best officers," he grumbled. "Once they get some experience under their belt, they want to head for the big city."

"Same crimes wherever they go."

He dipped a chip in salsa. "Can't convince 'em."

"I've been lucky," Daniel said. "My deputies all grew up around here, want to stay near family. It helps that they know everyone, and I like that they understand when we need to be flexible and when we can't be."

Having heard only the basics, he asked more about the armed holdup of a popular restaurant here in the county seat. The thieves had struck after closing and gotten away with a surprising amount of cash.

"Including the tip money out of two waitresses' pockets and what the staff had in their wallets." Ben shook his head in disgust. "The employees were all forced to lie facedown on the floor in the kitchen. I think they half expected to be executed."

"Nobody recognized a voice?"

"Nope. The consensus was they sounded like Northerners."

Daniel grinned. "Kind of like you?"

Ben laughed. "Afraid so." Once their entrées had

arrived, he said, "Got any suggestions for persuading an Amish man to testify even if he has 'forgiven' his assailant?"

"Not happening." Daniel took a bite of his burrito, enjoying the spicy flavor, before shrugging. "I shouldn't say that. Mostly, if the assault was personal, you won't get anywhere pursuing it. It's different if the Amish can see that the person you've arrested will continue to be a danger to other people. Cooperation might be possible. They can forgive him for whatever wrong they personally suffered, but testify as to the facts to ensure there are consequences. They hope a stretch in jail will give a wrongdoer time to repent."

Ben gave a sharp, hard laugh.

"Your best bet," Daniel continued, "is to speak to the bishop. Without his permission, no one in the church district will go along with you, whatever their feelings. It pays to try to build relationships with the bishops and ministers in every church district."

Lines in his forehead, Ben said, "My only dealings with them have to do with the businesses that are within the city limits. Not many actually live in Byrum."

Daniel hesitated. "I have more of a history with the Amish. If it's someone I know..."

They talked about the situation, and Daniel shook his head. He knew the bishop in question. "I think you have to let this one go."

"I was afraid of that." Ben gave him a speculative look. "I thought you'd been in office only three years."

"I have." He could, and usually would, leave it at that. But he didn't want to shut the door on potential friendship, not when he had been so aware lately of the distance between himself and others. "I grew up Amish," he said abruptly. "My family lives here in Henness County."

He explained why he wasn't under the *bann*, but that his relationship with his parents and brothers and sisters wasn't an easy one, either. "Jumping the fence is one thing," he said, "but being a cop is something else. We're taught to turn the other cheek, not fight back."

Ben winced, then pushed his almost empty plate away. "Do you mind me asking how it happened?"

Daniel couldn't remember ever telling his story. The reason his family had moved to Missouri from their previous home in Illinois and that he'd jumped the fence was known only among local Amish.

"You know Amish businesses rarely accept credit cards."

"Which means they tend to have a lot of cash on hand."

"Yes. This happened when I was a teenager. The father of a friend of mine owned a furniture and cabinet shop. He had just been paid for a big order, so he had an unusually large amount of money on the premises. He got a call that his mother had taken a bad turn and been transported to the hospital here in Byrum. As it turned out, she'd had a stroke." That part still made Daniel cringe. His friend Josiah had shrugged, insisting that his grandmother was always complaining and this wouldn't be any different than usual.

Ben's gaze never left Daniel's face.

"My friend was working for his dad by then. He promised to close up and take the day's receipts straight to the bank. But he figured, what was the hurry? He could take the money home and drop it at the bank in the morning. His *daad* would never notice. He had a cell phone, as plenty of teenagers do during *Rumspringa*. He called around, said, 'Let's party.' One of the other boys brought beer. There ended up being seven of us there, including two girls."

Daniel didn't like how vivid this memory was, but it wasn't surprising. In something like forty-five minutes, so many lives were damaged, his changed forever.

"It came out later that my friend's father had talked to a fellow merchant about when he was getting paid, and was overheard. Three young guys decided to rob him. When they stormed in, armed, my friend agreed to let them take the money. No matter our belief system, we couldn't have stood up to them bare-handed."

"But the money wasn't all they wanted," Ben said softly.

"No, it wasn't. We stood between those men and the girls, kept blocking them, but doing more than that is in violation of Amish beliefs. They slugged us, knocked us down. I...broke, I suppose you could say. I ripped one of the men off a girl, hit another. I was pistol-whipped and barely conscious from then on. Both girls were raped while the other boys watched. Every minute of it." Anguished, but abiding by their beliefs. "Ultimately, the girls and I were taken to the hospital, so the police were involved, but our bishop was rigid. I had recognized two of the assailants. All three were arrested and most of the money recovered. I was the only person who had been present when those girls were assaulted who was willing to testify against the assailants in court. The bishop reluctantly conceded that I should, but wanted me punished for transgressing our beliefs in fighting back. My father had more mixed feelings, but we still had raging arguments. I felt so guilty, so angry." Meeting Ben Slater's dark eyes, he smiled wryly. "I suppose, in a way, I wanted vengeance."

He still believed he had made the right choice for himself, but he had never entirely quieted doubt, either. "Vengeance is mine," the Lord had said. When would that vengeance be taken? he had asked himself. In the afterlife? How many women had those men already raped? How many would they have gone on to rape, had they been allowed to go free? And yet, his childhood beliefs ran deep. He still had moments when he feared God had tested him, and he had failed.

"My parents understood my decision enough to choose to leave our church district. They pulled up roots and moved here, to Henness County. I stayed at home for a while, but I no longer belonged."

Daniel had no idea what Ben saw on his face, but, after a minute, Ben said, "Becoming a cop hadn't even crossed my mind when I went to college. I was thinking law school. Big, prestigious firm, lots of money."

Both men smiled at the irony. There weren't a lot of zeroes on either of their paychecks.

"My older sister was raped," Ben said abruptly. "No arrest was ever made." His jaw muscles spasmed. "She was never the same. I changed my major to criminology."

Stunned to learn that such similar events had driven them both, Daniel could only nod his understanding.

Ben sighed. "And I have an appointment with the mayor in fifteen minutes, so I need to get moving."

Both dropped twenties on the table and they walked

out together. Ben held out a hand. They shook, nodded again and parted ways.

Daniel wondered how Ben Slater felt about baseball. Maybe he'd enjoy a drive to St. Louis to watch the Cardinals lose to whatever team came to town to whip their asses.

MATTHEW SQUIRMED ON the bench beside her. He had been restless almost from the beginning of the service. Rebecca could follow along in the *Ausbund*, the fat hymnal that held all the words but no scores. The hymns were sung from memory, passed down from one generation to the next. The *Ausbund* was in High German, not the dialect spoken day to day, but enough had come back to Rebecca that she was better able to follow along. She had sung these hymns before. Traditionally coming second in the service, *"O Gott Vater, wir Loben dich"*—"O God the Father, We Praise You"— came to her as if it had been last summer she'd attended the every-other-week services, not eighteen years ago.

Amish children were included in prayer from the time they were toddlers, held on a parent's lap with their hands clasped together for the prayer before meals. Only now that she was a parent did Rebecca realize that she had been coached in much the same way by her mother. Rebecca had never required Matthew to sit still without entertainment for more than half an hour at a time. TV was always available. Games, toys, books.

To him, the sermons in German had to be white noise. Even Rebecca had forgotten how hard it was to sit for hour upon hour on a backless bench. Very young children were sometimes taken out, nursing mothers were excused if they slipped out midway and the elderly were known to fall asleep, but everyone else remained attentive.

Rebecca gently rubbed Matthew's back and hushed him quietly a couple of times. But he kept squirming. Right in the middle of the sermon, he slid off the bench to his feet, his voice ringing out.

"Mommy, I'm bored!"

The minister fell silent. Heads turned.

She closed her eyes in mortification but recognized defeat. Grimacing an apology at the women she had to pass, she hustled him outside and a short distance across the packed gravel to the scanty shade of an apple tree.

"Being bored is not an excuse for rudeness," she said quietly. "You knew from last time what church would be like. I would have held you on my lap, or you could have leaned against me and napped. You're a big enough boy to know better than to interrupt like you did."

His face crumpled, but instead of crying, he spit out, "I want to go *home*! *Dad* wouldn't make me come here." Then he wrenched himself free of her hands and raced toward the house.

Feeling helpless, Rebecca stayed where she was, watching until another woman bent to catch him, spoke to him and led him to the long tables being set with food for the fellowship meal that followed the service. Confident he was safe and desperate to steal a moment to collect herself, she walked behind the parked buggies, then slipped between two of them and rested her arms on the fence. The fawn-brown dairy cows grazing in the pasture beyond the fence continued grazing, uninterested in her.

Had Matthew been using her to twist Tim with guilt into doing what he wanted? She would have liked to ask Tim, except…well, for the fact that he might be going along with a decision to kill her. She laughed without any humor. Yep, just a little complication in their ability to co-parent.

It stunned her that Matthew seemed so angry at her. She hadn't seen any displays of stubbornness or defiance with his *aenti* and *onkel* or grandparents. Perhaps she should ask Mose. Especially now, with *Grossdaadi* failing, Mose frequently kept Matthew with him along with Abram. Matthew was proud because he was learning some farm chores. He had helped throw hay into mangers and even, in a small way, to harness a horse. Yesterday, Mose had put the two boys to work scrubbing a buggy. Matthew hadn't seemed to mind.

So, why the anger at her? Had he guessed that she might really be taking him away from his father forever?

At the sound of an engine in the somnolent heat of the day, she turned her head. A marked police SUV approached slowly along the road. Feeling a flutter in her chest, she thought of stepping back between buggies. Would the driver see her?

When the vehicle eased to a stop on the shoulder of the paved country road, she knew he had.

CHAPTER SIX

THIS WAS STUPID. Daniel knew he should drive on. But he'd already set the emergency brake and turned on the warning lights. Ignoring his better judgment, he hopped out and strode up the lane to where Rebecca Holt stood, alone, hidden from the rest of the fellowship by the row of black buggies. The service couldn't possibly be over. Why wasn't she still in the barn?

"Rebecca."

She eyed him skittishly. "Sheriff. What brings you out here today?"

"My deputies and I make a point of patrolling before and after church services. I worry with so many buggies on the roads."

Fortunately, she didn't point out that he was more than a little premature.

"Where's Matthew?" he asked.

She turned back to face the dairy herd, her shoulders slumping. He hungrily studied the graceful line of her neck, bared between the simple, collarless dress and the *kapp*.

"He threw a temper tantrum in the middle of a sermon," she said. "I had to take him out of the barn. When I let him know I was disappointed because he couldn't be any more patient, he yelled at me and ran off."

Daniel went on alert despite the stultifying heat. "You're looking for him?"

"No, one of the women setting out food has him. I should be helping her since I didn't go back into the service."

"Do you understand the sermons?"

She smiled a little. "I'm afraid not. The Deitsch is coming back to me. Just everyday conversation, you know. But I can't claim to be grasping the subtleties."

Daniel leaned on the fence, too, but facing her. "It's hard for a little boy when he doesn't understand a word."

Rebecca wrinkled her nose. "Are you chiding me? You don't have to. *I'm* the one who was impatient. And everyone there knows—" She came to a sudden stop, the whites of her eyes showing.

"That neither of you are Amish?" he said sardonically. "That he doesn't speak Deitsch, far less understand the High German used by the ministers?"

"I don't suppose he'd appreciate what they were saying even if he did."

He laughed. "No, I remember being hideously bored during church services. I was glad when I was old enough to sit with friends and not be under my father's eagle eye. We managed to pass a few notes and poke each other with our elbows, unseen by our elders."

Rebecca smiled at him, her eyes sparkling, the curve of her lips tempting. "I'll bet *you* didn't announce how bored you were out loud."

"Is that what he did?" Chuckling, Daniel shook his head. "I wouldn't have dared. Was it Bishop Jonas speaking? My impression is that he, at least, has a sense of humor."

She rolled her eyes. "Of course not. It was Amos King."

The stern owner of the custom butcher shop. Daniel hid a grin. He had sometimes wondered why Amos hadn't moved to southern Missouri, where the Amish settlements were considerably more conservative.

"I should go back."

He leaned against the fence. "I've been meaning to catch up with you, anyway. Unless someone will worry?"

He could tell she wanted to make an excuse to escape, but after a moment she shook her head. "No, I doubt anyone will miss me for a few minutes."

She returned her gaze to the cows. He looked at her.

"I searched for your ex-husband and father-in-law online." When he saw the alarm flaring on her face, he shook his head. "I read newspaper articles on my personal tablet, that's all. There were plenty of them. Even your house was featured in a Sunday supplement."

She must have heard the question in his voice, because she said, "Tim built it for me. Only, he never asked what I liked." Her sigh was almost soundless and somehow…sad. "It's hideous. The house, I mean."

"Wouldn't appeal to me," he admitted, thinking that was more tactful than an outright agreement.

For a minute, the familiar drone of cicadas was the only sound. Then Rebecca glanced at him. "I suppose you read about the embezzlement."

"Kind of jumps out at you. I couldn't help wondering if you were still married during that mess."

She nodded. "The worst was the several months before it all came out."

"All came out? You mean, when Stowe took off."

Her eyes skipped away from his, then came back. "Yes. I knew something was wrong. Tim was…tense, all the time, but he would never say why. He just… withdrew. I found myself living with a stranger. If I pushed him to talk, he'd get angry. Once he—" she sneaked a look at Daniel "—he shoved me so hard, I slammed into the corner of a kitchen cabinet. That was the only incident I'd call violent, and he horrified himself." She hunched her shoulders. "Weirdly, once everything came to a head, I could tell he was relieved. He became, I don't know, more himself again."

"Relieved?" Not the usual reaction to finding out a trusted partner had just ripped off a significant portion of the assets of the company you'd built.

Rebecca nibbled on her lip. "It…seemed odd to me, too, but I decided that the hardest part had been knowing something was wrong, but not what. I'm guessing he and Steven and Josh were arguing. Blaming each other for financial problems. Once Tim knew what he had to deal with and could make a plan, he seemed certain they could ride it out."

Daniel supposed that made sense. The unknown was the most frightening. He couldn't feel a drop of sympathy, however.

"So he gave a sigh of relief and took you out for a romantic dinner?"

"Something like that." Now she met his eyes squarely. "He thought we could go happily on, as if the past few months hadn't happened. That's when I left him. I supported him through the worst, but I no longer liked or respected him."

A sudden burst of voices from the direction of the barn signaled that his time was up.

"Do you have a cell phone?" he asked.

"No, I left it behind so it couldn't be used to trace us. And I promised my *aenti* and *onkel* that, while we're with them, we will live plain."

"You might talk to them. If you agree not to use it except for emergencies, they might agree. We could get you a cheap, pay-as-you-go phone."

"But I'd have no way to charge it," she pointed out. "And the phone shanty isn't far."

No, it wasn't; it sat right between the Grabers and the neighboring farm, owned by Noah Yoder. But getting to it meant cutting through a cornfield and squeezing through strands of a barbed-wire fence or walking down the road. The small wooden enclosure was open to the road, too—no place to hide if someone was hunting you.

"All right," he said reluctantly. "You've been here, what, two and a half weeks? And there hasn't been even a hint that your ex-husband has located you? He may just be waiting, assuming that because of Matthew you'll eventually get in touch."

"Maybe," she agreed, but doubt leaked through. She didn't believe Tim Gregory would wait, maybe because she knew the man to be impatient by nature. Daniel could understand a father frantic to find his missing child.

He would really like to see the custody agreement. Something about Rebecca Holt got to him, which made him vulnerable to being manipulated. Her family here would have accepted whatever she said at face value. But what if *Tim* had primary custody, not her at all, and she was the one breaking the law by fleeing with her son? The rest of her story could be a smoke screen.

Except he'd seen her bruised face. And seen how afraid she was, how haunted. He half lifted his hand, wanting to comfort her, to touch her cheek, rosy now like the sun-kissed skin of a ripe peach.

"When you looked online," she said suddenly, "did you see anything about me taking off? It might have made the news if he'd reported Matthew and me missing."

"Nothing," he said. "Custodial interference would be taken seriously, of course." She didn't noticeably react, so he continued, "I doubt the police would have taken a missing-persons report if it was obvious you had packed up and left voluntarily."

"We…didn't take all that much with us. Because I knew we wouldn't need electronics or our *Englisch* clothes, and handling heavy suitcases when we kept changing buses didn't seem like a good idea."

"In other words, someone glancing around your apartment—house?—might not have been able to tell you had packed at all."

"Except I had my purse, of course. And I paid the rent a few months in advance. Oh, and I got rid of all the disposable food." Her nose wrinkled. "I couldn't leave stuff rotting in the refrigerator or molding in drawers."

"Who else had a key to your place?"

"Only the building management. They have to let themselves in for maintenance sometimes."

They both heard a woman calling her name.

"I have to go." Without so much as a goodbye, Rebecca whirled and hurried away. He lost sight of her as soon as a buggy blocked his view.

Daniel didn't linger. He wouldn't be welcome here

on a church Sunday. If he was spotted, it would be an embarrassment to his parents. Getting into his patrol vehicle, he wondered if Rebecca had gotten to know his mother or sisters at all. It was a strange thought. As members of the same church district as Samuel Graber's family, they had known she and her son were hiding from a bad man and weren't really Amish long before he did.

As always, thoughts of his family made him aware of the hollow, chronic ache in his chest.

THE FOLLOWING SATURDAY, Daniel sat by the window in the Hadburg Café, idly watching the very occasional passerby as he sipped iced tea and waited for his burger and fries. Hot as it was, no one much wanted to be outside. Sometimes a heat wave led to an increase in crime, but this one seemed to have made people too enervated to cause trouble. His radio had been mostly silent today.

A few cars had passed, as well as some horses and buggies. While he watched, a few Amish men in their dark trousers, blue shirts, suspenders and straw hats had gone into the harness shop, some carrying straps of leather and buckles that probably needed to be repaired or replaced. From this angle, the only one Daniel had recognized was Isaac Bontrager, a man with a distinctively stork-like build and jerky gait.

Daniel's food still hadn't arrived when a silver sedan pulled to the curb across the street in front of Olde Country Antiques. The man who got out wore chinos, a powder blue polo shirt and sunglasses with a gold sheen. Everything he wore looked expensive. He closed his door, then took his time studying the businesses lining Grove Street. Odd to park before he'd spotted his destination, Daniel thought.

Deborah Chupp set his food down in front of him, but he kept an eye on the stranger even as he thanked her. If the man had been accompanying a wife eager to browse gift and quilt shops, Daniel wouldn't have paid the same attention. As it was, the guy looked out of place.

Apparently making up his mind, the stranger walked halfway up the block to Miller's General Store. Heck, he might have just stopped on his way through town for something cold to drink or a snack. Still—why hadn't he parked right in front, or in the lot to the side?

He strolled out a few minutes later, hands empty. Daniel popped a French fry in his mouth and watched as the man went into the fabric-and-quilt store, the harness shop, the creamery and an Amish furniture store. In fact, every business he had entered was clearly posted as Amish. He skipped the liquor store, the gas station and the town's one-and-only real estate agency.

Then he crossed the street so that Daniel lost sight of him.

Done with his meal, Daniel dropped bills onto the table and called his thanks to Anna Mae Kemp, a distant cousin and widow who ran the café. When he stepped out on the sidewalk, he couldn't see the stranger, so he crossed the street and went into the general store.

Slow day like this, Yonnie Miller seemed to be alone, desultorily stocking shelves that held single-serving snack foods.

"Yonnie." Daniel nodded. "A fellow came in here a minute ago."

"*Ja, Englisch.*"

"Looking for something you don't sell."

"Seemed so."

"Mind telling me what?"

Yonnie considered for a minute. "Said he heard some Amish hereabouts breed Percheron horses." He shrugged. "I told him about Willard Hostetler and Big Ike and Little Ike Mast."

"Not Samuel Graber?"

"No. Thinking two was enough."

"Did he ask for directions?"

"I offered and wrote them down. He shoved the piece of paper in his pocket, not so careful."

Daniel had no trouble with the subtext of this conversation. Yonnie wasn't a member of the Grabers' church district, but he had heard something, enough to know not to send a stranger to Samuel Graber's farm.

"*Denke.*" Daniel then said in Pennsylvania Dutch, "Just curious, I am. He seems to be walking around town asking questions."

"*Ja*, lots of questions, that one."

Back out on the sidewalk, he took the time to jot down the license-plate number and make and model of car, although he felt sure it would turn out to be a rental. Then he went into the fabric store, where his appearance created a flutter of interest in the group of ladies seated around a quilt frame in the back room. A log-cabin quilt in sunny colors was stretched in the frame.

"Don't get up," he said when Gloria Wagler started to stand. "Just wondered what the *Englisch* man wanted. He seems to be checking out all the businesses."

The women exchanged glances. Rose Chupp, sister-in-law of Paul Chupp and *aenti* of Deborah, who had just served Daniel at the café, spoke up.

"He said he thought to buy a quilt to surprise his wife. He looked at the ones displayed—" she nodded toward the front room, where quilts hung from wooden dowels on the walls "—but not as if he saw what he wanted. He said he was told Ruth Graber was an especially fine quilter."

"Which she is," one of the other women chimed in. Rebecca's grandmother.

Gloria, whose shop this was, said, "I showed him two quilts she made, one for a bed, one smaller. He barely looked at them. He wanted to speak to her, ask her to make a custom quilt."

Rose Chupp, who it so happened was a good friend of Daniel's mother, said, "I told him Ruth's husband is in poor health and she has no time to make new quilts."

"We suggested other quilters. So many fine ones whose quilts I sell." Gloria's gaze was opaque when it met his. It appeared that she was aware of Rebecca Holt's situation, but didn't know *he* knew. "I said if he didn't like these, there are places in Byrum and River Grove for him to look. Or he could go to Jamestown. He said he just wanted to talk to Ruth."

"Hope you didn't tell him how to find her. She doesn't need to be bothered right now."

"I didn't, but someone else might."

"Thank you."

He stepped out to see the man crossing the street toward him. And not pleased to see a uniformed police officer, Daniel decided.

He waited on the sidewalk, smiling pleasantly.

"Don't know how you can resist buying something," he observed.

"I always like to look first, think about what I saw," the man said. His salt-and-pepper hair was cropped short, the crease in his chinos sharp. Thin but athletic, he was likely in his forties. He pulled his keys from his pocket. "Not a lot here, in a town this size."

Daniel really would have liked to see his eyes. Hard to judge a man hidden behind dark glasses.

"If you're looking for Amish crafts," he suggested, "you might prefer Jamestown."

"You're the third person to say that." He sounded irked. "Thought I might get better prices off the beaten track."

"Are you staying locally?" Daniel asked pleasantly.

His face tightened. "Haven't decided. Now, if you'll excuse me…"

"If there's anything I can do to help, you let me know."

The man took a couple of steps, then stopped and turned. "Maybe there is. I'm looking for a young woman who might be staying with her grandparents. Ephraim and Ruth Graber. You wouldn't know them, would you?"

"Amish, are they?" Daniel scratched his head. "We have a lot of Grabers in these parts. You know how many kids they tend to have. I imagine you could find some Grabers down in Daviess County, too, and probably Livingston. Of course, they aren't listed in any phone book. Don't believe in having phones."

"Ruth is a quilter, I'm told."

"Did you check at the quilt shop? They'd probably have heard of her."

"The woman there said her husband is ill and she's not taking commissions right now. Really, I'm more interested in her granddaughter and great-grandson who might be visiting."

"Did you tell the ladies that?"

He hesitated. "No. This is…a delicate situation."

"If that's so, why don't you come on over to the station and we can talk. I'm the Henness County sheriff, Daniel Byler."

"I appreciate the offer, but I'd rather keep this casual for now. I'd just like to talk to the woman, that's all."

"May I ask why?"

"Nothing you need to be concerned with," he said, sounding a lot less friendly. "Excuse me."

Daniel watched as he got in his car and drove past without his head so much as turning. Pondering, Daniel started down the sidewalk toward the sheriff's department headquarters, two blocks east and one block down a cross street.

The stranger wasn't Tim Gregory, Robert Gregory or Josh Griffen. Daniel would have recognized them. He wasn't Steven Stowe, either, assuming the missing man would have any interest at all in Rebecca or her son. A PI, Daniel suspected. He surely had stood out in this small, dusty town. Daniel wanted to think the guy would widen his search to Byrum and beyond, but something told him they wouldn't be that lucky. The fact that he had Ephraim's and Ruth's names, knew she was a quilter and that Ephraim had bred Percheron horses meant he was too close to his target.

Daniel wished Yonnie had pretended not to know anyone who bred Percherons. Either Willard Hostetler or one of the Masts, father or son, might generously share the name of a competitor.

Speaking of names... First thing he'd do was run the plates. Call the rental company, if the car was indeed a rental.

And then he'd better take a drive out to talk to Rebecca and Samuel.

REBECCA WAS RETURNING from the *grossdawdi haus* with a tray of dirty dishes when she saw the familiar sheriff's department SUV turn into their lane. Feeling a squeeze of fear, she prayed Daniel Byler was here only to ask more questions. Nosy as he was, that was likely, she told herself.

She slipped into the house and set the tray beside the kitchen sink. Her *aenti* smiled at her. "*Denke* for fetching those. It's *gut* to see Ephraim must have finished his soup, at least."

"He looks a little better." She smiled. "He scolded me for not wearing my *kapp*, so I asked why he wasn't wearing his hat."

Aenti Emma chuckled. "A stickler he always is." She sobered. "It's this hot weather. When it turns cool, you'll see, he will feel better."

Rebecca knew that nobody except possibly her grandmother really believed that. They all knew the end was coming. The inevitability made Rebecca glad she had had a chance to see him again, and that Matthew was old enough to remember meeting his great-grandfather.

A rap on the door had her *aenti* starting. "Who—"

"The sheriff is here again."

"Ah." Her face relaxed. "Then it is you he wants to see."

"Is Matthew actually asleep?" He only occasionally napped, but had been droopy today in the afternoon heat.

"I haven't heard a peep."

Nodding, Rebecca went to let the sheriff in. She hoped each time she saw him that the impact of his presence would lessen, but once again she felt breathless the minute he stepped into the kitchen. Aside from his strong build and too-perceptive eyes, he had an air. He wouldn't be a very good subordinate, she thought—people would always assume he was in charge. She bet that even as a boy, he had been the leader of his crowd.

"Let me cut you a slice of raspberry pie," *Aenti* Emma said briskly. "The coffee is always on, but we have lemonade, too."

"Thank you," he said, "but nothing this time. I ate at the café in town." He patted his stomach.

"*Ach*, if it's Rebecca you need to see, why don't you two sit out on the porch? There might be a breeze, *ja*?"

Of course there wasn't a breeze. *Aenti* Emma was offering a degree of privacy.

"I'd hoped to speak to Samuel, too," the sheriff said, his tone grave.

Rebecca's heart constricted. "I'll run and get him."

The farrier had come to shoe several horses, so she found her *onkel* where she'd expected, in the barn holding one of the massive beasts. Mose was there, too, as was Samuel's youngest son, apprenticed to the farrier. When she told them her errand, Mose gripped the horse's halter and Samuel accompanied her out of the barn.

"Did the sheriff say why he needs to speak to me?" he asked.

"No. But he looked worried, I think."

With his big, callused hand, he patted her shoulder. "Trust in God, Rebecca. You take too much on yourself."

She managed a smile at him and kept her rebellious thoughts unspoken.

Daniel was waiting for them on the porch, his shoulder resting against an upright. He watched as they approached, lines scoring his forehead. He exchanged nods with her *onkel*. Samuel urged her to sit on the porch swing, and even joined her when Daniel said, "I sit too much of the day already."

Then *Onkel* Samuel asked, "What is this about?"

"A man came to town today looking for Rebecca and Matthew."

Rebecca pressed her hand to her mouth.

Regret darkened Daniel's eyes when he saw how stricken she was, but he continued, telling them about the stranger who went to most of the Amish businesses in town, framing his questions differently in each. "At the quilt shop, he had heard what a fine quilter Ruth is and wanted to talk to her about taking a commission. At Miller's and in the harness shop, he was asking about breeders of Percherons. He wasn't satisfied by the names he was given, the Masts and Willard Hostetler. In each store, he tried a different story. Only with me did he admit he hoped to locate Ephraim and Ruth's granddaughter, maybe here for a visit."

A sound escaped from behind her fingers, one she didn't recognize. Daniel straightened. Her *onkel* took her free hand in his.

"We have to leave. Right now." She started to stand.

Onkel Samuel pulled her back down. "Let Sheriff Byler tell us the rest. Was this man Matthew's father?"

"No." His eyes locked on to hers. "He was a private investigator. I looked up the license-plate number on his car, determined it was a rental and called the company. The woman there gave me the man's name and I found him online. He owns a private investigation firm based in San Francisco. If he doesn't get any co-operation, he may not want to stay here long. Nobody in town I spoke to told him how to find this place. They went out of their way *not* to, Rebecca. Some aren't in your church district and probably don't know, but they didn't trust the man today, and they didn't want to give him what he asked. Everyone sensed there was something wrong with his interest."

"Somebody will tell him," she burst out. "*Onkel* Samuel's Percherons are well-known. Even in Byrum, people will say, go talk to Samuel Graber."

Her *onkel* didn't express his usual humility, because she was right. He had buyers from up in Iowa and down to southern Missouri, maybe farther away.

"Your ex-husband was only making a guess when he sent the PI to check here." The father-in-law was another possibility, Daniel had realized. Tim Gregory might have shared what he knew about Rebecca's grandmother being a quilter, her grandfather breeding the magnificent draft horses. The guy had paid more attention when she talked about those summers spent here than she'd believed. "It might be best if this man does get this far. If there is no sign that you and Matthew have ever been here, they'll move on to searching elsewhere."

She stared at him, aghast. "You're suggesting…
what?"

"That you stay close to the house and keep Matthew
out of sight, too. If Samuel and Emma are willing to
mislead him…"

He was careful not to say "lie to him," Rebecca
noticed.

"*Ja*," Samuel said. "No one needs to know we have
family visiting."

"He'll try to insist on talking to Ruth or Ephraim,"
Daniel warned.

Her *onkel's* expression became forbidding. "Bothering them, I will not permit."

"How is Ephraim?" Daniel asked, his voice becoming gentler, as if he really cared.

Samuel shook his head. "Not good, no. His heart
is giving out."

"So my mother said. I'm sorry. He will be missed."

"*Ja*." Her *onkel* cleared his throat. "I still need his
advice. No one knows horses like my *daad*."

His grief touched Rebecca even through her fear.
Did she dare stay? What if the PI didn't drive openly
up to the house, but sneaked across the field, instead,
and saw her or Matthew outside?

"Did that man look like someone who would sneak
around in the woods or fields?" she asked, surprising
both men.

Daniel's mouth curved. "He looked like he'd never
been out of the city. He wouldn't want to snag his fancy
trousers on a fence or step into a pat of manure. I don't
think you need to worry about that."

Onkel Samuel was chuckling. "The horses would be
curious about a stranger in their pasture. They would

follow him, lip his hair thinking it might be a new kind of hay, even step on his heels."

Daniel laughed out loud. "I'd like to see that. This man didn't seem the type to have ever been in touching distance of a horse. And such a big one?"

Rebecca still felt reassured despite her exasperation at the two men's open merriment. Daniel was right—if they could fool the PI, he'd go back to San Francisco and tell Tim she wasn't here. The challenge would be keeping Matthew close.

"Thank you," she said, letting herself meet Daniel Byler's dark blue eyes. "It was good of you to let us know someone was asking about me."

He stayed still for a moment that felt a little too long. "Did you think I wouldn't?"

"No, I—"

He gave her no chance to explain or apologize, only dipped his head, said, "Samuel, Rebecca," and walked away.

CHAPTER SEVEN

"REBECCA GREGORY?" *ONKEL* SAMUEL repeated the name the stranger had given him, then seemed to ponder. He took off his straw hat and slapped it against his thigh. "I have a cousin Rebecca," he said helpfully. "She married Marvin Bontrager, over Hickory Creek Way. But she was a Troyer before she married. This Gregory…" He shook his head.

Rebecca could see only the strange man's back from where she stood tensely to one side of the window in Sarah's bedroom, looking out to the driveway. Would he turn so she could catch sight of his face? She didn't recognize the mix of dark and gray hair, salon-cut in contrast to her *onkel's* thick bowl-cut. He had to be the private investigator Daniel Byler had told them about Saturday. Truthfully, she was surprised it had taken him two days to find them.

Rebecca, who had been in the kitchen when the car drove up the lane, had seen how quickly her *onkel* strode from the barn, intercepting the man as soon as he got out of the silver-gray sedan. *Onkel* Samuel hadn't so much as glanced toward the house.

Aenti Emma had flapped her dish towel at Rebecca. "Shoo! Upstairs with you, but not to worry."

How could she not? Matthew was playing with Abram, and though Mose's wife, Esther, knew to keep the boys close, would Matthew come over if he heard the car?

Sarah's window was open but screened, so Rebecca could just hear the voices drifting up. Even as she strained not to miss a word, she kept glancing toward the cornfield or creek where Matthew would appear if he returned unexpectedly.

"I should have said Rebecca Holt," the stranger said. "She went back to her maiden name after the divorce."

"Rebecca Holt," Samuel repeated, sounding enlightened. "*Ja*, her I remember. Little girl, used to visit summers. My niece, she is. Loved to fish and run wild with the boys. Her *grossmammi* tried to teach her to quilt, but that girl had no patience for sitting down." Smiling, he shook his head.

"I'm told she's visiting you now, her and her son, Matthew." The quick, sharp voice suggested the private investigator was struggling for the same patience Rebecca had lacked as a girl. *Onkel* Samuel's deliberate way of speaking would be driving the outsider crazy.

"Visiting?" *Onkel* Samuel sounded surprised. "Who told you that? She came… Let me think." He stroked his beard. "My Mose was having his *Rumspringa*. He might have been sixteen? Seventeen? He has four *kinder* of his own now, a blessing they are. So I think my niece Rebecca was eleven or twelve. Such a nice little girl. My *mamm* and *daad* were real sorry when she didn't come again. Her *mamm*—who was my sister, you know—wrote to say that Rebecca wanted to stay close to her friends. She writes sometimes, Rebecca does."

"Recently?" The question shot out with the explosive force of a gun firing.

"She did write of her divorce. It might have been in January or February the letter came. Sorry we were to hear about it, but he wasn't such a good man." He shook his head in obvious dismay. "Is it him who sent you looking for her?"

"Yes. She took off with his little boy. He is desperate to find his son."

"She might be afraid he would hurt the boy, seems to me."

"He loves his kid," the PI snapped.

"Men who say they love their wives and children sometimes hurt them, anyway," *Onkel* Samuel observed, an edge in his voice for the first time. "A man like that might hire someone like you to find a wife and son who ran away because they were afraid."

"You're saying that's why she took off?"

"No, no. How would I know?" Samuel did *perplexed* well. "No, I was asking *you*."

"I'm told they were having a custody dispute. She didn't want Matthew spending time with his father, which is wrong. A boy should grow up knowing his dad, don't you think?"

"Usually that is so, *ja*. But I can't help you find her so you can ask." He shrugged and clapped his hat back on his head. "Is that all?"

"No. If you'd point me their way, I'd like to talk to Ephraim and Ruth. They may have heard from her and not told you."

"Not so. They would have shared such news. And I will not let you bother them. My *daad's* heart is failing, and it's all my *mamm* can do to care for him. She does not need to worry more, this time about her granddaughter." There was no give in his voice. The PI was fortunate he hadn't been foolish enough to come here yesterday. Sundays were not to be defiled by such errands. *Onkel* Samuel took a step back. "I have told you what you need to know. I think you should leave now."

The PI, at least temporarily accepting that he'd worn out his welcome, handed *Onkel* Samuel a business card and asked for a call if he heard from Rebecca, thanked him for his time and got back in his car. Still hovering out of sight in case he looked up at the house, she watched as he backed up a couple of times to turn around, then drove down the lane, dust rising behind him.

Still without a glance toward the house, *Onkel* Samuel returned to the barn. Knees suddenly weak, Rebecca let herself sink onto the edge of the bed. Her breath came fast. Had the man been convinced? She wished she could have seen his face.

When she thought back, she realized that *Onkel* Samuel hadn't once lied. He'd never said *I haven't seen her in years* or *I've never even met her son*. Would the private investigator run through the conversation in his mind as he drove, and realize there had never been a denial, only reminiscences about those long-ago visits? If so, would he dare come back?

The panicked part of her wanted to grab Matthew and run. The more rational part asked where she would go, and how she would get there. With this investigator prowling around town, she couldn't catch the bus here. And what if he decided to watch the farm? He might follow if Mose or *Onkel* Samuel set off with a woman and child in a buggy.

And even if she succeeded in getting away, what then? She was back to the same worries about the future that had been keeping her awake nights. She had money, but it wouldn't last forever. And going on the run would mean not enrolling Matthew in school.

Stay, she decided, even though when she looked down, she saw that her hands shook. All she could do was hope Daniel was right, that the PI would go back to San Francisco now and tell whoever had hired him that she and Matthew weren't here.

Staring at the bright rectangle made by the window but not focusing on the blue sky outside, she wondered whether they would be satisfied if she mailed the ring and wallet to Tim. If she no longer had the proof that Tim had been involved in Steven's likely fatal disappearance, would he still consider her a danger?

Maybe not…but what about Josh? She was still a witness—and she believed Tim when he said it was Josh, always an enigma to her, who was the real threat. If Tim had been sincere when he claimed he hadn't had anything to do with Steven's death or the threats against her, that left Josh. Even if she relinquished the physical proof, she *knew* Steven wasn't out there dodging cops and somehow enjoying his embezzled millions. And she trusted Josh considerably less than she trusted Tim.

Besides, there was still Matthew. Tim *couldn't* let his son go, not without standing up to his father in a way he'd never been able to do. Squeezing her fingers together until they were bone white, she realized how foolish she'd been to take the ring and wallet in the first place—and to succumb to the temptation to use them in a kind of blackmail.

But I might have lost Matthew.

And she couldn't go back and do anything differently.

She ached to tell someone the whole story, ask for advice. She knew who she wanted to tell, but she was too afraid to take such a risk. All the same qualms nipped at her like hovering mosquitoes. He would want her to go to the police in San Francisco, which meant Detective Estevez. If she did that, she would again be within Josh Griffen's reach. Tim would likely be tried and convicted for, at the very least, aiding and abetting in a murder—assuming she lived long enough to testify. With Matthew's father behind bars, Robert would gain custody if anything happened to her. No court in California would award custody to an Amish *aenti* and *onkel* over a respected, wealthy local businessman, and that was assuming her family asked for custody. Going to court wasn't something the Amish did.

The dilemma hadn't changed. The wallet and the possibility of her testifying were all she had to hold off the man who had made those calls, as well as Robert's hunger to control his grandson.

Gradually, she succeeded in calming herself. She needed to help start dinner. She could let herself believe that she and Matthew were safe here now. It made sense to stay cautious, yes. But living in fear wouldn't keep them any safer.

And it would be best if Sheriff Byler didn't drive out here again. If anyone was watching, that would only draw attention. If she was going to keep quiet about what she had done and the secret she had cached beneath a floorboard in the barn, she needed to avoid drawing *his* attention.

So far as Daniel could tell, Clint Myers, the private investigator, had left town. Later in the day, after Daniel had spoken to him, Myers had checked into a bed-and-breakfast in Byrum. Waiting, unable to do anything beyond give Rebecca the warning, Daniel had spent a restless, edgy day and night until the owner of the B and B called on Monday to inform him that Myers had left after a two-night stay.

That same morning, Anna Mae Kemp rushed out of the café as Daniel walked past, calling his name.

"A message," she said, sounding breathless, "from Sarah Graber. She brought her *mamm's* sticky buns for me to sell, and asked me to tell you that the man came out to the farm and her *daad* talked to him. She said Samuel sent that man away, no problem, and you would know what she was talking about."

"I do," he agreed, wishing he could feel more relief. He'd give a lot to drive out to the Grabers' and find out exactly what was said. How had the PI justified his search for Rebecca? Disturbed, Daniel knew she might take off again with him being none the wiser. No way to stop her. Why hadn't he told her to stay in touch with him, no matter what happened?

Not that he'd have believed a promise. Rebecca didn't trust him, not yet. Maybe because her troubles were more complicated than she had admitted. Maybe because she hadn't told the truth at all—or, at least, not the entire truth.

Frowning, he got into his patrol car and sat for a minute. How could he be so attracted to a woman he knew might be lying to him? Going as far as thinking he might scrap his integrity and help her escape even if she was the one in the wrong?

Yes, she might be stealing her son when she didn't have full custody. It happened. If that was so, he felt strangely certain she had a good reason. After seeing her battered face, yes, he believed she could very well be afraid that her ex-husband would abuse her little boy, too.

During the night, he'd had the uncomfortable thought that she might have something to do with the embezzlement. Her flight could be out of fear her role would be discovered. Or she could have had an affair with Steven Stowe. What if they had arranged to meet up later, when they thought it would be safe? Would another stranger, a handsome blond one, show up in Hadburg? But Daniel trusted his own judgment of people enough to instinctively reject any scenario where Rebecca had stolen millions of dollars. It was stupidly credulous, maybe, to be so certain, but he was.

He would help her if he could, but he needed to quit thinking there could be anything between them. If she'd been Amish, that would have been a nearly impossible obstacle. She wasn't, but that only meant she had no reason to stay in this remote corner of Missouri once she could safely leave. And that was assuming her life didn't become a series of temporary stops, one step ahead of the men who were hunting her.

Or that she didn't go to jail.

There were plenty of pretty women around, he told himself. He ought to start looking instead of focusing on one consumed by fear and a fierce need to protect her child. A woman with trouble at her heels.

Somehow, this minute, he couldn't think of a single other woman who might interest him.

Growling under his breath, he fired up the engine

and decided it was time to visit the Shaver brothers, just to remind them that he was watching. He wanted no meth labs in his county.

And tonight…he might visit the Grabers, after all. If Rebecca didn't know him beyond superficialities, how could she trust him with whatever it was she was afraid to say? Building relationships, that was what his job was all about.

Daniel snorted at this weak effort to justify doing something he shouldn't, and pulled away from the curb.

THEY SAT IN the darkness on the porch steps this time. Venturing farther might have offended *Onkel* Samuel's sense of propriety. Besides, no one in the house could possibly hear them. She and Daniel were both speaking softly, even though nothing they had said was really intimate.

In the kitchen, Samuel had told Daniel in more detail about the private investigator's visit. Then Daniel had asked if he could speak to Rebecca privately. She had tensed. Could he have learned something new about the intruder? Or about Tim? Had he violated his promise not to make inquiries?

But so far, all he'd done was listen to her talk about how deftly *Onkel* Samuel had deflected questions without actually lying, and how frightened she'd been.

"I never really saw his face."

"Just as well." Soothing, he placed a hand atop hers, which she realized had been clenched in a fist.

That touch, simple and kind, was more comforting than it should have been. She felt the strength in that hand, so much bigger than hers, and let herself return his clasp. Still, she couldn't relax, not when he, too, was a threat. She didn't dare give him even a hint about why she was such a target. But…maybe she and Matthew really were safe, now that the PI was gone. Rebecca wanted so much—too much—to believe that was so. Even if eventually she would have to surface, she was desperate for a reprieve.

"Tell me about yourself," he said unexpectedly. "And your parents. Did your mother let go of her Amish beliefs?"

Rebecca shook her head. "As little as possible. My father didn't mind. He understood, because he'd spent enough time in various Amish settlements to have sympathy for their way of life and values. He wasn't really a modern man himself, not in the way the Amish mean it as a negative. Neither of them were interested in partying, or going out often, or fancy cars." She paused. "We did have electricity. *Mamm* accepted that."

"That's what you called her?"

She smiled into the darkness. "*Ja*. None of my friends ever realized I wasn't saying Mom like they did."

He chuckled.

"We hardly ever watched television. We read, we played games, we talked and debated. I rolled my eyes when I got to be a teenager when my parents still insisted we sit down to dinner every night as a family, but now I'm glad we had that time. We'd debate the day's news, talk about why people made the decisions they did." Rebecca fell quiet for a moment. "I don't think *Mamm* ever really understood worldly ways. She would shake her head and say, *'Auslanders,'* so bemused. Dad…" She choked up a little. "He was gentle with her, as if she was something so wondrous he couldn't believe she was his."

Daniel's hand tightened on hers, silent encouragement for her to continue.

"One of *Mamm's* favorite biblical quotes was from John. 'My little children, let us not love in word or in tongue, but in deed and in truth.' That was her. I swear I never went out the door without her calling after me, *'Da Herr sei mit du.'*"

"The Lord be with you," Daniel murmured.

"I miss them both every day, but especially my mother. *I* became so modern, I wonder how disappointed she was in me. She never said."

"Don't be ridiculous." This briskness was comforting, too. "I've seen you with Matthew enough to know that, like her, you love 'in deed and in truth.' And isn't that what is most important?"

"Yes." She blinked against the sting of tears in her eyes. "Of course it is." At least she knew that what mistakes she'd made had been made out of love. It had all been for Matthew, even her defense of Tim.

"Would you have gone to them, if you could?" Daniel asked suddenly. "Instead of here?"

Chilled, she said, "No. No, Tim knew them, of course. I wouldn't have wanted to expose them to his anger or even the possibility of violence." She shivered. "Instead, I've brought those troubles to my *aenti* and *onkel* and grandparents, who are even less equipped to understand something so alien to their framework of belief."

"I'm not sure that's true," Daniel said, sounding thoughtful. "Your *onkel*, for sure, has dealt with enough outsiders to see clearly their thinking even as he holds to his faith. Perhaps not your *aenti*."

"No, she's not even curious about the world outside her everyday experiences, not the way Sarah and *Onkel* Samuel can be. Even Mose," she added. "*Grossmammi*… She seems effortlessly able to forgive, to count the blessings of each day. Right now, her world has shrunk. Holding on to each moment with *Grossdaadi*, that's what matters."

"And you, and the rest of her family."

"Yes, of course. Having me home with Matthew, that's one of the blessings she counts."

"As she should."

Rebecca wished she knew more about Daniel's childhood. She would have asked, except she was very aware that they'd been out here awhile. Her *onkel* would soon check on them or send her *aenti* to do so. She felt at peace in a way she hadn't in a long time, even if the man beside her was a police officer who would disapprove of so many decisions she'd made.

Right now, she thought of him only as a man, one who seemed to share her contentment in the moment. Her eyes had adjusted to the darkness enough for her to see him tip his head up to look at the moon.

Indulging herself in his company too much, however— that could be risky. She stirred and said, "I need to get back inside before someone comes looking for me."

"I know you do." He swiveled on the porch step to face her, still holding her hand. "Rebecca…"

Suddenly he was close. So close, she could reach up and touch his jaw, feel the rasp of a day's growth of beard. She could make out the fascinating shape of his lips, which seemed softer than usual. The tempo of her heartbeat had quickened, and warmth curled in her lower abdomen. *This* was why anticipation quickened in her every time she thought of him, however foolish that was. "Yes?" she whispered.

He made a muffled sound and bent his head. Her reaction came without thought. She rested her free hand on his shoulder and lifted her face to his.

THE FIRST TOUCH of her lips jettisoned any common sense. Daniel knew he should keep this kiss gentle, noncommittal, something he could later tell himself had been meant as reassurance. It didn't happen that way.

He nipped at her intriguingly full bottom lip, savored the sweetness of apple pie. Her eager answer awakened his blinding need. The skin on her nape was silky beneath his rougher hand. His other hand slid upward from her waist.

It was she who ripped her mouth away, her body suddenly rigid. And then Daniel heard it, too—footsteps, the sound of the door opening so close behind them.

"Good night," she said hastily, leaped to her feet and was at the door by the time it opened.

As he stood, Daniel said his good-nights to her and Samuel, framed in the doorway. Then he strode away into the night, praying Samuel hadn't looked closely at him.

The dogs decided to accompany him when he crossed the lawn. After bending to slide between rails on the fence, he was greeted by the nicker of horses and the muted thud of giant hooves. Aroused and not thinking clearly, Daniel was grateful for the level, grazed pasture. At least he didn't have to stumble through a stand of woods. A pair of the enormous horses, appearing pale and ghostlike in the darkness, joined the dogs to accompany him all the way. Next time, if there was a next time, he ought to bring carrots and dog treats, he thought. Fortunately, all the animals seemed pleased enough with the unexpected company, stopping at the fence on the far side to watch him out of sight.

He had parked at the next property, tucking his SUV behind Willard Kemp's barn. He had heard talk in the café about the Kemps visiting a daughter in southern Iowa, and had indeed found the house dark.

Reaching his SUV, he flattened both hands on the roof, groaned and let his head fall forward.

He had promised himself he wouldn't touch her. He'd had complete faith in his self-control. *Idiot*, he castigated himself. Rebecca was on the run from her ex-husband. She was depending on his protection. He still wasn't sure how honest she'd been with him. No, that cast his doubts in a positive light—he suspected she *hadn't* been honest. He'd known he really just wanted to see her again, but the surface plan had been valid. Build trust with her so that she *would* open up.

Amazing, the power of lust.

Maybe it wasn't Rebecca at all; maybe it had just been too long since he'd had a relationship. The recent, self-imposed celibacy had been a mistake.

Shaking his head, he unlocked the SUV and got in, still taking another minute before starting the engine.

No, Rebecca Holt was his problem. But he *couldn't* go anywhere with this until the full truth came out and she and her little boy were safe to resume their lives as she chose.

Too bad all he wanted was to sneak back across the

pasture and toss a pebble at her bedroom window, invite her outside and keep on kissing her.

HELD IN REBECCA'S gentle clasp, her grandfather's hand was frail, the dry skin like crepe paper. Like other members of the family, she took turns sitting with him to relieve her grandmother. Today, *Aenti* Emma had insisted *Grossmammi* come to the main house for lunch instead of picking at her food and eating almost nothing while she hovered over her husband.

Rebecca was glad of any distraction. Three days after the kiss, Daniel hadn't returned—not that she'd expected him to. She kept reliving the unaccustomed peace he had given her. And the kiss, of course.

Right now, she was glad to be useful.

Her grandparents owned a sofa with built-in recliners that overpowered the small living room and looked new. She wondered if it had been purchased after *Grossdaadi*'s health had begun to decline. Comfortably ensconced at one end with his feet up, he peeled off the face mask that had been delivering oxygen from the portable tank and smiled. "Such a good girl you are," he said. "We are so glad you came, Rebecca. We missed your *mamm* so much. With you here, when you came, it is like having her back, almost."

Sitting beside him, she returned his smile despite a sudden sting of tears. "I wish I had come sooner."

He shook his head. "Never too late."

Except, sometimes it was. Rebecca's mother had been able to see her parents when she dropped off and picked up Rebecca. That had given her an excuse to visit. Young and as insensitive as children often were,

Rebecca had never understood why her mother cried every year as they drove away. "But we'll be back next year," Rebecca would say, and her mother would try to smile and say, "Of course we will," but even at that age Rebecca could tell she wasn't so sure.

"You only saw *Mamm* a couple of times after I quit coming, right?"

His expression grew sad. "*Ja.* Whoever thinks their child will die before them?"

Rebecca touched her cheek to his shoulder, so thin now. "I miss her."

"But it is good to know she is at peace. God had His reasons for taking her and your *daad* when He did. It does us no good to question those reasons. We must accept and know that however sad we feel, there was a purpose and we will see her again."

His certainty comforted her, let her almost share his faith, if only for that moment.

He shuffled off to the bathroom using his walker and, after he came back, felt well enough to sit at the kitchen table and sip half a mug of homemade chicken noodle soup before pushing it away.

When he stood again, he jerked and grabbed his shoulder. His eyes were wild, and although his lips moved, he couldn't seem to form words. Spittle dribbled from his lips.

Rebecca half carried him to the sofa, strapped the mask over his face and made sure the oxygen was flowing, then flew out the front door of the *grossdawdi haus* for help.

TWO HOURS LATER, the hospital waiting room was packed with family and friends. Rebecca sat between Sarah and Mose, whose wife, Esther, was on his other side. Mose's eyes were on *Grossmammi*. She held herself stiffly, staring at nothing. Rebecca had seen her respond as each newcomer paused to say a few words, but those responses seemed to come automatically, as if she was only partly in the here and now.

"I thought we were agreed," Mose grumbled, for the fourth or fifth time.

Not even Esther said anything. The family *had* been in agreement that they would not allow Ephraim to be hauled off to the hospital again. He had asked to die at home.

But *Grossmammi* had insisted her son run to the phone shanty and call for an ambulance. It was not her husband's time; the *Englisch* medicine could help, give him longer.

Now, Rebecca suspected she regretted her decision. She couldn't even be at his side while doctors worked over him. He'd have a tube down his throat and others going into his collapsible veins, causing enormous bruises.

The atmosphere in the room was funereal, nothing like other gatherings Rebecca had been to. The men's faces were stern, set so that they didn't reveal emotion. The women wiped at tears and chided children who squirmed and whined.

Matthew had been whispering with Abram, but now he slid from his chair and came to her. "I gotta go to the bathroom," he said.

She managed a smile as she rose to her feet. "Then let's go find one."

She'd noticed one down the hall, almost as far as the lobby, as they came in. After checking to be sure it was a small, single-toilet bathroom, she let him go in alone. Hearing water run after he flushed the toilet surprised her. Just because she insisted he wash his hands after using the toilet didn't mean he would do it when she wasn't there to see. Maybe he felt her stare through the bathroom door. *Supermom's X-ray vision*, she thought. If only.

He had just come out when she heard a man's voice from the lobby.

"I'm looking for the Grabers?"

Oh, no. That was *Tim*.

Rebecca grabbed for the bathroom door handle even as she reached for Matthew. They could hide inside—

But he cried, "Dad! That's Dad!" and, before she got a hand on him, raced down the wide corridor.

CHAPTER EIGHT

BONE-DEEP SCARED, Rebecca ran after Matthew.

Too late. Too late. Tim turned from the information desk and saw Matthew, who cried again, "Dad! You came!"

Tim saw her, too, his gaze first startled then searing, before he crouched and held out his arms. They closed tightly around Matthew, and Tim stood, lifting him to sit on his hip. "Of course I came," he said. "Your mother knew I would."

Fingers biting into her palms, she resisted the need to snatch Matthew out of his father's embrace. "How did you know we were here?"

"First thing I heard when I stopped for a bite to eat at some little café on the main street. 'Ephraim Graber has had another heart attack, sad to say. The whole family is gathered at the hospital.' Of course I came here." His eyes met Rebecca's. "What else would you expect?"

"This isn't a good time. My grandfather—"

"I'm here now, Rebecca. Let's go outside and talk. I didn't come all this way to sit in a waiting room and pat your hand."

He turned, still holding Matthew. The glass doors slid open for him and he walked out to the small shady area under a portico, his son on his hip. She could do nothing but hurry after them, only distantly aware of the wall of heat outside.

"Let him down, Tim. He can go back and sit with his cousins while we talk."

Lips compressed, eyes cold, he wasn't the man she'd known. She'd seen him angry, yes, but not savagely determined. "You're both coming with me. It's time to go home. Although you'll have to change out of that ridiculous getup."

"Dad?" Matthew suddenly sounded uncertain. "We can't go now."

"You're wrong," Tim snapped, and kept walking toward the visitor-parking area.

Almost running to catch up, Rebecca didn't see another soul. Would anyone hear if she screamed? And then what? He hadn't threatened her. He had a right to see his son. What could she say? *He might have murdered his friend, but I didn't go to the police.*

"Wait!" Surely she could make him see reason. Agree to sit down with him, even to return the damn ring and wallet.

He kept walking because he knew she'd go anywhere he led as long as he had Matthew.

And he wouldn't let Matthew go. The only way she'd get him back would be to give evidence that would ensure he was arrested. And even then, she would have to fight Robert on his home territory. Robert, who could afford better lawyers, who probably socialized with some of the judges.

She heard a beep as he stopped beside a rental car. He opened the back door and tossed Matthew inside.

"Put on your seat belt."

Matthew stared at his father in shock. "But—"

Tim slammed the car door and opened the front-passenger door, then grabbed her arm. "Get in, Rebecca."

Trying to wrench herself free, she called, "Matthew, run back to the hospital."

Tim turned his head enough to snarl, "Stay where I put you." Then he dragged Rebecca toward the front seat.

She was screaming now, she knew she was. Swearing, Tim slammed her toward the front seat, and her face smashed into the top of the door frame. Pain exploded from her cheekbone and the ridge of her eyebrow throughout her entire head. She heard a car coming. Would anyone see? Stop?

Matthew was the one screaming then and she looked down to see him head-butting his father. "Let my mom go! You're mean! I hate you! Let Mommy go!"

The slam of a car door and running footsteps, and suddenly Tim threw her aside and raced around to the other side of his rental. Reeling against the fender of the car parked beside his, she blinked against the encroaching darkness. Matthew? Where was Matthew? But he was clutching her leg, and it was Daniel running between cars and bursting into the open, right in front of Tim's car.

Which accelerated forward, going straight at Daniel. As he leaped aside, Daniel was yelling, too. He'd pulled his gun, but then his head turned toward her.

Legs like noodles, she let herself slowly slide down the side of the car. And then Daniel was there, catching her in his arms.

DANIEL CARRIED REBECCA in through the front entrance, snapping to the volunteer behind the desk to call for a gurney. Having to let that guy drive away infuriated him, but she was more important. He'd catch up to Tim Gregory eventually and take great pleasure in snapping on the cuffs.

Matthew hovered, tears running down his face. "That was my dad. He was so mad. Why did he hurt Mommy?"

Rebecca's head rested against Daniel's shoulder. Her lashes formed dark fans against her cheeks. He couldn't tell if she was conscious or not, but rage filled him at the sight of the discoloration and swelling that had already begun.

From one direction, nurses or orderlies raced toward him with a gurney. Down the cross corridor, an Amish man appeared, then broke into a run at the sight of Daniel carrying Rebecca. *Mose*, he realized with relief.

They arrived almost simultaneously. Even as he gently laid her on the gurney, Mose was at his side.

"Rebecca?"

Her eyelids fluttered open. Daniel could tell she was struggling to focus. "Matthew?"

Her cousin took her hand. "He's fine. Right here." He bent and lifted the boy so mother and son could see each other.

"Thank goodness," she whispered. Her eyes closed again, then almost immediately opened, seeking him. "Daniel?"

He gripped her hand, noticing her *kapp* was gone, revealing gleaming chestnut hair gathered into a mass at her nape. "I'm not going anywhere," he told her. "I'll stay with you, and Mose will take care of Matthew."

"Thank you." She tried to smile, first at him, then at Mose. "*Denke.*"

"You will be fine, Rebecca," her cousin said. "Just a headache, *ja*?"

Daniel nodded at the two attendants and said, "I'll be right behind you."

They pushed the gurney away. The last he saw, Rebecca lay heartbreakingly still, eyes closed.

Now he had things to do.

"It was her ex-husband," he told Mose. "He tried to force Matthew and Rebecca into a car." He reached out and stroked blond hair back from the boy's forehead, finding a smile. "Matthew was very brave. He fought to protect his mother."

Matthew sniffled. "He didn't *act* like my dad! Sometimes he gets grouchy, but…not like that."

"We worried when Rebecca and Matthew did not come back," Mose said.

"Any word on Ephraim?" Daniel asked.

"No." He scowled. "*Grossdaadi* should not be here."

Daniel sympathized. They had all known Ephraim was dying. It was unlike the strong woman Ruth Graber was to have permitted this.

"You will arrest that man?" Mose asked.

"That's my intention."

Mose only nodded, his mouth tight. If Tim had been Amish, would Mose have protested? Daniel wasn't sure, but thought Rebecca's cousin wasn't in a forgiving mood. With a last nod, Mose led Matthew away, holding his hand and telling him that they would come back to see his *mamm* as soon as the doctor said it was all right.

Already striding toward the emergency room, Daniel took out his phone and called Dispatch. Chances were good the guy would bolt for an airport. The closest was St. Louis, but there were other options. If Daniel had anything to say about it, Tim Gregory wouldn't escape.

WHEN DANIEL DROVE Rebecca and Matthew to the house in his own SUV rather than the marked one owned by the police department, Samuel came out to talk to them. The ER doctor had noted that Rebecca had a crashing headache and was sick to her stomach, but he'd decided, reluctantly, to release her because she had never actually lost consciousness. He'd also been swayed by Daniel's explanation that she needed to be placed in a safe house before her ex-husband had a chance to rebound and look for her again.

"Stay put," Daniel ordered.

She might have taken offense if she didn't feel so wretched. Instead, she rolled down her window as he got out and walked around to meet her *onkel*, who braced a hand on the roof of the SUV and looked down at her.

"You just missed the ambulance," he said. "Ephraim is back in his bed, but not so good. The doctor said his heart was damaged too much this time. He said maybe hours, maybe days. *Mamm* wanted him home again." The relief in his voice couldn't be mistaken. Whether he would have gone toe-to-toe with his mother over his father's wishes, Rebecca didn't know, but he wouldn't have wanted to be put in that position. She knew he shared Mose's unhappiness that Ephraim had ever been taken to the hospital in the first place.

"Sarah is packing up your clothes and Matthew's things, too," he continued. "You are to go stay with

Amos and Barbara Troyer. Glad to have you, Barbara told me to say."

A fleeting expression crossed Daniel's face that she didn't understand even as he nodded. Did he dislike the Troyers? She knew he and Samuel had agreed that she and Matthew should move to another household, preferably to someone not closely related to the Grabers.

The Troyers were members of Rebecca's family's church district, so they weren't complete strangers. She couldn't picture Amos but had liked Barbara, who said she and Rebecca's *mamm*, Miriam, had been *gut* friends as girls. Perhaps that was why she and her husband had agreed to hide Rebecca and Matthew.

"They know it could be dangerous?" she asked anxiously.

"*Ja*, they know what happened today. But I think Tim won't be able to find you," her *onkel* said.

Daniel was clearly furious that Tim hadn't been located. Coming and going from her side all afternoon and into the evening at the hospital, Daniel had been on his phone nearly constantly. He'd kept her updated, his expression grim.

Tim hadn't checked into any B and B or hotel within a three-county radius. His rental car had not been returned, or spotted by a Missouri State Highway Patrol officer or local cop. He'd disappeared, either by ditching the rental car and getting his hands on a different vehicle, or because he'd had a bolt-hole prepared. That was the theory Daniel was going with, which was why he was determined to move her and Matthew tonight.

Rebecca also had a suspicion he was afraid if he didn't, she might take off without telling him where she was going. He already knew her well enough to guess that would be her first instinct. Only…here she and Matthew had so many people determined to protect them, who cared. One of whom, inexplicably, was the county sheriff. That perplexed and worried her, even as the knowledge warmed her deep inside. Turning to him today had felt natural. The evening that they had sat close together in the dark, holding hands, had apparently switched off all her internal warnings.

Sarah hurried out of the house with her arms full, *Aenti* Emma behind her carrying more. Daniel popped the hatch so they could stow everything. *Aenti* Emma came around to the open window, looking first to the backseat.

"*Ach*, Matthew is asleep. *Gut*, *gut*, after such a day, he needs the rest."

Rebecca hoped he regained at least some of his confidence. He had been clingy and frightened since the awful scene with Tim. As furious as she was with Tim for scaring their son, she kept thinking how dumb he'd been. Matthew would never trust his father or feel the same about him again. And for…what? Had he really believed he could force them into the car and somehow get them back to San Francisco without them drawing attention or running away?

Maybe that wasn't what he'd intended, she thought queasily. What if he had the use of a house locally? An isolated one? He could have taken them there to force her to tell him where the ring and wallet were hidden. He might have intimidated Matthew into going home with him, but not her. And he couldn't have just let her go.

Maybe she'd never known him at all.

Her *aenti* and *onkel* and cousin took turns to lean in

to hug her gently and murmur reassurances. Rebecca accepted them all, tears stinging her eyes. Staying with people who were no relations of hers couldn't be anything but temporary. Panic stirred, but she pushed it down. She'd feel better tomorrow. Surely she would. Then she could come up with a plan.

Right now, she wanted nothing but to lie down in bed and close her eyes.

"Tell…tell *Grossmammi* that I wish I could be with her. That I will be praying for her and *Grossdaadi*."

"She knows already," Samuel said kindly. She made herself nod, then expressed thanks that they turned aside the same way they always did. "You're family."

A moment later, Daniel was driving them away, and the family and farm she had believed would be a refuge fell behind them.

HAVING WAITED ONLY until darkness fell the following evening, Daniel drove out to Amos Troyer's place. He hoped Rebecca felt better because he was determined to get some answers out of her.

Didn't it figure that her new protectors were members of his own family. He'd seen Rebecca's surprise when he greeted her hosts as *Onkel* Amos and *Aenti* Barbara. Barbara was his father's sister. She and Amos had chosen to move their young family to Missouri with Daniel's parents, eager to find affordable land.

What mattered was that Amos and Barbara had welcomed Rebecca and Matthew generously. Even Daniel's *onkel*, a dour and generally humorless man, had expressed his willingness to help. When she tried to thank him, he had shaken his head and said, "With our last child gone, it will be good to have young people in the house, not so?"

The sight of strange faces had alarmed Matthew, so Daniel was elected to carry the half-awake boy upstairs in the traditional, two-story house and lay him down in a room that had once been shared by two of Daniel's cousins. Leaning heavily on Amos's arm, Rebecca had followed. In the light of the gas lamp, he had seen her pallor and wished she was leaning on him. But Barbara rushed to her, so he helped Matthew take off enough clothes to sleep comfortably in his twin bed, then tucked the covers over him. He'd murmured, "Sleep tight," before turning to the other twin bed and taking Rebecca's hand. "I'll be out to see you tomorrow night. Rest. Don't try to leap out of bed in the morning and help."

"Bossy," she mumbled.

Barbara chuckled. "We won't let her, don't worry."

There hadn't been much he could do but leave.

Tonight, Daniel parked in a tractor turnout a short ways down the road from his aunt and uncle's, slipped up their neighbor's driveway and made his way through a greenbelt, *Aenti* Barbara's orchard and at last to the kitchen door. Through the glass, he saw only Amos, apparently nursing a last cup of coffee. When he rapped lightly, his *onkel* rose and let him in.

"Coffee?"

"*Denke*, but no. I've had enough for one day."

"That never stops me," Amos said, deadpan, making Daniel wonder if he had a sense of humor, after all. "Rebecca said you would come for sure."

"We still haven't found her ex-husband, and I'm hoping she can help."

Amos studied him, taking his time before nodding. "If she is up."

Had she spent the day in bed? Alarmed, Daniel wondered if he'd made a mistake pushing for her to be released from the hospital.

Amos left without another word, and Daniel felt constrained to wait in the kitchen. His *aenti* treated him like family, but his *onkel* maintained more reserve. It might only be his personality, but Daniel knew him to be rigid in his beliefs. Beliefs Daniel had violated.

It was a good ten minutes before Rebecca entered the kitchen, her appearance causing him to grind his teeth. This time, her eye had escaped the damage, but otherwise she looked like she had when he'd first seen her getting off the bus. Except that this time the bruises were fresh, mounting from her cheekbone over her temple and onto her forehead. Purple and black instead of fading to yellow. Even the good side of her face was wan, and he had the feeling she wasn't focusing well.

He had half risen at the sight of her, but now forced himself to resume his seat. "Amos didn't get you up, did he?"

"Yes, but I was just lying on top of the covers, not sleeping." Moving gingerly, she sat across the table from him. "The headache is bad, but I'm not dizzy or seeing double or anything else the doctor warned me about. I count my blessings."

"How very Amish of you," he said drily.

For an instant, her gaze sharpened. "Seems like there's something *you* never mentioned."

He ignored that. "Are you taking the pain pills the doctor gave you?"

"Mostly. I'm a mother, you know. I can't expect Barbara to take over entirely."

Stubborn woman, he thought, not for the first time. "Where are they? You need one right now."

"I…" She closed her eyes. "Ask Barbara."

He came back a minute later with one in his hand, poured her some milk to protect her stomach and watched her down the pill. "Go back upstairs and lie down, Rebecca. You're not ready for this."

"No. But…will you stay for a few minutes?" She sounded timid. "Just talk to me?"

Daniel hesitated, even though he knew he'd agree— despite the risk of letting her get under his skin enough to shake his resolve. He'd come here to wring a straight story out of her.

"It's okay—" she started to say, but he shook his head.

"Of course I'll stay."

"Can we go out on the porch?" Rebecca offered a weak smile. "The dark would be soothing, I think."

"We seem to do all our talking on front porches."

He kept his hands to himself, but stayed close as she went to the living room to tell his *aenti* and *onkel* where they were going. Once they were outside, she headed toward the porch swing, then stopped.

"I think I'll sit on the steps."

He watched anxiously as she eased herself down, resting her head against an upright supporting the porch roof. Sitting beside her, he swiveled so he could keep an eye on her.

"Where's Matthew?" he asked.

"I already tucked him in. I was keeping him company until he fell asleep."

The air felt, if not cooler, at least less stuffy than inside. The moon was three-quarters, and the golden squares of the kitchen and living-room windows provided some illumination. Fireflies darted through the night.

"How's he taking the change?" Daniel asked.

"I don't know." He heard worry in Rebecca's voice. "You saw him yesterday. He's still the same, not wanting to be more than two feet from me."

Silence enveloped them. Daniel braced himself.

EVEN WITH THE throbbing in her head, curiosity had eaten at Rebecca all day. Daniel knew so much about her that it seemed only fair to ask him to reveal a small part of himself. It would be different if he had always approached her as the sheriff, but the attraction they both felt made everything they said and did personal.

Finally she said, "You were Amish." She couldn't deny the craving she felt to really know him.

"Yes," he said readily, as if he'd expected her to ask. "You know my parents, Isaac and Susan. They're in your aunt and uncle's church."

"I remember them. I should have guessed. You look like your *daad*."

"*Ja*, so people tell me," he said in Deitsch, sounding rueful.

She laughed, then moaned. "Don't do that to me!"

His quiet chuckle felt like a touch.

She waited for the sharp pain to subside before asking, "When did you leave the faith?"

"In every important way, when I was sixteen. I stayed at home for a couple more years—we moved here from Iowa during that period—but I never accepted baptism, and my parents weren't surprised when I packed up one day and left."

"I'm assuming it has something to do with why you went into law enforcement." Before he could answer, she said, "Just tell me to butt out, if you want. It's really none of my business."

He shifted on his step, but said, "No, it's okay. Many of the Amish in the area know something of my history. Otherwise, I've kept quiet about it until recently. Away from here, all I wanted was to erase my roots."

"Starting with the accent and the tendency to say *ja* or my *daad*."

She caught his smile. He'd stretched out long legs.

"Starting with those, *ja*."

Rebecca had the startling thought that, if not for the confession she needed to make, she could have been completely happy right now. There was something about Daniel Byler. She clasped her hands together, wondering how it would feel to be tucked against his side, his arm around her. He had kissed her, yes, but to be held lovingly, that was different.

What she ought to ask herself was how he'd look at her when he learned about the wallet and ring. Would he understand her decision?

Just for now, she shoved her worries aside, letting the tension ease from aching muscles.

Daniel started talking, gazing out over a field of hay to the woods beyond. The minute he described the impromptu party put together by a teenager who didn't think it important to deposit the day's business receipts the way his father had asked him, she knew what had happened was bad. She tensed again when he told her about the boys' ineffectual efforts to keep the thieves away from the girls. When he reached the rape, she heard the remembered rage bubbling beneath Daniel's matter-of-fact recitation. The rest was terse, but she had enough history with the Amish to read between the lines.

Finished, he let out a long breath and scrubbed a hand through his short hair. "My parents hoped I would regain my faith if we lived in a less conservative settlement. My mother sent letters far and wide, trying to find the right place. She has a distant cousin who lives near Jamestown. This settlement in Henness County was fairly new, the farmland cheap compared to Iowa. *Mamm's* cousin had heard good things about the bishop."

"Is he still here?"

"Bishop Jonas."

She blinked, picturing the man with a long white beard and a twinkle in his eye. "He does seem nice."

"He's a good man."

"But you'd seen what you'd seen, and done what you'd done."

"That pretty well sums it up."

Studying his face in profile, she said tentatively, "Was it hard? Out there, I mean? With only an eighth-grade education?"

He turned his head, eyes a dark charcoal in this light. "Yes."

He'd said all he meant to, she realized. Maybe more than he had meant to. She closed her own eyes and let herself drift.

She didn't know how long had passed when she felt a touch on her shoulder.

"Bedtime, Rebecca," Daniel said in that impossibly gentle voice. He wrapped an arm around her waist and set her on her feet, turning her toward the front door. "Sleep tight. And if you wake up hurting, take the pills."

A kiss on the cheek, and he ushered her inside, where Barbara took over.

Swaying, Rebecca wished for foolish things before deciding all she really *needed* was to be prone.

DRIVING HOME, DANIEL wondered how she'd softened him up when he knew she hadn't told him anything close to the truth. Did she think she could keep playing him?

He grimaced. Maybe he was a sucker for a delicate face framed by chestnut hair and a *kapp*. But at thirty-five, he had never yet allowed himself to veer from a path he considered right by a pretty face or a lush female body. Or, truthfully, by anyone or anything, unless he were to count the sight of girls he'd known all his life being raped on the cold concrete floor in front of him. The bishop and even his parents believed he had chosen the wrong path from that moment.

But, for all his sometime regrets, he knew he couldn't have done anything but fight. Or to find a different meaning in his life from that moment on. He did respect the Amish choice to live by Jesus's teachings to be harmless as doves. But he'd found enough passages in the Bible to know God had given His blessings to warriors, as well as men of peace. Most of all, he took comfort in the knowledge that God called men according to His purpose. That didn't stop him wondering, at his darkest moments, if he was only trying to justify his decisions.

But it was an old debate, and he had mostly made his peace.

Daniel's mouth tipped up when he remembered a passage from Matthew that he ought to bring to Rebecca's attention tomorrow: "Fear them not, therefore, for there is nothing covered, that shall not be revealed; and hid, that shall not be known."

Somehow, he didn't think she'd appreciate his bit of piety.

CHAPTER NINE

THE MEMORY OF Rebecca's pallid, bruised face stayed with Daniel that night, sleeping and waking, and was on his mind from the minute he got up. He'd seldom struggled more than he did that day to concentrate on his job.

He trusted that Amos or Barbara would have let him know if she had a bad turn. But did they understand the dangers of head trauma? Were they watching her closely?

He chafed at having to wait until nightfall to return to the Troyer place, but also felt dread. Had Rebecca done anything he couldn't accept? How hard would he have to push to get the truth from her? He might lose his temper if she kept defending her scumbag of an ex, the man who had brutalized her.

As he'd done last night, he parked in a tractor turnout, at last reaching the kitchen door.

When he knocked, it was Rebecca who appeared, letting him in.

"Hi," she said shyly. "I've been waiting for you."

"You look better." He studied her. "I think."

Rebecca made a face at him. "I do feel better." Apparently seeing doubt, she said, "Really. It's just…" She touched her cheek carefully. "I think it's getting more colorful."

It was, but her eyes were clear, and she didn't hold herself as if she feared an incautious movement might make her head explode.

So he nodded. "I'm glad." He glanced around the otherwise empty kitchen. "Do you want to include Amos in this discussion?"

Distress replaced the gladness he thought he'd seen when she first let him in. "Do we have to?"

"Of course not." He hesitated. "In that case, let's go outside again."

They paused on the way so he could greet his *aenti* and *onkel*, sitting in the living room. Never idle, Barbara was knitting, the needles flashing beneath the propane-powered lamp. With one finger, Amos marked his place in the bible passage he had been reading aloud, took in the uniform Daniel had worn to emphasize his purpose tonight and said only, "Nephew." Barbara smiled a greeting.

"We'll sit out front again," Daniel said, and Amos nodded.

Daniel was glad, once the front door was closed behind them, to realize he could no longer hear Amos's voice, which meant his family inside wouldn't be able to hear him and Rebecca, either.

This time she chose the glider, while Daniel remained on his feet, leaning against a porch upright.

Assuming Matthew was asleep, Daniel asked how the boy was adjusting.

"I don't know." Worry sounded in Rebecca's voice. "He's shy with Amos and Barbara, and she's really tried with him. Mostly, I think he's scared. And, of course, he misses Abram. I'm having to sit with him until he falls asleep every night."

"Seeing his father hurt his mother has changed him," he said gently.

"Yes. So stupid of Tim."

"Under stress, he seems to have poor impulse control." Daniel congratulated himself for describing inexcusable behavior so clinically.

She gave a half laugh that held no amusement. "That's truer than I knew. Matthew had seen a few outbursts, but nothing awful until yesterday."

"I'd guess Tim's stress level is cranked even higher now."

She started the glider rocking, perhaps to comfort herself. "I…suppose so."

"You need to tell me why, Rebecca." He kept his voice soft, but with no give. "Your hideout has been blown. It suggests that your ex-husband paid a lot more attention than you thought he did to your reminiscences. It's also clear he's not going to back off. If this was all about him getting Matthew back, he wouldn't have been trying to stuff you into that car. He'd have grabbed his kid and taken off."

She stared at her hands. In this light, the garish bruises were less obvious. She appeared demure, her heart-shaped face set off by her gauzy white *kapp*.

Daniel let the silence stretch, acquire a weight.

Finally Rebecca sighed and lifted her head. "No, it's not all about Matthew, although he's a big part of it. And I got to thinking about how Tim found me. I still doubt he paid any attention to what I told him about my family. But when we left to come here, I couldn't take much from the apartment."

Daniel nodded for her to continue.

"I had a box of family stuff in my closet. A bible,

letters from my mother and from *Grossmammi* dating, oh, way back. The *kapp* I wore that last summer.
If Tim got into the apartment…"

"I think we can assume he did."

"Yes." Her shoulders sagged. "Have you heard anything about Ephraim?"

Was she trying to distract him?

"Last I knew, his condition was unchanged. Word
will spread fast when he dies."

"I suppose that's true." She pressed her lips together,
then chewed on the lower one for a moment. "Why Tim
wanted to find me. You won't be surprised to hear it
has to do with that whole mess at G, G & S."

No, he wasn't surprised. But he had tensed, his body
suddenly battle ready.

"Were you involved in any way with the company?"

"Me?" Her eyes widened. "Heavens, no! Tim didn't
even talk about work, which made me feel as if I was
on the sidelines of his life." Sadness infused her voice,
although it had the patina of something long accepted.
"He'd brag sometimes about a new project, and show
off anything in print about him or the company. But
when things went wrong, he closed up. Until he and
Josh had to call the police, I didn't even know there
were money troubles, just that he was worried and…
angry. It wasn't until quite a bit later that I knew more
than what was in the newspapers."

He raised his eyebrows. "Except for the fact that
your husband was relieved, when a normal person
would expect about any other reaction."

"Well, yes, but there might have been legitimate
reasons for him acting that way."

He'd conceded as much the last time they talked

about this. Now he was only annoyed that she kept making excuses for the creep.

Possibly reading his expression, she looked away from him, toward the moonlit pasture. She fiddled with one of the long ties dangling from her *kapp*.

"What happened is, during a meeting with our attorneys before the divorce, Tim gave me permission to take anything from the house that I wanted." She told him about deciding she wanted to keep a particular necklace, and opening a hidden safe her husband hadn't known she could get into.

Oh, hell, was all Daniel could think.

"I opened it and, well, there was something at the front. Now I wish I'd never looked, but then... It was Steven's wallet. With his driver's license and credit cards. The thing is, the police had been tracing him because he'd been *using* those credit cards." Very softly, she said, "Or someone was."

"He's dead, and your husband was encouraging the police to believe he's alive," Daniel said slowly. Having seen pictures of the two men, he immediately understood how easily Gregory could have gotten away with using the partner's ID and credit cards.

"Yes," Rebecca whispered.

"How did he know you'd seen the wallet?"

She bent her head. Her rocking picked up speed. "I was dumb. I, um..."

"You confronted him." Daniel felt sick.

She didn't want to look at him, which made him immediately suspicious. But after a moment, she said, "He walked in the door just as I was leaving. He was surprised to see me and, well, kind of hostile. A week later, when he was picking up Matthew, I begged him to tell me that he hadn't had anything to do with Steven getting hurt."

"That sounds more suicidal than dumb," he said, infuriated that she'd taken a risk so huge. *Hurt?* Really? How about *dead*? And she was *still* making excuses for this guy?

She glared at him. "He was my husband. I didn't believe—" After a few seconds, her shoulders sagged. "What I did was stupid, okay? I didn't give myself time to think through what I really should do."

Truth, Daniel thought.

"He insisted he didn't have anything to do with Steven dying, and I believed him."

More truth. So what *had* she lied about? He crossed his arms. "But he didn't deny the guy is dead."

"Not exactly. I was…pretty freaked. If Steven hadn't taken the money, where was it? And if he had…well, I guess Tim and Josh could have been frantically searching for it."

"That makes no sense," he said brutally. "Once law enforcement was involved, the two of them wouldn't have been able to recover the money without explanation. If they did explain, there would be a lot of questions. Starting with why the man who'd embezzled it didn't have the money." He frowned. "When did the police become involved?"

"A good friend of Steven's reported him missing after he didn't show up for their usual game of tennis. He went to Steven's town house, called around, found out he hadn't been at work for a couple of days."

"If Josh and Tim had had their way, they'd never have involved the cops. If anyone else within the company knew money was missing, they could have blamed Steven but said they didn't want clients to know the foundation of the firm had a giant crack." Major businesses did often keep financial disasters secret.

"I suppose I didn't think it through," Rebecca said. "All I can say is that I once loved Tim. We'd been together for nine years."

That precarious dignity of hers got to him, although he didn't want it to. Not now.

"That's a long time," she said. "And, no matter how I felt about Tim, I didn't want to see Matthew's father go to prison. It's not like I *knew* what happened."

"You didn't go to the police."

Her chin came up. "The lead investigator grilled me right after Tim and I separated. He was so nasty I didn't *want* to cooperate with him. I know I should have. But I justified it to myself, and then... The truth is, we'd been arguing about custody. Tim backed down and said he'd allow me primary custody."

"If you kept your mouth shut." Crap.

Back to examining her hands, she said, "Matthew is everything to me. I couldn't let Robert have him. Tim and his father could afford better lawyers than I could. They're successful community leaders. I wouldn't look like much in comparison."

Frustration with the woman mingled with his fear for her. She'd danced with the devil and was now paying the consequences.

Feeling cruel, he said, "Did you give a thought to Stowe's family, waiting for news about him?"

She lifted her head for a fleeting look at him. "He doesn't have any family. He wasn't even in a relationship. If he had been..." Her throat worked. "I'd like to say I would have called the police."

Sucker that he was, he wanted to believe her.

"So then you and a bullet had a near miss," he said wryly.

"No, it was quite a while." She kept her eyes on her clasped hands. "Since we were in agreement, the divorce went through. Tim seemed...mostly like himself when I saw him the next few months. I think he believed I wouldn't say anything. He had Matthew every other weekend. I got mad once when Matthew came home upset. His grandfather had spanked him for standing up for me. Matthew didn't like the bad words Robert used about me. But I don't think anything else like that happened. Then suddenly Tim told me that Josh didn't like me knowing so much. Josh felt threatened, too, Tim said."

"Too."

"That's what he said. I thought Tim believed I'd never go to the police. Maybe if he'd never told Josh..." She trailed off.

"He and Josh were coconspirators. *You* are an ex-wife."

Sounding unhappy, she said, "Josh wasn't the only one angry at Tim. His father was, too."

"And you have primary custody because you had knowledge to hold over his head."

Her chin came up. "He offered. I didn't ask."

"Doesn't change the reality."

The chin came back down. "No."

"You know what we have to do now."

"Tell the investigator something I'm sure he already suspects?"

"You can give him someplace to start. With that focus, they'll find proof Tim was out of town when the other guy's credit cards were used. With luck, he'll have left some trail that will allow them to put him right where the card was used."

"But I *don't* believe Tim had anything to do with Steven's dying, if that's what happened." She was pleading for him to believe her. The glider action became agitated. "And it's *not* because I have some kind of lingering feelings for Tim. I don't. Right now, I'm furious. But I do know him. I believe he got sucked into something bad by Josh. Because of his father, Tim is all about impressing people, showing he's the big man— even if that means doing something he wouldn't otherwise. Only, the way things stand, it will be *Tim's* face that appears on some security camera using Steven's cards. *He'll* take the fall for Josh. I'd feel different if I really thought Tim had killed Steven."

She might as well be wearing blinders, like the harness horses that pulled the buggies. Daniel would have been disgusted except a lot of this sounded familiar. He could have been talking to one of his sisters who'd gotten herself into a similar spot. It was as if Rebecca shared the Amish reluctance to go to the law. She certainly hadn't wanted to turn to *him*.

He was willing to bet she had determined to forgive her ex-husband for any and all sins, too. The Amish believed that if a man repented of a wrong he'd committed, he should be accepted back into the faith and the community, forgiveness absolute, past actions left behind. Rebecca wanted to believe Tim really was a decent man, influenced by the truly wicked.

He shook his head. She'd spent enough time among the Amish. It wouldn't be surprising if their attitudes had worn off on her. And her mother hadn't rebelled from her childhood beliefs, not the way he'd done. She would have gently influenced her daughter to believe that forgiveness was right, that people deserved second chances.

Fine. Daniel believed the same, up to a point. And maybe Tim Gregory really wasn't the bad guy. But he'd had his second chance now, and he'd blown it. Never mind that, at the very least, he had helped cover up a death that had likely been a murder.

"He's a dangerous man, Rebecca."

"The thing is, something else happened."

"Besides you almost getting shot?"

The strain on her face found an echo in her voice. "After the shooting, I was still lying on the sidewalk when my phone rang."

He tensed.

"It was this sort of metallic voice. He said I'd had a warning now, to keep my mouth shut. That if I went to the cops, Matthew would die."

Gripped by now-useless fear and anger, Daniel could only articulate one word. "He?"

"I'm pretty sure. Um." She didn't want to look at him anymore. "Tim wouldn't have threatened his own son. He does love Matthew. When I called him about what happened, he sounded really shocked and mad. He said he'd try to find out more and, well, make sure there wasn't a repeat."

And she'd believed him, because the guy was so trustworthy.

"Except…" She chewed on her lower lip. "When he called back, I could tell he wouldn't be able to stop Josh, if that's who was behind it."

Huh. A dose of common sense.

"I packed to take off, but that same day, I got hit by the car," she said. "There was another call. This one said, 'Lucky for us, you have a weakness.' I couldn't risk Matthew!" she cried. "I couldn't."

"It didn't occur to you that telling the truth to the investigators in San Francisco would have taken the pressure off?"

"Would it?"

"I can't see your father-in-law going the route of threatening Matthew," Daniel said slowly. "I wouldn't let your ex off the hook. Threats are cheap, and he of all people knows how to get to you."

Her mouth formed a circle of outrage. "He wouldn't! You don't know him!"

"Think about it. Would Josh really do anything to his buddy's son? He'd have risked Tim turning on him."

She was still angry, but thinking. "What if he's set up the money trail to make Tim look guilty? I don't have anything but Tim's word that points at Josh. No matter what, if I'd gone to the police and they'd made an arrest that day—and how would they have proved Josh was behind the attempts on my life?— a trial would have been months away. Would I really have survived to testify?" She glared at him. "Besides, there's still Matthew."

"With Tim under investigation, he wouldn't have had a chance of gaining custody." Daniel couldn't let himself soften. "You have good reason not to allow him visitation. No court would dispute that, under the circumstances. And Josh wouldn't have dared go after you or Matthew, not if he was trying to look like the bewildered innocent. Sounds to me like you're still trying to protect your ex."

She hesitated. "Not for his sake, but…is it so bad to want Matthew to be able to respect his father?"

Daniel shook his head. "After yesterday, I think that ship has sailed."

"I'm also afraid of Robert."

He thought that over. "You believe what you're holding over Tim is also what's keeping your father-in-law from taking you on in court."

Her hands twisted in her lap. "Yes. He belittles Tim, but he's all about status. To have his son *arrested*? I think he'd do anything to prevent that."

"But does Robert know why Tim didn't fight for custody?"

"You mean, does he know what Tim's involved in?"

"That's what I'm asking."

Her beseeching gaze met his. "I don't know. I kind of doubt it, but… I can't be sure."

"It's time to talk to the detective," Daniel said flatly.

She crossed her arms, almost hugging herself. "If I do, if I give him everything, I'm defenseless." She hesitated. "The thing is, I have—"

Losing patience, Daniel shook his head. "Tim, at least, has already come after you. You're kidding yourself if you think anything you can do protects either you or Matthew. Once the San Francisco investigator knows—"

Rebecca surged up from the glider. "You won't call that detective yet, will you? Promise me!" Tension vibrated through her. "I need to figure out what to do—"

Daniel resisted the need to push away from the railing and take her hands in his. Pull her into his arms. *This* was why he should have kept his distance from the beginning.

Body rigid, he said, "I can't make that promise. This will become a murder investigation, Rebecca, and you've left the detectives so in the dark they don't even know they should be looking for the body." He understood her turmoil, up to a point, but he couldn't let it sway him. "I have to do my job."

"Please! Just give me a day."

He made himself shake his head. "You've had too many days already."

She let out a cry that pierced him. "I trusted you!"

"You know who and what I am," he said, his jaw tight. "Have you given any thought at all about what the *right* thing is?" The question came from both sides of him: Amish and cop.

"A thousand times," she whispered. Her voice gained strength. "But, obviously, what I think or feel or fear is irrelevant. After all, you have to do your job."

A hand seemed to grip his throat. "I do, but that doesn't mean—"

"All of this—" a wave of her hand encompassed them both "—was nothing but you doing your job." Her stare burned. "Then go do it."

The next second, the door banged closed behind her, and he was left alone on the porch.

SHE WAS AMAZED that she was able to speak normally to Amos and Barbara once she went into the house. Amos invited her to join them, and she managed to sound regretful when she said she had a headache and thought she needed to go to bed. Not that she expected to sleep.

Wrestling with her conscience, trying to deal with her wrenching and probably unfair sense of betrayal, Rebecca lay awake through much of the night. Tim's terrible behavior had built in slow increments. In contrast, Daniel's scathing words and expression left her devastated.

It wasn't as if she'd refused to talk to Detective Estevez. She was past the point of being able to navigate a booby-trapped maze alone. All she'd asked was a little time to think about what she should do once she handed over the only thing she had to bargain with. Daniel's reaction told her the truth. He'd been nice to her, kissed her, only so he could uncover what she was hiding. The irony was he had cut her off just when she'd been about to tell him she *had* the wallet and ring.

Of course Detective Estevez would insist on talking to her himself. She would tell him what she had, not just what she knew. It was true that Tim hadn't earned her silence. If she needed to do the right thing, that went double for him. He should come forward, accept punishment for what he'd done rather than condone threats against his own son.

For her, admitting what she knew to Estevez would be a small way of making up for her sins.

But Daniel… She wished she never had to see him again. A day—that was all she'd asked for. What difference did one day make now? He'd refused her even that. So arrogant, he thought the little woman couldn't do anything to protect herself. *Shouldn't* do anything. As if he could protect them.

Her conscience pointed out that he had come to her rescue in the hospital parking lot. Well, fine, but it was pure luck he'd been in the right place at the right time. What was he going to do, take a leave of absence to be their bodyguard? Of course not! His *job* was more important than her, that was for sure.

Anger at Daniel balled in her stomach, but she felt at peace with her decision. Soon it would all be out of her hands. Ironically, he'd be unlikely to reach Detective Estevez tomorrow, it being a Sunday. How foolish of him not to realize. To think he could have given her the day she'd asked for, and she'd never have known how much contempt he really felt for her.

Her eyes dry but burning as she stared at the dark ceiling and listened to Matthew breathe in the other twin bed, Rebecca comforted herself that at least tomorrow she would be able to pray with a clean heart, truly give herself to God instead of holding back. The rest…she would deal with when it came.

CHAPTER TEN

DANIEL PULLED OFF the road midafternoon when his phone rang. Shorthanded today, he had gone out on patrol himself, as he often did. Truthfully, he'd had no desire to attend church. He wouldn't have been able to pay attention to a sermon or feel any of what he ought to when he was in a house of the Lord. Helping keep the roads safe for the faithful felt more important.

He'd left a message that morning for Detective Estevez in case the guy was working on a Sunday. But this wasn't Estevez. The number was unfamiliar, but local.

"Byler here," he answered.

"Sheriff." The voice was unexpected. "This is Samuel Graber. I wouldn't usually call you about what has happened, but I think it must have to do with my niece."

"You're at the phone shanty?"

"*Ja*."

"What happened?"

"Today was church Sunday. We were at Levi Troyer's. Nothing wrong there, but when we got home, we found someone had broken in."

Stiffening, Daniel said, "If Emma and Sarah are already cleaning up, please stop them. I want to see exactly what was done. I can be there in ten minutes."

"*Ja*, I will tell them to wait. They itched to set everything right, you know how it is, but they will understand."

Daniel had to force himself to stay under the speed limit during the drive. Nobody had been hurt, he reminded himself, before remembering that Ephraim and Ruth might have been on the property in the *grossdawdi haus*. Surely Ruth, at least, would have heard intruders. He shuddered at the idea of the tiny old lady confronting them. But Samuel would have said if something like that had happened.

He made an effort to brake gently rather than slide to a stop in front of the Grabers' house. Samuel and his son Mose strode out to meet him immediately. Sarah sat on the front porch, but Emma wasn't in sight.

Daniel got out. "I worried all the way here about Ruth. If she heard anything—"

Samuel shook his head. "They were with us. Ephraim was too *agasinish* to stay home with the oxygen the doctor says he must have."

The word meant *contrary* or *stubborn*, and Daniel smiled.

"He did fine." And Samuel was clearly marveling that Ephraim had been able to accomplish such a thing. "Maybe *Mamm* knew best and it was not his time."

"God didn't need him yet, which is a blessing for Ruth," Daniel said automatically.

"The blessing," Mose said more grimly, "is that *Grossmammi* and *Grossdaadi* were not home when these people came."

"You're right," Daniel agreed, still appalled to think what would have happened if Ephraim hadn't stubbornly insisted on attending the service. "Did they go only into the house?"

"No, everywhere. The house, the *grossdawdi haus*, the barn, even the chicken coop. Usually, I would have been thinking it was *Englisch* teenagers, tearing the place up for fun. But they would have stolen, or written on the walls, or…" He stopped. "This has us *fernhoodled*, it does. Makes no sense."

"Show me," Daniel said.

They started with the house, and he saw immediately what Samuel meant. This wasn't pure vandalism, although things had been broken. The crocks that held sugar, flour and oats were smashed on the floor, as were other containers. The counters and floor were a mess. The refrigerator door stood wide open as did many of the kitchen cabinet doors.

"They were searching for something," Daniel said after a minute.

"*Ja*, it is like that everywhere," Samuel said. "They had to have been here for hours. Mattresses off the beds, clothes all over the floor, boxes upended. There are many smashed jars in the cellar." Grief filled his voice.

Daniel understood. Cleaning up the bedrooms, that would only be a *bodderation*, as the Amish put it. But Samuel was thinking of the enormous amount of work his mother, wife and daughter had put into the canned foods—planting, weeding, picking, even before the fruits and vegetables reached the kitchen. Because they were taking care of their family, it had been a labor of love, now smashed and trampled. His impression was that Samuel and Emma were comfortable enough financially that they could still afford to eat well, but that wasn't the point.

Daniel skipped the *grossdawdi haus* during his tour,

guessing that Ruth had already begun to clean up. But he saw that straw had been pulled out of the hen's nests, tools flung everywhere in the shed. The destruction was the worst in the barn, as if the intruders had grown frustrated or had recognized the impossibility of finding whatever they sought if it was hidden here.

He stood looking around at what he knew had been an orderly space. Tack was now tossed in heaps, some pieces cut. Neatly baled and piled hay had been flung against walls, bags of grain dumped out. Thank the good Lord the horses had been out to pasture, Daniel thought.

"Even the buggies," Mose said with a gesture.

They would have driven the large family buggy to church service, but both Sarah and Emma had their own, smaller ones. In Sarah's, the velvet seat covers had been slit with knives, the filling ripped out. Side panels were torn out. This damage would be costly to fix, though Daniel guessed Harvey Stolzfus, who built and repaired buggies, would not charge Samuel.

At the sound of steel wheel rims approaching, he glanced toward the open barn door. It would be a neighbor arriving, the first of many who would help with the cleanup. No Amish man or woman, however unlikable, was ever left to face troubles alone. Everyone in the church district, and some people from beyond, would pitch in. By evening, the women would have a feast laid out on tables on the lawn, and the kitchen, barn and bedrooms would be neat as a pin.

"I'm going to call for a deputy who does fingerprinting." Seeing the two men's expressions, Daniel continued, "Not in the house. I think he can get clear impressions from the tool handles and the doors and panels in the buggies. If these men are smart, they will have worn gloves, but people aren't always smart. Or a glove could tear, the man not noticing. We can at least find out if these are known criminals."

Samuel nodded with clear reluctance. "Could this have something to do with Rebecca?"

"I can't be sure." Oh, he knew, all right, but didn't want to admit as much, not yet at least. "But I think so. These were not thieves, and they didn't commit the kind of vandalism teenagers do. Whoever they are, they think something is hidden here."

"*Fernhoodled* we are, for sure," Samuel said for the second time, shaking his head. "Glad I am they don't know where to find Rebecca."

Even September's heat had done nothing for the icy chill Daniel had felt since he'd received the phone call. "You and me both." He nodded toward the barn doors. "I'll make that call and wait for my deputy. You can go ahead with the house and the henhouse. Even the barn, except for the buggies and tools with smooth handles."

"*Denke*," Samuel said, his disquiet undiminished. He and Mose walked out to greet whichever neighbor had arrived first, while Daniel took out his phone.

Would Rebecca be quite as *fernhoodled*? he wondered, his molars grinding. Or would she only pretend to be?

He should have known she was still lying.

Since the moment they had returned from the church service and fellowship meal, Rebecca felt the weight of tomorrow's inevitable visit from Daniel. She bustled in the kitchen, unable to settle down even though she knew Amos was waiting for her to join everyone else in the living room for a Bible reading. She seemed to be the only one aware of how thick the air had felt today, as if a storm approached. She kept remembering a time when she was only eight or nine. *Grossdaadi* calling, such urgency in his voice, as he shepherded them into the cellar. She'd felt as if she'd been electrified, every tiny hair on her body standing on end.

That day the tornado bypassed the farm by half a mile. They'd been lucky. She had gone with the rest of her relatives to help another family rebuild. In the years since, she never saw mention of a tornado on the news without feeling a shiver of dread and remembering that barn, flattened, the house missing its roof. And the dead animals.

Amos and Barbara trusted in God's will and His mercy in a way she didn't quite. Perhaps Amos had chosen a particularly appropriate Bible passage to read tonight. She would do her best to find comfort in it.

A sharp rap came on the kitchen door behind her. She jerked, then spun to face the danger.

Not danger—Daniel. But why come on Sunday evening?

Apparently her reprieve was over.

She hurried to let him in even as she heard footsteps behind her. Daniel stepped inside, nodding at her but addressing his *onkel*.

"Have you heard what happened at the Grabers' today?"

"Ephraim?" Amos said.

"Oh, no." Rebecca realized she had splayed a hand over her chest, as if to calm her speeding heartbeat. One thing she hadn't thought to worry about. Her grandfather had looked surprisingly sturdy at the service this morning.

"Ephraim is still fine," Daniel said. "As fine as he can be."

Amos said, "Sit down, Daniel. Rebecca, he would like coffee, I think. I will ask Barbara to take Matthew up to bed, *ja*, so he doesn't hear."

To compose herself, she focused on removing two ceramic mugs from the cupboard and pouring the coffee that was almost always on the stove.

She had just set one mug in front of Daniel at the kitchen table when Matthew flew into the kitchen, his sun-streaked hair tousled. She had the thought that soon it could be trimmed to look like the other Amish boys' hair. And how tan he'd gotten! Rebecca bent to hug him, closing her eyes for a moment at the sheer joy of holding his long, bony body close.

But anxiety filled his eyes. "Do I really have to go to bed? You'll come up to say good-night, won't you?"

"You do, and of course I will." She found a smile for him. "Say hello to Sheriff Byler."

He looked at Daniel with suspicion, which made her heart sink. He must sense her tension. But after a moment he said, "Hi. Why do I hafta go to bed?"

"Because I need to talk to your mother," Daniel said.

"And because Barbara said you must," Rebecca added sternly.

He grimaced, but went.

"Good night," Daniel called after him, but got no response.

"It's not quite dark yet," Rebecca said as she glanced out the window at the deep purple of dusk. And then she really let herself look at his face. Her apprehension became dread. He was all cop.

No, she reminded herself, he was just letting her see the truth, now that he had what he wanted from her. *This* was who he was. She fastened her gaze on Matthew's artwork decorating the front of the refrigerator and sat silent, nerves taut. Had Tim gone to the Grabers' today looking for her? What could he have said or done?

Amos reappeared and settled with a sigh on the chair beside her, facing Daniel. It was probably wishful thinking to believe he was allying himself with her.

"What is this about, nephew?"

"While you were all attending the service this morning, someone ransacked the Grabers' house, barn and outbuildings." His jaw muscles kept flickering, his gaze shifting between her and Amos.

Rebecca sat aghast, speechless.

"Even the *grossdawdi haus*. There was destruction, but none of the usual vandalism I'd expect of teenagers. Nothing stolen, so far as we can tell. It would appear they were hunting for something small, because they dumped out kitchen canisters, swept jars off the shelves in the pantry to see behind them, tipped mattresses off beds, yanked panels from the buggies, slit the seat covers. They lifted and flung hay and straw bedding. Even searched the henhouse. It must have taken hours."

Her fingernails bit into her palms and her teeth wanted to chatter. Realizing both men were now looking at her, she said, "What if *Grossmammi* and *Grossdaadi* had stayed home?"

"The intruders might have made some excuse for

being there and left. But they might not have, too. This search was ruthless, Rebecca."

"It's because of me." Of course it was.

"You have another idea?" he asked, voice hard. "Unless it's drug related, we don't have this kind of crime in Henness County."

Head spinning, she asked in an absurd last hope, "Do you think they expected Matthew and me to be there?"

"That's possible, but this wasn't just a temper tantrum because they'd been thwarted." Daniel suddenly looked weary, the lines in his face deepening. "They hoped to find something, whether you were there or not."

Shame flooded her. This wasn't how she'd wanted to make this admission, but it had to be done. A just punishment for her pettiness.

Amos said nothing. So much for being her ally. And why would he be, when Daniel was family? Daniel's connection to them was the only reason he and Barbara had taken her in.

Tears burned at the back of her eyes, but she refused to let them fall. Instead, she focused on Amos's face, which didn't help. The dry humor and occasional twinkle she'd seen in his eyes before were no longer apparent.

"I did hide something at my *aenti* and *onkel's*," she said baldly. "Something I should never have had. I thought it would keep Matthew and me safe, but..." She didn't bother finishing, although her gaze sought Daniel's.

He was looking at her, all right, with cold judgment. "The men might have taken it."

Fear sprang from nowhere, spreading with sickening speed. What if he was right? Daniel said they had flung hay bales. They might have seen the loose board beneath one of the bales, just as she had.

If the wallet and ring were gone, she wouldn't be able to make anything right.

In a voice not her own, she managed to say, "It's possible, but… I found a good hiding place."

Devastated by the trauma her family had suffered today, she couldn't worry about herself or feel crushed by Daniel's condemnation. Even if she'd told *Onkel* Samuel up front that she was hiding something as a kind of insurance, this would have been bad. Now, all she could do was confess to her *aenti* and *onkel* and cousin Sarah, to Mose and Esther who'd been so kind. They would offer forgiveness, of course, but trust once lost was rarely extended again. Except for Matthew, they were her only family. She hoped her grandparents could be left with their illusions.

Amos's stern regard had her wondering if he would ask that she and Matthew be moved again.

She said quietly, "I'm sorry, Amos. I know that's not adequate, but… I believed I was protecting Matthew. And I never thought anyone would be at risk but me."

Amos nodded, still gravely. Kindly? She hoped so. There was certainly no kindness on Daniel's face.

She made herself look at him. "Can we…go see?"

THE GASP AND small thump coming out of the darkness compelled Daniel to turn and help Rebecca, despite his lack of sympathy. Navigating the woods along the creek wasn't easy without using a flashlight, but at least he wasn't wearing skirts to midshin.

He could make out her shape, and he could tell she was still upright.

"You okay?" he whispered.

"Just—" She shook her head hard. In such moon-light as there was, he saw her *kapp's* white ties swing. She waved him forward.

He hadn't wanted to bring her. Not because he believed whoever had been watching the Grabers' farm still lurked in the woods. Any city boy would be scared witless out here the first time an owl with full wing-span dropped from the sky or a deer crashed through the undergrowth. Even so, Daniel couldn't entirely discount the possibility—thus this trek from three farms over.

No, being mad at her was his real problem.

Rebecca had tried to describe the exact location of the loose board in the barn, but since it apparently wasn't close to the stalls or any other obvious land-mark, he'd had a vision of himself crawling around that huge barn until dawn. No saying she could go right to it, either, especially by flashlight, but she would have a better chance than he did.

They should be able to slip in without announc-ing themselves or scaring everyone. Barn doors were never locked, not with the fear of fire in these huge, old wooden structures filled with hay and straw. The long dry spell increased the risk when the next light-ning storm swept through. Being able to get animals out as quickly as possible, that was what mattered. This being an Amish homestead, there wouldn't be any motion-sensitive floodlights, either.

And since, for the first time all day, he was being glass-half-full here, he should also be glad that if the horses were to trumpet a challenge and Samuel came to find out what caused the racket, unlike an *Englischer* he wouldn't shoot first.

At another snapping sound accompanied by a rustle and a tiny whimper, he reached back for Rebecca's hand. A branch had whipped toward her—not into her face, he hoped. He couldn't let her be hurt because he was sulking. Her hand felt icy cold and stiff in his, but she accepted that she needed guidance.

He made out the bulk of the barn roof at last, veering so that they would emerge behind it.

"Side door," he murmured.

She nodded and moved silently along with him. He groped his way along the stone foundation until they reached the door. He hadn't expected it to be locked any more than the main entry, and it wasn't.

As they stepped inside, a soft whicker greeted them. Big feet thumped as horses shifted in stalls.

After gently closing the door, he took the flashlight from his belt and turned it on, keeping the beam low. Rebecca went to the first stall and stroked the nose that poked over. Daniel joined her. It was worth taking a few minutes to calm the horses.

Her quiet voice came to him. "Yesterday, I started to tell you I had the wallet and ring, but you interrupted and I didn't make myself try again. Last night, I made the decision to tell Detective Estevez when you came back with your phone. You may not believe me—"

"I don't," he said shortly.

If anything, she stretched her neck to hold her head higher. There was her dignity again, fragile though it was.

He was being a jackass, he knew, and was afraid his

fury was all because she hadn't trusted him, not because he didn't understand why she'd held back.

After a moment, she nodded, then said, "I need the flashlight."

He handed it over, and she swept it across the floor of the cavernous barn.

"It doesn't look anything like it did!" Her voice rose in dismay.

He kept his mouth shut, tempting though it was to say, *Gee, I wonder why?* Okay, he hadn't gotten over being mad.

After a minute she advanced toward the center of the barn, not far from a ladder that rose to the loft above.

"I think…" She crouched and began pushing loosely piled hay aside. When she reached for a burlap bag of oats, he hefted it aside before she could. He kept moving them out of her way until she gasped.

"This is it!" Her certainty seemed to diminish. "I think this is it." She directed the beam of light at a joint where two boards met, and he saw that nails were missing. He also saw her hands ball into fists. She was girding herself to find an empty space beneath the floor. "I need a hoof pick or something like that."

Daniel took his Swiss Army knife from his pocket, flipped open the longest blade and handed it to her.

He held the flashlight as she lifted the board. The wood squeaked, and then she breathed, "Oh, thank God."

Daniel had his doubts whether God would want any part in this mess, but he could be wrong. It didn't seem that anyone else cared much about Steven Stowe.

Crouched beside her, he watched as she eased a clear

resealable plastic bag through the crack the knife blade held open.

The bloodred light of a ruby winked at them.

BACK IN THE SUV, Daniel set the small bag on the floor by Rebecca's feet. Without saying a word, he reached to start the engine.

Seat belt secured, Rebecca twined her fingers together on her lap and stared straight ahead. He wasn't talking to her any more than he had to. This silent treatment was worse than being berated.

He probably only saw her now as a witness requiring protection. Just think how much he'd have to tell Detective Estevez in the morning. Triumph was probably all he felt.

But the engine didn't start, and, after a moment, his hand fell to his thigh.

"Please tell me you know how stupid it was to take those things." His voice wasn't quite a roar, but close.

Watch what you wish for.

"I know it was, but—" No, no, don't argue.

Too late.

"But?" Frustration filled that deep voice. "Did having them keep you safe?"

She shook her head.

"Did it keep Matthew safe?"

And then she lost it. "Yes! *Yes*, a thousand times, yes. Don't you see? If I hadn't had Steven's wallet, not only would Tim have gone on fooling the police, he would have won joint custody. Which means *Robert* would have had Matthew most of that time! At least I got primary custody out of it. The rest of this... I never imagined..."

His snort of disgust cut deep.

"I had barely a minute to decide what to do when I heard Tim walk in," she defended herself.

"But you had months to decide you weren't going to the police," Daniel countered.

Rebecca swallowed. He was right. Why was she arguing? She *ought* to be contrite.

"You know my reasons. And… I'd given my word."

"To a man who conspired in a murder." Daniel just kept scowling at her. "You know you could face charges of withholding evidence."

She swallowed and nodded. That had always been one of her terrors.

If she had volunteered all this to Detective Estevez rather than having it dragged out of her, the investigator might have been more sympathetic. Daniel might have, too. She understood his abhorrence for lies. A deep core of him would always be Amish, plus he must get frustrated day in and day out with the ease with which people lied to the police. *Like I did.*

He shook his head. "Blackmail wouldn't have worked, any more than it did the first time around."

The attempts to kill her, the threat against Matthew, suggested he was right. In the end, though, it didn't matter. She couldn't keep endangering her family, and Tim no longer deserved anything from her.

"I've been scared," she said finally. "What other weapon did I have?"

"The entire San Francisco Police Department!" Daniel snapped. "Tim and Josh would have been behind bars in no time."

To her astonishment, anger swelled inside her, blistering hot. How many times did she have to say this?

"You mean, *Tim* would have been. My word wouldn't be enough to provide grounds to arrest Josh, not without…without some corroborating evidence. You know that! And how long do you think Tim would have *stayed* in jail? Twenty-four hours? He'd have been out on bail before I had time to pack a suitcase. No matter how high it was set, he or his father would have paid it! And what if that detective had arrested me, too? What would have happened to Matthew?"

A moment of silence descended. Daniel flexed his fingers a couple of times on the steering wheel before finally gusting a sigh.

"You're right." His voice had softened, in a rumbly way. "I do understand why you made the choices early on."

Still stinging from the anger, Rebecca said, "But once I met you, I should have cast myself at your feet? Turned gratefully to you to get me out of this mess?"

"I would have tried, you know."

She almost believed that. He *had* tried. But even though the anger had left her with a whoosh, she shook her head.

"I do trust your intentions as a police officer, but… Thirty seconds more, and Tim would have had me in that car. You *can't* provide twenty-four-hour-a-day security for me and a six-year-old who needs to play and have at least a little bit of freedom."

"Your trust doesn't go very far, does it?"

She couldn't read his tone, but what did it matter?

After a moment, he fired up the engine and released the emergency brake. "I need to get you back. *Onkel* Amos will be waiting up for you."

A lump in her throat, her vision blurred, she nodded.

He drove in brooding silence, his brows drawn together. She averted her face so she could swipe surreptitiously at her damp cheeks.

When he finally pulled off the road, she unclicked the seat belt. "You don't have to come with me. I know the way."

Waste of breath.

"I'll see you to your door," he said shortly.

Even if they'd felt inclined, talking wasn't an option as they passed through the neighboring farmyard and sneaked behind the hay field and through Barbara's orchard. Daniel seemed to have eyes like a cat, or maybe he'd just learned this route by heart. She acquired a couple of new scratches and stubbed her toe painfully.

Only when they approached the back door, where a light showed, did Daniel stop her with a hand on her arm.

"Rebecca..."

She didn't let herself look at him, but she didn't pull away, either.

"Are there any more secrets?"

"No."

"Whatever you think, I wanted to spend time with you, get to know you. It wasn't all about this mess you've gotten yourself into."

Rebecca gave a broken laugh. How could she believe him?

His hand dropped from her arm. "Expect me tomorrow after I talk to Estevez."

She only nodded and let herself into the house, never looking back.

CHAPTER ELEVEN

"DETECTIVE ESTEVEZ HERE, San Francisco PD. What can I do for you, Sheriff?"

Considering the caseload the guy probably had, Daniel was impressed to have gotten a call back by ten in the morning. Pacific time on a Monday morning.

Daniel gave his usual silent thanks to God. Spinning his wheels waiting would have made this day awful. He was already suffering with remorse for his attitude last night—and because Rebecca thought he had betrayed her. He felt like he had a splinter working its way so far beneath the skin it would require a scalpel to dig it out. He'd swear it was inching toward his heart, the sharp end deadly.

Don't think that way. He couldn't in good conscience have kept her confession to himself. He was a cop. He had to believe God had called him to this job.

Leaning back in his desk chair, Daniel swiveled to look at the branch of an old oak tree through his tall casement window. The leaves were already turning colors after the exceptionally hot late summer.

"It's more what I can do for you," he said.

"That so." Estevez didn't sound impressed.

"Tim Gregory's ex-wife has taken refuge here in my county with relatives of hers. Ms. Holt has some knowledge that implicates her ex-husband in the mess she says you're investigating."

"What does she know?"

Daniel told him, including the fact that he had Steven Stowe's wallet and ring in an evidence locker.

Estevez growled, "Do you know how much time she would have saved us?"

Daniel had a good idea.

"Why didn't she call me?"

"I think that's better coming from her." Into the silence, Daniel continued, "She felt her life was in danger after she had a near miss in a drive-by shooting followed by a hit-and-run accident in your city, Detective. After each incident, she received threatening phone calls." He described both, feeling a change in the quality of the silence. "Since she left Gregory, she's also dealt with pressure from his father-in-law, whom you may have encountered. Robert Gregory would like his son to have custody of Matthew."

After talking about the PI's appearance, Daniel went on to describe Tim's attempt to grab his boy and Rebecca, detailing the findings of the doctor who had treated her in the ER. "The guy has gone to ground here, unless he's reappeared in your city."

"I've spoken to him on the phone, but he claimed to be out of town on business." Estevez sounded intrigued. "Wasn't sure when he'd be getting back."

"He had a little glitch getting his hands on Ms. Holt."

"If she's decided to come forward, why use you as a go-between?"

"She's in hiding with an Amish family." He explained her family history, the fact that they didn't permit phones in the house and that she'd agreed to live plain while here. "I can take a phone to her. Anytime today, if you want."

Was her forgiveness even a remote possibility? If he extended it to her in turn? And what kind of idiot was he, to feel so much for a woman who had lied to him from their first meeting?

The detective huffed out an exasperated breath, then said, "I just pulled up reports of the hit-and-run. Doesn't appear she mentioned the drive-by when the police came after the hit-and-run."

"She took seriously the threat not to go to the cops." Estevez grunted.

"There's something you should understand." He rubbed the back of his neck. His explanation of Amish attitudes was necessarily brief, and he expected skepticism, but at least Estevez listened. "You mind telling me if you've gotten anywhere in your investigation? I admit to having developed a dislike of Ms. Holt's ex-husband."

"The forensic accountant started digging deeper after Stowe dropped entirely from the radar and we began to wonder if he hadn't been a scapegoat. One who'd been slaughtered," he added drily.

So Rebecca had succeeded in that much, Daniel thought.

"Our guy is still hip-deep in numbers and who knows what," Estevez continued. "He has pinned down a string of G, G & S's supposed projects that never really existed. In each case, there are blueprints and sketches on file. Money appears to have been paid to suppliers and workers. There are just no buildings, or at least not ones that match the plans."

"And presumably the suppliers and workers are fictional, too."

"Oh, yeah."

"I gather Stowe was the money man."

"Which was why we initially zeroed in on him as the embezzler. Along with his disappearance, of course. But once he disappeared from the radar, I started leaning on Gregory and Griffen a lot harder, as well as other employees at the company. I'll be able to get a warrant for Gregory's house now, at least, although what are the odds he has anything else incriminating there?"

Daniel grimaced. "Not high. Make sure you include both safes in the warrant."

"Both?"

"She says there's one in his home office as well the smaller one in a walk-in closet in the master bedroom."

"Good to know. Let's make the phone call one o'clock my time," Estevez asked abruptly.

Daniel glanced at the wall clock. "Sure. I'll call you once I have her available."

They signed off, leaving him apprehensive. He was biased toward Rebecca, whether or not she believed it, and she felt Estevez's interrogation style was aggressive. Plus, the San Francisco cop had good reason to be frustrated with her. He might even press charges because she'd hidden critical evidence.

Daniel told himself the best course was to step back, not stay stuck in the middle. His emotional entanglement appeared one-sided now, if it hadn't been all along. And even if she felt anything but anger for him, Rebecca wouldn't be staying in Henness County when this was all over.

All his tension exploded. He hammered a fist on his desk, then shoved his chair back violently. Who was he kidding? Whether she appreciated it or not, he'd keep fighting for her. He couldn't stand an arm's length from her, absorbing those wide blue eyes or the generous curves beneath the theoretically plain Amish dress, the delicate lines of her face and the bruises that had yet to fade, and allow Estevez to threaten her.

He groaned and rolled his tight shoulders, then grabbed his gun from a drawer, holstered it and strode out of the office.

REBECCA REFUSED TO look at Daniel as she defended herself to Detective Estevez. Daniel's stance, while outwardly relaxed, still managed to be intimidating, so she focused on the dried bird's nest tucked beneath the eaves. Because this was daytime, Daniel had parked out of sight and ushered her behind the house where they couldn't be seen from the road.

Since he'd already told the detective everything, Estevez had barely snapped out questions that she could only answer with a "Yes" or "That's true" or an occasional "I don't know."

Now, clutching Daniel's phone to her ear, Rebecca said with what dignity she still had, "I know it seems foolish to you, but Tim will forever be the father of my son. I suppose I wanted to believe he's at least close to being the man I thought he was when I married him."

Detective Estevez grunted.

"He assured me he had nothing to do with Steven's death," she continued.

"He admitted his partner is dead?" he asked sharply.

"Well, not in so many words."

"What *did* he say?"

Very conscious of Daniel's presence despite her best effort to pretend he wasn't there, she struggled to cast her mind back. "I said something like, 'Tell me you wouldn't hurt anybody,' and he said, 'It wasn't me.' Then he said misleading the cops—" specifically, the one to whom she was speaking "—was the only way to save the company."

"He just came out and told you that."

She closed her eyes. "He was angry. We were arguing. What was he supposed to do, insist I hadn't seen Steven's wallet?"

"No one else heard him."

Stiffening, she said, "He'd just brought our son home from a visit, and Matthew had gone to his room." Detective Estevez would interview Matthew over her dead body.

"It was months before the shooting. If you're telling the truth, nobody had threatened you at this point. You expect me to believe your tender feelings for the guy you'd just dumped kept you from giving me evidence you knew was critical to our investigation?" The sneer came through.

This was the explanation she had dreaded most. She took a deep breath. "I don't expect you to understand, but Tim had been demanding joint custody of our son. He worked too many hours to be any kind of parent. I knew his father was behind it. Robert is a harsh, demanding man who never thinks Tim has performed up to his standards and tells him so frequently. He wanted control of Matthew. I suppose he thought he could mold him into the perfect grandson to replace his inadequate son."

If Tim had stolen money from his own company, she felt sure it was because he was so determined to appear wildly successful to his father.

Daniel shifted, uncrossing his arms and rolling his shoulders. She sneaked a look. To her surprise, his expression wasn't hard, as she'd seen it when he was all cop. Some small lines had formed on his forehead, and the deep blue of his eyes mesmerized her.

"When he learned I had taken the wallet, he offered to back off and let me have primary custody as long as he got reasonable visitation. I'm not proud that I understood he was offering a bargain, or that I took it. But I believed I'd lose in court. My ex-husband's family has a great deal of influence in San Francisco. My attorney thought the request for joint custody would seem reasonable to a judge. I was afraid to allow Robert to have any more access to my son than he had during the every-other weekends with Tim."

"So you abetted your husband's cover-up in what's very possibly a murder," Estevez said, making no effort to hide his contempt.

Past the lump in her throat, she said, "As I told Sheriff Byler, I do not believe Tim killed Steven. He's just... not the kind of man who'd do something like that."

"And yet, not much later, you believed he was trying to kill *you*, either to silence you or to gain undisputed custody of his son."

She found herself shaking her head. "No. I never thought it was Tim. My best guess is that Josh Griffen was behind it. Tim apparently told Josh that I'd seen

Steven's wallet. Tim told me once that Josh felt threatened, that he didn't trust me to—"

"Keep your unsavory little bargain?"

Feeling sick, Rebecca bent forward. "Think whatever you like about me," she said in a shaky voice just above a whisper. "Protecting my son is the most important thing in the world to me."

The lengthy silence increased her nausea.

"I'll be out there to pick up the evidence as soon as I can arrange it. I want a face-to-face with you." His growl sounded like a threat, and she took it as one.

"Do you think I haven't told you everything? You're wrong. But I'll see you whenever you come. Goodbye, Detective Estevez." She thrust the phone at Daniel, whirled away and started walking, not caring where she ended up.

Beyond the trellised green beans in the garden, she reached the rows of raspberries, soon to be pruned, the new shoots tied up. There, she plopped down on the grass, bent her head to her knees and listened to the *rat-a-tat-tat* of a woodpecker, seemingly answered by an odd cry that sounded like "Peter, peter, peter." A bird—what had *Grossmammi* called it?

A shadow fell across her. She didn't look up.

"He was doing his job," Daniel said.

"Is that how it's done?" She didn't look up. "If so, I doubt he ever elicits genuine cooperation from a witness. You, at least, *pretended* to understand."

He crouched, bringing himself down to her level. From the corner of her eye, she saw the khaki of his trousers pulled tight over powerful thigh muscles. His bare forearm, lightly dusted with hair, was braced on his knee, his big hand dangling. Relaxed.

"Rebecca, you know he can ask for obstruction-of-justice charges to be filed against you." Suddenly his voice sounded hard. Because she'd refused to continue buying into his slick manipulation? "You should be thankful he didn't mention the possibility."

Thankful? "Let him try," she snapped, and finally did raise her head to glare at him. He wore dark glasses to hide his eyes. "Please leave. I'm not in the mood to answer any more questions."

She didn't let her glare waver. After a minute, he tipped his head and rose effortlessly to stand over her.

"I've tried to help," he said quietly. "If you want to talk, I'll be behind the barn at about eight tonight. Your choice." And he turned and walked away.

Rebecca dropped her forehead to her knees again, her arms squeezing her shins, pulling her body into the classic fetal position.

You know he can ask for obstruction-of-justice charges to be filed against you.

Fresh terror ricocheted through her body. Knowing vaguely it was a possibility was one thing, the reality another. *She* could end up going to jail instead of Tim. Given how long she'd taken to tell what she knew, would a jury think the worst of her and refuse to believe her testimony about the wallet and the things Tim had said?

She heard Daniel's voice, as if he still stood above her. *I've tried to help.*

Sure he had. Earn a woman's trust—if she's scared enough she'll crack and spit out the whole story, right? What a shame nobody had ever taught Detective Estevez the technique, she thought bitterly.

She had to go inside, but not yet.

Her stomach roiled. How could she have been so stupid? So careless with her own integrity? When she had stuffed Steven's things in her purse and walked out of the house, she'd thought she was striking a compromise between the public good and her private need to protect the man she had once loved, Matthew's father. She'd meant to stop him from misleading the police. But then she'd made the whole thing ugly by accepting Tim's custody deal.

For Matthew's sake, not hers. Wasn't it?

She pictured *Onkel* Samuel, so kind, so good, with his determination to live as his savior had asked. How would he look at her if he knew everything she'd done?

Her cheeks were wet now. When had she started to cry?

It was a long time before she could work around to thinking about the future. Hurt pride and the sting of betrayal made her want to take Matthew and run again—far, far beyond the reach of Sheriff Daniel Byler.

With puffy eyes, she watched an ant struggling to mount a blade of grass.

What right do I have to be hurt when I got myself into this mess? Rebecca asked herself harshly. Daniel was a cop; *of course* he'd felt compelled to do his job, to persuade her to tell him the truth. Even if being nice was just his technique, wasn't that better than Detective Estevez's belligerence?

Anger spiked again. Fine, but he shouldn't have kissed her. Had he imagined he'd get her into bed before her legal troubles came to a climax?

If you want to talk. To him? Oh, sure. Top of her list of things to do tonight.

DANIEL GROWLED A word that hadn't crossed his lips in three years even as his hands tightened on the steering wheel until his knuckles showed white.

Estevez would have gotten a lot further if every word he spoke wasn't tinged with contempt and aggression. Even standing several feet away, Daniel had heard enough. Making witnesses cringe was no way to persuade them to open up. A degree of empathy, understanding, were more effective.

Rebecca had accused him of *pretended* empathy and understanding.

He flinched, because he did pretend sometimes when he interviewed a suspect. With her, he had been sincere. She'd been in a tough spot, pulled too many ways. He did understand her early decisions, whatever she believed of him now. Women would kill to protect their children. In comparison, covering up someone else's crime was nothing. He also recognized that her continuing insistence that Tim Gregory really was a good guy rubbed him the wrong way for personal reasons. Keeping her mouth shut about his sins in front of her kid, that was different. The right thing to do. His own mother would have made many of the same decisions had his father done something equally bad. She would have refused to lose faith in the man she felt she knew on a fundamental level. She certainly wouldn't have gone to the police.

Daniel would have almost been grateful for the call that came in just then from Dispatch letting him know about a two-car accident on the highway, had the last thing Jennie said not been "possible fatality."

MATTHEW SPUN IN circles in the middle of the lawn until dizziness toppled him, then stood up and did it again. Rebecca watched helplessly. Neither of them could go on much longer if she couldn't find a way to distract him.

"You'll throw up," she warned, the next time he flopped on the grass.

"Uh-uh!" He staggered to his feet and started spinning again, his arms outstretched.

Once she'd tried catching him, but he had struggled wildly. This frenzy wasn't like him. *Her* stomach churned, just watching him.

Again he fell. This time, she sank down beside him, staring up at the sky.

"Look," she said, pointing. "There's a red-tailed hawk. I think that smaller bird is chasing him."

"How come?"

"The hawk might have gotten too close to a nest." Except this wasn't the right season, was it? But Matthew wouldn't question her.

Because moms were supposed to be all-knowing, she thought sadly. It would never occur to him that she could be wrong about something.

She and Matthew stayed on their backs as the long shadow from one of the apple trees reached toward them.

"Why was Daddy so mad?" her little boy asked in a small voice.

She'd been dreading the question but couldn't see a way out of telling him the truth.

"Your dad has been mad at me for months." She turned her head so she could watch Matthew. "I saw something to do with his business that he thought he'd hidden. He was afraid I'd tell someone."

Matthew's forehead wrinkled and he met her eyes. "What did you see?"

"Right now, I don't think you're old enough to understand. Your dad's business is pretty complicated, you know."

"That's what *he* says when I ask *anything*."

She smiled a little. "He never liked it when I asked questions, either. That's part of why your dad and I aren't married anymore. Being married, you should be partners and best friends. I felt more like something pretty he'd bought to show off to his friends."

"But you're a person, not a *thing*," he protested. "You're a *mom*."

"I am." She ruffled his hair, a lighter blond now than when they had arrived in Missouri. His face and hands were tanned, his forearms less so. The strict Amish garb protected most of his body from the sun. His sleeves, he sometimes rolled up. The hat, Rebecca had almost given up on except on church Sundays. He managed to "misplace" it about two minutes after she set it on his head.

"Back to your dad being mad," she said. "He didn't like that I brought you here to visit family. I was starting to be scared about living there in the city. You know how I got hit by that car."

"Yeah. And your face was all purple."

She touched her cheek. "I guess my face turns purple pretty easy, huh?"

"He was mean." Matthew's voice had become small again.

"Your dad loves you, but he's really angry at me, and upset with things happening at his company. I bet your grandfather especially wanted him to come get you."

Matthew suddenly didn't want to look at her. "I like *Grossdaadi* lots better than Grandpa Robert."

"Me, too."

They lay quiet for a minute.

"How come we couldn't stay with *Aenti* Emma and *Onkel* Samuel? Abram was my *friend*."

"I know." She found his hand and squeezed. "We're sort of hiding right now, from your dad *and* your grandpa Robert. I know it's boring here, without any friends, but I can't let your dad take you. Not until we work lots of things out."

"I don't want to see him ever again!" he said with sudden passion, rolling toward her to hug her. "I'll scream and kick if he tries to make me go with him."

Tears in her eyes, she said, "I'll be screaming and kicking, too. But…just remember that you've always loved your dad, and he loves you. I think eventually you'll want him to be your dad again."

But he buried his face against her and didn't say a word.

To her surprise, when she helped Matthew to his feet a while later, she saw Amos on the porch. He was watching them, his face shaded by his straw hat. He must have come down to the house for a cup of coffee and seen the two of them out on the grass. Otherwise, he would have used the back door, as he always did. In most Amish homes, front doors were for guests and to be used on formal occasions like weddings and funerals.

"I wish it was time for dinner," Matthew mumbled, kicking a hummock of grass.

"You're hungry already?"

He shrugged, which indicated discontent rather than

a growling stomach. *We can play a game*, she thought desperately. If only they weren't both sick of the few they had. They could work on reading and writing…

Amos came down the steps and said, "If Matthew is willing, I could use his help in the barn."

Rebecca could have kissed him.

One of Amos's sons had bought a farm down the road and now grew hay on his father's acreage, in addition to the crops on his own place. Amos, she learned, had never been interested in farming. Barbara was the one to tend their large produce garden and small orchard. He built beautifully crafted cabinets in his barn workshop. Cabinetry and furniture stores in Hadburg and Byrum carried examples of his work.

"Me?" Hope in his eyes, Matthew looked up at the taciturn man.

"*Ja*, you."

Amos returned Matthew to the house after an hour, his hand resting lightly on the boy's head. "Big help he was. He swept and organized my bins of small pieces of wood."

The six-year-old grinned. "I could help more."

Amos shook his head. "I will be using saws that are dangerous to small fingers. And soon it will be dinnertime. I will have jobs for you other days."

Rebecca smiled at him. "*Denke*."

"No need for thanks," he said gruffly, and went back out the door.

She took Matthew's hand and said, "Now we need to help Barbara get dinner ready, *ja*?"

"*Ja*," he said with a big grin.

And me, I need to decide whether I'm willing to

stomp on my pride to meet Daniel. A man she had so recently wanted to hate.

Whether she remained angry or not, Daniel was the only person she really *could* talk to. Rebecca couldn't deny that he still drew her. Was she brave enough to find out if everything he'd said and done really was about the job, or whether some of it might conceivably have been about *her*?

CHAPTER TWELVE

AT DINNER, REBECCA tried to push aside her tension and indecision. Only politeness made her lift her gaze from her plate when Barbara began to talk in her placid way.

"You know we have a grandson almost Matthew's age. His *mamm* and *daad* don't live as close as we'd like, ain't so, Amos?"

She probably already had a dozen grandkids, Rebecca couldn't help thinking.

Her husband's response was a predictable grunt. Rebecca hid a smile as he shoved a forkful of pickled beets into his mouth.

"Is he six, too?" Matthew piped up.

"No, he is five. His birthday is in November, so he couldn't start school. I've been thinking Caleb must be as bored as Matthew. So I wrote to Grace—she's my daughter—and asked if Caleb could come stay with us for a little." She beamed at them both. "Today her letter came. She is happy to have him visit. Amos is to go get him tomorrow."

"That's wonderful of you to suggest. But…what if—" she stole a look at Matthew "—this isn't a good time for him to be here?"

"*Ach*, who would think Rebecca and Matthew were here with us?" Amos asked. "Two boys here, not only one, that is better."

Rebecca's eyes stung. "It's so kind of you to think of it."

Barbara chuckled. "It makes no trouble."

Matthew looked worried. "Does he talk like me?"

"No, but you will both learn, *ja*?"

Rebecca smiled at him. "Don't be so doubtful. Wasn't Abram learning some English? And you some Deitsch?"

"For sure you were," Barbara said. "Do you remember what I said to you this morning?"

He shook his head.

"I said, *'Setz der disch,'* and you did. You didn't say, what does that mean?"

"Abram's *mamm* always makes us set the table."

"See? You are learning to speak like we do." She nodded at his half-full plate. "Now, eat yourself full."

Matthew applied himself to his dinner. Watching him, Rebecca noticed that he was a lot less picky than he used to be. *Silver linings.* One of many, she had to believe, starting with reconnecting with her family.

AN OWL HOOTED, providing companionship of a sort for Daniel.

Of course she hadn't come out to meet him. He shouldn't have bothered to come. Rebecca had been furious at him—and hurt. Picturing her face, he shifted uncomfortably on the crude bench behind Amos's barn.

Weariness kept him leaning against the side of the barn. The woman he'd pulled from her totaled car and performed first aid on had died, leaving her baby motherless. That news had put the cap on his crappy day. Or was he doing that himself, sitting here pathetically waiting for a woman who had lied to him from day one, then was furious when he called her on it?

Tonight was noticeably darker than last night. The moon was waning, suiting his mood. He'd probably clobber his head on a tree branch or get caught in a barbed-wire fence on his way back to the car. Yeah, he was in a mood.

Daniel shoved himself to his feet—just as he heard a rustle. He grabbed the butt of his gun as he spun around.

A small gasp told him who was here even before he made her out.

"You came," he said, stunned.

"I didn't think *you* would."

"Then why did you come out here?"

"I thought I would enjoy some solitude."

"Then I'll leave you alone," he snapped.

He'd taken several steps when her low voice stopped him. "I wasn't fair today. Or Saturday."

Daniel squeezed the bridge of his nose, needing the pain to counteract the flood of relief. He took a minute before he slowly turned. "Given my oath of office, I didn't see how I could delay passing on information regarding such a serious crime. Or cooperating with a detective from another jurisdiction."

"I get that," she said wearily. "Today, Matthew spun in circles until he made himself dizzy and fell down. Lately, I feel like that's what I've been doing."

"You've dealt with a lot." She sat, and Daniel walked back toward the barn and settled a foot or two from her.

"That's no excuse." She looked at him, making him wish he could see her face better.

"When I talk to Estevez again, I'll lean on him to

cut you some slack. If nothing worse comes to light, I think he'll agree. He has bigger fish to fry."

He sensed as much as saw her shiver, realizing belatedly that one of those "fish" was her ex-husband. The one she'd been protecting.

"You still don't know where he is?" Rebecca sounded timid. "Tim, I mean?"

"No." The muscles in his shoulders and neck were in knots. "I have to admit, I didn't get much looking done today."

"I don't blame you," she whispered.

"No." He reached almost blindly and found her hand. "It wasn't just you. Right after I left here this afternoon, I was called to a major vehicular accident out on the highway. Ended up with two fatalities."

"Oh, no." Her fingers twined with his, perhaps unconsciously. "But...why you?"

"I was closest, which made me first responder." He started telling her about it but stopped before he got too graphic. "You don't need to hear this."

"I think you need to tell someone. I'd...like it to be me. It's only fair, you know."

The lump in his throat surprised him. He'd never had anyone he could talk to about the things he saw on the job. From what he'd gathered, even most married cops didn't talk to their wives about the gory or brutal or senseless stuff. Why he had this compulsion, he didn't know. He'd seen plenty of dead bodies before, and tried and failed to save lives.

After a minute, he said, "One of the drivers died almost instantly. It appears he was speeding. Don't know yet if he was drinking or why he lost control. The other driver was a woman. I tried to control her bleeding while I waited for paramedics. She died on the way to the hospital." He paused. "Her baby was in a car seat. She's fine. Her grandparents picked her up because her dad—" The guy had been twenty-three. Practically a kid, his world turned on end.

"Was too grief stricken," she said softly.

"Yeah."

"I'm sorry." Suddenly Rebecca scooted closer to him. Close enough to rest her head on his shoulder.

Afraid she'd flee if he so much as tried to put his arms around her, he savored what she did offer. They sat there for quite a while, providing and receiving comfort with the contact, no more words necessary.

AMISH RARELY TURNED to the police, but now he'd received his second call in a matter of days from Samuel. Troubled, Daniel set his phone on his desk. Rebecca's *onkel* had told Daniel that Noah Yoder, the next-door neighbor, had seen a man with binoculars tramping through the woods behind his place.

"He could be only a bird-watcher, but after the break-in, we are all worried." He paused. "Other people I know say that cars they didn't recognize slowed down to pass their buggies. Might be only tourists, curious, but the men in the cars stared, wanting to see every face."

"I hope you'll spread the word to have the *Leit* call if they spot someone who seems to be spying," Daniel had said. "If a car slows so men can stare, a license number would allow us to find out whether these are tourists or something more dangerous."

Hesitant, Samuel had nonetheless agreed he would tell others.

In the meantime, about all Daniel could do was make cruising the back roads in the heavily Amish areas of the county a higher priority. How much good that would do was another question. Visitors frequently came to the area to crane their necks at the Amish in their buggies.

He was still at the office trying to decide where to position the even-skimpier evening shift of deputies when his desk phone rang. Melissa Sue, one of the dispatchers and general assistants, said, "There's a gentleman here to see you, Sheriff. His name is Robert Gregory."

Now wasn't that interesting. Did that mean the senior Gregory knew everything his son was up to? Or did he believe Tim was searching only for Matthew?

"Thank you. Let him know I'll be out in a moment," Daniel said, hanging up the phone.

Robert Gregory hadn't bothered to take a seat in the small waiting room. When he heard the heavy door opening, he swung to face Daniel, raking him with an assessing look. Easily recognizable from the pictures Daniel had seen online, the man fairly crackled with impatience and intensity.

"Mr. Gregory?" Daniel held out his hand. "I'm Sheriff Byler."

"Sheriff." They shook. "I'd like to sit down with you in private."

Daniel let his eyebrows climb, but said, "Certainly." He nodded at Melissa Sue, who buzzed him back through the always-locked door. He waved Gregory ahead and into a small conference room just inside.

As soon as they had taken seats, he said, "Now, what is it you think I can do for you, Mr. Gregory?"

"I know you're aware my daughter-in-law is here illegally with my grandson," the man said tightly. "I'm asking you, as head of law enforcement in this county, to hand over the boy to me."

Daniel leaned back in his chair as if taken aback. "You might want to tell me what makes you think this woman is here."

The man failed to hide his contempt. "I know that my son and Rebecca—" he said the name with distaste "—had an encounter."

"An encounter. Interesting way to describe it."

"I'm aware my son may have behaved somewhat… impetuously. I'm not defending him."

Daniel let his voice harden. "Good, because I saw your son slam his *ex*-wife into the door frame of his rental car. She could easily have suffered brain damage or lost an eye. *Impetuous* isn't the word I'd have used."

Robert made a sharp gesture and snapped, "That's beside the point."

"No, I don't think it is. I would have arrested him for assault had my first concern not been Ms. Holt's injuries and her terrified little boy. Unfortunately, your son escaped while I was assisting her."

His eyes glittered. "So you do know where they are."

"If I did, Mr. Gregory, I wouldn't tell you. In fact—" he leaned forward, wishing his size advantage would intimidate the creep "—I need *you* to tell me where Tim is. He has to answer to the charges laid against him in this county before we can have any further discussion."

Robert snorted. "I neither know nor care where he is. I want my grandson, Sheriff. Ms. Holt did not have the legal right to take Matthew out of the state without informing the boy's father. She has not made my grandson available for court-ordered visitation. Tim has himself in a mess I want nothing to do with." His lip curled. "My concern is removing Matthew from a mother who has shown herself to be unable to care adequately for him." His eyes narrowed. "And I *do* expect cooperation from you."

What a prick. Daniel felt no guilt over thinking the word. No wonder Rebecca wanted to keep her kid out of his grandfather's hands.

"Tell me, Mr. Gregory, do you have a court order indicating your custody rights to this boy?"

Gregory glared at him. "I will certainly demand full custody once I have the boy home in San Francisco."

Daniel quirked an eyebrow. "I take it that's a no?"

"Matthew's only family is in California. You cannot possibly be taking the side of a woman who has attempted to disappear with him."

"Strange you should say that." Daniel let himself smile. "As it happens, besides his mother, young Matthew has maternal great-grandparents here in Missouri, as well as any number of aunts and uncles and cousins. It's my understanding he has been warmly received by his family."

"Amish," Robert spit.

"I find them to be good folks," Daniel said. "Law-abiding and generous."

"It might as well be a cult," the man sneered. "I will not lose my grandson to those people."

"I don't mean to be unhelpful, but it seems to me that right now you don't have a leg to stand on, Mr. Gregory. You might be smart to go on back to California and try to figure out what your son has gotten himself mixed up in."

Robert shoved back his chair. "What would you know about it?"

Did he believe the sheriff of this small county was an ignorant hayseed? Very possibly, Daniel realized.

"I do know that your former daughter-in-law barely escaped from two attempts on her life back in your fine city. I've spoken to a Detective Estevez there. Those incidents had something to do with the troubles at G, G & S. Or with someone's desire to remove Ms. Holt from the equation so that his father—or grandfather—might have custody."

Robert shot to his feet, his face dark with fury. "You're accusing *me*…?"

"No, no, not at all." Daniel took pleasure in appearing placid. "Only letting you know any discussion of the best placement for Matthew is unlikely until some questions are answered. As I said, unless you're interested in helping us locate your son, I recommend you go on home." He, too, stood, smiling. "Although I feel sure Detective Estevez would be glad to talk to you. I have his number if—"

Robert stalked out of the conference room. Daniel ambled after him, pleased to see that Melissa Sue had waited for his nod to electronically unlock the heavy door.

Only a few feet into the waiting room, Robert turned a burning look on Daniel. "You'll be hearing from me again."

"I'll look forward to that, Mr. Gregory."

"Made him mad, did you?" the dispatcher said cheerfully after he left.

"I did."

"Course, he was mad when he walked in the door," she mused.

Daniel hoped that wasn't the language she used when speaking to the fine citizens of Henness County, but he let it go. The truth was, he had *enjoyed* making Robert Gregory mad.

THE STURDY YOUNG boy perched beside his *grossdaadi* on the driver's seat of the black buggy stared at Matthew, who stared back. Like Matthew and Amos, Caleb wore black trousers, a long-sleeved blue shirt and suspenders, all in more diminutive sizes. Unlike Matthew, he also wore a straw hat identical to his *grossdaadi's*.

When the staring contest failed to end, Barbara intervened, chuckling with delight and sweeping her grandson down while chattering away to him in Deitsch. Rebecca couldn't help thinking that Caleb Lapp was a very brave boy. From what she'd gathered, he hadn't seen his grandparents since Christmas, which was a very long time ago in the life of a five-year-old. And now he was confronted with a strange boy whom he had undoubtedly been told didn't speak his language.

But Caleb finally eyed Matthew and said, "Hi." Had he rehearsed it?

Matthew's face brightened. "Hi. Do you want to play catch? I even have a bat, if you want to hit the ball." Barbara had driven to town this morning to grocery shop, returning with a bright blue plastic bat and ball, as well as bags full of food.

Caleb transferred his gaze to his grandmother, who

translated. Then he grinned at Matthew, showing a gap in his front teeth. "*Ja!*"

The two boys ran for the porch, the three adults looking after them in amazement.

"He is not a shy boy," Amos finally commented, his tone odd. "A *blabbermaul*, more like. Don't know why he hasn't lost his voice." Then he clicked his tongue, and the horse started toward the barn.

Barbara laughed. "Poor Amos, hours stuck with a *kind* who talks all the time."

Rebecca had to laugh, too. "And look at Caleb and Matthew!" They had taken the bat and ball and started around the side of the house, where the ground was flat and uninterrupted enough for baseball.

"*Brederlich* already," Barbara agreed, sounding just a little smug. Rebecca couldn't blame her. Her idea to bring Caleb for a visit had been splendid, even if Rebecca still worried about Caleb's safety.

Amos deserved a good deal of the credit. Until Rebecca had seen him spending time with Matthew, she wouldn't have been able to imagine him entertaining a five-year-old boy for several hours.

Then she laughed again. It was entirely possible he hadn't had to do a thing but nod and grunt from time to time.

Hiding her hand in her skirts, Rebecca crossed her fingers. *Please let them become best friends.*

IN PREPARATION FOR DINNER, Barbara put both boys to work snapping green beans, fetching a jar of applesauce from the cellar and setting the table. Along with bible stories after dinner, Rebecca played games with them, translating for them to their merriment since her own

Pennsylvania Dutch still wasn't fluent. Even so, the games were more fun with three.

Nonetheless, all she could think about was seeing Daniel again. The last thing he'd said yesterday evening was, "Eight thirty?" She had promised to try.

After tucking the boys into the same twin bed, she went downstairs and paused in the living room doorway. "I'm going outside for a while."

Barbara and Amos smiled in understanding. Perhaps she should have told them she was meeting Daniel, but as an adult she wasn't about to bow to Amish restrictions on women, even if she had agreed to live plain to blend into their lives.

What she couldn't understand was her excitement whenever she thought about meetingDaniel.

Had she let go of her anger so easily?

She had felt betrayed most to think he had fostered the sense of intimacy between them only to extract confidences. But last night, he had turned to her in his grief. She hadn't been a witness or a suspect to him, only a woman he needed.

Outside, she strolled briefly toward the deserted country road, although not so close a passing driver would see her, before turning back and continuing toward the barn.

Just as she reached it, a dark figure stepped around the corner. "It's me," Daniel said quietly.

Relief and that same excitement filled her.

He took her arm even though her eyes had adjusted to the moonlit darkness. They sat on the bench, really only a board laid across a couple of upended stumps. She pictured Amos taking breaks out here, enjoying the quiet and solitude.

They had to stay quiet. If she was caught sneaking out to meet a man, she and Matthew might lose their current refuge.

"I haven't told your *aenti* and *onkel* I'm meeting you. They probably think I'm just enjoying some peace and quiet."

He grimaced. "Maybe tomorrow you should tell Amos that I asked you to meet me outside so nobody watching would see me near the place."

Something in her relaxed, both at the suggestion and at the knowledge that she would see Daniel again. "I'll do that."

She sat, Daniel beside her. He'd laid a flashlight down but did not turn it on.

"I do have news."

She held her breath.

"Your father-in-law marched into the station today." He told her about Robert's demands, and how he had routed him, if only for now.

"Here. He's in town, so close."

"No, I followed up. He caught a flight to San Francisco out of St. Louis earlier in the evening."

"Where he'll file for custody."

"Relax." A large hand lifted hers from her lap.

After letting him lace their fingers together, she looked down, seeing their clasped hands in moonlight, her skin paler than his even after the hours she'd spent working in *Aenti* Emma's garden and hanging out laundry. His hand engulfed hers. The bones in his wrist were so much bigger than hers, his forearm strong with muscle.

"How can I relax?"

"He won't be filing for anything, not yet. He isn't

that stupid. His son is in deep trouble. You're hiding out of fear of Tim—and don't say it's not Tim, because he's part of it. I pointed out that Matthew has lots of relatives here."

"They're Amish," she said tightly. "I'm betting judges are leery of them."

"In your part of the country, probably. But Robert has a big problem right now—his son. Until that's resolved and you and Matthew are safe, there won't be any hearings."

It was a long moment before she could let herself believe he was right, before the rigidity gradually seeped out of her body.

"Hey." Daniel bumped his shoulder against hers. "Caleb make it?"

She smiled despite everything and repeated what Amos had said about his grandson being a *blabbermaul*. "Although your *onkel* has surprised me."

"How so?"

"Yesterday afternoon after you left, I was about to go nuts when he took Matthew for an hour to 'help' in his workshop."

"Amos?"

She couldn't help laughing at his amazement. "Matthew came back feeling really proud of himself."

"Huh." Daniel shook his head. "How are Matthew and Caleb getting along?"

"Amazing, considering they can barely talk to each other. I had no idea how much I'd miss Abram. And Mose and Esther. They treated him like one of their own."

"What's one more in that household?"

"And I doubt they're done."

"No, I think the *kinder* will just keep coming for those two," he agreed.

"Caleb is your cousin," she realized, then corrected herself. "First cousin, once-removed."

"I guess he is." The words came slowly. "I've never met him."

"I suppose you have a lot of cousins."

"Nieces and nephews, too." He sounded sad. "Some I've never even met."

"Why not?" she asked, indignant. "You're not under the *bann*."

"No, but I'm not quite part of the family, either. Two of my three sisters have married out of the area. Both were visiting in Iowa when they met their husbands. My next younger brother is still angry at me. We were close growing up."

"He thinks you rejected him."

Daniel sighed. "Yes. He had no trouble convincing himself that he's really mad because I broke with the faith, and in such a conspicuous way." His shoulders moved. "I do see *Mamm* and *Daad* and most of the family who live locally on occasion."

"Is it awkward?"

"Not as much when it's just my parents and my one sister, Rachel. Otherwise…yes."

"I'm sorry." She gave his hand a little squeeze.

"My choice," he said curtly.

"But it can still hurt."

There was a moment of silence before he nodded. "You're right."

"Do you ever wish you hadn't come back?"

He gave a short laugh lacking any humor. "You have a way of getting right down to it, don't you?"

Shrinking, she said, "I shouldn't have—"

But Daniel tugged on her hand and said, "Come here."

She barely hesitated before scooting close enough for him to put an arm around her. His willingness to tell her about his life, to share the things that hurt him, had restored her trust in him. He'd known too much about her, while remaining the cop. Now, they were achieving the give and take that put them on the same footing.

"The answer to your question is, sometimes, even if I usually think I'm right where I should be."

Reassured by what felt like honesty, she said, "They may all be conflicted about you, but it's obvious they respect you, too. *Onkel* Samuel told me you're a good man."

A smile in his voice, Daniel said, "I think he is, too. And Amos, or I wouldn't have brought you to stay here."

She sat quietly for a minute, feeling the need to remind them both of the real reason for this meeting. "You didn't magically find Tim today, did you?"

"Far as I can tell, he's vanished into thin air."

Rebecca didn't know how she could smile, but suddenly she did. "Maybe a doorway into another dimension opened."

"If so, I hope some truly hideous monsters were waiting for him, and I don't care if he *is* Matthew's father." He pressed a kiss to her head. "Read a little sci-fi, do you?"

"And fantasy. You?"

"Same. Otherwise, mostly mysteries and nonfiction." He chuckled, then turned serious. "My best guess is that he's still around, and I doubt he's here alone."

She frowned. "Why?"

"Who's buying the groceries? If he's rented a house or a cabin at a resort or a hotel room, whose name is it under?"

"The PI?" she suggested.

"His name hasn't popped up. Neither has your father-in-law's or Josh Griffen's. Which doesn't mean Josh isn't in the area, or that Robert can't come back. I've asked for help from neighboring jurisdictions, but they may not be looking as hard as I am. And, for all we know, Tim could be camping out in the woods, or in a vacant house on a dead-end road."

"I can't stay here for too much longer. It's a huge imposition."

"Have you gotten the feeling you're not welcome?" Daniel asked.

Rebecca sighed. "No, of course not. Actually, I think Barbara is enjoying having someone to talk to. Your *onkel*, well, he isn't very chatty."

He laughed, low and rusty. "I've noticed."

She pulled back a little to look up at him. "Do you have electricity at home?"

"I do. I got spoiled. And, yes, I even have a television."

Rebecca chuckled. "And tablet and smartphone. You're a thoroughly modern man."

"In some ways." He sobered. "I watch baseball and occasionally football. Sometimes the news. I can go days or even weeks without turning the TV on. I use the internet primarily for work-related research. Most people would find my house…bare."

Rebecca squeezed his hand. "In other words, the

man may leave the Amish, but he still carries the beliefs wherever he goes?"

"And where did I go?" He made a sound in his throat. "Home, but not quite. Ambivalence in action."

"But you do what you couldn't as a boy," she said thoughtfully. "You keep the people you love safe."

CHAPTER THIRTEEN

THE NIGHT SEEMED darker as Rebecca waited for Daniel to say something. Anything.

Tim had hated her attempts to get him to talk about his feelings. He'd accused her of trying to pry him open like a tin can, determined to find out if the contents matched the label. Maybe she was just nosy, and his desire to keep a big part of himself locked down completely natural.

Even in the dark, she felt Daniel's eyes boring into hers. Suddenly, he made an inarticulate sound, and then his arms were tight around her and he was kissing her. She felt his anger and desperation along with passion, and she threw her arms around his neck and kissed him back with equal ferocity. Maybe because *she* was still angry, too. And afraid.

Moments into the kiss, he groaned and gripped her around the waist, lifting her as if she weighed nothing and setting her sideways on his thighs. Then he went back to kissing her with passionate single-mindedness. One of his hands kneaded her hip.

His mouth left hers to string kisses over her cheek, to nip her earlobe, taste her throat. Daniel growled when he reached the high neckline of her modest dress.

Daniel groaned again. She felt the vibration in his chest. More than that—his hands were shaking. *She* was shaking. For a moment he didn't move except to rest his forehead against hers.

"I want you," he said raggedly. "But we can't—"

"No." But she wasn't sure she'd have had the self-control to stop. Imagine the scene if Amos had come looking for her! "I told them I wouldn't be gone long."

"I'm sorry." He rubbed his nose against hers. "I shouldn't have started that. I didn't mean to."

"It was me being pushy."

"It was you reading me as if—" He stopped suddenly.

She was afraid to ask him to finish. Asking him to bare himself to her just because she felt so vulnerable wasn't reasonable. Because his job was to protect her, he had to hear about her problems. She didn't have an equal right, even if she wanted that right.

Daniel stayed silent until his chest lifted and fell with another long sigh. Somehow she wasn't surprised when he said, "You should get back inside."

Unreasonable hurt had Rebecca pulling free and jumping to her feet.

But Daniel stood, too, so close she could feel his body heat. His breath was a whisper against her cheek. "This is dangerous," he murmured. "Meeting in the dark, alone."

"You don't have to come." It hurt to say. "If you have something to tell me, you could leave a note. I can check here every morning."

He pressed a hard kiss to her mouth. "I need to see you."

The hurt dissolved. "Oh. Then…"

"Tomorrow night." He made a sound deep in his throat. "Maybe it's lucky you're dressed plain. Between your *kapp* and that dress, I'm forced to remember our circumstances."

"I wish…"

"I wish, too." His knuckles brushed her injured cheek with aching tenderness. "Go, Rebecca."

Head bobbing, she turned away. She felt sure that he watched until she slipped inside the house and he knew she was safe.

DANIEL'S DAY STARTED with a call from Little Ike Mast.

A man had visited the Mast father-and-son horse farm, but hadn't seemed very interested in the draft horses. He claimed to have heard good things about Samuel Graber's operation, but also that Samuel was too busy right now with his niece visiting to seem interested in selling horses.

Not part of the Grabers' church district, Little Ike knew only that Samuel's place had been ransacked. That made him wonder about someone more interested in Samuel's family than in the horses he had claimed he wanted to see. "The bishop said I should call to tell you."

Little Ike hadn't liked the *Englischer*. No, not a tall man, but strong, with dark hair and eyes. Not very friendly.

Josh Griffen? "What did you say to this *Englischer*?" Daniel asked.

"That I didn't know what he was talking about. Visitors? How would I know?"

Whoever these men were, they were taking risks, letting themselves be seen. Daniel thought about checking in with Estevez, but the information didn't really add to what they knew, and he expected to hear from the detective soon, anyway.

In fact, that call came a couple hours later.

"Finally got clearance for the trip and have a reservation for Saturday morning."

They discussed logistics, then Daniel told him about the apparent hunt for Rebecca and her son.

"If the stupid woman had just come to me in the first place..." Estevez sounded as if he was grinding his teeth.

"She might be dead."

Silence. Then he said, "You know I should slap her with every charge I can think up. She's wasted so much of my time."

"I'd be happier if you didn't," Daniel said mildly.

"You're kidding."

"No. I do believe Ms. Holt has suffered remorse even as she believed the items were the only way to hold off her ex-husband and his partner. I have the impression it's the father-in-law most of all that had her panicking. Having met the guy, I can understand."

"You met him?" Estevez asked, surprised.

"Oh, yeah. He marched into the sheriff's department headquarters yesterday and demanded I hand over his grandson. All but disowned his son. Didn't care what Tim was up to, or that he'd battered Ms. Holt. When I inquired whether he had any paperwork showing legal custody, Mr. Gregory assured me that the minute he had his grandson back in the state of California, he'd go to court to get that custody. Didn't seem to have any doubt of his success."

The San Francisco detective snorted. "Guy's an asshole. He's almost enough to make me sorry for his son."

"I don't know about Tim, but the grandson is a great kid," Daniel remarked. "Funny, smart, sensitive." Well, he'd agreed that he didn't want a siren to frighten the horses. That qualified, didn't it? "Got to say, the idea of him in Robert's hands gives me a chill."

"Thus your sympathy for the kid's mother."

"I suppose so." *And, by the way, I'm falling for her. Have fallen.* Not something he intended to share. "Like she told you, if she'd immediately gone to you with the wallet, you'd have arrested Tim. But you wouldn't have had enough to arrest Griffen, too, unless Tim rolled on him. And either or both of the men would have been out on bail within twenty-four hours. Meantime, the custody issue was still on the table, slowing Ms. Holt's divorce, and Robert was maneuvering in the background."

More silence, followed by a huff that combined frustration with acceptance. "I may get pushback from my boss and from the DA."

"Introduce them to her father-in-law."

Estevez gave a bark of laughter. "There's an idea."

"How did he get to be so influential?" Daniel asked.

"Money, what else?"

"Inherited, or did he earn it?"

"A little of both, from what I know. Sounds like he's smart enough." The admission was grudging. "There are a couple of software powerhouses that wouldn't have gotten their starts without him. Face it, money trumps personality."

Daniel's turn to laugh. "Can't say I'd know. I wouldn't call anybody in Henness County rich." Although he'd tangled with a few like that when he worked in St. Louis.

"Count yourself lucky." The detective sounded sardonic. "Means you don't have to tiptoe during an investigation the way the rest of us do."

Did Estevez know how to tiptoe? He might have gotten further with Rebecca if he'd approached her with some finesse.

This mess made Daniel grateful that the crimes he typically saw were straightforward with easy-to-understand motives. He frequently pitied the people he arrested, like the Shaver brothers. What could have led Tim Gregory and Josh Griffen, successful by anyone's standards, already wealthy in their early thirties, to kill a friend and partner—or at least to cover up his death? Daniel would never understand the greed behind that kind of embezzlement.

Daniel ended the call with a tap of his thumb and then leaned back in his desk chair, looking at the clock. Counting the hours until Rebecca would slip around the corner of the barn and into his arms.

That evening, Rebecca resolved to be *airlich*—honest—with her hosts, although she prayed they wouldn't make an attempt to forbid her from going out to meet with Daniel. Out of gratitude for their kindness and generosity, she would comply with most requests from them, but not that one. If they were shocked and disapproving, staying with them would be tense. But she had to see Daniel.

When she told them Daniel intended to sneak onto the property this evening to talk to her, Amos and Barbara looked at each other. After a moment of silent communication, Amos nodded brusquely and didn't ask how Daniel had set up this meeting with her in the first place.

"We would not like a daughter meeting a man in the dark, but it is not our place to tell you what you can do. And I can see why he doesn't want anyone to see him come here."

"Thank you. I won't be long. I wish I thought he would have good news."

"*Ja*, it would be good if he could find that man," Barbara agreed.

The moment Rebecca stepped out, she felt the muggy air. The latest promised thunderstorm had bypassed them, nothing but distant rumbles late in the afternoon. She walked straight to the barn, not surprised to find Daniel there before her. He reached for her hand first thing. "I told Amos and Barbara I was meeting you," she heard herself say. Self-defense—or was it defense against self? A reminder that her time was limited and her hosts knew she was with Daniel?

"And they didn't lay down the law?" Daniel sounded surprised, even though he had been the one to suggest she be honest with Amos and Barbara.

"No. They weren't thrilled, but Amos said he had no right to tell me what to do."

"I can hear the whiff of disapproval."

Her forehead wrinkled. "No, he also said he understood you can't come here openly."

"Estevez will be here Saturday."

Her heart gave a single, unhappy kick. "Oh, joy."

"I think he's more bark than bite."

"Right."

Daniel smiled at her sarcasm. "I'll come to the back door tomorrow night so I can talk to Amos about how to sneak you to town for the meet. Not sure a big city detective would enjoy beating his way through the fields and woods to come here."

She clasped her hands together. "Okay."

"Little Ike Mast called to say a man who was more interested in Samuel Graber's visitors than his horses showed up asking questions. He pretended complete ignorance." Daniel hesitated. "His description of the man could match with Josh."

"Doesn't Detective Estevez know where Josh is?" Wonderful—she sounded semi-hysterical.

"He doesn't have grounds at this point to watch the guy. Josh may do some traveling as part of his work. And remember, Robert, Josh and Tim can all afford to fly with private charters, which makes tracking them harder. I'm surprised Robert flew commercial, now that I think about it."

"Will this ever end?"

"Hey. Come here." He held out an arm that closed around her when she slid closer. "You know we'll get them eventually."

He was asking for another form of faith from her. Faith in law enforcement, in justice and in him. It was still a struggle for her, but she finally nodded.

"Last night," he said suddenly. "I shut down on you. It's uncomfortable to feel clear as glass."

She turned within his encircling arm to look at him. "I'm sorry. I was nosy."

"Curious," he corrected. "Curious is good."

That let her relax. "You aren't easy to read. It's me. I think… I've felt pulled both ways, too. Not as strongly as you, I'm sure, but…my mother tried to instill her values in me. I never connected my stays here with home life. I didn't know why the television was rarely on in our house, why we played games in the evening or talked or cooked instead. Why she was never comfortable chatting on the phone. After the summers here, I tried to be like all my friends, and I guess I succeeded, in a way." A smile twisted on her mouth. "I'd see Mom's disappointment. And then there was my choice of Tim."

"You've felt some culture clash, too."

Rebecca nodded against his shoulder.

When he asked, she talked about growing up, and her brief rebellious stage when she'd cut her hair spiky short and dyed it various neon colors. She wondered what he would have thought of her if they had met while he was still an earnest Amish boy—or even later, when he was struggling free of the cocoon of his faith and family.

"Mom never forbade me to do anything," Rebecca said softly. "She wanted…"

"You to have a freedom she didn't?"

"I suppose that's it. She told me so many times how proud she was of me." In his embrace, her grief found solace.

DANIEL HAD HAD guarded conversations with others who had left the faith. He'd discussed the difficult transition before. But most of the people he'd met had craved a different life, some looking back with contempt that felt too much like how many non-Amish reacted. He had always wondered if they really felt no regret. He'd never heard anyone acknowledging the inner conflict he felt every day of his life. But Rebecca made it easy for him to start talking.

"I sometimes think I'm like an immigrant to this

country. Someone who knows he'll never be able to go back, but will never feel quite at home here, either."

She pulled away from him at that raw honesty so she could lay a hand on his cheek. "To the Amish, you may be a…a bridge."

He grunted. "Nice thought, but they're determined to stay apart from the world. You know that. They don't want a bridge."

"That may be where some of the tension comes from. But they do trust you, and they know if they have to cross over, the bridge is solid."

Daniel expelled a breath as if he'd been punched. He had never thought of his relationship with his family and the Amish community that way. If it was true…

He didn't like to think about his first few years after leaving all that was familiar, but when Rebecca asked more questions, memories spilled out. He'd hated feeling so stupid, stumbling when everyone else ran. Too much had been new, shocking and frightening, and he had existed in an adrenaline-fueled state that had probably shortened his lifespan.

He'd lived on the street until the weather grew too cold, then in a homeless shelter, before finding work, mindless and physical. The pay had been enough to rent a room. A social worker at the homeless shelter had steered him to educational resources, and he had begun studying for his GED.

As he continued talking, he realized he and Rebecca were still holding hands. Comfort and connection.

He told her about the classes he'd taken at a community college that helped him pass the GED, and how he'd continued on until he had a two-year degree. Scholarships and a nearly full-time work schedule had gotten him through the final two years at the University of Missouri–St. Louis.

Even then, he had been ill prepared for the realities of policing a major city with crimes that once would have been unimaginable to him.

He talked until he was hoarse, giving no thought to whether Amos would come to check on them. When he finally fell silent, he gathered Rebecca into his arms and just held her, soaking in this closeness to another person.

After he'd left her with a gentle kiss that required every ounce of self-control he could summon, he watched until she entered the house through the back door. Then he set off through the small orchard in what was becoming a familiar trek. This time, the owl's soft *whoo* sounded like a greeting between friends.

Tonight, an odd thought struck him. In roughly the last hour, he and Rebecca had shared much more than he ever had with any woman. In fact, all of their hushed meetings in the dark, sitting on porch steps or the bench behind the barn, were building a stronger foundation than a more intimate physical connection ever could.

And yet he still felt helpless, unable to arrest the men hunting her. Or even to be sure she would stay once she was safe. He also knew he couldn't let himself ask until she really had a choice.

GRATEFUL FOR THE slight padding provided by the horse blanket Amos had thoughtfully laid on the floor of the buggy, Rebecca started out cross-legged, skirts covering her to her stocking-clad ankles. But no position was very comfortable, and she had to keep shifting.

Even though the buggy was well sprung, it hit a hole in the road hard enough to bounce her. Wincing, she squirmed into another position.

The drone of the metal tire rims on the paved county road and the swaying of the buggy made her drowsy. Several cars passed, but she didn't think any of them slowed to a crawl to allow someone to peer in the windows.

But the sound of increased traffic, cars and other buggies, banished her sleepiness. The dread she'd been trying to suppress poked its way free. Would Daniel stay or hand her over to Detective Estevez? Silly to be so anxious about talking to the man in person when she had already told him everything. The tightness in her chest didn't ease. Detective Estevez had become a bogeyman, as frightening as all the other ones currently populating her head.

Possibly because *he* could arrest her.

Thank goodness for Caleb, Rebecca thought for at least the hundredth time. One of Amos and Barbara's daughters had brought her children over, and Matthew had hardly noticed when his mother left.

Now, the buggy made several turns, Amos clucking once to his bay mare and saying, "Almost here," ostensibly to Barbara but loudly enough for Rebecca to hear. A minute later, the mare slowed to a walk and then stopped when Amos said, "Whoa, Jessie."

The buggy swayed some more as the two got out. The clank of a bucket and a sloshing sound suggested Amos was providing water for Jessie. Then Barbara's voice drifted to Rebecca, receding as she spoke.

"I need a few things in Miller's. And flannel and thread for a new nightgown."

Amos's answer was barely a rumble.

Rebecca got to her hands and knees, afraid to lift her head in case someone walked by.

Not a minute later, what sounded like a truck came slowly down the alley, stopping right beside Amos's buggy. She had to believe it was Daniel, as planned, not Tim or Josh or one of their confederates. If she was wrong…she'd scream and struggle.

"Rebecca," said a quiet voice.

She rose to a crouch and opened the door, scrambling ungracefully out and into the backseat of the black SUV with tinted windows. The door slammed shut, and no more than a few seconds later Daniel drove them away. He turned right out of the alley to avoid the main shopping street, then kept going.

Detective Estevez swiveled in the passenger seat and looked sourly at her. "Interesting getup."

That stiffened her spine. "My family is Amish. I'm living plain."

One of his heavy eyebrows lifted as he surveyed her with dark eyes. "You're full of surprises, Ms. Holt. I sure never expected to have to travel halfway across the country to see you again."

Her cheeks heated. "Staying in the city didn't seem to be smart."

"So Sheriff Byler tells me. I wish *you* had."

"I should have come to you," she made herself say. "But I didn't think I'd live long enough to testify in any trial."

"The sheriff here suggested you might be more afraid of the senior Mr. Gregory."

"I never thought it was Robert trying to kill me. Just that if anything happened to me, he would swoop in and claim my son." Discovering her arms were wrapped as tightly around herself as she could manage, Rebecca tried to make herself loosen them. Under that sour gaze, she failed.

"All right," the detective said, still irritable but less aggressive. "We need to cover some of the same ground again. Let's start at the beginning."

First, he turned on a recorder and asked her to acknowledge that she knew she was being recorded and had given her permission.

Her eyes met Daniel's in the rearview mirror. She drew strength from his presence.

The real beginning, she knew now, had been months before she'd discovered the wallet, when Tim became so tense and angry, so secretive. But what Detective Estevez needed to hear...

"Tim had told me to take a look and decide what I wanted from the house," she said, grateful that she sounded almost composed. "So I let myself in..."

DANIEL FRETTED FOR what remained of the day. He'd told Rebecca to expect him tomorrow night, but not tonight. He didn't want to stretch his *uncle's* tolerance. But he had underestimated how stressful Rebecca would find today's meeting—and maybe the uncomfortable trip to and from town on the hard floor of the buggy.

What was she thinking? She had to be going a little crazy. He wished suddenly that they'd talked more about the future instead of concentrating on the past. He knew why he had—he saw her future here, with him, and had been afraid to find out she didn't. She'd said nothing to make him think she would do something dumb like take off or try to contact her ex, but he'd be reassured to hear that from her.

Sneak out there tonight? No, Rebecca wouldn't know to meet him. Anyway, he thought he'd like to see her face when they discussed the meeting with Estevez and where they'd go next.

He considered openly stopping by for once. Amos and Barbara *were* family. Why would anybody pay attention? While he was out, he'd make other stops, as was his habit. Just to remind people that he was willing to help…or, in a few cases, that he was keeping an eye on them. One of his deputies had reported seeing some traffic coming and going from the Shaver brothers' place, not a good sign.

But he was shaking his head even before he'd consciously made a decision. No. He couldn't risk drawing any attention at all to her location.

Go after dark and knock on the kitchen door again, then. Sit down with her *and* Amos.

With luck, she'd walk him out when he left and he could sneak a kiss to sustain him.

CHAPTER FOURTEEN

REBECCA WAS JUST tiptoeing out of the bedroom after tucking the boys in when she saw Amos at the head of the stairs.

"Asleep?" he asked in a low voice.

"Caleb is," she whispered.

He nodded. "You are needed downstairs."

What on earth? She hurried after him.

Not until they reached the main floor did he say, "My nephew is here, wanting to speak to us."

Her pulse rate rocketed. What could have happened?

She almost ran for the kitchen, brushing by Amos on the way. It was an anticlimax to find Daniel sitting at the table polishing off a piece of apple pie swimming in cream while Barbara unnecessarily wiped kitchen counters and chattered about what her daughter had told her about the boys' doings today.

They were surmounting the language difference with astonishing speed. Matthew, Rebecca was beginning to think, had already picked up more Deitsch from the Grabers, and especially Abram and Mose, than she'd realized. "Hi" had been the extent of Caleb's English when he'd first arrived, but increasingly he mixed English words and phrases into his Deitsch. However the two boys accomplished it, they seemed to understand each other.

Matthew still needed a hug or just the knowledge his mom was there, but the clinginess had passed. Rebecca was grateful for his resilience. If only she could feel as strong.

Seeing Amos and Rebecca, Barbara exclaimed, "*Ach*, here they are! You need to talk, *ja*? I will go back to my knitting."

"You're welcome if you'd like to stay," Daniel said unexpectedly. "I have nothing to say you can't hear."

Amos raised an eyebrow but, as was his way, wordlessly pulled up a chair to the table. He nodded his thanks to his wife for the cup of coffee she poured. Rebecca found herself directly across the table from Daniel.

They all stared at him until he scraped his plate clean and sighed. He smiled at his *aenti*. "I should steal you away. My cooking is nowhere near as good as yours."

Rebecca's fingers bit into her palms. Was he trying to torture her? "Why are you here?" she burst out.

Amos gave her a reproving look, which she ignored. Daniel focused on her, his expression calm.

"I wanted to tell you that Estevez and I talked after we dropped you off, and he says he, er, appreciated your cooperation and won't be filing charges."

Her breath whooshed out of her. At the same time, she couldn't help saying, "*Appreciated*? Detective Estevez?"

Daniel grinned. "He may have expressed it more begrudgingly than that."

Amos and Barbara stared at her as she laughed, which suggested she didn't sound quite sane. She couldn't decide if her relief was even proportional, given that someone who wanted to kill her was still on the loose.

Daniel just waited her out, his gaze steady. If they'd been alone, she felt sure he would have at least taken her hand.

"Thank you," she said. "I mean, for coming here to tell me."

"I also wanted to find out how you're holding up." He hesitated. "You've had all the control taken out of your hands, with nothing to do but wait."

It was as if he'd bulldozed a barricade holding back a toxic brew of emotion. "I keep wanting to *do* something! This is my mess, and now I'm completely helpless, waiting to be bailed out." She glared at him, even though none of it was Daniel's fault. "I *hate* feeling like this."

"I understand." His mouth twisted. "I wish I could suggest a way for you to help, but I don't know what that would be."

She looked down at her hands. "I could...take off. Make sure they know I'm not here anymore."

"With Matthew?" Daniel's voice sounded as if it had been run over a grater.

"Well...no, I couldn't do that to him. But if he could stay here—" she flicked an apologetic glance at Amos and Barbara "—I could lead them away." Yep, great idea.

He groaned. "How would they know to chase after you?"

"I could call from someplace like a bus or train station, where departures are being announced over a PA system. If he heard it in the background..." Seeing Daniel's expression, she mumbled, "It was...just a middle-of-the-night scheme. I know it's stupid. It's just…"

Amos surprised her by setting a big, work-roughened hand over her knotted fingers. "We have thought of you like a daughter, Rebecca. Stay as long as you must. You and one small boy make no trouble."

Through the blur of tears she saw Barbara smiling encouragement.

Rebecca sniffed. "Two small boys and a woman like me can make a whole lot of trouble."

"The good kind," Barbara said. "Enjoying you all, we are."

"Is common sense all that's stopped you from embarking on this great plan?" Daniel asked, his blue eyes penetrating, his voice almost harsh.

She couldn't look away from him. "I couldn't really have left Matthew and—" *you* "—everybody who cares about me."

"I'm one of those people, you know," he said quietly.

The floodgates opened. She mumbled, "I do know," and buried her face in her hands. She didn't see him move, but suddenly he had circled the table, pulled out the chair next to hers and wrapped his arms around her, right there in front of Amos and Barbara.

Rebecca let herself cry on his uniform shirt for only a minute, then gave herself another minute to steep in the pleasure of being held close. His smell was mingled sweat, a hint of aftershave. Man. His arms were so strong, his shoulders reassuringly broad. She hated to look up, because now she'd be blotchy and puffy and she'd have to see how shocked his *aenti* and *onkel* were, but finally she had to.

"It's just me, you know," she said in a soggy voice,

"Matthew seems really happy." She smiled shakily at Barbara. "Thanks to your brilliant idea. It's just... I hate knowing I've brought danger to all of you. I never meant—"

Amos stirred. "Here, you have our nephew to keep you safe."

She did. The miracle was, despite the fact that she felt trapped, she did believe in Daniel.

"Yes," she whispered, but wasn't sure he was convinced.

MORNING BROUGHT THE usual distractions from the minute Daniel walked into headquarters. Plus, a deputy had called in sick, leaving them shorthanded at a time when they could ill afford it. Lucky he hadn't planned to take this Sunday off, Daniel thought, since he'd be replacing his absent deputy.

He hadn't driven two miles during his patrol when a voice crackled through his radio. "Found a buggy. Nobody in it. Horse seems upset."

After a quick glance in the rearview mirror, Daniel braked. "You've searched in case the driver got thrown out?"

"Drove back a ways," Deputy Sloan responded. "Nothing."

This couldn't be good. He could only pray whatever had happened was unrelated to the reports of men studying the faces of Amish traveling the roads. Today was the "off" Sunday for the Amish, who used it for visiting instead of church.

"Location?" he asked.

"Westwood Road, 'bout half a mile this side of the river bridge."

The Thompson River took a curve into Henness County, the banks sandy in that stretch. Fishermen could often be seen in their waders, lines cast. Westwood Road narrowed to cross a rusting steel bridge preferred by the Amish to the busier and more modern bridge to the south.

"On my way."

On cresting a gentle hill, he saw two buggies ahead, as well as a sheriff's department vehicle. Daniel parked behind his deputy and got out to find an Amish couple he knew only slightly, the man soothing a sweating, wild-eyed bay gelding hitched to a small, open buggy, while the woman had stayed in their own buggy. The deputy was almost in the ditch, keeping a wary distance from the horse. If this had been a busier road, the scene would have been considerably more chaotic. If the horse had run in a panic out in front of a car…

He shook off the image.

"Paul Glick?" Daniel ventured.

"*Ja.*" The man, perhaps forty, was unusually dark-haired and dark-eyed for the Amish. "You are Sheriff Byler, not so?"

"I am. Do you know whose buggy this is?"

"*Ja*, Anna Lantz lives with her husband and children on Sandy Creek Road." His accent was stronger than most. "Her *mamm* and *daad* live near my wife and me, half a mile over the river. She and her oldest boy, I saw them when they left her parents' to go home, maybe half an hour ago." His head turned, his eyes sweeping the woods on one side and the overgrown pasture on the other. "Where could she be?"

"Let me call this in and make sure she and her son weren't transported to the hospital."

Dispatch checked; no Amish woman had arrived at the hospital in Byrum or as an emergency at the medical clinic in Hadburg, although if an *Englischer*, local or tourist, had found her or her boy in distress, they could still be in transit. But would even an anxious or suddenly ill mother simply abandon her horse and buggy without at least turning them into the next lane?

Daniel returned to Paul Glick. "How old is the boy who was with her?"

"Luke is five, I think. Just too young to start school."

Daniel didn't like being proved right. The dread felt like a too-tight band around his rib cage. "What does Anna look like?"

Paul stared at him like he was *ab im kopf*—off in the head, for sure. But seeing something in Daniel's expression, he said, "She is a pretty woman. Even after two children, she is thin. Her hair is…" He hesitated, obviously floundering.

"A red-brown," his wife called. Daniel had assumed she was too far away to be able to hear them talk. "Wavy, sometimes curling out from under her *kapp*."

His deputy had been shading his eyes and looking back down the road. "I think I see something," he said suddenly, and jogged along the shoulder.

"She has blue eyes," the wife added.

In other words, she met the basic description of Rebecca Holt.

"Her boy?"

"Blond, like his *daad*."

The dread coalesced into naked fear.

Seeing that Sloan was jogging back, something in his hand, Daniel said, "Excuse me a minute," and walked to meet him.

"A bonnet," the young deputy said, holding it out. "One strap is torn off. I didn't see this from the car."

It was black, the kind of bonnet any respectable Amish woman wore when out in public. Picturing rough hands ripping it from her head, Daniel said tensely, "Start canvassing. Go back as far as the river. Let's hope we find some people who were outside and noticed passing vehicles. I'll bring in help."

He allowed Paul Glick to unhitch Anna Lantz's mare and tie her to his buggy. He would detour to take the horse home, he promised, before he and his wife continued into town. Daniel walked a few feet away and made his calls to bring in every possible deputy and volunteer.

Knowing how much he had to do, he still stood beside his car for a minute, paralyzed with fear for Rebecca. The Lantz home wasn't a mile from Amos and Barbara's. That suggested the hunt was closing in. Daniel wanted her out of there.

Not Matthew, at least not yet. One more Amish boy would pass unnoticed, once his mother wasn't in the picture. The kid today wouldn't have been grabbed, and probably not the woman alone, either. It was the combination that had put them in danger.

We'll never find them in time. No wonder Rebecca hadn't wanted to give up her bargaining chips.

And that was when he had a lightbulb moment.

He couldn't get away himself, so he called a deputy whose shift hadn't yet started. After that, he drove to the Lantz home, passing Paul's buggy on the way.

Out in a field, two men seemed to be inspecting the enormous bales of hay, but both turned to look when the marked police car drove up the driveway. As he came to a stop, one of the two strode across the field toward him. Out of the corner of his eye, Daniel saw that a heavy, older woman had stepped out onto the porch with a toddler on her hip.

Being the bearer of bad news was a part of the job Daniel couldn't push onto others, but he hated it nonetheless.

The man, no older than Daniel himself, had wheat-colored hair and beard. Daniel took a few steps to meet him. "Eli Lantz?"

Worry filled the blue eyes. "*Ja*, I'm Eli."

"Mr. Lantz, one of my deputies found your wife's horse and buggy abandoned on the road this side of the river. Paul Glick and his wife came along. He's bringing the horse to you. You can retrieve the buggy later." After Daniel's one crime-scene technician had gone over it. "He says Anna had your son Luke with her."

Eli nodded, his gaze straying to the woman and child on the porch. "The little one stayed home."

"I've received no word from emergency services, and the hospital and medical clinic have both promised to let me know if an Amish woman or child is brought in by anyone. Failing that—" he hesitated "—I have to worry that Anna and your boy have been abducted."

Eli called, "*Mamm!*"

The older woman hurried from the porch.

Soon the other man was approaching, as well.

Daniel explained the situation again to all of them, then asked Eli to go to the nearest phone shanty and check for messages. The families nearby always shared an answering machine as well as the phone.

"*Ja, ja,*" he said, and ran. But only minutes later he returned, shaking his head. "No messages at all."

"Keep checking every once in a while," he advised.

Daniel didn't want to tell them the possible connection to Rebecca and Matthew yet. The implications were too ominous. What would happen when Tim or Josh saw that the wrong mother and son had been snatched? She'd all too likely seen the faces of her abductors. And the boy was old enough to be able to describe their captors. These men weren't likely to guess the Amish wouldn't go to the police if she and the boy were immediately released, uninjured.

Were those guys cold-blooded enough to murder a young mother and child inadvertently caught up in their hunt for Rebecca?

REBECCA MASHED POTATOES while Barbara took sourdough biscuits from the oven. As they prepared the midday meal, Caleb and Matthew contentedly sat at the table drawing pictures and giggling at each other's efforts.

Both women turned in surprise when Amos walked in the back door. He had gone out to feed their two horses only a minute ago.

"Rebecca," he said, expression grave, "*komm*. I must speak to you."

Alarmed, she followed him to the living room without argument.

"Harvey Zook's boy, Mark, just ran over." His accent had thickened, making the "just" more of a "chust." "A sheriff's deputy came to his house, says Daniel asked him to pick you up. Wants you to pack a change of clothes and sneak with Mark back to the sheriff's office. Says he needs you to do something, and that maybe you not being near Matthew right now would be good."

She listened to this speech, heart drumming. The Zooks' farm was probably half a mile down the road. "Something happened. This Mark doesn't know what?"

"No, but my nephew would not ask this without reason."

Even through her panic, she noted his calm faith in Daniel. A bridge, indeed. "No," she said. "I mean, yes. Okay." She drew a steadying breath. "I'll go pack some things into my duffel. Where's Mark?"

"The barn. He came in the back, so he would not be seen."

She ran upstairs, stuffed another of her plain dresses into the duffel, as well as the limited wardrobe with which she'd begun her journey.

Matthew took the news well. He held her only a little longer than usual when she hugged him. Then she hugged Barbara and hustled out the back door with Amos before she burst into tears.

IT WAS A *huge* relief to crawl out of the police car. Of course, she'd had to lie on the backseat, behind the grill. The car rode a whole lot better than the buggy, and moved faster, too, but the upholstery stank, an awful mix of cleansers and something really gross. She found herself staring at stains, too.

Annoyingly, the young deputy refused to tell her *why* he had been sent to pick her up. Maybe he didn't know. When he helped her out and she discovered he had pulled right up to the back door of the sheriff's department, she asked, "Do people throw up in your backseat?"

He flushed, making him look about sixteen. "Uh…
yes, ma'am. I've even had drunks, uh…" He thought
better of what he'd almost said, but Rebecca could fill
in the rest. She desperately wanted to scrub herself,
head to foot.

He did allow her to detour into a restroom and wash
her face with a paper towel, then her hands. She almost
went back out, but instead locked herself in a stall and
changed to her alternate dress and apron. She needed
to stay plain until she knew what Daniel needed, but
at least she felt almost clean now.

She was tying her apron when a knock came on
the door.

"Ma'am? Are you all right?"

She jammed the clothes she'd just shed in the duffel bag, zipped it and opened the door. "No, I didn't
squeeze through that tiny window and make a getaway," she said drily.

He blushed again. "I didn't mean…uh… I never
thought…"

How on earth did this poor boy ever make an arrest? Or did he believe she *was* Amish and therefore
had delicate sensibilities?

He handed her over with obvious relief to a recep-
tionist, who introduced herself as Melissa Sue and ushered her into a conference room.

"Sheriff says he'll get here when he can. He doesn't
want anyone to see you, so if you don't mind…" She
looked uncomfortable.

"Don't stick my head out?"

"Something like that."

She did bring Rebecca a can of pop and a small bag
of peanuts in case she was hungry, then left her alone.

DANIEL HAD DRIVEN back to the scene of the abduction, where he started knocking on doors himself. Even the make of the vehicle would give them something to go on. Nobody had had reason to note a license-plate number, and out-of-state plates were commonplace around here because of tourism, but there might have been something distinctive about the vehicle—a bumper sticker, damage from an accident. Anything.

What they got was nothing. Not a single person along the road had happened to be working in a field close enough to notice traffic.

"*Ach*," said one Amish woman with a shrug, "cars pass all the time, and buggies, too. If someone doesn't turn up to our house…"

Finally he let everyone know he was returning to the station. Anna and Luke Lantz had only one hope: Rebecca.

He found her stashed in one of the small conference rooms. Hand on the knob, he paused for a minute, looking through the wire-mesh window. She sat at one end of the table with a book open in front of her, but she wasn't reading. Instead, she gazed straight ahead, toward a wall that held nothing but a blank whiteboard.

Her head turned when she heard the door opening. Worried blue eyes met his.

"Sorry to put you through that," he said. "I know you had to hike cross-country again, but I didn't want a deputy seen stopping too close to Amos's."

The sound she made was something like *pfft*. "It was nothing. As your *onkel* said, you wouldn't have sent for me without good reason."

"He said that?" Maybe he shouldn't be surprised, but Daniel was.

Rebecca smiled and nodded, although the smile disappeared too quickly, her eyes searching his face. "You don't look good. What happened?"

"An Amish woman and boy were abducted this morning," he said bluntly. He went on to explain about the buggy and horse abandoned on a road and that Anna Lantz at least superficially resembled Rebecca, as her boy did Matthew. "Her bonnet had been ripped off—we found it in the ditch—probably so that whoever grabbed her could see her face better."

"Oh, no," Rebecca whispered.

"Nobody saw what happened. That stretch of road isn't in sight of any house. A few people along the road have noticed slow cars lately, but figured tourists were out looking for Amish or were just lost. So far, we haven't found a trace."

She stiffened, anger transforming her face as she thought about the woman and boy who had been taken in place of her and her son.

"You brought me here to call Tim."

He should have expected her to make that leap, and knew she would have offered if he hadn't thought to ask.

"Yes."

CHAPTER FIFTEEN

DANIEL WISHED THERE was a plan C, one that didn't put Rebecca right in the bull's-eye. The very blackmail he suggested hadn't worked to hold off her enemies, but he prayed it would save two lives.

Fortunately, he'd already purchased a cheap phone loaded with minutes, and his intention was to persuade Amos to let her carry it. He'd meant to give it to her this evening.

He bounded upstairs to get the phone, grateful he had charged it last night, knowing that Rebecca would have no way to do so at the Troyers'.

After handing it to her, he drew up the chair beside her. "I won't ask you to put the phone on speaker, because he'd be able to tell and wonder who else was listening."

Not even blinking, she nodded.

He bent forward to kiss her cheek. "You know his number?"

"Yes. But what if he isn't carrying his cell?"

"He was until not long ago. Estevez spoke to him. Tim was evasive about his whereabouts, implied he was away on business."

"Wait. Can't you use the GPS in his phone to find him?"

"Estevez is getting a warrant to do that. Griffen's phone, too."

They talked for a minute about what she should say. Then she took a deep breath, murmured, "Okay," more to herself than him and dialed.

Looking tense, she waited through the rings followed by a message Daniel could hear. "Call me. This is Rebecca. I have something important to tell you. You need to call me. The number is—"

Daniel slid a piece of paper with a phone number written on it in front of her.

She read it aloud and ended the call. Her hand shook as she set down the phone. "He didn't answer," she said unnecessarily. "Should I try Josh?"

He took a hand that was ice-cold into his, rubbing to try to restore her circulation. "No. Now we wait."

"Do you think he knows Detective Estevez came here?"

"I doubt it, but even if he does he can't know you've already handed over that wallet, if that's what you're thinking."

Rebecca nodded, her gaze staying fixed on the phone. They waited in near silence, Daniel willing Gregory to have heard the ring, to be checking his messages.

Not even five minutes had passed when the phone rang. Rebecca jerked. "It's him."

"Okay." He laid his hand on her back, moving it in gentle circles. "You can do this."

HIS STEADY VOICE and gaze, his confidence—confidence in *her*—had a calming effect. She wouldn't let him down—or Anna and Luke Lantz.

Rebecca fixed her eyes on Daniel's as she answered. "Tim."

"You know I didn't mean to hurt you when I was helping you into the car, don't you?" Contrition and sincerity rang in Tim's voice. "I lost my temper and screwed up again. But, damn it, Rebecca, all I want is to see my son!"

"Really?" She spoke coldly. "Somehow, I doubt that's all you want."

"Where are you?"

"You think I'm going to tell you?" She hoped her laugh was as jagged as broken glass.

"If you'll just hand over the things you took from me, let me see you and Matthew, give him a hug."

She might have been touched if she didn't remember all too clearly what had happened outside the hospital.

"Here's the deal," she said crisply. "An Amish woman was kidnapped this morning along with her son. I'm told she looks like me, and her son is about Matthew's age and coloring."

"I don't know what you're—"

"I think you do."

Daniel nodded encouragement.

"Why would I—" Tim tried.

Rebecca interrupted again without compunction. "If she and her son are not released, alive and well, in the next hour, I will hand over Steven's ring and wallet to the police. The county sheriff has already been in touch with Detective Estevez after your attempt to force Matthew and me into your car. He doesn't know the whole story, but he will if Anna Lantz and her son aren't released."

"But I don't know anything about them!" Panic infused her ex-husband's voice.

"Find out," she said flatly. "I will promise that, if they are uninjured, they won't go to the law. The Amish don't, except in the case of serious crimes." Like kidnapping, but she didn't say that. "Whoever took her doesn't need to worry if she or her little boy saw faces."

"How can you accuse me—"

"One hour, Tim." She ended the call, dropped the phone and let out a shuddering breath.

"Well done." Daniel's big, warm hand moved up to her nape. When she let her head fall forward, he kneaded until she had to stifle a moan. His hands moved on, working her shoulders, until she felt so limp she wasn't sure she could lift her head at all.

But at last, with a sigh, she made herself straighten and, to her regret, Daniel's hands left her.

"Do you think it will work?" she asked—no, begged.

"I think what you just did is Anna's and Luke's best chance."

Only chance was what he meant. Fear curling in her stomach, she said, "What if Tim was telling the truth when he claimed not to know anything about them?"

"He'll call his partner and deliver the message."

She shivered. "This is a nightmare. It's completely insane! These are businessmen. Pictures of them make it into the newspaper when they attend a charity event. How can they be willing to kidnap and maybe even kill to protect…what?"

"My guess is that they stumbled into this. One or both got an idea of how they could short the third partner, maybe keep salaries down company-wide while padding their own income, just by tallying up some extra expenses. It could be Josh was the one doing the financial tricks, but Tim found out and he let him in. More likely, the two of them dreamed it up. It might have even seemed harmless. It was their own company, after all."

"Not quite. They were all equal partners, which means Steven owned a third."

Daniel probably had other things he should be doing—he'd silenced his phone twice in the last five minutes—but he didn't make any move to leave. Instead, he asked, "Did Tim like Stowe?"

"Originally, he must have. But by the time we were married…no. Steven did come off as arrogant, although I used to wonder if that wasn't a cover for major insecurities. He had a lousy childhood. And, yes, he did make sure everyone noticed his Harvard ring, and that they knew he was the money man for G, G & S. I had the feeling he and Tim had a sort of mutual-resentment thing going. Tim because Steven was an Ivy League grad, Steven because he thought Tim had grown up privileged and spoiled."

"And Josh?"

She hesitated. "Tim implied that both of them found Steven irritating, but that's secondhand. We socialized more with Josh than Steven, but I never felt like I really knew Josh. Steven and I would talk sometimes, but if only Josh was over, the minute we finished dinner he and Tim would close themselves in his office or the media room."

"The media room." Daniel had a bemused expression.

She made a face. "It scared me. I knew how to turn the TV on and put in a DVD when I let Matthew watch something, but I was afraid to push buttons. Tim would come scowling to say, 'How many times have I explained how to use the remotes?' But there were at least four of them, with all those buttons." She gave herself a shake. "It doesn't matter."

They both knew what *did* matter now.

"I wonder," Daniel said, "if one component of the embezzlement was putting something over on Steven. He was supposed to be the financial genius, and he didn't even notice all the fake expenditures?"

Oh, yes, she could see that. Their secret pleasure, because in their eyes they were proving themselves smarter than Mr. Harvard.

Daniel's phone rang again. This time, after a glance, he said, "I should take this call."

"Go." She flapped her hand toward the door.

He smiled, kissed her lightly and went. He was already talking on the phone by the time the door swung slowly shut behind him. A minute later, he popped back in to dump some change on the table.

"Last door on the left is the break room. Get yourself something to eat or another soda."

And then she was left to watch the second hand jerk slowly around the big wall clock. And pray.

Dear Lord, don't let an innocent woman and child suffer in my place.

THE CALL DANIEL had hoped for came fifty-seven minutes after Rebecca had spoken to Tim Gregory.

"Daniel, we have something here you've been looking for," said Ben Slater, Byrum police chief. "An Amish woman and kid. They're shaken, but not badly hurt so far as we can tell."

Daniel murmured a silent thank-you to the Lord. "I'll drive over and pick them up. You have them at the station?"

"I do."

"Where were they found?"

"They were dumped out of a van on the outskirts of town. Nobody was close enough to get a license plate, even though half a dozen people saw the van brake just before two people came tumbling out. One witness told me she'd seen someone throw a cat and kittens out of a car once, and this was just like that. Mrs. Lantz's apron was caught in the door and ripped and she's moving a little stiffly. The boy skinned his hands when he hit the pavement, but we've cleaned him up."

"Thanks, Ben. I don't have to tell you what a relief this is."

"Is there more going on than you've told me?"

Daniel didn't hesitate. He quickly summed up recent events, leaving out only his personal involvement with Rebecca.

"Well, damn," Ben said.

They signed off, and Daniel bounded down the stairs. He went first to tell Melissa Sue to call off the search, that the Lantzes had been found, then opened the door of the conference room.

If Rebecca had moved since he had left her, he couldn't tell. Her book lay closed on the table. But when she saw his jubilant smile, she sagged.

"They're safe?"

"They are. Thanks to you." He circled the table to draw her out of her chair into a hug, not caring whether anyone passing in the hall saw. He shared what Slater had told him, and said, "I'm going to pick them up and take them directly home unless they need any medical attention."

She let out a shuddery breath.

"Your phone call worked, sweetheart."

"But we're no closer to catching Tim or Josh."

"I'm hoping Anna can tell me something that will help. How many men she saw and who. If she has any idea where they were held."

"I did say—"

"That they wouldn't be charged with kidnapping Anna and her son, and they won't. Even without your promise, I can't imagine she would be willing to testify in court."

"No." Rebecca sank back into the chair.

He frowned. "I hate to leave you stuck here, but I don't see an alternative."

"No, I suppose I can't go anywhere until after dark."

Oh, crap. Had he given her the impression she'd be returning to his aunt and uncle's? Daniel grimaced.

"Rebecca, at this point, I'd rather you keep some distance from Matthew, and the Amish in general."

"But…"

"I'd rather keep you closer." Would she trust him enough to go along with his plan? He had to say it. "I want you to stay with me for now."

She gaped, finally managing to say, "You mean… your house?"

"Yes. I have plenty of room, and there's no reason anyone would suspect you're there." He shook his head when she appeared ready to object. "I need to get going. We can talk about it when I come back. Yes, I know Amos won't approve, and probably your *onkel* won't, either. But you'll be safe. Anna's kidnapping tells us these scumbags will do anything to get their hands on *you*. I doubt it will occur to them that you'd leave Matthew behind. He should be safe with Amos and Barbara. For all anyone but their church members know, they have two grandsons visiting."

"Yes, but—"

Daniel smiled. "Store up your arguments for later."

She blinked a couple of times. "Okay. You're right. Go."

"If you need anything—"

"I'll ask the woman out front."

"Melissa Sue." And he wanted to kiss her before he left, but with an inarticulate sound he made himself leave Rebecca in that bare conference room and jog out the back to his SUV.

DANIEL COULD AGREE that Anna Lantz was a pretty woman, but with a pleasantly rounded face she didn't look much like Rebecca, whose features were delicate. Anna's hair was closer to auburn than Rebecca's chestnut, too, and far curlier. Any of the men who knew Rebecca wouldn't have mistaken this woman for her, which meant her abductors had been hired muscle.

Shy with him and obviously overwhelmed by events, Anna hesitated to get into a police car, but finally did so. Daniel fastened her son's seat belt in back, the mother craning her neck to watch. She managed her own, but awkwardly. Not all Amish had ridden in cars. Anna might not have been rebellious enough to have *Englisch* friends during her running-around years, and perhaps as an adult, she'd never had need of a taxi or a ride from an *Englisch* neighbor.

Learning that they hadn't eaten since morning, he

detoured into the drive-through of a burger place, and soon Luke was slurping happily on a milk shake in the backseat while Anna devoured a burger in the front. She didn't say a word until she'd finished it.

Then, voice soft, she asked if her husband knew what had happened.

Daniel stuck to English so the boy wouldn't be able to understand. "Yes, I talked to him and your mother-in-law after your horse and buggy were found abandoned. I know he's scared."

"Colleen—my horse—was she hurt?" Anna asked anxiously.

"No, pretty upset, but Paul Glick came along. He got her calmed down and then took her to your place."

"So nice," she murmured.

"I sent a deputy out to let Eli know you two had been found. Your family will be glad to see you."

With a half-hour drive, Daniel was able to let her finish her fries and float, and to see young Luke had fallen asleep, before he started questioning her.

"*Ja*," she said, "I saw faces, but I didn't know those men. Two of them, there were. Outsiders. They talked different, not like *Englisch* here." She produced descriptions that could have fit half the male Caucasian population between thirty and fifty years old. She had no idea where she had been held, only that it was a bare bedroom with a boarded-up window.

The room had to be pretty bare indeed if it seemed so by Amish standards. They often had nice furniture, but didn't put up wallpaper or decorations. This bedroom hadn't been dirty, but wasn't clean by her exacting standards, either, he gathered from her wrinkled nose. The floors were wood but scratched and scuffed, the old chenille bedspread threadbare.

Twice, she had had to knock and ask for her and Luke to use a bathroom, which had been right beside the bedroom where they were held. Fixtures were clean but stained, linoleum old and cracked. No window. Yes, she said, it was one of the same men who had taken her from the buggy who escorted her back and forth.

Then she said, "Another man came, maybe an hour after we were locked in that room? All he did was stare at us. Then he left."

"Can you tell me what he looked like? How old he was?"

"Older than Eli," she decided. "Your age?"

"I'm thirty-five," he told her.

"*Ja*, something like that." She described the man's brown hair—much darker than Daniel's—and brown eyes. He was shorter than her Eli, she was sure, but more muscular. "And mad! Even after he slammed the door, I heard him yelling at the other men. I covered Luke's ears." She gave Daniel a perplexed look. "Why was he mad? Why did they do this, if we weren't what the man wanted?"

So he told her the basics—that a young woman and her son, relatives of a local Amish family, had been hiding here in Henness County from those men. That Anna looked enough like this other woman, and Luke enough like the woman's son, that they had been abducted by mistake.

"They let us go, at least," she said, giving a small nod as if satisfied that "those" men had behaved decently in the end. Daniel didn't have the heart to tell her Rebecca's threat had bought her release.

Her entire family and likely most of the members of her church district swarmed his vehicle the minute he pulled in. Tears ran down Eli's cheeks as he enveloped his wife and son in his arms. An older woman who had to be Anna's mother hugged Daniel and kissed his cheek before saying, "*Denke. Denke.*"

He wasn't allowed to leave until he'd had a cup of coffee and a slab of shoofly pie. A huge meal was being laid out as he made his excuses. Enough food to feed a family of ten was thrust on him. Thanking the Lantzes, promising to return the dishes, he finally escaped. At least he wouldn't have to worry about what he'd feed Rebecca tonight.

FROM HER POSITION crouched on the floorboard of Daniel's own SUV, Rebecca heard the garage door rolling down. The lighting dimmed. Wow, she was getting good at this.

"You can get up." Daniel turned in his seat to watch as she squirmed out from behind his seat. "I wasn't sure what you'd brought, so I picked up some clothes for you. I'm going to get out and turn my back while you change." Seeing her surprise, he said, "This is a detached garage. We have to cross the yard to the kitchen door. I don't want a neighbor or anyone else to catch a glimpse of an Amish woman entering my house."

"Oh." She blushed. "No, that would be bad."

His smile made her tingle. "I'm not trying to protect my reputation. I just don't want even a hint to get out that you might be here."

"No. Of course not."

While she was peeking in the plastic bag he handed over, Daniel got out. Rebecca found he'd bought an airy cotton skirt, a scoop-necked peach T-shirt and flip-flops. Cool, pretty and he'd guessed her sizes perfectly, which was interesting.

She hurried to change, one eye on his broad back, then set the athletic shoes she'd been wearing into the bag, followed by her stockings and the neatly folded dress and apron. On top she laid her *kapp*. It would feel odd not to wear it. After a moment's thought, she pulled pins to let her hair down from the distinctly Amish style and dropped them in the bag, too.

When she got out, Daniel surveyed her, a glint in his eyes. "Good" was all he said, but not all he wanted to say, she thought.

She brought her clothes, and he opened the rear hatch to grab her duffel, which he slung over his shoulder, and a large bag filled with plastic containers. Food given in thanks from the Lantz family and friends, he told her.

His lawn, like most this summer, was brown, crackling underfoot, the leaves on two sheltering trees in the yard turning autumn colors. The house was a white two-story with an enclosed back porch. He let them directly into the kitchen, with its aging cabinets painted yellow and a black-and-white checkerboard floor.

"Place could use some work," he said, glancing around as he set the food on the counter. "I keep telling myself I'll get to it."

If he'd bought this house immediately upon returning to Hadburg, he had been here for three years. Remodeling wouldn't be much of a priority for a single man, though, Rebecca supposed. One whose family probably never came to see him here.

"Let me put the food away," he continued, "and then I'll show you your bedroom."

On their way, she caught glimpses of a living room that held a sofa, recliner, television and not much else, and a dining room. Upstairs, he said, "We'll have to share a bathroom, since the only other one is a half bath downstairs. There are four bedrooms, but only one of them is set up for guests." He opened the wood-paneled door and showed her inside.

The room was prettier than she might have expected. The wallpaper, sprays of flowers against a white background, must already have been here when he bought the house. Sheer curtains framed a tall casement window that also had a roller shade. A beautiful old quilt in a churn dash pattern covered the antique wood bed. The other two pieces of furniture were antiques, too: a bedside table and an armoire notable for its simplicity.

Sounding stiff, he said, "There's no closet, so…" He gestured toward the armoire. "It has some drawers inside. And hangers, too."

"I don't have that much." After a moment, she set her plastic bag on the bed, stroked the quilt, then said, "This is really nice. Thank you."

He dropped the duffel bag on the bed, too, then retreated to the doorway. Strangely, she was reluctant to face him. Maybe it was knowing they were alone in the house. And that there was a bed, right here.

"My room is just across the hall." He cleared his throat. "In case you need me during the night."

She did. But she was afraid of the force of that need. Finally, she turned to see that he hadn't moved. He was watching her, his eyes darkened to navy.

"You look different," he said quietly. "Like I imagined you, but...not quite."

What a strange thing to say. "How you imagined me?"

He shook his head. "It's disorienting. I knew you weren't Amish, but seeing you like this...surprises me."

Did he mean that she looked wrong now? "I appreciate the clothes. I only have a couple other outfits. What I set out with."

He nodded, his gaze unwavering.

Why was this so awkward? He'd held her, he'd kissed her passionately, and now he was keeping his distance.

Because of the bed, she realized. She wasn't the only one aware that they were alone in the house, and in a bedroom. He wouldn't want her to think he had any expectations.

Daniel gave himself a shake. "Take your time. I'll go see about heating some of that food for dinner." He backed into the hall, raking her with one last, sweeping, somehow incredulous look before disappearing.

She let out a tiny whimper and sat on the edge of the bed—although she had to hop up to get onto it. Then she pressed a hand to her throat and waited for her racing pulse to slow before she even *thought* about going downstairs to join him.

CHAPTER SIXTEEN

"It's probably okay if you watch TV tomorrow," Daniel told Rebecca as he helped himself to a third piece of corn bread.

She blinked. "What would I watch during the day?"

Truthfully, he had no idea. "CNN? Doesn't it run news all the time?"

"I don't know."

"There are talk shows." He was sure about that. And soap operas, which he knew about even though he had never watched one. Come to think of it, Rebecca's life could be used as a script for one. "Keep the volume down. Same for the radio. Just in case somebody comes to the door, we don't want anyone outside to be able to hear it."

Her confusion suggested it hadn't occurred to her to turn on anything electronic. Such habits had been broken in recent weeks, he supposed, if she'd ever adopted them at all.

When he looked at her, he kept seeing double. The frame of her *kapp*, hiding much of her heavy mass of hair, the plain-colored dress and apron, only hinting at curves. And here she sat now in the knit shirt that clung to her and bared the wings of her collarbone and a creamy chest as well as a hint of cleavage. Even her slim, pale arms looked sexy to him. And she'd found something to tie her hair with, because she'd gathered it into a high ponytail that spilled below her shoulders.

Thinking about her safety was the best distraction he could come up with.

"Don't walk in front of windows." He frowned, foreseeing problems. "You'd better not lower the shade in your bedroom, even at night. I'm sorry. We can switch rooms, if you want. I wake up early, anyway. I won't mind the sun coming in."

Her lips curved. "Me, I've been sleeping in until ten or eleven every morning at your aunt and uncle's."

He laughed, relaxing. "Right. I suppose *Aenti* Barbara has you out collecting eggs at six a.m."

"She does." Her forehead crinkled. "I worry about her having to keep up with everything, and now taking care of the boys, too."

Daniel hadn't thought about it because Amish women were such hard workers. His *aenti* had raised four children without much help—but she was in her late fifties or even sixty now, and he'd seen that she got to her feet more slowly than she used to, sometimes pressing a hand to her back as if it ached.

"I'll go by my parents' tomorrow," he said. "Ask them to spread the word quietly that Barbara could use some help." He could stop tonight, after he'd sneaked in to talk to Amos, but he knew he wouldn't. He could already taste his eagerness to get back to Rebecca, and he hadn't even left yet.

Worry showed on her face. "That would be nice, as long as nobody talks about who Matthew is."

"You know they won't."

After a minute, she nodded.

"I'll leave the drapes closed in the living room." He

rarely opened the curtains here in the kitchen. They were thin enough not to shut out much light, but he doubted anyone could see in.

"I'll be careful."

"I know you're going to be bored," he said.

"Oh, Daniel. You worry too much. It will be quiet and peaceful! I haven't been sleeping well, so I might even take a nap tomorrow."

"If you do, sleep in my bed. I won't open my blinds in the morning."

Some emotions shimmered through her eyes. Her teeth closed on her lower lip, but she only nodded. Daniel wondered if she was thinking that his sheets might carry his scent, just as he was enjoying the picture of her in his bed.

He glanced irritably at the window, not wanting to leave, but seeing that darkness was falling. "Once we clean the kitchen, I'll run out to tell Amos what's happening."

Her gaze followed his. "Go now. I can take care of the kitchen." Her smile flickered. "It'll keep me from getting bored."

"I have books—"

"Shoo."

Daniel laughed. "At least you didn't say 'get lost.'"

Her smile faded. So quietly he could only just hear her, she murmured, "I would never say that."

His heart skipped a beat. All he could do was give a single, jerky nod before he went out the back door, checking to be sure it would lock behind him before he closed it.

WHILE HE WAS GONE, Rebecca indulged herself by exploring. He did own a smallish flat-screen TV, but no

DVD player. CDs were something else again, but the collection was unexpected. Classical and jazz. She pulled out a number of CDs with crayon-bright covers, all featuring music from other parts of the world.

The two bookcases in the living room were packed with fiction, including sci-fi and mysteries, and an eclectic mix of nonfiction. Whatever had interested him at any given moment, she suspected.

The dining room lacked even a table. He must eat all his meals in the kitchen.

Tucked beneath the stairs was a half bath and a closet, and he was obviously using a small additional room as a home office. The tablet was the one modern note, left out on one of those acre-wide oak desks that businesses had jettisoned half a century ago. A filing cabinet sat beside the desk, and another bookcase dominated the back wall. This one held mostly nonfiction, including a shelf of home repair and how-to books.

She had noticed the wood floors on this level gleamed. Had he refinished them himself? It made her sad to think he'd have to do all the work on his own. If he were Amish, family, friends and neighbors would turn out for a work frolic. Among them would be all the skills needed. The women would prepare a feast while the men tore out old cabinets and replaced them with new, reroofed, repaired the sagging fence, stripped molding and painted.

Rebecca started to get mad. Had his family ever even *seen* his house?

Don't judge when you don't know, she reminded herself, but his loneliness spoke for itself.

Upstairs, she opened the two closed doors. One room served for storage, holding boxes, a bathroom vanity cloaked in thick plastic and some unused or unwanted furniture. The fourth room, a small bedroom, was completely empty, lacking even curtains, although these walls were papered with ivy twining into patterns.

Really, this house was too big for him. An ache took up residence beneath her breastbone as she realized he must, even if unconsciously, want to marry and have children.

When Rebecca got to his bedroom, she didn't let herself go beyond the doorway. Not that she thought it held any secrets. His room had a large antique armoire like hers, as well as an oak dresser. The queen-size bed had no headboard. It was covered by a log cabin quilt that was, presumably, Amish, as no print fabrics had been used. If the room had ever been wallpapered, he'd steamed it off, just as a good Amish man would, since wallpaper was unacceptably decorative. The walls in here were now painted a warm cream color that contrasted with the refinished wood molding. The room was pleasing and plain. Only the digital clock, the lamp beside the bed and the overhead light showed he had embraced any part of being "modern."

His parents would say he hadn't kept up the faith, but Rebecca wondered.

If she lived here, she'd add some art, but not much. In retrospect, she realized that living in the house Tim had built for them had felt like wearing a too-tight garment. Always a little uncomfortable, even though most of the time she suppressed the awareness. Her parents' house hadn't been as old as this one, but the simplicity of the decor made it almost plain. Her father hadn't minded. He had loved *Mamm* so much and had studied the Amish enough to understand what would feel right to her. She allowed electricity; he didn't expect art on every wall.

I was so foolish, she thought sadly, absorbing this house, taking in a full breath that felt clean.

CHANCES WERE GOOD Rebecca had already gone to bed. He should hope she had, removing temptation. But he couldn't quell anticipation he hardly recognized, living alone as long as he had. These feelings were too powerful. Not since he was a child had he had someone to come home to. Someone who was *his*, who would be waiting with eagerness to match his own.

But Rebecca wasn't his. He couldn't be sure how she felt about him. He hadn't liked wondering how she saw his house, after living in such luxury with her husband. When he'd showed her around, it had suddenly appeared even shabbier than usual, and he'd had to say something about meaning to remodel, as a kind of apology.

Turning the last corner, he saw that the same lights were on in the house as when he'd left, which didn't mean she had stayed up, only that she was using common sense.

His talk with himself hadn't lessened the hungry anticipation that had him leaping out of his SUV once he was in the garage and covering the distance to the back door with long strides. Stupid as it was, he had a vision of her jumping to her feet the minute she saw him, stepping into his arms as if she couldn't do anything else.

The kitchen was bright and empty, and spotlessly clean. But as he closed and locked the door, he heard quick, light footsteps. Her face lit up at the sight of him, but he also saw nerves and shyness and a whole lot more on her expressive face.

"Daniel! That was quick."

"Was it?" He glanced at the clock above the kitchen table. "I was gone an hour and a half."

"I didn't know if you had other things to do." She stayed a good ten feet from him. "Did you see Matthew?"

His pleasure was dampened by knowing she had met him so eagerly because he would bring news of her son. But he understood and sympathized.

"I did. I gave him a hug from you, and told him you weren't far away, and were thinking about him all the time."

Her eyes filled with tears, but she wiped them with the back of her hand and smiled, too. "Thank you. You knew the right thing to say. He already likes you, you know. You'll make a good father." Her gaze shied from his. "I mean, when you're ready. Um, to have your own kids."

He was ready. Not something he could say, so he only nodded.

"Barbara said he'd been good, and he only worried about when his *mamm* would come back. Amos took the boys to a pond on Rudy Bontrager's place just up the road. They swam and splashed him, he said."

"Oh." Eyes brimming with emotion, she laid a hand on her chest. But then she said, "Do you want coffee? Or something to eat? That rhubarb cobbler, maybe?"

Daniel laughed and shook his head. "I was stuffed before I left, and coffee would just keep me awake. Let's go sit down."

They went to the living room, where he saw his stereo was on, an open CD case lying beside it. She'd been listening to music.

She sank onto one end of the sofa and waited until he lowered himself into the recliner. "What did Amos say?"

"He wasn't happy I hadn't taken you to another family, but he understood." Actually, he had lectured Daniel, saying that, while Rebecca was not a *maidal*, she was a good woman, modest and knowing right from wrong. Daniel took offense at the suggestion that *he* didn't know right from wrong. He and his *onkel* had gone at it, shouting until his *aenti* rushed into the kitchen to remind them that there were *kinder* in the house. He thought he wasn't the only one to be ashamed, then.

"He didn't really understand, did he?" Rebecca said unhappily, obviously having read more on Daniel's face than he had meant her to see. "I suppose he's shocked."

He tipped the recliner forward, resting his elbows on his knees. "Not that, I think. Just…struggling with the reminder that you aren't really Amish."

She nodded after a moment, her gaze fastened on his. "Like you."

"What?" He sat up.

"Isn't that what you were telling me? Earlier, I mean, after I changed into this." She waved at herself.

"No!" Wasn't it? "The first couple of times I saw you, when I thought you *were* Amish, I was…disappointed." A mild word for what he'd felt, out of the blue. "When you admitted you weren't, that you were dressing plain only to hide—"

"And out of respect for my family," she interrupted.

Daniel nodded. "To be respectful, too. When I found out you weren't Amish, and were not married, either, I was relieved, because something about you called to me even before I knew you."

She had quit moving, maybe even breathing. They stared at each other. That was more honesty than he'd intended to give, but it was something he had needed to say.

Finally she drew a shuddery breath. "I...felt the same."

His heart began to hammer.

"I didn't want to," she said softly. "You scared me. You saw too much. I told myself you could help, but... the danger seemed too great."

"You thought I'd hurt you?"

Rebecca's ponytail swayed when she shook her head. "See right through me." She tried to smile. "Be able to tell when I was lying."

"Mostly, I could. You're not a good liar."

She made a face.

"It frustrated me that you kept withholding things."

"I'm sorry, but... I was pulled so many ways."

What he wanted to know was whether she could imagine a life here, with him, rather than returning to the city. But he couldn't ask that yet. "You never said how your parents died."

"A drunk driver. *Mamm* was gone right away. Dad... lingered for a day, but never regained consciousness. It was so hard to lose them. I wasn't ready."

This time he didn't fight temptation. He rose and went to her, sitting beside her on the sofa so he could take her hand in his. "Is anyone ever?"

She grimaced. "Probably not. But it hurt, knowing

Matthew wouldn't remember them, that they'd never be there again when I had questions. Not having any other family…"

"But you did," he said gently.

Rebecca nodded. "Then…well, I was married, and the gulf seemed too great to cross. I let my grandparents know *Mamm* had died. Ever since I got over being an awful teenager, I had written them regularly. *Grossmammi* was good about writing back."

He smiled, moving his thumb gently across her palm. "The Amish are excellent correspondents."

"It's true." She looked painfully vulnerable when she met his eyes. "Have you heard anything about my grandfather?"

Daniel didn't like to tell her, but knew he had to. "He's failing. *Onkel* Amos said he was told it won't be more than a day or two now."

"Oh," she breathed, stricken. "Do you think—"

He shook his head. "You know it's not safe. He has family around him, and the joy of having gotten to know you again. He's had weeks longer than the doctors expected."

"Yes. I suppose…" Rebecca ducked her head, probably to hide tears.

Daniel tugged her toward him. "Come here."

As she laid her cheek against his shoulder, her body held no tension, as if she were trusting herself to him. Even though it would be easy to let himself become aroused, Daniel felt such contentment he didn't want to move, to lose the tickle of her hair on his throat and chin, her scent.

"Something I've wondered." *Obsessed about* was

more like it. "Were you happy in your marriage until the problems at work came up?"

Daniel wasn't sure he really wanted to know. He wished he hadn't asked when she pulled away so she could see his face.

"Only at the beginning." A different kind of sadness clung to her now. "I believed marriage was forever. I didn't let myself acknowledge how disappointed I was. Tim put in such long hours. He was excited about building the company, and I was excited for him, but it was lonely. Especially since he never really talked about decisions he made or any of the important stuff. He had Josh and Steven for that. He never let me feel we were in it together. I wish I'd worked longer before I had Matthew." Rebecca sighed. "The end result is, here I am, thirty-one years old, and I only had my own classroom for a year. Getting my foot in the door now won't be easy."

"Maybe in San Francisco," he said, trying to sound casual, "if you're determined to go back there. But it's not like that in a lot of rural areas. Last year, a fifth-grade teacher here in Hadburg had to quit suddenly, and the school district ended up using substitutes all year. Shiny new grads don't want to come here. It's not so different from my problems replacing a deputy. To young people especially, life here looks backward. And the pay doesn't equal what's offered in a city."

She asked a few questions, and he took the opportunity to tell her that the county had three school districts with a total of eight schools, which didn't sound all that impressive. Still, he hoped for enthusiastic interest, but her response was noncommittal. That made him decide it was time to end the evening before he let himself do something foolish. He wanted her in his bed—but if the idea of staying in Missouri wasn't on her radar, he needed to protect himself.

If that was still possible.

THE NEXT MORNING, Daniel sat in his squad car studying a house that had been for sale for months. Backing on a creek, the property was good, eighty acres with a small woodlot and old fruit trees. The house wasn't much—dating from the 1940s, at a guess, with probably no more than two bedrooms. The place would take work—the fields were overgrown, blackberries claiming large swaths of land, and even from here he could tell that if the roof on the barn wasn't replaced soon, the whole structure would be lost. Amish were no strangers to hard work, and this would be ideal for a young family wanting to farm. The problem, as Daniel had heard it, was that the owners wanted too much money.

This house had been next on his list of empty homes that were potential hideouts for the men he sought. Ever since Tim Gregory's assault on Rebecca in the hospital parking lot, deputies had been visiting properties like this. Ben Slater had his men doing the same in Byrum, as did the chief in River Grove, although Daniel didn't think Griffen and Gregory would have gone to ground anywhere near neighbors who would be likely to notice their comings and goings.

With real estate moving slowly in northeastern Missouri, Daniel doubted local agents had shown this house in some time. Still, squatting here would be a risk. If the owner had been approached about a short-term rental, he would be crazy not to have grabbed it.

Daniel had tried calling the man, who now lived in Virginia, but hadn't gotten a return call.

He lowered his window and listened, hearing nothing but birdsong. After a minute, he got out and walked toward the house, but with each step his uneasiness grew. He rested his hand on the butt of his gun. There was no reason to think he wasn't alone here, but he'd learned to listen to his instincts. Besides, what he saw lined up with Anna Lantz's description of where she had been held.

If he hadn't been listening so hard, he might not have heard a squeak as if a porch board were protesting. Going completely still, Daniel let his eyes rove. The sun off the front windows hadn't let him see until now that shades had been drawn, giving the house a secretive look that didn't fit with it being for sale.

One of the barn doors stood open, although the interior was too shadowy for him to tell if a car might be parked there. What he knew was that he felt exposed, certain that somebody was watching him.

Given his department's staffing issues, deputies all patrolled alone.

He eased one foot back, then the next. He could wait the ten or fifteen minutes it would take for backup to arrive.

At a flash of movement in the corner of his eye, a glint of sun off metal, he spun to face the woods and started to draw. That was the moment an engine roared to life.

A white van exploded out of the barn, its driver barreling right for him. He got off one shot before he had to dive out of the way, landing hard on what had been lawn. Even as he rolled, he saw the van swerving at him.

His next shot went through the windshield, but he knew he hadn't hit the driver. Another roll and he got his feet under him enough to leap away—but not before the driver's-side mirror struck his shoulder, sending him flying.

Even as he jumped to his feet and lifted his Glock, the van turned onto the road. He ran down the driveway, hearing the squeal of brakes. A car door slammed. Then the van took off again.

By the time he reached the road, the vehicle was receding. Too far away for him to shoot out a tire.

But he'd taken in most of the license-plate number—and he'd seen the driver's face.

A LITTLE AFTER seven that evening, Daniel let himself in the back door. Unless Rebecca was imagining things, he was moving stiffly as he turned to lock.

She waited until she saw his face, heavily lined with weariness and something else. Her heart cramped.

"You're hurt." She gripped the large spoon in her hand tightly.

"Nothing major." He came to her and nudged her hand back over the stove. "You're dripping on the floor."

"Tell me."

A shadow crossed his face. "Some SOB tried to run me down. Clipped my shoulder. I picked up a few bruises and scrapes."

Some SOB?

"Was it…about something else?"

His eyebrows rose. "Besides you, you mean?"

She bobbed her head.

"No, it definitely had to do with you."

When she moaned, Daniel took the spoon away from her, turned off the burner and steered her to a seat at the kitchen table. Then he pulled up a chair himself, his knees touching hers.

"You know we've been hunting for your ex and Josh." He went on to tell her about realizing the house he was walking toward could be the one in which Anna Lantz and her son had been held. And the wrongness of the shades drawn and the barn door left standing open, followed by a sound that didn't belong if the house was empty.

"You saw the driver," she said finally.

He could tell what she was asking. "Nobody I recognize, but I'll know him the next time I see him." He told her that he'd called in deputies and searched the house, finding evidence that at least two men had been staying there, perhaps more. One of the deputies had taken pictures of the bedrooms and bathroom with his phone and driven to the Lantz farm so Anna could see them.

"She made a positive ID." His eyes, that unusual, deep blue, never left Rebecca's face. "The kitchen was stocked. When they saw me out front, they must have packed fast and run, but we found a few things. A razor and two toothbrushes left in the bathroom, a few scraps of paper." Daniel paused. "One of them had a phone number. Josh Griffen's cell number."

"But…nothing leading to Tim?"

His expression darkened. "Because he couldn't possibly be involved?"

Her temper flared, but she waited it out because he

was right. She did keep trying to stick her head in the sand. "No," she said at last. "I know he is."

Daniel's eyes searched hers. "I'm sorry for jumping on you. I don't like thinking you're still—"

"Still what?" she whispered.

"Holding on to any love or regret, I guess."

Her heart drummed at his intensity. She couldn't look away from him. "How can there not be regret after a divorce? You start out so filled with hope. And…we have a child together. I can't walk away and never see him again, however much I wish I could."

"Do you really want to let him influence Matthew?"

She didn't, but… "I think Matthew needs to have some kind of relationship with him. Matthew needs to see that his father has good qualities."

Daniel bent his head suddenly and rubbed a hand over his face and through his hair, leaving it ruffled. "I'm being a jerk. This is hard for me."

"Being attracted to a divorced woman with a kid?" Okay, her temper was still simmering.

His head came up sharply, his eyes pinning her again. "Not knowing how you feel about him." His voice became huskier. "Or me."

CHAPTER SEVENTEEN

"I DON'T KNOW how *you* feel!" Rebecca cried.

"I want you."

"That's not…" Her throat clogged.

"Enough?" One side of his mouth tipped up in an odd smile. "I want you to tell me you won't leave when this is all over. That you'll…give me a chance."

The feelings swelled in her until her chest actually hurt. "You've…forgiven me?"

"Forgiven you?" His face cleared. "You mean for not being truthful." .

"Yes."

"Of course I have," he said, in a voice filled with tenderness. "No, that's not right. Forgiveness isn't necessary. I understand why you were afraid to tell me everything."

She couldn't cry. Not at a moment like this. *I will not.* "Thank you for saying that."

"Will you?" He took her head. "Give me a chance? Consider staying?"

She had to blink hard. "Yes. Of course I will." A smile trembled on her lips. "I'd be crazy not to."

Just like that, they were grinning foolishly at each other. A chance. He was giving *her* a chance. What more could she ask?

DANIEL'S MOOD SOARED. Perhaps he shouldn't read so much into so few words, but he let himself believe she had meant them.

He ate the stew she had produced from what she'd found in his cupboards, and more pie given by Anna Lantz's family. He and Rebecca talked while they ate, but not about anything important. These words didn't seem to matter. The warmth in her eyes, the occasional shyness, the color that tinted her cheeks—those things spoke to him. He felt young and in love. That might sound naive by modern standards. Standards that might be hers, although he thought not. They fit so well because they had both lived with the confusion of not quite belonging where they'd found themselves.

Rebecca insisted on putting away leftovers and cleaning the kitchen while he sat at the table drinking a cup of coffee. He tried to object—he had spent enough years taking care of himself to shake the belief that the kitchen was strictly a woman's domain. Her ex-husband hadn't wanted her to have any life outside the home. Daniel knew better than to make that mistake. She wasn't Amish, and neither was he anymore. As he watched her move around the kitchen with a dancer's grace, he conducted an internal battle.

Would she come to his bed if he asked? A part of him thought it would be wrong to ask. He should wait until she wasn't dependent on him to keep her safe.

But his gaze lingered on the sway of her hips before moving to her long, slender neck, bared when her ponytail swung. He imagined how the strong hands she was now drying on a dish towel would feel kneading his shoulders and back.

Suddenly he realized she had quit moving and was

watching *him*. Her eyes were dilated, her lips parted. Without thinking, he shoved back the chair and took the few steps he needed to reach her.

"You're so beautiful," he said roughly. "I don't think you know that."

She shook her head in instant denial. "No more than plenty of other women."

"In my eyes, that's not so. But it isn't just your lips—" he rubbed his thumb over them "—or your eyes or…" He was the one to shake his head this time. "It's the way you carry yourself. The softness I see on your face when you look at your son, the determination to protect the people you love, the shame you can't hide when you think you wronged someone. The way you guard yourself, even as your eyes give you away." He bent his head until their foreheads touched. "Emotions so open. You've…troubled me from the minute I saw you."

Now dampness shimmered in her eyes. "You've troubled me, too. I couldn't understand why I was so sure I could trust you. Why, when I should stay away from you, I was so happy every time I saw you."

"Yes," he murmured, and kissed her.

REBECCA COULD NO more have prevented herself from responding than she could have stopped loving Matthew. Daniel's passion for her was compelling enough, but the tenderness in his every touch had brought so much to life in her. There was no need for her to ask herself whether she trusted him completely.

She had fallen in love with him so quickly, so hard, she had to believe she wasn't wrong about him.

His lips brushed hers, his tongue dampened them.

She wrapped her arms around his neck, bringing her body in full contact with his, muscular and solid. His hands roved, warm and strong. He explored every dip and hollow, his fingertips lingering on the bumps of her vertebrae.

Daniel groaned and deepened the kiss. Suddenly, her back was against something hard. Startled, she realized he had walked her backward. By some instinct, she wrapped one leg around his. Her rubber flip-flop dropped to the floor, and he growled something.

"Your shoulder."

"Don't care," he muttered. He pinned her to the wall and kissed her deeply with a driving passion that made her melt. Her fingers had slid into his hair, feeling its heavy silk.

An indescribable sound vibrated from his chest. When he went completely still, Rebecca almost whimpered.

He rubbed his bristly jaw over her cheek. "Rebecca." His voice was guttural. "If you're not ready…"

For an answer, she closed her teeth on his earlobe.

Another of those raw sounds escaped him.

He carried her out of the kitchen and up the stairs, pausing twice along the way to kiss her again with ravening hunger.

In his bedroom, they undressed each other. He removed his belt first, laying it with the holster and gun on the bedside table. After that, he let her undo one button on his shirt at a time. Despite their growing urgency, neither was hasty. Once she'd tossed the short-sleeved shirt aside, she squeezed the muscles between his neck and shoulders, stroked the powerful planes of his chest dusted with hair a shade darker than that on his head, kissed the horrible bruise that capped one shoulder. His muscles jerked at her every touch.

He flattened a hand on her stomach before his fingers slid beneath the waistband of the skirt. Rebecca bent her head and watched him tug the skirt over her hips, letting it fall to pool at her bare feet. She was even paler than she'd been when they came to Missouri, except for tanned forearms and face. The contrast looked odd to her, but nothing in his rapt expression suggested he was disappointed. When finally he looked up, his eyes were pure heat, the blue at the center of a flame, while dark color ran across his cheekbones.

"You're the most beautiful thing I've ever seen."

He was the most beautiful thing she had ever seen, broad shoulders, sleek muscles, the arrow of hair disappearing beneath his uniform pants.

Embarrassed at the compliment, she said, "Where's the Amish in you?"

He nuzzled her face. "Amish boys dream about naked girls, too, you know. But this isn't like that."

"I'm glad," she whispered shakily.

They looked at each other, naked in a way that went far beyond unclothed bodies.

And then he reached for her.

DANIEL NEEDED TO keep her close.

He was shaken in a way he hadn't expected. But this, what he and Rebecca had just done, was something more. Something out of his control, as Rebecca had been from their first eye contact.

He stayed silent because he didn't know what to say. What seemed extraordinary to him might not to her. Feeling like an uncertain boy didn't sit well with him. But this silence could be damaging. What was she thinking?

She stirred. "Say something."

Did that mean she felt as vulnerable? Daniel wondered. "I'm still speechless."

"You don't look down on me because I said yes, do you?"

"What?" He rolled again, so that he was above her with his weight on his elbows. "How can you think that?"

"*Grossmammi* would think I behaved like an *Englischer*, making myself cheap."

Was she joking? But her eyes were dark and serious, her teeth closed on her lower lip.

"I think your grandmother would be angry at me, not you," he said honestly. "I know I should have waited until you didn't need me to keep you safe."

"You don't think... I came to bed with you so you'd keep helping me?"

"No." He pressed a soft kiss on her mouth. "You don't hide what you feel that well."

Rebecca wrinkled her nose, altering the mood. "I'll have to practice."

"Don't." His voice lowered. "I like seeing your emotions passing through your eyes."

"Oh." She lifted a hand to cup his cheek. "I've never felt like this before."

That was all the reassurance he needed. In fact...he was so happy, he felt as if the hollow inside him had been filled to overflowing.

REBECCA WALKED DANIEL to the back door before work the next morning. She'd put on the same skirt with a camisole from her duffel bag, explaining she'd die of heatstroke in the clothes she set out from San Francisco with.

"Do you think you could buy me a pair of shorts?" she asked, sounding hopeful.

"Sure." Her hair was still wet from a morning shower. It was hard to tear his gaze from the droplets shimmering on her neck.

Of course, he couldn't exactly buy shorts for a woman at Miller's General Store without giving away a whole lot, but he wouldn't mind taking the time to drive to Byrum.

Determined to do some research today and call or email Estevez, Daniel had his tablet tucked under his arm. The situation had become frustrating. What had happened with the warrant? He wanted to get his hands on Josh and Tim both and wring the identities of their confederates out of them, too—especially the one who'd tried to run him down.

Seeing her glance at the tablet, he said, "I'm sorry I can't leave it so you can go online today."

Her head tilted like a bird's. "Why are you so worried I'll be bored?"

Her question poked at his deepest core of insecurity. If she thought Hadburg was dull, she'd want to leave. Going with her...that would be like trying to transplant a deep-rooted tree. She understood that; he didn't think she'd ask it of him, but that didn't mean she'd be content here.

"I don't know," he lied.

Rebecca went on tiptoe and kissed his jaw. "You have everything here I need to entertain myself." Her lips flirted with a tiny, mischievous smile. "I think I'll start browsing those books on remodeling. It might be fun to learn to tile or who knows what else."

Because she meant to stay, to work on the house with him? He hoped the insecurity was gone, once and for all.

"Okay." He kissed her goodbye and drove to work, parking in back.

The first couple of hours were consumed by administrative necessities. Scheduling for the next week, always a juggling act. Given the current tension, he denied a request for leave. Worked on a budget request asking for some improved technology he intended to submit to the county council, even though he knew it would be denied. All the while, he kept an eye on the clock.

At nine in the morning West Coast time, he called Estevez.

"Just walked in the door. I was going to call you first thing," the detective claimed. "Warrant came through yesterday for Tim and Josh, denied for Gregory senior." He didn't sound surprised, as Daniel wasn't. "We pinged their phones. We got nothing on Griffen's phone. I did a little leg work. Turns out both Gregorys are here in the city."

"You talked to Robert?"

"You better believe I did. I got an icy reception. He said his only interest is in his grandson, that he's 'pursuing legal remedies.' Tim was home, said he wouldn't talk to me again without his attorney being present, but a blind man would have known he's falling apart. I told him he's wanted for assault in Missouri. He tried to claim that's ridiculous, his ex-wife's bruises were the result of an accident and she's accusing him maliciously, but he's scared out of his mind."

"You think he'll crack."

"Oh, yeah. My gut feeling is he got in over his head. He's furious with Ms. Holt, but the possibility of being implicated in the abduction of an innocent woman and child has him shaking in his boots. I told him to be smart and stay put. That taking off, and especially setting foot in Missouri right now, would not look good to investigators, prosecutors or the judge and jury when he appears in court."

"You'll know if he takes off?"

"If he flies commercial. I'll try to keep an eye on him, but you know how overextended we are."

It was a sad truth in any jurisdiction.

"When do you intend to pull him in for an interview?"

"This afternoon. I'll call you after."

They signed off, Daniel wishing he could feel relief. Josh Griffen, likely still here in the county, was the dangerous one. He was willing to bet the partnership between Josh and Tim was irreparably broken. Tim had gotten greedy, and then panicked and tried to cover up what he'd done. But Josh had killed and was willing to kill again to save his own skin.

Knowing it was Rebecca Josh intended to kill sent rage running like an electric current beneath Daniel's skin. He had to find the son of a bitch.

THUNDER GRUMBLED IN the distance, increasing Rebecca's sense of unease. She didn't understand herself. Daniel had worked yesterday, too, leaving her alone, and she hadn't felt the tiny hairs on her nape prickling, hadn't been so aware of how quiet the house was, hadn't been unwilling to play music to fill that quiet.

He'd mentioned not having a landline, but she hadn't expected the lack of a phone to scrape at her nerves. Daniel had tossed the one she'd used to call Tim into a Dumpster, saying it wasn't safe for her to keep using. She wished she'd thought to ask him to replace it, but she hadn't expected this uneasy awareness that she had no way to call him for help, or for him to let her know if anything happened.

She did read, but kept imagining small sounds. Or maybe the house was settling, as old houses did. Each time she heard a noise, she'd walk a circuit through the downstairs, peeking through blinds or around curtains in a way that wouldn't show if anyone was watching the house. It was dumb to have let her imagination run wild. Tim and Josh couldn't possibly know she was here. Besides the woods in back, there wasn't a good place for a watcher to hide, either.

But instinct said *something* was going to happen.

And all she could do was wait and listen as the storm drew closer.

THEY NEEDED RAIN, but did it have to be today? Answering the internal line on his desk phone, Daniel stood at the window in his office looking at the ominous clouds filling the sky to the north.

"What's up?"

Melissa Sue said, "Bert at the corner store called. He says some young guys are hanging out in the parking lot hassling customers. He's losing business. He sounded mad."

Daniel sighed. "I'll walk over."

Forget what he'd been thinking about the storm. With some luck, he decided, the skies would open up and soak the little jackasses. A lightning bolt somewhere in their vicinity wouldn't be a bad thing, either, so long as nobody was hurt. He looked up at the sky as he turned the corner. *How about it, God?* he asked, while acknowledging that He had more important things to do. *If this is my purpose, then He trusts me to do my job*, he reminded himself.

His jaw tightened when he recognized Billy Shaver at the center of the cluster of young men, pants hanging low, cigarettes dangling from several of their mouths. Damon wasn't with them—maybe he'd acquired a little sense. A woman had pulled up to get gas in front, but two of the boys circled her car, slapping hands on the roof, hood and trunk. She jerked in fear with each ring of metal, afraid to get out. Daniel couldn't figure out why terrorizing a woman on her own could possibly be fun.

The boys saw him approaching and retreated to their pack. The woman seized the chance to drive away without filling her tank. Daniel saw Bert, the stocky store owner, standing behind the glass doors, arms crossed, glowering.

Not boys, Daniel told himself. Not this group. He knew them all. They were troublemakers, none younger than eighteen. At least two, including Billy, were over twenty-one. Old enough to know better. An Amish man of their age would have committed to his church, be marrying and starting a family, working hard at his profession.

He knew they'd seen him across the parking lot, but Daniel turned when he heard the fast clop of horses' hooves on pavement and the hum of wheels. Not much reason for Amish to be passing down this road.

It was Samuel Graber who reined in the horse at the curb beside Daniel. This couldn't be chance.

"Amos says Rebecca is with you. *Mamm* sent me to find you, to say that Ephraim has died peacefully, and at home, God be thanked. If she can come, the funeral—" He stopped midsentence, his gaze going past Daniel, who swung around in alarm.

Oh, no. He hadn't seen Billy break away from the group, or heard his approach.

"The sheriff has hisself an Amish girlfriend," Billy taunted. "She putting out, Sheriff?"

Ignoring the rest of the crowd, which was growing brave enough to swagger forward, too, and arrange themselves behind Billy, Daniel skewered the punk with a hard stare. "You don't know what you're talking about. Back off. You and your buddies."

Hate flickered in Billy's brown eyes. "We're just being friendly. Curious, you might say. This the lady some men want to find? You ought to be more careful, *Sheriff.*"

Temper filled Daniel, as dangerous as the storm but slow moving, too. He had always been able to control it. He took out his phone, wishing he'd called sooner for backup. He hoped Bert had made the call for him.

But he kept his voice calm in hopes of preventing an escalation. "I've tried to work with you, Billy. Give you a fair chance. But that's not what you want, is it?"

"Fair chance?" Billy snarled. "That what you call it? Riding my ass, sticking your nose in my business?" He spit a glob of something brown in Daniel's direction, then told Daniel where he could put his fair chances.

Would Samuel's presence make any difference? The horse was shifting uneasily, hooves clattering and harness creaking. Samuel stayed silent.

Daniel looked from one to another hostile face. "You boys need to go home. This is your warning. You have no reason to be here. I can arrest you for trespassing if you don't get moving, *now*." He made sure they heard the steel.

Billy didn't even blink. Daniel didn't dare look away. He felt as if he was engaging in a staring contest with a venomous cottonmouth.

A couple of the others were backing away, and a guy right beside Billy said, "Hey, man, what are you doing?"

Billy shrugged insolently. "Must be the girlfriend that has the *sheriff* so hot and bothered. I'm going." He started to turn away, then, with the speed of a striking snake, he lashed out, sending Daniel's phone flying. He took off running, followed by the others.

Daniel growled something Samuel would find abhorrent, but let them go. He could track them down later. It was the threat that mattered.

This the lady some men want to find? You ought to be more careful.

If Billy knew who to call…

The horse danced, Samuel murmuring reassurance. Even so, the buggy rocked forward and back—and Daniel saw his phone just before a steel wheel rim rolled over it with a *crunch*.

Daniel's decision to arrest the punk set, concrete hard.

CHAPTER EIGHTEEN

THUNDER RATTLED THE window glass. Rebecca cringed. No more than a second later, the shocking flash of light momentarily blinded her. Rain hammered on the roof and enveloped the house in gray sheets. The light was murky, even if it was only five thirty and sunset was almost two hours away.

With her ears still ringing, she wasn't positive she'd heard the car engine, but then the door rattled and Daniel walked in. He was drenched—hair plastered to his head, uniform to his body.

Stopping just inside, he said, "Would you mind getting me a towel? I don't want to drip all the way through the house."

Rebecca ran upstairs and brought a couple of towels. Daniel was already stripping. She watched as he tossed the shirt to one side in the tiny mudroom that also held a stacked washer and dryer. The chill she'd felt all day lessened at the pleasure of seeing that muscular body as he scrubbed himself with the first towel, ending up with his hair poking every which way.

And then she really looked at his face, and the chill returned. "What's wrong?"

"You mean, what new and fresh disaster do I have to report?"

She nodded.

"I have to move you again. A conversation I had with your *onkel* was overheard by an ex-con who hates me."

"But he couldn't know—"

"He does." Definitely grim. "He instantly associated you with 'the lady some men want to find.'"

She dropped into a straight-backed kitchen chair. "Right now?"

He unbuckled his belt and dropped his holster and gun on one end of the counter, then stripped off his shoes, socks and soggy pants, leaving him in nothing but shorts. "By morning. With this weather, I have to stay available. Creeks and river were so low, we shouldn't have any flooding, but there'll be car accidents and fires. I need to change, get out my rain gear and go back to headquarters."

Leaving her here, alone. But she could only nod because, of course, he had to do his job.

"You'll have to come with me," he added. "I hate to stick you in that conference room again, but you'll be safest there. If you don't have something warmer to put on, I'll find you a sweatshirt. I have an extra rain slicker, too."

Not alone. *Thank you.*

Thunder rolled, but not overhead. The lightning flash wasn't as immediate or as bright. And...had the rain let up a little, too?

"The stupid truth is, I lost my phone," Daniel grumbled. "Should have stopped for a new one, but I was too worried about you. I'll have the police radio once I get back to the station, but—" His expression changed, the compassion as powerful as a touch, and somehow she knew what he would say.

"Samuel drove to town to let me know your grandfather died, Rebecca. Peacefully, he said." Daniel padded across the kitchen to her and crouched beside the chair, laying a cold hand over hers. "I'm sorry."

Tears threatened, but she held them back. She bobbed her head. "It was coming."

"Yes." His blue eyes searched hers. "Samuel sounded almost relieved. His *daad* went the way he should, at home, his family around him. It would have been harder on all of them if Ephraim had died that night at the hospital."

"Hooked up to all those machines." She still wanted to cry, but Daniel was right.

"You okay?"

She pulled herself together. "Yes. Go change."

After another, thorough scan of her face, he rose. "I need to take a quick shower. Then we can go." He grabbed his gun and took it with him.

Rebecca followed him upstairs and went into the guest room to dig through her duffel bag. Fortunately, she had jeans and athletic shoes, a T-shirt, with a hoodie over it, she decided, pulling out what she needed.

She heard the shower across the hall and indulged herself in the sensual memory of showering with Daniel before she sighed, stepped out of the skirt and reached for the jeans.

More thunder, and the rain was still coming down, but she went still, listening. Was that a car? Maybe a deputy coming to get Daniel because he couldn't call?

Quickly fastening the jeans, she sidled until she was beside the window and dared to take a peek. The sedan that blocked the garage was silver, not sheriff's department green and white. And a dark-colored SUV was coming up the driveway, going fast. It veered to cross the lawn, disappearing around the front of the house. Car doors opened and men climbed out, carrying rifles.

Heart drumming, she tore across the hall. The bathroom door opened just as she reached it and Daniel walked out.

"There are men with guns outside," she gasped. "They're surrounding the house."

Daniel said a word she'd never heard him use. He ran to the bedroom, eased the shade aside and swore again. A second later, he had a big, evil-looking weapon in his hand.

"Look in my closet," he said. "There's a gun safe. I have a backup handgun and ammunition in there." He told her the combination, which she dialed with a shaking hand.

The smaller gun was already loaded but only held six bullets, he told her.

"I need to call—" He gritted his teeth. "No phone. That punk did it on purpose."

Rebecca didn't ask for explanation. "Your tablet?"

"Kitchen."

She vaguely recalled seeing him set it down.

They were completely isolated.

Glass shattered downstairs.

"The bathroom is the safest place for you," he told her with unnatural calm, gaze steady. "Sit down in

the tub. It's cast iron, and will stop bullets. I'll identify myself if I open the door. If somebody else tries
to come in, shoot them. Aim for the torso. It's hard to
miss at close range."

"What about you?"

Even as she asked, he pulled on a vest, fastening it
with Velcro tape. She'd seen those before, black with
POLICE in white across the back. Thankfully he had
one here, only…it didn't seem to protect enough of
his big body.

A voice came up the stairs and she knew her chance
of scuttling into the bathroom had been lost. "Rebecca,
you know what I want." Josh. "Hand it over, and we'll
go away."

Sure they would. But when her lips parted, Daniel
shook his head. So softly she barely heard, he said,
"They can't be sure you're here."

Oh.

Daniel stood just inside his bedroom door, where
he could see the hall and staircase. He raised his voice.
"You're armed and you've broken into a police officer's home. If you thought you were in trouble before,
it was nothing."

A shot rang out. He didn't even flinch, although she
heard wood splinter and plastic crumble. Daniel leaned
forward and fired. One, two.

Swearing came from down below.

He looked at her with those eerily calm eyes and
whispered, "Lie down behind the bed."

She did, her head at the foot of the bed where she
would see approaching feet. And then she waited.

HE SHOULD HAVE gotten her stowed in the bathroom quicker.

He had a ladder in the garage. If they found it, they could climb the side of the house and come in through one of the windows. There were at least four of them, one of him. And no way for him to call for help.

He peered around the door frame and saw the top of a head. This time, he deliberately aimed high as he took a shot.

After hearing an obscene word and a clatter on the stairs, Daniel raised his voice. "Last warning."

He faced the knowledge that he might have to kill, something he'd avoided in his career so far. Fighting back was one thing. Taking warning shots. But killing another human being? Even cops with no religious faith struggled after having to commit that act. For him, it could be soul destroying.

His jaw tightened as he pushed the devastating realization away. To keep Rebecca safe, he'd do whatever these men forced him into. Even as a boy, he hadn't been able to turn the other cheek. Now, the weight of the gun in his hand told him what he had become.

A barrage of gunfire had him stepping back. Then he thrust his hand around the door frame and opened fire blindly.

"Daniel?"

He glanced over his shoulder and saw that Rebecca had risen to her knees to look out the window. Damn it, she knew better.

"There's a horse and buggy coming."

"What?"

In a voice filled with fear, she said, "I think it's *Onkel* Samuel."

Had he come to apologize for betraying Rebecca's location today? Or had he heard something? *Please,* he prayed, *don't let them kill such a good man, and in front of Rebecca.*

Some cursing and a flurry of voices came from below. Rebecca, who had stayed on her knees beside the window, said, "There's another buggy behind him. And...another turning in."

Samuel, he realized suddenly, would never have driven out here to say a few words, not when doing so would confirm Rebecca's presence.

Gripping his Glock in both hands, Daniel stole another look down the hall and saw nothing.

"What's happening?" he asked, unable to risk crossing to the window.

"They're driving onto the lawn. Oh, Daniel." Emotion swelled in her voice, because she knew a miracle was being performed right in front of her. "More are coming. The men are parking the buggies and just sitting there. I can't see the gunmen, but..." Her voice broke. "There must be a dozen buggies now. They've formed a line, and they're blocking the driveway. It's as if..."

"They're saying, *Kill us all, or know anything you do is being witnessed.*"

Her "yes" came out soggy.

Daniel heard a siren. And then...that had to be a second.

He let himself look at the woman he loved, who looked back, her eyes brimming with both emotions and tears. And then he continued to do his job. He slipped into the hall, keeping his back to the wall, and edged toward the staircase. He couldn't relax until he knew Rebecca was truly safe.

"It was Mike Bontrager heard," Samuel explained.

Daniel listened, stunned. He had yet to allow Rebecca to emerge from the house and make herself vulnerable. Until police cleared the area, they couldn't be positive a sniper hadn't set up to pick her off if she appeared framed in a window or stepped outside. And, yes, he knew how unlikely that was, and that he was being absurdly overprotective.

"Mike heard that Billy make a call, thinking himself alone. He told someone where he could find Rebecca and that he had taken care of your phone."

Mike was the teenage son of Eli Bontrager, the harness maker who had lost so much in the fire this summer. Daniel knew Mike to be enjoying his *Rumspringa* with his gang, but was still a good kid. He'd know who Billy was, and about his prison term.

By good luck, Mike had seen Samuel, who had still been in town informing others about Ephraim. Mike had used his cell phone to call several Amish businesses as Samuel rounded up what other Amish men he could find.

"We thought those men wouldn't do anything bad if they knew they were being watched," he said in his stolid way. "Mike and his friend David went to your police station. We were afraid the deputies working might be too far away, or too busy with something bad to come, but they must have driven very fast."

In fact, the two deputies who had arrived on the heels of the last Amish buggy had been joined in the next ten minutes by an off-duty deputy, followed almost immediately by officers from the Byrum police department, including Ben Slater, who was currently listening to one of his officers talking and gesturing toward the woods.

Three of the intruders now sat in police cars, hands cuffed behind their backs, heads hanging. Two of the four men had bolted for the woods, but one had gotten hung up on a barbed-wire fence almost immediately. Daniel recognized him as the driver of the van that had nearly run him down. No wonder he'd tried to escape. Only Josh Griffen had made it to the cover of the trees.

Floodlights had been set up in the back, and deputies and two more late-arriving Byrum police officers were situated along the back roads where Griffen would emerge if he made it that far.

Shortly after the police cars arrived and the first two intruders surrendered, the Amish had nodded to Daniel and, one by one, circled their buggies, trotting down the driveway and returning to town. They had done what they were called to do and didn't want to be mixed up any more with the law than they had to be.

He knew all those faces, some stern, some usually smiling. Reuben Gingerich, Harvey Stolzfus, Yonnie Miller, Isaac Bontrager, even the humorless minister, Amos King. And among them was Daniel's *daad*, whose eyes had smiled as he bent his head to his son.

Only Samuel remained, apparently feeling obligated to explain their presence.

"We'd be dead if you hadn't come." Daniel choked

up as he thanked the man who had acted so decisively to rescue his niece, and done so without violating any of his principles. "I might have had to shoot to kill. You saved me from that."

Samuel looked gravely down at him. "I will pray you never have to do such a thing."

One of Daniel's deputies called for him, and Samuel looked at the house. "You will bring Rebecca to us?"

It was more an order than a request. Her family would not permit her to stay with him. Rebellion rose in Daniel, joining his burning need to go back into the house and just hold her. Yet he also felt driven to do his job with dignity. Rebecca would understand, he told himself.

Now he said, "I'll bring her to see you."

Samuel's eyes narrowed at an answer that wasn't what he wanted to hear, but he finally nodded. "Then I must go. Emma and *Mamm* will be worrying, me being gone so long."

Daniel backed away, watching as the buggy swung in a U-turn. Then he walked across the wet grass to join Ben.

The rain had passed, he was surprised to realize. When he tipped his head back, he saw a few scattered stars between shredded clouds. A very faint rumble and flash of light in the distance told him the storm had moved south.

"Thanks for coming," he said, holding out his hand.

Ben shook it. "What those creeps did was downright crazy."

"My place is isolated enough, they must have thought they could get in, kill us both and get out quick.

My guess is they were prepared to kill any deputy who showed up, too."

"You got lucky with that Amish kid not only hearing what he did, but acting on it. From what I've learned, that's not usual."

"No." He hesitated. "It's Rebecca's connection to them. Everyone who knows her situation has joined to protect her."

"And you," Ben said shrewdly.

"Maybe." Something to think about. Had he held himself apart unnecessarily, thinking he wasn't welcome when he might have been?

Ben's phone rang. Eyes meeting Daniel's, he answered immediately. "Yeah?" After a moment, he said, "Good work. Yeah, hold on a second." He lowered the phone. "Griffen walked out of the woods with his hands up."

Relief profound, he said, "Tell them to go ahead to the jail. I'll follow in a few minutes to interrogate all four of these guys."

"Good. See you there."

The cars started to clear out, including the ones transporting the prisoners. Daniel walked back to the house, pausing to release the deputy standing guard on the front porch, and went inside.

Rebecca jumped up from the sofa, her face anxious. "Is it—"

"Over? Yes. Griffen was just arrested."

"Thank God," she whispered, and rushed into his arms.

He probably held her too tightly, but he couldn't seem to loosen his grip. He rubbed his cheek against her hair. So much emotion welled inside him that his rib cage hurt.

"I made so many mistakes," he finally said. "I think you'd have died tonight if we hadn't been lucky. So lucky."

Rebecca shook her head vehemently, lifting her chin so she could see him. "What are you talking about? How could you possibly have predicted something so insane?"

"Griffen couldn't stop. He should never have come to Missouri. The ring and wallet connected to Tim, not him. But he decided you were a threat and couldn't stop. Maybe his ego wouldn't let him."

"I think he always felt he had to prove himself. He and Tim were friends, but…"

"Josh resented Tim for having the advantages he didn't."

"Yes. And maybe Steven for overcoming even more obstacles and becoming a man who was satisfied with what he'd made of himself."

Daniel shook his head. So much of that made no real sense to him, even if he understood it intellectually. Money or what college a man attended had nothing to do with what made him worthy of respect from friends and family. Now Griffen would be stripped of such outward signs of success when his time came to be judged.

Rebecca shivered. "When they first showed up, I was so afraid Tim was one of them."

He didn't allow himself to think that she was again being protective of her ex-husband. "That would have been hard," he agreed, instead. "When he told you on

the phone he hadn't had any part in the abduction of
Anna Lantz and her son, it was probably true. Stealing
money, trying to get out of trouble—those he would
do, but not more."

"Yes, except…" Doubt tightened her voice. "If he'd
gotten me into the car that day at the hospital, where
did he intend to take me?"

He didn't want to make excuses for her ex-husband,
but the fact that he had gone home to face Josh—and
Robert—softened Daniel's anger. "Probably to talk to
Josh," he said, "but I wonder if he understood what his
friend was capable of doing."

"On one level, I think he did. He hinted once that
Josh was the real threat to me. He might have even been
trying to serve as a buffer. He was just…"

Weak. She didn't want to say it, and Daniel didn't
blame her. It would be hard on a boy to know what his
father was really like, but she could shield Matthew
only so far. She must know that.

"I didn't mean to leave you in here alone for so
long."

"I understood." She laid her head on his chest, showing trust and acceptance that threatened to break his
control.

"I have to go to Byrum to interview all four men.
It's better if I talk to them before they have too much
time to think about how they can get out of this."

Her fingers bit into his back, but then she straightened, making an effort to hide her tension. "That's
your job."

"On my way, I can drop you at my aunt and uncle's.
You can see Matthew, stay the night."

Tears filled her eyes. "You wouldn't mind?"

He would, because he wanted her here, waiting for him when he got home, but leaving her alone now wasn't an option. And... Samuel was right.

Hiding his reluctance, he said, "Of course not."

"Should I pack everything?" she asked, sounding... he wasn't quite sure. "I mean, to stay?"

Neither his family nor hers would find it acceptable for her to remain here with him now. Letting her go was something he had to do. He could court her, take her out to dinner, for drives. Think of things they could do that would include Matthew.

"You probably should."

She gave a jerky nod and whirled away.

"I love you," he said to her back, surprising himself. She didn't move.

His heart clenched. It was too soon. He'd presumed too much.

And then she turned back, smiling and crying both. "I love you, too. I do, Daniel."

Somehow, he was across the room, kissing her. She tasted of salt but happiness, too. He tried to let her know everything he felt: passion, desperation, tenderness.

When he could make himself release her lips, he said, "We can't offend our families." But to make himself wish her a polite good-night in front of his *onkel* Amos or Samuel... Daniel didn't know how he would be able to do that.

"I know." Rebecca sounded equally sad.

"I'll come to see you every day. We can be like other courting couples." Minus the courting buggy, he thought. And those couples hadn't already made love, didn't have to take a step back.

"Date." She smiled, if tremulously.

"I should get to know Matthew."

"He already likes you, but…that would be good."

Daniel took a deep breath. "That's what we *should* do. But I want you here, with me. Will you marry me?"

Again her eyes flooded with tears. "Of course I will!"

"Soon?"

"Tomorrow, if you can arrange it."

He laughed. "Not that soon. There's Ephraim's funeral, for one. And we should be married in my church, which means talking to my pastor. Our families will want to be there. Matthew should have a chance to get used to the idea. I can survive a few weeks."

"I'm not sure I can. Oh." She swiped her tears on his shirtfront.

Even though he ought to hurry, they kissed and made plans and kissed some more. And when she said, "Poor Tim," he only nodded his understanding. The Lord's Prayer, made before every meal throughout his youth, said, "Forgive us our trespasses, as we forgive those who trespass against us."

And on this night, they had certainly been delivered from evil.

Yes, he could forgive and help a man who had been led into temptation to remain important to his son.

"I love you," Daniel said again, before giving her a nudge. "Leave your *Englisch* clothes here. You won't need them where you're going."

Soon he would have a wife and family. He searched

inside but could no longer find the fear that he would never quite belong anyplace, with anyone.

They held hands all the way to the Troyers'. Witnessing Rebecca's reunion with her son moved him more than he'd expected. Matthew even flung his arms around Daniel and whispered, "You brought my mommy back."

That made it not so hard to say a quiet goodbye and drive away.

What were a few weeks out of a lifetime?

* * * * *

HER AMISH PROTECTORS

Dear Reader,

The story that became *Her Amish Protectors* sneaked up on me while I was writing *Amish Hideout* (originally published as *Plain Refuge*). First I became intrigued by a character, then by an idea.

Ben Slater came to life only because Daniel, the hero in *Amish Hideout*, needed a friend, someone he connected with on a deep level. Thus we got Ben, who had inexplicably left an urban police department in New Jersey to take a job as chief of a small-town department in rural Missouri. The "why" didn't matter in *Amish Hideout*, but it began to bug me. I'd created the guy. Why *would* he do something like that?

And then there was the quilt auction. I chaired a large charity auction (benefiting a no-kill animal shelter) for fifteen years. It was a *huge* amount of work. The week leading up to the auction was insane. Auction day, I started with setup first thing in the morning and kept going through wrap-up at eleven o'clock or so at night. Then the drive home, and I'd topple into bed, so exhausted I slept like the dead for twelve hours. And here's the thing: someone had to take all that money home. Of course, that was me. It always made me just a teeny bit nervous to keep it from Saturday night through Monday morning. What I had in a box in the bedroom were mostly credit-card slips. But the Amish deal primarily in cash, so the proceeds of the quilt auction…are a temptation!

Janice

PROLOGUE

HEARING *HIM* TALKING on the phone behind her, she risked opening her eyes a slit. Her best friend still looked back at her with the shock and vacancy of death, a line of blood drying where it had trickled from her mouth. Without moving, she could see only Colin's legs and feet where he lay sprawled on creamy plush carpet. Carpet splashed with scarlet splotches, as was the glass-topped coffee table. Keenan, now...

His fingers twitched. His shoulders rose and fell slightly with a breath. In. Out.

Her terror swelled. If his father saw any hint of life, he'd pump another bullet into his eight-year-old son. He thought they were all dead—Paige, eleven-year-old Colin, Keenan and the baby of the family, six-year-old Molly.

And Paige's friend, who had happened to drop by this evening with a book of quilt patterns that Paige had wanted to look through. Wrong time, wrong place.

Except, she'd managed to inch over when Damon's back was turned so that she could shield Molly's small body. Molly was breathing. Damon couldn't be allowed to see. Once she'd laid a hand over the little girl's mouth to stifle a moan.

She ached to whisper reassurance to Keenan, who wasn't within reach. To beg him to stay absolutely still.

Every breath was agony, searing pain flaring from her abdomen. Blood had spurted when the bullet struck and she had gone down with that first shot. She vaguely remembered hearing Colin's terrified scream. Damon had turned away to shoot his son and forgotten her. Probably, she thought dully, her wound would be fatal. But she desperately wanted Molly and Keenan to live. All three of them might survive if the police stormed the house soon.

There'd been a bullhorn earlier, before Damon answered his cell phone. That could have been fifteen minutes ago, or two hours ago. She floated in a dreamlike state. Only the pain anchored her here.

No. Not only pain. Molly and Keenan.

It took an enormous effort to comprehend what Damon was saying.

"No, I'm not going to let her talk to you! If you don't quit asking, that's it. Do you hear me?" The savagely angry voice bore little resemblance to the smooth baritone she knew from phone calls and the times Paige had invited her to dinner with her family.

Pause. "They're with their mother. No, I'm not going to upset them by putting them on the phone, either."

They're dead or dying. Paige is dead. Please, please. We need *you.*

Time drifted. Occasionally, she heard him talking.

"I lose my job and she's going to *leave* me?"

Molly was still breathing. Keenan…she wasn't sure.

Whoever was on the phone with Damon listened, sympathized, gave him all the time he wanted to air his furious grievances.

While we die.

She quit listening, quit peeking at a dying boy. She let herself float away.

CHAPTER ONE

"Now, WE BOTH know you want that quilt." The auctioneer had strolled down the aisle between folding chairs until he was only a few feet from one of the two bidders on a spectacular album quilt. "And for a cause this important, you can spend a little extra. Isn't that right?" He thrust the microphone toward the woman next to the man holding the bid card.

She giggled.

Nadia Markovic held her breath. She'd put in a huge amount of work to make tonight's charity auction happen, and it was paying off beyond her wildest dreams. The ballroom in this restored pre–Civil War house was packed, and bidding had been lively on the least-coveted quilts, intense on the stars of the evening. Watching from beside the temporary stage, she felt giddy. Profound relief had struck when the trickle of first arrivals had appeared two hours earlier then had gathered strength, until her current ebullience made her wonder if she'd bob gently toward the ceiling at any minute.

"We're at twenty-eight hundred dollars right now," the auctioneer coaxed. "What do you say to twenty-nine hundred?"

The poor guy glanced at the woman, sighed and raised his bid card again.

The crowd roared.

The other bidder's number shot up.

The silver-haired auctioneer, lean in his tuxedo and possessing a deep, powerful voice, looked around at the crowd. "Three thousand dollars, all for the victims of the recent tornadoes!"

This time, he couldn't persuade the second bidder to go on. He declared the album quilt sold to the gentleman holding bid number 203.

Sturdy, middle-aged Katie-Ann Chupp, the Amish woman who had been Nadia's assistant chair, exclaimed, "Three thousand dollars! Colleen will be so glad."

Colleen Hoefling was a superb quilter. Standing at the back of the room and smiling at what was presumably congratulations from others clustered in her vicinity, she did look pleased, but not surprised. Nadia had recently sold another of Colleen's quilts through her shop, that one in the classic Checkers and Rails pattern, for twenty-eight hundred dollars.

As the bidding began for a lap-sized Sunshine and Shadows quilt, Nadia found herself trying to add up what they'd already earned but failed. She should have made notes in the catalog—

A woman in the ballroom doorway signaled for her, and Nadia slipped out to the foyer where the reception and cashiers' tables had been set up. The auction software program being used tonight was new to all of them. Nadia had entered the original information—the quilts, estimated values and the names and addresses of all registered bidders—which made her the de facto expert.

A woman who had won the bidding on two quilts

was trying to check out, but her name didn't appear on the computer. Realizing the woman was an unexpected walk-in, Nadia added her to the software, took her money then printed a receipt.

"Quite an event you've put on," the woman said, smiling. "I don't really *need* any more quilts, but one of those April tornadoes missed us by less than a mile. Could have hit our house."

Nadia thanked her again, realizing anew that she'd hardly had to sell the cause to the people who lived in northern Missouri. They saw the devastation, year after year.

The good news was that at least a third of tonight's attendees had come from outside Missouri, either as a way to help or because they were passionate collectors excited by the mix of antique and new quilts being offered tonight. The Amish-made were among the most prized.

Nadia added the check to the gray metal lockbox. At her suggestion, they'd offered an express pay option, but surprisingly few auctiongoers had taken advantage of it. At charity events she'd helped with in Colorado, hardly anyone had paid cash. Here, apparently people were used to the fact that few Amish businesses accepted credit cards. The piles of actual cash already in the lockbox, much of it from the earlier sales tables, bemused her. It awakened something a tiny bit greedy, too. She itched to start counting the bills, even though the software would supply totals.

Able to hear furious bidding on a queen-size quilt from an elderly Amish woman, Ruth Graber, Nadia lifted her head. She expected this one to surpass the three thousand dollars that had been the evening's high so far. The Carpenter's Square pattern was intriguing but not complex; it was the elaborate hand quilting with incredibly tiny stitches that made this one stand out.

"Do you mind covering for me while I race to the bathroom?" one of the volunteer cashiers asked.

Nadia smiled. "No, I'll be glad to sit down for a minute." With a sigh, she sank into the chair behind one of the three networked laptop computers, not so sure she'd be able to get up again.

Of course, she'd have to make herself. Closing out and cleaning up after the auction would be a job in itself, all those display racks to be dismantled, chairs to be folded and stacked onto the rolling carts, the vast ballroom to be swept. It had to be pristine by morning. This gorgeous historic home was open to the public from 9:00 a.m. until 4:00 p.m. daily except Sundays. Tomorrow was Saturday.

She couldn't crash until she got home, however late that turned out to be. Lucky adrenaline was still carrying her.

The cause was what mattered, of course—she'd seen for herself some of the devastation left in the paths of giant twisters. She had hoped, too, that her willingness to take on organizing the event would help earn her a place in this town that was her new home.

And, okay, she was selfish enough to also hope that the success would bring in more business to A Stitch in Time, the fabric and quilt shop she had bought and was updating. If the quilters in Henness County adopted her and came first to her store both for their fabric *and* to offer their quilts on consignment, she would survive financially. Otherwise…she'd gone out way too far on a brittle limb when she moved to the county seat of

Byrum in a part of the country she'd never been until she decided she needed to begin a new life.

She had quickly discovered the local Amish kept a distance from everyone else—the *Englischers*—that was difficult to erase. Their goal was to live apart from the world, to keep themselves separate. But Nadia felt she was making friends among them now, Katie-Ann being one.

Just then, Rachel Schwartz appeared, hurrying from the direction of the bathrooms. She was another Amish woman Nadia counted as a friend. When she saw Nadia, she headed toward her instead of the ballroom door. Tonight she wore a calf-length lilac dress and apron of a slightly darker shade as well as the gauzy white *kapp* that distinguished Amish women.

"Have they gotten to Ruth's quilt yet?"

"They're bidding on it right now," Nadia said.

A swell of applause coming from the ballroom made her realize she'd missed hearing a total for Ruth's quilt. But the cashier beside her leaned closer. "Thirty-five hundred dollars! Boy, I wish I had that kind of money to throw around."

Nadia laughed. "I'm with you, but what a blessing so many people who do showed up tonight."

Rachel beamed. "*Ja!* Didn't we tell you? Trust in God, you should."

Her Amish volunteers had all insisted that any endeavor was in God's hands. They *hadn't* insisted the night would therefore be a success, which was quite different. They'd all worked hard on making tonight happen, but they were unwilling to worry about the outcome. If a thunderstorm struck so that the auction-goers stayed home, that would be God's will. A person couldn't be expected to understand His purpose, only to accept that He *had* a purpose.

No thunderstorm, thank goodness.

But Nadia only smiled. "You did tell me."

Rachel rushed toward the ballroom, brushing against a man who happened to be strolling out at just that minute.

He drew Nadia's immediate attention, in part because of his elegant dark suit, a contrast to what everyone else was wearing tonight. The Amish, of course, wore their usual garb. Otherwise, most of the people who'd come to bid or volunteer were dressed casually, some in khakis, some even in jeans.

Along with being beautifully dressed—although he'd skipped the tie, leaving his crisp white shirt open at the neck—this guy personified tall, dark and handsome. His every move suggested leashed power. From a distance, his eyes appeared black, but as he approached she saw that they were a deep, espresso brown. And those eyes missed nothing. Nadia had caught occasional glimpses of him all evening, strolling or holding up a wall with one of those broad shoulders. His gaze swept the crowd ceaselessly.

She had yet to meet him, but another volunteer had identified him when she asked. Byrum police chief Ben Slater was a Northerner, Jennifer Bronske had murmured, as if the fact was scandalous. From New Jersey. No one knew why he'd sought the job here or accepted it when it was offered.

Apparently, Chief Slater felt an event of this size and importance demanded his watchful presence. Or else he was suspicious of all the outsiders. Who knew?

She hadn't had so much as a shoplifter in her store, but he might have been conditioned to expect the worst.

His dark eyes met hers for the first time. It felt like an electrical shock, raising the tiny hairs on her arms. Nadia couldn't imagine why she'd responded that way. His expression was so guarded, she didn't have the slightest idea what he was thinking as he walked toward her.

She was peripherally aware she wasn't the only one transfixed by his approach. The other two cashiers were staring, too, although she couldn't tear her own gaze from him long enough to tell if they were admiring a gorgeous male specimen, or frozen the way a small mammal is when a predator locks on to it. Nadia wasn't even sure which one *she* felt.

He stopped on the other side of the table from her, his lips curved but his eyes remaining watchful. And he held out a hand. "Ms. Markovic, we haven't met. I'm Ben Slater, chief of the Byrum police department."

She focused on that hand, long-fingered and powerful enough to crush a man's throat—and she knew what her reaction meant. That was a spike of fear she'd felt. When she made herself accept his handshake and looked into his eyes again, she saw a flicker that told her he hadn't liked whatever he'd seen on her face.

"Chief Slater. Several people have pointed you out," she said pleasantly, suppressing her completely irrational response. The antipathy she felt toward law enforcement officers was one thing, this was something else altogether. Although she had to wonder if he wore a holster beneath that perfectly fitted jacket. The sight of a handgun could send a shudder of remembered pain and terror through her. "Thank you for coming tonight.

I don't suppose you're planning to bid on one of those quilts, are you?"

She was pretty sure he was amused now. "As beautiful as they are," he said, in a velvet deep voice, "I'm afraid I can't bring myself to spend thousands of dollars on a bed covering."

"They're more than that," she protested. "They're works of art."

"I won't argue." His smile was devastating in a lean, beautiful face. "Unfortunately, I don't spend thousands of dollars for wall art, either."

"A Philistine," she teased, even as she marveled at her daring.

He laughed. "I'd call myself a man who lives on a modest paycheck."

She heaved a sigh. "Oh, well. I guess you're excused, then."

"What about you? I didn't see you bidding, either."

This time, she made a face. "I can't afford what the quilts are going for, either. I do own several beautiful ones already, though." She hesitated. "Actually, I'm a quilter. I donated one of the lap-sized quilts that already sold. That was all I had time to do, what with getting a business up and running."

"The fabric store."

"That's right."

"Not someplace I'm likely to shop."

She chuckled. No, he would be wildly out of place amidst the riot of color and femininity in her store.

But then she had an odd thought. The previous owner of her building had died in a fall. She'd heard a rumor that the police suspected the elderly woman had been pushed down the stairs, but rumors had a way of sprouting from the smallest of seeds. Still, even when an accident resulted in a death, the police responded, didn't they?

"You must have been in my building before."

His gaze became opaque. "I have."

"Did you…know Mrs. Jefferson?"

"No. I was new on the job when she died." One side of his mouth tipped up. "And, you know, she did run a fabric store. As we've established, not my kind of place."

Nadia smiled again, but it took a bit of an effort. When she heard the rumor, she'd seriously considered backing out of the sale. She'd have been within her rights, if there was any real reason to believe Mrs. Jefferson had been murdered. That was the kind of information the Realtor should have disclosed immediately. But then she'd told herself not to be an idiot. The location was perfect for her business, and she loved the idea of being able to live upstairs from it. What, did she think no one had ever died in the town of Byrum?

But she heard herself say, "I came here thinking this was a peaceful community. Learning about Mrs. Jefferson's death really disturbed me."

More thunderous applause from the ballroom had the police chief glancing over his shoulder, but his dark gaze returned to her. "No place is completely peaceful, Ms. Markovic. Humanity being what it is."

"I know that." Wait. Was he *confirming* that awful rumor?

No, he was speaking in generalities, of course. And, no, she absolutely would *not* ask him what he thought about the elderly woman's death. Since she went up and down those stairs several times a day, the last thing she needed was to obsess about the older woman who had plummeted to her death on them.

Or to think about how intimately *she* had seen death.

Nadia was rescued from trying to think of something pleasant to say by renewed excitement from the ballroom. Even the police chief looked around. Nadia noticed the third cashier hovering, the one whose seat she was occupying. A stream of people started out of the ballroom, so she stood and said, "Looks like it's time to go to work."

Chief Slater had stepped back, but was waiting when Nadia came around the table. "Pleasure to meet you," he said.

She forced a smile and lied. "Likewise. Except I hope I never need to call you."

"There are other reasons for two people to talk," he murmured, nodded—and walked away.

INTRIGUING WOMAN, BEN REFLECTED, as he stood at the back of the ballroom and watched the last few quilts be auctioned for staggering prices.

Beautiful woman, too. Hair as dark as his, white, white skin that would give her trouble in the hot Missouri sun and haunting eyes he'd label as hazel, inadequate as the word was to describe the seemingly shifting colors: green, gold, whiskey brown. And lush curves. The woman was built. Breasts that would more than fill his large hands, tiny waist, womanly hips and long legs that weren't sticks. Scrawny women had never done it for him.

For just a second, he'd thought she returned his interest. But something else had darkened her eyes. Wariness? Okay, he was a cop. Some people reacted that way to him, although usually they had a guilty conscience. She didn't look like the type.

He frowned. He wasn't so sure what he'd seen *was* wariness. She'd almost looked...afraid.

The minute the thought crossed Ben's mind, he knew it was right. She'd moved here because she'd believed the community to be peaceful, which suggested wherever she'd come from wasn't. Still, you'd think if she'd been the victim of a crime, law enforcement presence tonight would have reassured her.

For a moment, he didn't see the still-full ballroom, the auctioneer, the spotters. He saw only her face, gently rounded rather than model beautiful. And he saw that flare in her eyes, and knew whatever she'd felt had been for *him*, not what he represented. Or, at least, not only what he represented.

He grimaced. Maybe he bore an unfortunate resemblance to some scumbag who'd beaten her. Mugged her. Stalked her. Or what if she'd had an ex who'd been a cop *and* violent?

Bad luck. What Ben would like to do was drop by the fabric store and persuade Ms. Nadia Markovic to take a break for a cup of coffee. But scaring women... that wasn't a feeling he enjoyed. He'd keep his distance, at least for now.

He abruptly refocused on the stage, because Nadia had taken the microphone and was thanking everyone for coming and letting them know how much money had been raised. Over a hundred thousand dollars just from the auction, plus an additional twenty thousand dollars from the sale hall open today, where many more quilts had been available as well as other textile arts.

A drop in the bucket compared to the need, but a nice sum of money nonetheless.

"And, finally," she said, "we all owe thanks to the artists who donated the work of thousands of hours, their skill and their vision, to help people whose lives were devastated by nature's fury."

The applause was long and heartfelt. Ben joined in, watching as Nadia made her way from the stage and through the crowd, stopping to exchange a few words here, a hug there. She was glowing. Nothing like the way she'd shut down at the sight of him.

Even so, he hung around until the end, thinking about how much money was stashed in that metal box behind the cashiers. He couldn't shake the big-city mentality. Hard to picture anyone here trying to snatch it—but better safe than sorry.

He clenched his teeth. That had been one of his mother's favorite sayings. She had, once upon a time, been firm in her belief she could keep her family safe by adequate precautions. Until the day she found out bad happens to everyone.

Keeping that in mind, he stepped outside and waited in the darkness beneath some ancient oak trees until he'd seen Nadia Markovic safely in her car and on her way.

THE FOURTH STAIR *always* creaked, and it always made her start. Which was silly. Older buildings made noises. Nadia had had an inspection done before she bought this one, and there wasn't a thing wrong with the structure. Yet the creak made her think of clanking chains, moans and movement seen out of the corner of her eye.

Had the stair creaked before Mrs. Jefferson's fatal

fall? Nadia wrinkled her nose at her own gothic imagination. Only then she got to wondering if the police had noticed that one step creaked. Because nobody could sneak up those stairs—unless they knew to skip that step. Or the person hadn't bothered, because he or she was expected, even welcome. Either way, it suggested the killer wasn't a stranger.

She rolled her eyes as she set the money box on the dresser in her bedroom. If Mrs. Jefferson had the TV on, she wouldn't have heard anyone coming. Or she could have been in the bathroom, or maybe she was going a little deaf. No one had said.

Or, oh, gee, she'd stumbled at the head of the stairs and fallen. There was a concept. A neighbor had said that the poor woman had suffered from osteoporosis. Tiny, she had become stooped with a growing hunch. She should have moved to an apartment or house where she didn't have to deal with stairs.

And Nadia did *not* want to think about tragedy of any kind, not tonight. If she hadn't encountered Ben Slater, she wouldn't have felt nervous for a minute going upstairs in her own home.

While she was at it, she'd refrain from so much as thinking about him, too. She'd forget that odd moment of fear, or her surprising physical response to the man. Instead, she'd let herself enjoy satisfaction and even a teeny bit of triumph, because tonight they'd exceeded their original goal by a good margin. She could hardly wait to deposit the money in the bank tomorrow morning.

Normally, she didn't like to have money lying around. She made regular deposits to limit how much cash she had on hand in the store. But whatever Chief Slater said, Byrum seemed to be a peaceful small town.

She read the local paper, and most of the crimes mentioned in it were trivial or had to do with teenagers or the weekend crowd at bars.

Nadia had locked up as soon as she was inside, checking and rechecking both the building's front and back doors as well as the one at the foot of the staircase leading to her apartment.

Worrying came naturally to her, and the tendency had worsened drastically after— Nope, not gonna think about that, either.

Instead, she removed her heels and sighed with relief. Most people hadn't had to dress up at all, the event having been advertised as Missouri summer casual, but since she'd opened the evening and closed it, she'd felt obligated to wear a favorite silk dress with cap sleeves while hoping it wasn't obvious her legs were bare.

She took a cool shower, brushed her teeth and went to bed wearing only panties and a cotton camisole. She threw even the top sheet aside. The small air-conditioning unit in the window helped, but she usually turned it off at some point during the night. It didn't just hum, it rattled, which was really annoying.

Maybe *that's* why Mrs. Jefferson didn't hear someone coming up the stairs.

Nadia groaned, but even as exhausted as she was, it was bound to wake her up later. Replacing it was on her wish list.

So, as she often did, she basked in the scant flow of chilly air until her eyelids grew heavy, then forced herself to crawl out of bed and turn off the air conditioner. Tonight, not even a sultry ninety degrees would keep her awake.

THE SCREECH OF the alarm jolted Nadia to enough consciousness to slap the button to shut it off. Then she moaned and buried her face in the pillow. Why hadn't she planned to close the shop today?

Dumb question. Saturday was her busiest day in a typical week, and she bet lots of people would stop by just to share the excitement generated by last night's event. Plus, she needed to slip out before noon to deposit the money, since the bank's Saturday hours were so limited.

"Ugh." Her eyelids felt as if they were glued shut, or maybe weighted down with a thin coating of cement. She *had* crashed last night. Unfortunately, her body wasn't ready to reboot.

Another cool, or even icy-cold, shower would help, she decided. She just had to get up and make it that far.

With a whimper, she rolled out of bed. It only took a minute to gather clothes. Heading for the bathroom, she tried to decide why her entire body ached. Yes, she'd worked hard yesterday doing setup, and she'd been on her feet for hours on end, but she wasn't in *that* bad shape.

Nadia had gotten all the way into the bathroom before her brain stuttered. *No, no. I just didn't see because I wasn't* looking.

So she set the neat pile of clothes on the countertop, then very slowly turned around. Through the open bathroom door, she could see her dresser. She could even see her reflection in the beveled mirror above the antique chest of drawers.

She just didn't see the money box.

CHAPTER TWO

HAVING SLEPT POORLY last night, Ben was not happy when his phone rang while he was in the bathroom trying to scrape off the whiskers he'd grown since he last shaved at approximately 6:00 p.m. yesterday. He glared at himself in the mirror and groped for the phone. Half his face still covered with foam, he snapped, "Yeah?"

"Um… Chief?"

Recognizing the voice, he sighed. "Sergeant. Sorry. What's up?"

"Ah, just had a call I thought you'd want to know about. Since you said you were going to that event last night."

Tension crawled up his spine. "The quilt auction."

"Yeah. The lady who organized it says somebody stole the money. She's next thing to hysterical."

How in…? "I know where she lives. I'll be there in fifteen minutes."

Incredulity and worry spinning in his head, he finished shaving, got dressed and went out the door without his usual second cup of coffee. In front of her building, he parked directly behind a squad car.

After he rapped lightly on the door that had a closed sign and no one came, he went in. An astonishing array of colors filled the space. Rows and rows of fabric on bolts flowed naturally from one shade to another, while quilts hung on every wall. At the rear was a door leading into another space that had been a storeroom in the past, but he knew Ms. Markovic was offering classes now, so maybe she'd converted it. The store was a whole lot more appealing than it had been the last time he'd been here, after Mrs. Jefferson's death.

To his right, a wide doorway opened to a hall that gave access to a restroom for customers, ending at a back door. He was all too familiar with the layout, including the oddly shaped closet beneath the staircase. Ben stopped long enough now to examine the lock on the apartment door.

Voices came from above as he mounted the stairs. One step still creaked, resulting in abrupt silence above. Sure enough, Officer Grumbach appeared at the head of the staircase.

"Chief." He looked relieved.

Ben nodded a greeting and entered the apartment.

Nadia sat in an easy chair, arms crossed and held tight to her body. Her mass of dark hair was loose and unbrushed. She wore a stretchy camisole with no bra beneath—he had to make a conscious effort not to let his gaze drop to those generous breasts—and what looked like thin sweatpants. Her face was pinched, even paler than last night. And her eyes fixed on him, unblinking.

He sat on the coffee table right in front of her. "Okay," he said in a deliberately gentle voice, "tell me what happened."

"I don't know what happened!" she cried. "Like I've told *him* over and over."

Hovering by the doorway, the young redheaded officer flushed.

"Let's put it another way," Ben said. "I saw you drive out of the parking lot last night."

Her eyes widened. "You were still there?"

"I was. That was an awful lot of money you had."

Her teeth chattered. "It never occurred to any of us that something like this could happen."

"Now I wish I'd escorted you home, too," he said.

Nadia shook her head. "I got home fine. I had the box. I thought of hiding it downstairs, but I decided to keep it close by instead. So I put it on the dresser in my bedroom."

He went very still, not liking the implication.

Officer Grumbach cleared his throat. "When I checked, the back door was unlocked. And Ms. Markovic says the door at the foot of the stairs was unlocked this morning, too."

"But I checked both last night!" Nadia's voice rose. "I locked my apartment door and verified that I had. I did!"

Unable to help himself, Ben reached out and laid a hand over hers, now writhing in her lap. She froze, took a couple of deep breaths and continued in a quieter voice, "I worried a little, because I always do, but how could anyone get in?"

He frowned. "Are you a heavy sleeper?"

"Not usually, but I don't think I've ever in my life been as tired as I was when I got home last night."

"That's understandable." He took his hand back. "So you were locked up tight last night. The money box was sitting on your dresser when you fell asleep."

"I had to have slept more deeply than usual. I never even got up to use the bathroom. I turned my air conditioner off because it's so noisy, but for once it might not have bothered me. If not for my alarm, I wouldn't have woken up when I did. I was still tired."

He nodded his understanding. He gave passing thought to whether she could have been drugged, but her eyes were clear, she was unlikely to have been drinking anything during cleanup at the end of the evening and he'd heard from more than one person that she'd been at the mansion from the beginning of setup early in the morning to the very end, at close to eleven. She had to have been dead on her feet.

Her teeth closed on her lower lip, the eyes that met his desperate. "Without the air conditioner, it was hot up here."

An upstairs apartment like this would be, even though it was still early summer.

"All I had on was this—" she plucked at her camisole "—and panties. I didn't even have a sheet over me."

Horror to match hers filled him. No, she hadn't been raped, but she'd been violated anyway.

"He—" her voice shook, and she swallowed "—he could have stood there and looked at me. And I never knew it." She went back to trying to hug herself.

"Officer Grumbach, please go find Ms. Markovic a sweater or sweatshirt."

He nodded and disappeared into her bedroom. She didn't even seem to notice until Grumbach handed her a zip-front, hooded sweatshirt. After a moment, she put it on and hunched inside it.

"This morning?" he nudged.

She accepted the cue. "This morning, I got up, grabbed clothes and started into the bathroom. That's when I realized the box was gone. I *knew* where I'd left it, but I ran around searching anyway. I don't know what I was thinking. That I sleepwalked? Hallucinated last night? Anyway, I searched this whole place, then I ran down to my car to make sure I didn't leave it on the seat. I parked in front last night," she added.

"That was smart." He nodded his approval. "Do you lock the car?" Not everyone in Henness County did. Law enforcement kept busy enough, but the crime rate per capita was substantially lower in what was usually a peaceful town and rural surroundings than it had been in urban Camden, New Jersey.

"I always do. And it was still locked, so I knew—" She gulped to a stop.

Ben straightened, careful not to let her see what he was thinking. Because there were two possibilities here, and the most obvious was that she was lying through her teeth. If so, she was a big liar, but he didn't know her well. Nobody in these parts did. The first thing he'd do when he got to the station was run a thorough search on Nadia Markovic's background.

Possibility two was that somebody had somehow unlocked two doors without leaving a scratch or making a lot of noise—because however sound her sleep, Ben was betting she'd have woken if she heard a strange sound right there in her apartment—and walked out with the money. And if that was the case…odds were good the thief had been a participant or volunteer at the auction. Who else would know who had the money?

What would have happened if she had awakened to see someone looming in her bedroom? Had the thief been prepared to kill if necessary?

A question he didn't need to ask himself until he eliminated the possibility that she had either planned the entire event with the intention of profiting from it, or had succumbed to temptation at some point and decided to keep the money.

"Have you had anything to eat or drink yet this morning?" he asked abruptly.

Comprehension was a little slow coming. "No. No." She shook her head. "I couldn't eat."

"You can," he said firmly. "Let's go in the kitchen, and I can at least pour you a cup of coffee."

"Tea. I drink tea."

"Tea it is." He rose and held out a hand. Just like last night, she stared at his hand for a split second longer than would be usual before taking it. He boosted her to her feet. "Officer Grumbach, I think you can go back to patrol now." On a twinge of memory, Ben glanced at her. "Unless you'd be more comfortable not being alone with me, Ms. Markovic."

"What? Oh, no. That's fine." She summoned a weak smile for the young officer. "Thank you. I'm sorry I yelled at you."

"You were understandably upset, ma'am." Grumbach nodded and departed in what Ben suspected was more relief. He was a new hire, barely experienced enough to be out on his own. He'd done fine, though; Ben made a mental note to tell him so.

Nadia wanted to make her own tea, but he persuaded her to sit and let him do it. Waiting for the water to boil, he investigated her refrigerator and cupboards, finally settling on a croissant he heated in the microwave before splitting it open and slapping on raspberry jam from a local Amish woman. He recognized the label. He added extra sugar to the tea before setting the cup in front of her, then the croissant.

Under his stern gaze, she did eat and sipped at her English breakfast tea. Finally, she admitted to feeling better.

"Then let's talk." He pulled a small notebook from his pocket. He thought being recorded might stifle her. "Who knew you were taking the proceeds home?" he asked bluntly.

She blinked. "I can't imagine…"

He cocked an eyebrow. "But the thief had to know."

"Oh, dear God," Nadia whispered. She stared into space for a minute. "Well, Katie-Ann Chupp, of course. Julie Baird, Karen Llewellyn, probably Rachel Schwartz."

Two Amish, two *Englischers*. Even he'd come to divide his citizenry that way. From what he'd learned since moving to Byrum, it would be a cold day before either of the warmhearted Amish women would so much as give a passing thought to stealing, never mind carrying out a heist like this. They'd have no need. If either woman's family was struggling financially, all they'd have to do was ask for help, and it would pour forth. That's how the Amish worked; they took care of each other. On the other hand, he knew both the other women, at least in passing, and felt reasonably sure neither made a likely suspect, either. Julie Baird's husband was a doctor, Karen's a representative for a farm equipment company. Still, he noted all four names.

Nadia reeled off a few more, then admitted that anyone helping with cleanup might have heard or guessed that she would be taking the money.

Yes, it would have been logical to suppose the event chair would deal with the evening's take, which could widen the suspect pool considerably. But would somebody really break in to look for the cash box without being 100 percent certain Nadia had taken it home? Ben didn't think so.

Of course, that somebody could have been lurking outside to see who carried the box out, and even though Ben had been watching for just that eventuality, landscaping around the historic mansion included a lot of dark bushes and trees.

"Did you see anyone around last evening who wasn't involved with the auction?" he asked.

Her forehead crinkled. "I don't think… Only Mr. Warren, wanting to be sure everything was going smoothly. He left after I promised to lock up and then return the keys sometime today, but I bet he went by after we were gone last night to make sure I had."

Ben would bet the same. Lyle Warren, head of the historical society that maintained and showed the house, was anal to an extreme. He fussed.

"Anybody ask questions about the money?" Ben asked.

She stared at him. "Well…of course they did."

"No, I was thinking about interest in how much cash you had versus checks or credit card slips."

Nadia moaned, and he didn't blame her. Once word got out, people would have to contact their credit card companies, maybe wait for new cards, put a stop on checks. Those among them with a strong conscience would then reimburse the auction committee, meaning the total sum wasn't lost. But if the thief made use of credit card numbers or altered and cashed checks, everyone would be angry, whether the credit card companies and banks took the loss or not.

Unfortunately, some inks were easy to "wash" from a check, allowing the thief to change the recipient's name and even the amount the check was made out for. Depending on what info the auction cashiers had written down, checks could be an aid to identity theft, too.

And anyone who had not just a credit card number, but also the expiration date, name on the card and the code from the back was home free to spend up to the limit.

When she finally answered, he could tell her thoughts had gone a different direction.

"Nobody asked," she said, her voice thin. "I think… most of them are so used to transactions with the Amish being primarily cash, nothing about the evening would surprise them. You know? But every time I opened the box, I was surprised. I mean, there were *wads* of money. So many of the sellers during the day were Amish, I bet three-fourths or more of that twenty thousand dollars was cash. And last night… I'll have to find out, but even if it was only half…"

In other words, somebody might have gotten his or her hands on between sixty and seventy thousand dollars in cash. Even if the thief didn't make use of the credit card numbers, the loss was substantial, even cataclysmic.

"Have you told anyone yet?"

She shuddered. "No."

He decided to ease into the personal stuff. "Will you tell me why you moved here, Ms. Markovic?"

That had her staring. "What does that have to do with anything?"

Was she really that obtuse? He studied her face and couldn't decide.

"I'm wondering whether you left behind somebody who dislikes you enough to want to do you a bad turn, and profit from it, too."

"Oh. You mean an ex-husband or something?"

"A stalker, anyone who feels wronged by you."

She started to shake her head again.

"Have you ever taken out a restraining order?"

"No. Never."

"Were you married?"

"No."

"Have you ever been in a relationship that ended badly?"

"No. Really."

He rolled his shoulders. "That takes us back to my original question. Why did you move and why here? And where did you come from?"

"Colorado Springs. I grew up in Colorado, even stayed there for college."

Big change, Ben mused, to leave a town of half a million residents at the foot of the Rockies for Byrum, with its flat terrain and 3,809 residents. He'd guess Colorado Springs to be politically liberal, too, while this part of Missouri was anything but. Of course, he was one to talk, coming from the urban jungle of Camden, New Jersey.

Nadia drew a deep breath. "I wanted—I needed—" The words seemed to be hitting a blockade.

Once again, he reached across the table and took her hand, which felt cold in his, considering the air temperature.

"I was running away," she whispered.

She couldn't have just said, *I needed a change*? But, no, the down-deep truth had slipped out. Nadia wanted to bury her face in her hands. Except one of hers was engulfed in his big, warm, comforting hand.

"From my family," she added hastily. Like that

helped. There was no getting out of this now, even if her past couldn't possibly have anything to do with the money being stolen.

"I…had something traumatic happen. I couldn't get past it. I thought making a change would help."

The intensity in his dark eyes made it hard to look away. "You wanted a peaceful small town."

"Yes."

"Surely there are nice small towns in Colorado."

His speculative tone unnerved her. Evading the question wouldn't be smart. "I wanted to get farther away from home. Everyone I knew either babied me, or they kept thinking of *fun* things we could do. And I know they were trying to cheer me up, but…"

"If I do some research, would I find out what happened?"

Had he even noticed his thumb was circling in her palm, which was way more sensitive than she'd ever realized?

"Probably," Nadia said. "But it really didn't have anything to do with this. I mean, the money."

He didn't say anything, just watched her. Why had she opened her big mouth?

She bent her head and looked at the tabletop. "It was a domestic violence thing I got caught up in by chance."

"Not your family."

"No. And…I have to tell you, I really hate to talk about it." Even trying to get *out* of talking about it caused the memories to rush over her, still shockingly vivid, colored in blood.

He saw more than he should, because his hand tightened. Or maybe it was because in his job he saw the horrifying aftermath of similar scenes. On a swelling of remembered bitterness, she wondered whether he would have made the same decisions those cops had.

"Will you give me the bare bones anyway?"

"You don't need to hear this," she said stubbornly.

He waited, his eyes never leaving her face.

"I stopped by a friend's house." Oh, heavens—she was going to do this. "I'd obviously arrived at a tense moment. My friend—Paige—tried to hustle me out, but too late. Her husband had gone to get his gun. He shot all three kids, me and Paige. I…pretended to be dead. It was, um…"

Ben Slater made a low, guttural sound. The next thing she knew, he'd circled the table and crouched beside her chair. So close. He laid a hand on her back. Nadia was shocked by how much she wanted his arms around her, to bury her face against his neck, but she made herself stay where she was, focused on the grain of the oak table.

"Did anyone but you survive?"

"Their daughter. She was six. She's seven now." The little girl's recovery was the only spark of hope emerging from the horror. "Otherwise…even he killed himself at the end."

Ben breathed a profanity. "How badly were you injured?"

"I was lucky." She touched the spot where she knew the scar was on her abdomen. "The bullet came at an angle and missed everything important. I bled enough that I guess my acting was believable." She even managed a sort of smile.

"How long ago was this?"

"A year and a half. It left me really jumpy, and I had bad dreams. And, like I said, my friends and family were driving me nuts. Plus, I'd been teaching quilting classes and selling my own quilts, but also working for the assessor's office. My dream was to have my own store. Property values and rents are lower here, so I could swing it with what I'd saved. And interest in quilts is high anywhere the Amish live." She might very well lose her store now. The reminder was chilling. If people didn't think she'd stolen the money herself, they'd see her as careless.

Not just *people*. Chief Slater. Of course he had to suspect her! Nadia couldn't believe she hadn't realized that sooner. He didn't think someone from her past had pursued her here to Byrum; he needed to investigate her, and she'd just given him a jump start.

So much for wanting to sink into the safety of his embrace.

Her spine stiffened and she felt his hand drop from her back. "As I said, what happened is irrelevant."

A flicker in his eyes told her he'd noted her withdrawal. He rose and looked down at her. "To the heist? Probably. But in other ways? Of course it isn't."

Pulled by the power of that velvety voice, roughened now, she couldn't help but look at him. His eyes were nearly black, the bones in his face prominent, his mouth tight.

She swallowed a lump in her throat, and waited.

"Aren't there a couple of other apartments on this block?"

He was thinking someone might have been awake to see an intruder. She wished that was possible.

"The one next door is empty right now. The florist went out of business."

He frowned. "Right."

"I heard a group of Amish furniture makers may have taken the lease. I hope so."

"It would work well with your business," he agreed. "And we don't want vacancies downtown."

"No. The next closest apartment is above the barber shop."

Slater grimaced. "Lester Orton."

Mr. Orton had to be eighty years old. He seemed to cut hair fine, and must handle the stairs to his apartment, but he was going deaf and she'd noticed his lights went out every evening by nine o'clock at the very latest.

"There are several upstairs apartments across the street, too, but it was my back door that was unlocked. Even if one of those neighbors had been looking out the window, they couldn't have seen anything."

"Unless he was using a flashlight."

"Yes, but that wouldn't tell you anything."

He did the neutral cop expression well, but she was already shaking her head.

"That's not true. It would…corroborate my story, wouldn't it? Isn't that the word police always use?"

"It is, and yes, it would." No discernible emotion there.

Nadia would have liked to resent his suspicion, his ability to shift from cool questions to compassion and back again. Maybe he'd held her hand because he was basically a nice man who really had felt for her. More likely, he'd been trying to make her believe they had a connection. Which was deceitful, but…he was doing his job. She couldn't dislike him for that.

He went back to his seat, and they looked at each other, him appraising her, Nadia gazing coolly back.

Finally she asked, "What should I do now?"

He hesitated. "I think you need to start letting your committee members know what happened. I'll be talking to them, too. One of them may have noticed someone expressing unexpected curiosity about the event, or someone hanging around who shouldn't have been there." He paused. "Do you have a list of attendees?"

"I can pull up a report from the software on people who preregistered and the walk-ins who made a purchase." She closed her eyes. "I need to let them know, too, don't I?"

"Certainly the ones who wrote checks or paid by credit card. They'll need to put stops on those payments. I'm guessing most of them will then make a new payment, so you won't be out the entire amount." The lines in his forehead deepened. "Ask them to let us know if their card number is run or their check already cashed, too."

"Isn't that awfully hard to do?"

"You mean the checks? Yeah, it's tougher than it used to be," he agreed. "I doubt that will happen. Credit card numbers…you know what a big business stealing those has turned into. Even so, my suspicion is that the thief was solely after the cash."

As much as two-thirds of the money so many people had worked hard to raise for victims who needed it desperately.

Well, the only cowardly thing she'd done in her life was pack up and set out across country to start over. She wouldn't add another now. Shower, she told herself, get dressed and begin.

Slater asked if there had been walk-ins who hadn't made a purchase, and she could only say, "I assume so, but I have no way of knowing. Also…most people came in pairs." Spouses were one thing, but some bidders had probably brought a friend instead.

He gave her his email address so that she could send him a list of attendees and the contact info. Even then, he wasn't done. He asked if she'd changed the locks since buying the building—no—and suggested she have it done immediately.

He gave her one last penetrating look with those disconcertingly dark eyes and said, "Think, Ms. Markovic. This wasn't a stranger. He or she had to know not only who had the money, but how to get into your apartment without making a sound. He could have had a penlight—probably did—but it's also possible our thief already knew the layout."

He also asked her to walk him to the foot of the stairs and lock the door behind him. Which, like replacing the locks, was closing the barn door after the horses were out…except, what if last night's intruder had been thinking about *her*, and decided to come back?

Alone, Nadia scuttled upstairs to an apartment that no longer felt like a refuge.

CHAPTER THREE

NADIA HAD BEEN to the Bairds' house several times, because Julie had hosted some auction committee planning sessions. Sprawling and open, it was the fanciest house in town except possibly for a couple of the huge nineteenth-century mansions. The interior was light and airy, the colors all pastels. Nadia had noticed before that Julie only purchased quilts in soft colors. She was currently taking a beginner-level class, having decided to take up quilting herself, and—no surprise—she'd chosen a creamy yellow fabric as centerpiece, to be accented with paler creams and delicate pinks.

Not much older than Nadia's thirty-two, Julie was an attractive, slender woman with a shining cap of blond hair. Nadia had wondered if she went to a salon in St. Louis or Kansas City. No other women around here had hair as skillfully cut.

Leading Nadia to the living room, Julie said, "I'll have Mary bring us iced tea. Or would you prefer lemonade?" Mary Gingerich was a young Amish woman who kept the house spotless and served as maid when Julie had guests.

"Oh, thank you, but no. I can only stay a minute," Nadia said, smiling apologetically. The smile probably looked as forced as it felt. "I...have something I need to tell you."

Looking concerned, Julie faced her. "What is it?"

Nadia blurted it out, just as she had half an hour ago to Katie-Ann. "The money from last night was stolen."

Julie stared, comprehension coming slowly. "What?" She gave her head a small shake. "How?"

Fingernails biting into her palms, Nadia told her.

"You've informed the police."

"Yes, of course. I called 911 as soon as I discovered the money box was gone. Sheriff Slater seems to be taking charge of the investigation himself."

"And what does he say?" Julie sounded…cool. She hadn't suggested Nadia sit down.

"He'll be talking to everyone working on the auction. I'm sure you'll hear from him. He's interested in who might have been hanging around without an obvious reason, and whether anyone was asking questions about the evening's proceeds."

Her perfectly arched eyebrows rose. "You mean, about who was taking charge of the money?"

"Yes, or seeming curious about how much of it was cash versus checks and credit card slips."

"I see." The pause was a little too long. "I don't really know what to say. I'm certainly…shocked."

And she wasn't going to be supportive, Nadia could tell that already. "I'm devastated," Nadia said frankly. "I don't know what I can do other than help Chief Slater to the best of my ability."

"Perhaps you should consider making some financial recompense," Julie said, her voice having chilled even more.

"Julie, I'm a small business owner. I have no cushion that would allow me to do anything like that." Feeling the burn in her cheeks, Nadia said, "I must be going. I need to tell everyone who was on the committee what happened in person."

"I appreciate you doing that. I'll walk you to the door."

In other words, if she didn't hustle, the door would slap her in the butt. She had no doubt that the moment she was gone Julie would start calling everyone but the Amish volunteers, who didn't have telephones. Nadia thought of asking her to wait, but keeping herself together was a strain already. She said, "Goodbye," without adding her usual, *See you Wednesday for the class*. Somehow, she felt sure Julie Baird would have an excuse for dropping out. Or she might not even bother with one.

Nadia drove half a mile from the Baird home, which was on landscaped acreage on the outskirts of Byrum, before she pulled over, set the emergency brake and closed her eyes. She had known—feared—that some people might react like that, but Katie-Ann's warmth and sympathy had given her hope that these women she had started to think were friends would believe in her. She wanted to go home, climb into bed and pull the covers over her head.

The image startled and dismayed her. This wasn't close to the worst thing that had happened to her. Nobody was threatening to hurt or kill her. This was all about shame and her sense of responsibility. *So suck it up*, she told herself.

Her appointment with the locksmith wasn't until four. She still had time, and she had to do this.

Karen Llewellyn next, then… Nadia made a mental list of who she needed to see and in what order, talked herself through some slow, deep breathing, then put the car back into gear.

WHEN LYLE WARREN saw Ben, alarm flared in his eyes. Now, why would that be? Ben asked himself, his instincts going on alert.

"Mr. Warren." He held out a hand.

The older man, tall and bony, eyed that hand dubiously before extending his own. Ben was reminded of Nadia Markovic doing the same last night. The shake was brief. Lyle said, "I'm surprised to see you here, Chief Slater. What can I do for you?"

Ben had first visited the Brevitt mansion, where Warren maintained an office, then tried him at home. At last he'd tracked him down to what he'd been told were the remains of a gristmill a few miles outside of town. Walking the distance from where he'd had to park, Ben had begun to think he should have waited until Warren returned to town. He'd done some hiking in Upstate New York and New England, but he wasn't much of an outdoorsman, and he'd had the unfortunate experience of encountering poison ivy not long after moving to Missouri. He *thought* that was Virginia creeper growing thick among the trees here, but wasn't positive. It and poison ivy looked too much alike. One of them had three leaves, the other… He couldn't remember. Five? But the answer was irrelevant, since he also didn't remember which was which.

He'd found Lyle Warren prepared for the trek in heavy canvas pants and boots, in contrast to Ben's dressier shoes and slacks. Warren hadn't seemed like the woodsy type.

Now Ben surveyed the ruins. "You're thinking you can do something with this?"

"If we can purchase the property. We could restore the building."

Okay, the brick walls still stood, although Ben wouldn't have risked leaning on one. Graffiti had been sprayed on a couple of those walls, and when he walked a few feet to peer inside, he saw cigarette butts and discarded condoms. Nice.

"According to records, the original mill on this site was built in 1837," Lyle said, in his precise way. "It was burned down in the Civil War. This one was erected using the original foundation in 1869, shut down at one point, then restarted in the 1890s. The steel rollers were, unfortunately, removed during World War II to be melted down. We do have some of the other equipment in storage."

"Huh."

Lyle's mouth tightened, making him look as if he was sucking on a lemon. "This land is owned by Aaron Hershberger, who is Amish. Although he isn't farming this strip, he is reluctant to sell any part of the land. He doesn't want a tourist site right next door, he says."

Ben wasn't about to say so, but he could sympathize. The Amish were tourist attractions themselves. They might take advantage of that fact commercially— their fine furniture, quilts and other products were profitable—but they had to be annoyed by the outright nosiness of visitors who didn't respect personal boundaries. Ben didn't know Hershberger, but he'd noticed the farm as he passed, with dairy cows grazing in a pasture, an extensive orchard, several acres of what Ben thought might be raspberries, neatly tied in rows, and a handsome huge barn with a gambrel roof and stone foundation. If the mill became starred on maps, he'd have a steady stream of cars passing his place and a lot of strangers tramping through these woods. Maybe through his fields, too, in a quest to get an up-close look at a "real" Amish farm.

Lyle planted his hands on his hips and gazed yearningly at the crumbling brick walls and burbling creek overhung with maples, sycamore trees, dogwoods and some others Ben didn't recognize. "The fool is too shortsighted to recognize how critical historic preservation is. If we dawdle another five or ten years, this site might be lost to intrusive vegetation and the teenagers who obviously use it for…for…"

Ben hadn't noticed any drug paraphernalia, only cigarette butts and beer cans, or he would have planned to speak to the Henness County sheriff, Daniel Byler. But what was going on here… Kids would be kids.

Of course, all he'd had to worry about was an unstable transient climbing in the same broken window he had. Here, the mill looked like a great hangout for cottonmouths and rattlesnakes.

"I don't suppose you came out here to look at the mill," Lyle said, shoving his hands in his pants' pockets.

"You're right. I didn't. I need to ask you some questions about yesterday's event."

He frowned. "I was told it went well."

"It did. Very well." Ben barely hesitated. "However, the proceeds were stolen during the night from the volunteer who had taken them home."

Lyle blinked a couple times. "Stolen? But…how?"

"It would appear somebody waltzed into the woman's bedroom and helped him or herself to the money box."

The guy took a step back. "But…why are you talking to *me*?"

Did he receive a salary from the historical society? Ben found himself wondering. Even if he did, the odds were it wasn't much. Did he have family money? Lyle might have the mannerisms of an elderly man, but he wasn't more than mid to late forties. He could be struggling financially, but didn't want to lose his status by quitting the historical society gig. Or…was he passionate enough about his cause to steal to benefit the historical society? Say, to buy this piece of property? Would he be making Aaron Hershberger a new, higher offer soon?

"Because I understand you were in and out last night," Ben said. "I'm compiling a list of who was present, particularly locals, and thought you might be able to add to it."

"Oh." His features slackened briefly in what Ben took for relief. "Well, it's true I've had people remark on how observant I am. I suppose…"

Ben suggested they walk and talk, so they made their way back to the cars. A couple of names did pop up in Lyle's recollections that surprised Ben a little. Lyle was quite sure no one had asked him about the money.

"Why would they? I didn't know anything about it. I don't even know who took it home." He unlocked his car door and opened it, stepping behind it as if to put a barrier between him and Ben.

"I'll bet you could make a good guess," Ben suggested, trying to keep the dryness from his voice. "Observant as you are."

"Well…" Lyle appeared briefly pleased. "I suppose I would have assumed that Ms. Markovic had it. She'd taken responsibility for locking up, you know, which means she was the last out. And she *was* in charge of the whole event."

"You're right. It was Ms. Markovic who was robbed."

His forehead creased. "She wasn't hurt, was she?"

"No, in fact. She never knew she had an intruder until she woke up this morning and found the money gone."

"That's…well, it's dreadful. So much work went into it. I never did hear how much money they raised."

That sounded genuine, although Ben took almost everything with a grain of salt. Which might be one reason his personal life was so lacking.

"Just over a hundred and twenty thousand dollars."

"Oh, my. Oh, my."

"That's one way to put it." Ben gave himself a shake. "I need to be going." He pulled a card out of his shirt pocket and extended it. "Here's my number. If you think of anyone you didn't mention, hear any rumors, please give me a call. It's my hope we can recover this money."

"That would certainly be best," Lyle agreed.

When Ben drove away, Lyle hadn't moved. He still stood beside his car, looking after Ben's marked BPD unit, his thoughts well hidden.

NADIA RETURNED TO her shop midafternoon to find her one full-time employee, Hannah Yoder, answering questions from two women whose clothing and colorful tote bags labeled them as tourists.

Nadia greeted the women and chatted briefly with them before deciding neither was serious about buying a quilt. Truth was, they were probably enjoying interacting with a real Amish person. She excused herself and went upstairs. She ought to leave her purse and go back down, even let Hannah go home, but what if people came into the store because they were excited about the auction? Or, worse, because they'd heard about the missing money and wanted to judge whether she was guilty or innocent for themselves?

All the more reason to hide up here.

With a sigh, she sank into a chair at her table and massaged her forehead and temples, pressing hard to counteract the pain that had been building all day. Her neck hurt, too, as did her shoulders. Tension made her feel as if she'd been stretched on a medieval rack.

She'd talked to—she had to count—nine people today, the ones she felt obligated to tell in person. Mostly volunteers, several quilters and the head of the relief organization that was to have funneled the money to the homeowners and farmers most in need of help.

The four Amish women had, while shocked and dismayed, also seemed genuinely distressed for Nadia. They had, one and all, plied her with sympathy and food.

Bill Jarvis, from the relief organization, had all but reeled, as if she'd struck him. "But…we had such hopes," he said, leaving her almost speechless. With the best intentions in the world, she had let so many people down. Bill didn't seem to blame her, at least, not yet; given a little time, he might circle around to anger.

Of the remaining women Nadia had told, one had been openly sympathetic, one scathing and two on the fence. If those were her odds, she'd be posting an out-of-business sign within a couple of months. Her Amish shoppers might stick with her, but her biggest competition was a nice, Amish-owned fabric store in Hadburg, the next-largest town in the county, and closer to where most members of the faith lived. Many worked in or owned businesses in Byrum, but their ideal was rural living and Nadia knew of only a few who had homes or apartments in town. She wouldn't even want the Amish to entirely abandon the Hadburg store just to support her.

Of course, going out of business was only one option. Another was the possibility of being arrested.

Now she was just being pathetic. How could Chief Slater arrest her? She didn't have the money. Full stop.

So now what? she asked herself drearily.

Help him to the best of her ability, even if the man had disturbed her both times they'd met, although for different reasons. And what she could actually *do* to help was a mystery.

When a knock on the door at the foot of the stairs came, Nadia pushed herself wearily to her feet.

Instead of Hannah, a man stood there patiently waiting. Medium height and thin, he had light brown hair graying at his temples and a face too lined for what she guessed to be his age.

"Ms. Markovic?" he said. "I'm Jim Wilcox." When she apparently looked blank, he tapped the embroidered insignia on his shirt. "Wilcox Lock and Key?"

"Oh! Oh, yes. Thank you for coming."

"You said you had a break-in?"

"Actually, what we suspect is that the intruder had a key."

He frowned. "Well, first thing I'd suggest is that this interior door require a different key than the front and back doors. I put these locks in myself, had to be seven or eight years ago. I suggested the same to Mrs. Jefferson, but she didn't want to be bothered to have to figure out which key went to which door."

"I actually meant to get this lock changed when I first moved in," she admitted, "just because it opens to my private living space. I've had so much else to do, though, and really the only other person who has a key is Hannah Yoder—"

"Who is trustworthy." He nodded. "Even so…"

"Even so," Nadia agreed.

"You want me to replace all three locks."

"Yes."

He backed up a step. "I'll get started then." But he didn't keep going. Instead, he cleared his throat. "I hope you weren't home when you had the break-in. I mean, that you weren't hurt or…frightened."

"I slept through it," she said wryly. "But I was scared to death come morning when I realized he'd been *right there*—" She cut herself off with a shudder.

"I'm real sorry, Ms. Markovic." He looked truly distressed, but Nadia had found most people in her new community to be kind. Or, she had until today.

She smiled with difficulty. "Thank you, Mr. Wilcox. I appreciate you coming so quickly."

He bobbed his head awkwardly and retreated, presumably going out to his truck to get the new locks and whatever tools he needed.

Nadia made herself go into the store, where she found a trio of women she knew.

"Is it true?" one of them said right away.

She had to say, "Unfortunately."

FRUSTRATED, BEN DECIDED to go by and talk to Nadia again before he called it a day. She might have learned something, or at least that's what he told himself. The underlying truth was that he wanted to find out how people had reacted to her disclosure. She'd gotten to him this morning, when she had explained why she needed to start over in a new place. He hadn't been able to help thinking about the parallels with his sister in her lengthy recovery from the assault that shattered her life, and hoped everyone Nadia talked to had at least been decent to her.

Online, he hadn't had any trouble finding articles about the horrific episode when she'd been shot. Turned out, she'd given him a very condensed version. It sounded like a real nightmare, and one that had gone on for hours. He also learned that she'd spent those hours using her body to protect the little girl, somehow keeping her quiet after she regained consciousness. Nadia had saved young Molly's life. She was labeled a heroine in news coverage. He'd seen a picture snapped from a distance away of her being brought out of the house on a gurney. The cops and EMTs in the photo all looked grim in a way Ben recognized. The sight of murdered children scarred the most hardened cop. And to know their own father had killed them…

He shook his head in denial, even though he knew better. Fathers, and mothers, too, regularly hurt and killed their own children.

Nadia was closing up when he arrived. She let him in, then turned the sign on the door to Closed. His gaze went to the shiny new dead bolt lock.

"I see Jim has been here."

"Yes. I don't think he charged me enough. He seemed to feel bad about what happened."

"Yeah, he was pretty upset when Mrs. Jefferson died, too."

"He told me he recommended she replace the lock on the apartment door, but she didn't want to be bothered with two different keys."

Ben nodded. "Jim felt guilty that he hadn't insisted."

"Wait." She gaped at him. "Do you actually think someone *killed* her? That she didn't just fall down the stairs?"

"I'm sure she was pushed," he said grimly.

"But…how can you know?"

"Because her head hit the wall a lot higher than it could have if she'd fallen. We found blood and hair in the dent. It took some real force to launch her up instead of down. The ME agrees, too. People who fall bump down the stairs, but her injuries are consistent with the greater force theory."

"Oh, no," she whispered.

He kept a snapshot of Edith Jefferson's body, just as he did one of every other crime victim he'd seen. Crumpled at the foot of the stairs, Edith had appeared shockingly tiny and hideously damaged.

He tried to shake off the picture. "It happened long before you came to town. What happened to her was personal. It had nothing to do with you."

"No, I know, but…" She shivered. "Even if she'd

changed that lock, it might not have made any difference."

"It might not have," he agreed. It stuck in his craw that he hadn't been able to make an arrest. Nothing had been stolen. Nobody seemed to have both motive to kill the old woman and opportunity. He hadn't closed the case, though, and wouldn't. He sure hoped this current investigation didn't end up in a similar limbo. So far, it wasn't looking good. "So, how'd your day go?" he asked.

She told him, but he had a feeling this was the condensed version, too. Her face was pinched, her luminous eyes clouded. It was especially disturbing because he'd seen her glowing on the stage last night as she thanked everyone. The contrast was painful.

She might have taken the money, he reminded himself, but couldn't quite believe it. Okay, didn't want to believe it.

He threw out names of people he had been told were there last night. Turned out several were playing a behind-the-scenes role or had good reason to be attending. A couple of the names had her shaking her head.

"I don't know any of them. Or, if I've met them, I didn't catch their names."

She didn't invite him up to her apartment, and since he hadn't come up with anything else to ask her, Ben finally said, "I'll bet you haven't eaten today."

Expression mulish, she retorted, "You made me have breakfast, remember?"

"A croissant. Did you stop for lunch?"

Her lips compressed.

"You may not feel like eating," he said quietly, "but

you need to make yourself. And take something for that headache."

Nadia stiffened. "How did you know?"

"You have all the signs." He knew he could have massaged some of that pain away, but he couldn't let himself put his hands on her. As the last person to have the money, she remained a suspect.

"You're right." She sagged slightly. "I'll follow your advice. I promise."

He left on that note. On the drive home, he called to let his dispatcher know where he'd be, then made another call to order a pizza for pickup.

Usually by the end of a day, he was sick enough of people to relish a few hours of solitude. Tonight, his house felt strangely lonely when he finally let himself in.

For once, he was glad when his phone rang shortly after he'd cleaned up when he was done eating, and especially when he saw the name displayed. His sister. Odd timing, when she'd been on his mind so much the past few days.

"Lucy."

"Hey," she said. "Did I get you at a good time?"

"Yep. Just had pizza and I was thinking of kicking back and watching some baseball. How are you?" He made the question sound light, but it wasn't. It never was. While he was in college, Lucy, only about a year and a half older than him, had been brutally raped and left for dead. The rapist was never identified and arrested. She was the reason Ben had changed his major from prelaw to criminology.

Lucy had remained…fragile. She was gutsy enough to move into an apartment of her own despite their parents' opposition, and she held a job, but to his knowledge she never dated, probably never went out at night, which limited any friendships. She lived a half life, because she could never forget. He saw hints of the same vulnerability in Nadia, but also more strength.

"I'm okay," his sister said now. "But I was thinking."

Ben waited.

"Would you mind if I came for a visit?" she said in a rush.

Traveling was something else she didn't do.

Hiding his surprise, he said, "What, you think I'll say no? I've only been trying to talk you into coming since the day I moved."

"I know. Something happened that shook me up—nothing big, just the usual—" which meant she'd had a panic attack "—and, you know, I've been reading about your part of Missouri. I'd like to see it."

"It's pretty country, but not spectacular."

"I'm curious about the Amish. They sound so gentle."

Ben had his suspicions that behind the facade even the Amish had their share of drunks and spousal and child abuse, but he had to admit that on the whole the ones he'd dealt with were straightforward, good-humored and honest. Their belief in forgiveness was profound. Okay, he still had trouble believing an Amish woman who had suffered what Lucy had could truly forgive her rapist. But then, he was a cynic.

"They seem like good people," he agreed. "Individuals, just like any other group."

"Yes. I just thought..." Lucy hesitated. "I don't know. That Byrum sounds like a nice place. Even..."

He braced himself. Don't let her say *safe*.

What she did say was almost worse. "Peaceful," she finished.

He remembered what Nadia had said, word for word. *I had something traumatic happen. I couldn't get past it. I thought making a change would help.*

She'd sought peace here, too, and hadn't found it.

"I'm a cop," he said, his voice coming out rough. "They hired me for a reason, Lucy."

"I know, but it's not the same as what you dealt with here, is it?"

The hope in her voice just about killed him.

"No." What could he say but, "When are you coming?"

She *would* be safer here. She'd have him, and nobody would hurt Lucy on his watch.

She never forgot, and neither did he.

CHAPTER FOUR

AT LEAST, WITH today being Sunday, Nadia didn't have to open her store. Too bad she had to spend her day doing something worse than facing the avidly nosy and the angry in person. Instead, she was going to call every single person who'd written a check or used a credit card for a purchase at Friday's event. Karen Llewellyn had offered to help, the reluctance in her voice only part of why Nadia had insisted on handling the entire task herself. The main reason was her sense of responsibility. She'd lost the money. To the extent she could, Nadia vowed to face the unpleasant consequences alone.

She knew a few attendees, and was well aware that some calls would prove more difficult than others. *Difficult* being a euphemism, of course.

Strictly alphabetical was the only way to go, she decided.

With a cup of tea steeping at her elbow, she opened her laptop and began. Her very first call was to the woman she'd added as a walk-in last night, Louise Alsobrook.

"Oh, you poor dear!" was the first thing Ms. Alsobrook exclaimed after Nadia's stiff explanation. "Didn't *somebody* among your volunteers have a safe?"

"Unfortunately, no," Nadia said. "And really…I

don't think any of us dreamed of something like this happening. The community has been so supportive. I've been involved with charity events in a larger city before and nobody worried about securing the money until the bank opened."

"Greed can happen anywhere," the woman said practically. "Well, I just looked online, and the charge to my credit card hasn't been presented. I'll ask my credit card company to put a stop on this number and issue a new card. In the meantime, I'll put a check in the mail for the same amount, or even some extra. Because a lot of what's gone must have been cash, wasn't it?"

"Yes, unfortunately. Thank you so much, Ms. Alsobrook," Nadia said fervently. "This is…such a nightmare, and you've been very kind."

"Oh, honey, I know all of you worked so hard. Now, should I send it straight to the aid organization?"

"Yes, please." She asked that Ms. Alsobrook add a note to let Bill Jarvis know that it was a replacement for the stolen credit card slip. He'd agreed to keep track so that the auction organizers knew who had sent money and how much.

"I'll send that check first thing tomorrow," Ms. Alsobrook promised.

Eyes stinging, Nadia ended the call, made a note and allowed herself a few sips of tea before she reached for the phone again.

ARMS CROSSED ATOP the white-painted fence, Ben watched foals with legs too long and spindly for their bodies gamboling in the field as their mothers grazed placidly. Gary Edgerton bred, raised and trained horses destined to be harness racers or to pull an Amish buggy. His wife was the quilt enthusiast, but both had attended the auction and spent a substantial amount.

Having heard approaching footsteps, Ben wasn't surprised when a man's voice came from behind him.

"A lot of money on the hoof."

Ben turned to see Edgerton watching him rather than the mares and foals. "Cute little buggers," Ben commented. "How old are they?"

"A couple weeks old up to three months. The last few brood mares are due any day."

Ben knew next to nothing about horses. He'd never thrown a leg over one in his life, although he'd now ridden in a buggy and had become accustomed to the splats of manure decorating the streets of his town, as well as to the hitching rails as common as they would have been in the nineteenth century.

"Why the age spread?" he asked. "I thought foals were born in spring."

"Mares don't all come into season at the same time. Some breedings don't take, so we have to wait until she's ready again for a second go-around."

Edgerton offered a tour, but Ben asked for a rain check.

"Guess you go at it hard when this much money is missing," the guy remarked.

"Ms. Markovic called?"

"This morning. She and Allison had words."

"And why is that?"

The horseman snorted. "Woman comes out of no-where, charms her way into taking the lead on the auction, leaves with the money and, oh, oops, reports it stolen the next morning. You're in the wrong job if you're credulous enough to believe crap that smells a lot worse than my manure pile."

From long practice, Ben hid his irritation successfully. "Allison thinks the same?"

"Yes!" Expression bullish, Edgerton glared at Ben. "Slick a scheme as any I've ever heard of."

"She put a lot of money into starting that business," he said mildly. "Sure, Ms. Markovic would walk away with some money, maybe sixty, seventy thousand in cash. But if most people think the same as you and your wife, her business will go under. I don't think she'd come out of it much, if any, ahead."

"Sixty thousand bucks on top of what she recovers by selling the building and the business? That's not a bad take. And then she can move on, pull the same stunt somewhere else."

Unwilling to argue the point, because, yes, he was already considering that very scenario, however unlikely he believed it to be, Ben steered him to recollections of Friday. Mrs. Edgerton had attended the quilt sale earlier in the day Friday and spent money there as well as a larger amount at the evening auction. Edgerton offered the names of a few people who weren't already on Ben's list but sneered at the idea that any of them would steal.

"These are folks who have lived around here their whole lives," he insisted, as if that was all Ben needed to know about them.

Choosing not to point out that he'd arrested more than a few longtime residents for crimes ranging from misdemeanor shoplifting to rape and negligent homicide, Ben ascertained that the missus was up at the house and went to talk to her.

She was even more sharper-tongued than her husband had been. Ben drove away without having learned anything useful, but with a sour taste in his mouth and a cramp of pity for what Nadia must be experiencing.

There were more people he should talk to, but he was increasingly doubtful that he'd learn anything new. He needed to get a more complete list of volunteers from Nadia… With a grimace, he corrected himself. He should get that list from Julie Baird or Katie-Ann Chupp. Because, much as he disliked the idea, Nadia remained his only potential suspect right now. Katie-Ann—yeah, he could count on her for complete honesty. But this, if memory served him right, was church Sunday for the Amish. With no child missing, no dead body, he couldn't justify bothering her before tomorrow.

BEN HAD WORKED before with Tricia Mears, the deputy prosecuting attorney who was waiting for him at the station. Thanking her for coming, he escorted her to his office. As soon as he shut the door, she said, "I have your warrant."

He needed to search Nadia's financial records, something that also would have to wait until morning, when banks opened. If she really was a thief, she'd hardly be brazen enough to deposit the money. If she found a secure enough hiding place, she could filter the cash slowly into her finances with no one having a clue.

"You drag a judge out of church to get this signed today?" he asked.

Maybe in her late twenties, tiny and blonde, she grinned. "Wouldn't dare. But I was parked in Judge Greenhaw's driveway when he arrived home after church. He asked if this couldn't have waited, but he didn't seem to really mind. And, like everyone else in town, he already knew about the theft."

"Did he have an opinion, too?" Ben asked drily.

"Hadn't had occasion to meet her, he said, but he understood why you had to look at her first."

"Thanks for getting right on this," Ben said.

Vibrating with energy, she perched on the edge of the seat she'd taken across the desk from him. "Anything else I can do for you?"

"Not yet. What I'd like is to find out where everyone who attended that auction stands financially, but I kind of doubt Greenhaw would go for such a sweeping warrant."

"That's safe to say." She rose to her feet. "Unless you'd like to…well, throw around ideas, I need to show my face at my grandparents' for Sunday dinner."

He waved her off. "Go."

Only a few minutes later, someone knocked on his door. When he called, "Come in," Officer Danny Carroll entered.

In his early thirties, stocky and stolid, Carroll had demonstrated the kind of judgment and work ethic that put him at the top of a short list for promotion. Today, he and Riley Boyd had gone to Nadia's block to speak to the neighbors who hadn't been home yesterday.

Ben leaned back in his desk chair. "Anything?"

"I found one woman, a Laura Kelling, who saw a light in Ms. Markovic's place during the night Friday. She'd gotten up to go to the bathroom, but has no idea what time."

Wonderful. "Overhead light?"

"She was uncertain about that. She lives across the street, but a few doors down. Not a perfect angle. She said the light was diffuse, just a glow coming from somewhere inside, downstairs. She claims it went out while she was watching."

"So something about it caught her eye," Ben said thoughtfully.

"That's my take," Carroll agreed.

"And she couldn't pin down the time at all."

"She went to bed at about ten because she needed to be up by six yesterday morning. She admits to getting up at least once, sometimes twice a night."

"Ms. Markovic was home just after midnight. Is it likely this Ms. Kelling would have needed to use the bathroom that quick?"

Officer Carroll shrugged. "Depends when she cut off liquids for the night."

That was true, unfortunately. Ben could imagine a defense attorney trying to persuade a jury that the witness's bladder would have held out longer than two hours and that, therefore, the light she saw had shone inside what should have been a dark building well after Ms. Markovich had gone to sleep.

After which the prosecutor would point out that they had only Ms. Markovic's word for when she turned out the lights and went to sleep, and that it was entirely possible she had gotten out of bed at some point during the night to hide the money in a location the police were unlikely to find in any initial search.

Something he probably should have had done yesterday, he reflected, although he had taken precautions to ensure she couldn't sneak the money out of the building and hide it elsewhere.

"Okay, thanks," Ben said. "Have you spoken to everybody?"

"Yep. Sundays are good that way."

Left alone again, Ben realized he was disappointed. He would have liked incontrovertible evidence to turn up showing that someone besides Nadia had taken the money. And he knew better than to develop feelings for a suspect, far less allow sympathy or any other emotion to influence him. Because of his usual objectivity, he'd been called cold; no one outside his family having any idea how much rage burned in him for one particular class of criminals. He'd succeeded in hiding it from the people he worked with until the day he came so close to crossing a line that would have ended his career and conceivably resulted in jail time.

The hatred for rapists was one explanation for why his blood boiled every time he pictured a man slipping uninvited into Nadia's bedroom, detouring from his main purpose to look his fill.

Statistically, the odds were that the thief was a man. In this case, the auction volunteers, who were most likely to know who had the money, were all women except for a few men dragged in to assemble the stage, do some heavy lifting and build quilt display racks. Imagining a woman in Nadia's bedroom instead of a man wasn't a big improvement. Either way, what sense of security she'd gathered around herself after the tragedy would be stolen again.

Unless, of course, nobody else had ever stepped foot in that bedroom, and she knew exactly where the money was.

He wondered whether she'd give permission for a thorough search of her premises.

Ben groaned, rasped a hand over his jaw and decided to call it a day.

NADIA ENDED THE day feeling battered. Sick to her stomach, bruised from head to toe. Remembering Ben Slater's chiding, she dragged herself to her kitchen and examined the contents of the cupboards and refrigerator. She'd skipped lunch and had no appetite for dinner, but he was right—she had to eat. Even a salad felt like too much work, so she settled for cottage cheese and a small bowl of strawberries. Finally, new lock or no, she carried a kitchen chair downstairs and braced it under the doorknob. In theory, there'd be an awful noise at the very least if someone tried to open the door.

Nadia watched TV shows that didn't really interest her until it was late enough to go to bed. If she'd had a sedative, she would have taken it. After very little sleep last night, she was mind-numbingly tired. But once she climbed into bed, lights out, she lay stiffly. The nausea soothed by her bland meal returned with a vengeance. As if she'd recorded today's phone conversations, they replayed in her head, some voices heavy with disappointment, others sharp. A few vicious.

Have you no shame?

I suppose you think we're country hicks, too dumb to see through your little story.

I won't be buying so much as a spool of thread at your shop again, and I hope every other woman in this county feels the same.

Plenty of people had been neutral, promising to let her know if the credit card had been run or check cashed. Perhaps half had promised to replace the money. A very small minority had been, like Louise Alsobrook, really nice.

Of course, it was what the nasty people said that was stuck in her head.

Nadia tried with the "sticks and stones may break my bones" thing, but still felt like an old woman when she opened the store come morning. Thank heavens she didn't have to teach a class today! She hoped makeup, applied more heavily than usual, disguised some of the signs of her exhaustion, especially the purple bruising beneath her eyes. The fact that her eyes appeared sunken…well, there wasn't anything she could do about that. Plus, her head ached, blinking almost took more effort than she could summon and she wasn't sure the muscles that would allow her to smile were functioning.

But this was the one day of the week she had no help, and the sign out front listed open hours that included Mondays, ten to five. If anything of her new life was to be saved, she couldn't hide in her apartment.

Mondays were the slowest days, businesswise, so she wasn't surprised, and was almost relieved, that no one at all came in to browse until after eleven. Then it was a husband and wife she pegged immediately as tourists. They exclaimed over the displayed quilts, gasped at the prices and bought a set of machine-quilted place mats.

Her next visitor was Colleen Hoefling, who wanted to hear what, if anything, the police had learned, and who purchased fabric for her next quilt, or so she said. Nadia suspected Colleen, like most serious quilters, already owned enough fabric for her next ten or twenty quilts. She was simply being nice.

Colleen also shooed Nadia upstairs to get some lunch, insisting she knew how to use a cash register.

After eating, Nadia came down to the sound of voices.

The first was scathing. "And who do you think stole the money if it *wasn't* her?"

"I don't know," Colleen said, hers distinctly cool, "but I'm appalled at the rush to judgment I'm seeing. Nadia has been nothing but friendly. She's warm and likable. Do you have any idea how much time she gave to make the auction a success? I'm not sure it would have happened at all without her." She talked right over the other woman, whose voice Nadia had recognized. Peggy Montgomery, whose consigned quilt was currently starring in the front window display. "What's more, Nadia is a fine businesswoman with a good eye for color. With the way she's selling our quilts online, she's giving all of us opportunities we haven't had."

"*And* making a sizable commission."

"This *is* her business. I, for one, am a terrible saleswoman."

Continuing to lurk out here made her a coward. Nadia girded herself and entered the store.

"Peggy," she said with a smile that probably looked ghastly, but was the best she could do, "how nice to see you. Is there anything I can help you with?"

"Thank you, but no," she said stiffly. "I just wanted a word with Colleen." She turned and strode out the door.

Nadia waited until it closed behind her before she turned to Colleen. "I expected more people like her today." She wrinkled her nose. "What am I saying? I'm nowhere near halfway through the day. There's plenty of time."

"You heard her?"

This smile felt genuine. "And you. Thank you for the defense."

Colleen shook her head. "I don't know what's wrong with everyone. Peggy is a good example. She's a nice woman. This wasn't like her."

"I'm the newcomer. The outsider." Nadia had figured out that much Saturday. "Painting me evil is better than imagining someone you've known all your life stealing money that would have helped struggling people hold on to their land or rebuild."

The other woman sniffed. "I've lived around here all my life, and *I* have no trouble imagining a few of my neighbors feeling justified in doing whatever they pleased."

Nadia was laughing when the bell on the front door clanged. She turned to meet a pair of very dark eyes. Ben Slater wore his uniform today, a badge on his chest and his holstered gun at his hip. The visible weapon had the usual effect.

Her laugh had already died before she saw his stone face. "Chief Slater."

He bent his head. "Ms. Markovic. Mrs. Hoefling."

"I'm happy to stay a little longer, if you need to speak to Nadia," Colleen offered.

"That would be helpful," he said. "Perhaps we could go upstairs, Ms. Markovic?"

As chilled as she was by the expressionless way he was looking at her, Nadia didn't see that she had any choice. She thanked Colleen and led the police chief through the side door. She sidled by the chair she'd left at the foot of the stairs, since she had every intention of bracing it in place again tonight—and every night, for the foreseeable future. She didn't look back to see what Ben Slater thought about her primitive defense.

In the small living room, she faced him, chin high.

She couldn't make herself ask how she could help him. Hating her awareness of him, she just waited.

"I'm here to ask if you would permit a full search of this building without my getting a warrant first."

"I feel sure you wouldn't have any trouble getting one," she said bitterly. "Given the local consensus on my guilt."

Something flickered in his eyes, but he said only, "You must realize this is something I need to do."

Nadia crossed her arms. "Shouldn't you have done it Saturday? Over the weekend, I could have taken the money box anyplace."

He didn't say a word. His expression stayed impassive. She stared at him, understanding embarrassingly slow to come.

"You've had me watched. Did somebody *follow* me Saturday?"

"I'm doing my job."

Air rushed out in what felt too much like a sob, but she clung to her dignity—and her anger and despair. "Do you know what it will do to my business once word gets out that the police suspect me to the point of searching my premises?"

"The sooner we can clear you," he said woodenly, "the sooner your reputation will be restored."

Her laugh was caustic. "What a nice, positive spin! I suppose practice makes perfect. I guess all that experience is why they made you chief."

The only satisfaction he gave her was the tightening of his jaw muscles and some tension at the corners of his eyes.

"When do you plan to do this search?"

"If you agree, immediately."

Nadia was so law-abiding, she'd never so much as gotten a traffic ticket. The police officers who spoke to her after the shooting in Colorado had admired what they called her bravery. Now, seared by humiliation, she wanted to tell Ben Slater to get a warrant. *I should have hired an attorney*, she realized. She would, first thing tomorrow morning. But not anyone local.

Knowing her cheeks were burning red, she said, "Fine. Do it."

He took a step closer. Lines deepened on his forehead and his voice came out rough. "This is not meant to suggest we believe you stole the money."

"No? What other homes and businesses are you also searching?"

"You know there aren't any yet."

"I didn't think so. If you'll escort me downstairs, I'll let Colleen go home. I'd just as soon no friends were here to watch."

Nadia walked past him, pride all that held her together. She heard his tread on the stairs right behind her. Naturally. He couldn't let her out of sight, in case she tried to move her stash.

Alone in the store, Colleen had been studying a quilt hung on the back wall. Her eyes widened. "Nadia?"

"I'm fine. Thank you for staying, but I think I'll close up now."

"I'm sure people will understand." Colleen obviously didn't, but she knew not to ask questions. "Call me anytime, okay?"

"I will." Nadia gave her a swift hug and retreated before she could burst into tears. "Thank you."

The other woman gathered her purse and bag full of fabric and thread, leaving after a last, worried look over her shoulder. Nadia hastened after her, flipping the sign to Closed and locking the door.

"Make your calls," she said, with frozen dignity, and went to the back room to sit in front of the quilting frame. With her hands shaking, she couldn't so much as thread a needle, far less work on the half-finished Bear's Paw quilt in the frame.

She heard Slater's voice, coming from just outside the doorway. Which probably meant he hadn't taken his eyes off her for a moment. "It's a go," he told someone. "I'll wait here for you."

CHAPTER FIVE

"If you'll allow us to search your car, I see no reason you have to be present while we're doing this," Ben said.

The woman sitting in the back room didn't even look at him. She'd gone deep inside; if he weren't watching carefully, he wouldn't have been able to tell she was even breathing. Horrified, he wondered if this was how she'd escaped a second bullet during the hours when she'd pretended to be dead.

"You wish," she said coldly.

"What?"

"I'm staying."

Ben almost stepped back, in case icicles had actually formed in the air. "Why?" he asked.

At last Nadia's head turned, and her gaze was the furthest thing from icy. Her magnificent eyes burned. "I intend to document every bit of damage you and your men do."

He might have taken offense, except he couldn't deny damage did sometimes occur. He knew of instances where a search left a house trashed. He'd never allow that, but in an old building like this, boards might have to be pried up. In the shop, the bolts of fabric sat on some kind of wood base. They had to be hollow, which meant his team would need to look inside however they could. Display quilts would be lifted or removed from walls in case Nadia had added a safe or cubbyhole beneath one. Nearly every possession she had, upstairs and down, would be handled. He couldn't help feeling some dismay when he looked at the hundreds of bolts of fabric. This space would be a nightmare to search. He'd remind people to wear gloves to avoid dirtying fabric that would then have to be cut off the bolt and discarded. And there were the quilts he now knew were each worth hundreds to thousands of dollars.

"My team will be here any minute."

Nadia turned her head away and stared straight ahead, although he knew she wasn't focused on anything. She couldn't see out to the alley through the large window, because a filmy blind covered it.

For just a minute, he looked at her straight back, squared shoulders and the pale skin and delicate vertebrae on her nape, visible beneath a heavy mass of gleaming dark hair confined in some mysterious fashion. Her complete stillness disturbed him anew. He couldn't see her forgiving him for this.

He had to do his job.

Teeth clenched, he left her, reaching the front of the store to see his sole crime scene investigator about to rap on the glass door. The couple officers Terry Uhrich had trained to assist him were only a few steps behind. Ben let them in.

"Ms. Markovic has chosen to stay," he said in a low voice. He nodded toward the back. "She's in there."

Uhrich didn't look happy. "You told her to keep out of the way?"

"I think she understands." Her sense of dignity

wouldn't allow her to do anything so crude as to physically obstruct the searchers. But they would, one and all, end up ashamed of themselves for intruding so unforgivably. Ben remembered her horror at the idea of a man studying her sleeping, nearly nude body, and knew what he was doing to her was worse. Did he really believe he was doing what he had to? Or was that simplistic crap, justifying the fact that his investigation had gone absolutely nowhere? Right this minute, he was at war with himself.

They started with her car, parked in the alley, in case she changed her mind and decided to flee. Ben, of course, remained inside with her. Terry decided then to do the apartment, undoubtedly hoping Nadia would take refuge in it once they were done.

She followed the three men upstairs, Ben trailing behind, and stood in the middle of the living room with her arms crossed, glaring at each man in turn as they searched her kitchen cupboards, refrigerator and freezer and antique buffet holding dishes. The two officers pulled out the refrigerator; one crawled beneath her table while the other lifted each chair to peer beneath the seat. Cushions were removed from the sofa and armchair, and both were turned over in case wads of money were stuffed between the springs.

Ben was tempted to help, just to speed up the process, but his role as lead detective was to make sure the search was thorough, clean and fell within legal parameters. Anyway, what was he going to do? Sift through her lingerie? Study the contents of her medicine cabinet and bathroom vanity? All he'd do is make any future conversations with her even more difficult. Instead, he had to watch as she lost every shred of privacy and yet clung to both dignity and fury.

Mercifully, his men managed to finish up here without doing any damage. They even, more or less, put everything back in place. The relative care they took didn't make Ben feel any better. His gut roiled as they continued with the necessary task.

The downstairs took hours. Just the peculiar closet beneath the stairs consumed an inordinate amount of time. It was jammed with plastic totes, all labeled, but each had to be opened, the contents examined. Nadia had installed cupboards and open shelves in the back room for some storage, but she needed most of the space for the quilt frame and to hold classes, so she had to live with the inconvenience of the oddly shaped closet. It must be a pain in the butt when she needed to find something that wasn't right in front.

Once they moved on to the store proper, Ben stepped into the hall where he could see the proceedings and Nadia while also making phone calls and checking email. He learned exactly how much money she had in checking and savings accounts as well as an investment account. Given her mortgage, he doubted she had enough put away to allow her to hold out six months if sales in her store tanked. Not at all to his surprise, there had been no suspect deposits.

Suddenly, she exclaimed in anger and anguish, "You can't put those on the *floor*! Do you know the work that went into them?"

Ben hustled into the store to see Officer Ackley straightening with an armful of quilts, expression chagrined. "But…we have to take them down, ma'am."

"Lay them carefully over a row of fabric, or hand

them to me and I'll find a place to put them temporarily. This one was made by Ruth Graber. Do you know her?"

Ben knew *of* her. The elderly Amish woman had lost her husband last fall. As it happened, the county sheriff, Daniel Byler, had married Ruth's granddaughter Rebecca in November. Who knew how many more quilts she'd make? Ben had also seen the tiny price tag pinned to the one Officer Ackley had been about to drop onto the floor. Twenty-eight hundred dollars. He cringed to imagine a dirty footprint in the middle of an intricately hand-quilted white block.

He stepped forward to take the quilt from Ackley, making a point of twitching the tiny price tag into view. The officer's eyes widened.

Watching, Terry Uhrich shook his head and went back to inspecting walls.

Ben turned to find Nadia had resumed her rigid stance. Unfortunately, she'd crossed her arms, plumping her breasts above them. He had trouble dragging his gaze from the sight.

"You have to be beat," he said in exasperation. "Why don't you go lie down? I'll keep an eye on them, I promise."

Not even looking at him, she said in a low, fierce voice, "You are the last person—" She shook her head, not finishing. She didn't have to.

He was the last person she would trust to look out for her interests. He couldn't blame her for feeling that way. She'd called the police for help, and, from her perspective, instead of looking for the real thief, they were subjecting her to this. They might as well have cuffed her, hauled her to the station and focused bright lights on her as they shouted questions.

He made a sound no one else would hear. *They?* Who was he kidding? In her head, the villain was *him*. And she wasn't even wrong—he had ordered this. He'd known they wouldn't find anything, any more than the warrant had turned up a grain of suspicious activity, and yet he still didn't know what else he could have done.

From what he was hearing, community opinion was solidifying against her. He wanted to be able to say, "Ms. Markovic is not a suspect." But would anyone believe him, after word got out about the search?

And it would—nobody had thought to lower the blinds in the front windows, and people had been peering in watching. A couple of times, the doorknob had rattled despite the closed sign. Nadia had kept her back to the windows, refusing to look at the curious.

Finally, Terry left his two men putting bolts of fabric back on the hollow bases and came to Ben and Nadia. "We're done, Ms. Markovic. I've lost track of which quilts hung where, but if you'll tell me, I'll be glad to put them back."

"I'd prefer you leave." Her voice was a husk of itself, dry and empty.

"But the ladders are out…"

She didn't say a word. Her gaze seemed fixed on a now bare wall.

Terry's eyes slid Ben's way. Ben gave his head a slight shake, and the other man sighed.

"Yeah, okay."

A minute later, the three left, the bell dangling on

the front door tinkling in their wake. Nadia didn't move, didn't speak.

"They didn't put the fabric back in the right order," he heard himself say. He didn't love the idea of her spending an hour or more perched precariously on a step stool while she rehung the quilts for sale, either.

At last she faced him, the devastation in her beautiful eyes acting like a kick to his belly.

"I assume you're satisfied?"

"I didn't expect to find the money. I told you."

"And yet you decided to ruin me. Because you haven't been able to come up with another suspect, I assume." When he held his silence, her lip curled. "Unless you have any other indignities to offer, you need to leave. I don't want you here."

He couldn't tell her what else he'd done, because he'd continue watching her financial dealings for the immediate future, just in case she now thought herself safe and deposited some of the money. When she found out, as she inevitably would… Yeah, she'd see that as another indignity.

"I regret having to put you through this," he said stiffly. "I can only tell you I was doing my job."

"I've lost everything." She looked around in despair.

"You haven't." He wanted to grip her upper arms and make her meet his eyes, but knew better. "You have supporters. People will realize you would never have stolen that money. Just…give them time."

"I can't afford to give them time," Nadia said in the dry voice that held no vitality. "And…do I want people who condemned me without a second thought to become good customers? They would have to pretend, and I'd have to pretend…" She shook her head. "I can't stay in Byrum, not after this. Whatever happened, I'll never dare call the police again, I know that."

"Nadia—"

She took a step back. "You've worn out your welcome."

Despite the renewed ice in her voice, he hesitated, but recognized he couldn't make this better. Not now, maybe never.

He dipped his head. "Things will look better tomorrow."

She didn't dignify that with any response whatsoever.

When he walked out, she immediately locked the door behind him. Ben got in his car, started the engine then tipped his head back and closed his eyes. *Things will look better tomorrow?* Had he really said that? Why would she feel one iota better come morning?

Muttering a foul word, he drove away without allowing himself a last glance at the storefront.

NADIA MADE IT upstairs to her own bathroom before she dropped to her knees in front of the toilet, her stomach heaving.

When her phone rang and she saw her parents' number, she let the call go to voice mail. They'd spent the past year worrying about her. She wouldn't give them a new reason. If they knew what was going on, they'd want to rush to Missouri to support her. As much as she loved both her parents, she couldn't bear their surreptitious monitoring of her every word and move, the false cheer, the constant little suggestions.

And look how well her escape had gone, she thought bleakly.

Her skin crawled as she thought about the day. She should have left. They'd done nothing but their jobs, even Ben Slater. She knew that. And yet her entire goal had been making them all feel guilty for what they were doing to her, as miserable as she possibly could.

Except she knew perfectly well they'd put her out of their minds by now. Any of them who were unmarried had probably stopped at a bar for a couple of beers and a game or two of pool once they clocked out. The married ones would have gone home to family chaos. And their chief? He'd done what he felt he had to, staying calm all day, and if he was a little ruffled by her contempt and pain, he would shrug it off.

She was the only one who couldn't. This was *her* life, or, at least, the one she'd been trying to patch together.

Some of this bitterness that edged toward hate had roots in Colorado, not present circumstances. But that was the only other time she'd *needed* the police, and they had failed her as completely as it was possible to do. So, no, she wasn't being fair, she knew she should hate the thief, not Chief Ben Slater, but she didn't care. It almost seemed as if he'd gone out of his way to make the search as conspicuous as possible. If he'd cared, he could have arranged it to be done after hours and not had multiple marked police vehicles sitting in front of her business. He could have pulled all the blinds.

But, no. He had likely intended for the search to be as visible as he could make it. *See? I listen to the citizens of my town. Watch me do my job, without regard to the woman I'm destroying.*

Feeling cold despite a sweltering temperature here

upstairs, she tried to shake off the debilitating effects of rage and humiliation so she could think clearly.

What was she going to do? Pack up and return to Colorado?

She revolted instinctively at that idea.

Okay, try to make yet another start somewhere else? She'd be able to do that only if she could fund the start by a quick sale of the building. Otherwise…even if she took a job after moving and found a new outlet for selling her quilts, she wouldn't be able to earn enough to make payments on her mortgage here while covering the rent wherever she found to live. Go bankrupt? Couldn't do that until she really did run out of money. What's more, bankruptcy would mean no possibility of getting a loan to start over.

Anyway, if she put a for sale sign out front, she would only increase Ben Slater's certainty that she had the money. If she was compelled to stay, for however many weeks, she had to keep opening the store every morning and hope she still had a few customers. At least she might bring in *some* income. It was safe to say nobody would hire her right now, making job hunting a non-option.

Panic joined the crowd of emotions elbowing for room inside her ribcage.

Nadia wanted desperately to run away. To pack a couple of bags and go. She could make long-distance arrangements for the quilts to be returned to their makers, for someone to clean out the apartment, to hire a real estate agent.

Her spine stiffened. She wouldn't run away again. Fail, have to move, maybe, but not quit when there was any possibility of salvaging what she'd built here in Missouri.

Making herself get practical, she decided she could get by for a while without replacing stock. No one would notice that the bolts of fabric were looser because no new fabric replaced what had sold. There might be stock in her store that could be returned to manufacturers, too, it occurred to her. Not much, she was afraid, but every little bit would help. The rest…she could donate it to Amish quilters. *My little bit of recompense*, she thought bitterly, remembering Julie Baird's suggestion.

Running the air conditioner after she went to bed so she could hide under the covers, Nadia made herself face reality.

Self-respect aside, taking off *would* make her look guilty. The smartest thing she could do, the bravest, was get up in the morning, do her best to restore her displays and open just as she did every other morning. If business was as slow as she anticipated, she'd have to let Hannah go. Maybe keep her or hire someone else just for the hours she was teaching classes—assuming anybody showed up for those classes. Unfortunately for her, given that the Amish were being supportive, they didn't need to take classes; they all had mothers and grandmothers and aunts to teach them the art.

One more thing she could do was refuse to talk to Chief Slater again without having an attorney present. Which put finding one next on her to-do list, after straightening up downstairs.

A little sleep would be really helpful right now, but every time she closed her eyes, she saw herself watching three strange men handle her most intimate possessions while she knew all the while that *he* was watching her.

If he expected his pressure would break her so she confessed all, he was going to be sadly mistaken.

LUCY'S CALL CAME the next day as Ben was leaving Aaron Hershberger's farm.

The poor guy was still scratching his head over Ben's interest in the gristmill on his property as he watched Ben get back in his car. *Ja*, Aaron knew Lyle Warren wanted to buy that land, but then he would not only restore the mill, he'd put in a parking lot and trails and signs, and Aaron did not want to live next to such a thing. He did say that Lyle had only repeated his initial offer, and not since spring. Warren apparently didn't have the money to increase it.

"I wouldn't sell it even if he offered double," the farmer had said with a shrug. "That building, it's falling down anyway. Already it's a nuisance. I chase teenagers away all the time."

Ben hadn't bothered telling him to call the sheriff's department. The Amish had as little to do with police as they could manage.

Braking at the foot of the lane, he answered the call.

"I'm ahead of schedule. I'll be there in about half an hour," his sister said with perkiness he knew was forced. She struggled with anxiety whenever her routine was altered. But he had to respect her decision to rent a car on her own after flying into Saint Louis so she wouldn't be totally dependent on him.

Had it taken the same grit for Nadia to make the move to Byrum?

"Can I stop by the police station and pick up a key?" his sister asked.

"I'll meet you at the house. You have the directions?"

"I printed them off," she assured him.

After promising to be there by the time she arrived, he turned onto the country road, noting where he'd parked Saturday but unable to see the mill from the road. Fortunately, it didn't take him over ten minutes to reach town.

When Lucy got out of her car in his driveway, he walked to meet her. "You've lost weight."

She made a face at him. "Most women would take that as a compliment."

"It wasn't meant as one." Yeah, Mr. Tactful, he wasn't. But his once slender sister had become painfully thin. Even since he last saw her at Christmas, she'd dropped weight.

His smart, pretty sister had always had an air of vulnerability. Sometimes Ben wondered if the rapist had picked her out from the herd because he'd seen her vulnerability. The thought never failed to enrage Ben.

Now, he hugged her, disturbed by the sharpness of bones he shouldn't be feeling. He'd always been protective where she was concerned, but it grated that he hadn't even been able to help her heal. "You look like crap," he murmured against her baby-fine light brown hair, "but I'm really glad you came."

She stepped back with a tremulous smile. "I'm glad I did, too. I miss you, you know."

"Yeah." He had to clear his throat. "Ditto."

He carried her suitcase up to the somewhat bare bedroom across the hall from his. He had bought the bed right after moving into the old house in town. Only his parents had slept in it. Just a few months ago, he had seen the dresser in the window of an antiques store in town and bought it on impulse along with a rocking chair that was in the living room. Otherwise…he guessed he wasn't much for decorating.

"This is perfect," Lucy said, sounding as if she meant it. "What a wonderful house."

"A place the age of this one has some drawbacks, but there aren't a lot of new houses being built around here. I liked the porch." He had been sold the minute he saw the porch running the full width of the house. One of the few furnishings he'd purchased right away was a glider. He'd liked the rope swing in the backyard hanging from an old maple tree, too, even though he didn't have kids. He rarely had time to sit out on his front porch, either.

"It's a family house," his sister said softly, as if she saw right into his head. She'd always been able to do that.

"Yeah," he said gruffly. "Maybe someday."

"You haven't met anyone?"

Ben flashed on Nadia, lush curves, glorious eyes and fierce pride. Not happening. "No."

Lucy tilted her head to one side. "You're lying."

He gave a short laugh. "Maybe I didn't miss you."

She giggled, the unexpectedly merry ripple of sound somehow also sharp enough to pierce his chest, between the ribs and up into his heart.

"Are you going to tell me?" she teased.

"No." He sighed. "Maybe. But fair warning—there's no happy ending."

Her smile fading, Lucy searched his eyes. Ben didn't know what she saw, but she rose on tiptoe and kissed his cheek. The ache in his chest was so acute, he had to fight the need to press his hand to his breastbone to try to ease it.

"She's a suspect in a crime," he said harshly. "We… searched her apartment and business yesterday. Right now, she hates my guts."

Still studying him, still seeing deep, his fey sister asked softly, "Did you find anything?"

Ben shook his head.

Expression troubled, Lucy said, "She may understand better than you think."

"She told me I'd ruined her. That she'll have to leave Byrum. She said…she'd never dare call the police again."

His sister flinched.

"You feel that way, too?" he asked, reeling. She'd never told him anything like this.

"They made me feel so ashamed. I knew they had to ask questions, but…" She shifted, looking toward the window as if she no longer wanted to meet his eyes. "Do you know how it feels, to have that happen, and then have the police officers asking how often you date, whether you've been flirting with anyone, why your door was unlocked, why—" She choked to a stop, and he was shocked to realize she was blisteringly angry. "Because of course it was my fault," she finished, suddenly sad.

That nearly killed him. He'd felt more in the past few days than he had in years.

"You never said."

"No." She tried for a smile. "I knew what to expect. Rape victims all say the same. I suppose the police officers believed they were just doing their jobs."

This kick to his chest emptied him of air. His sister stared at him in astonishment. He couldn't explain.

Wasn't sure, given her history, he ever would. Instead, he told her he had to desert her, but he'd be home as soon after five as he could manage.

After all, he had to go do his job, didn't he?

CHAPTER SIX

NADIA KEPT HERSELF busy restoring bolts of fabric to their proper places. Either the women signed up for today's class would show, or they wouldn't.

Business had been dismal. Yesterday, she'd held a session on enlivening quilt borders, for which only three of the seven participants showed, and that was the third of four sessions. She'd been sure they were all enjoying the class. Today's, focused on the Drunkard's Path pattern, was the opener, so no one was mid-project, or committed beyond the check written when signing up.

A couple of her regulars had come shopping and left with fabric. Otherwise, tourists browsed and left.

Now, when the bell above the door rang, Nadia turned.

The petite redhead who entered wasn't signed up for any class. She didn't need to be. Somewhere in her fifties, although she didn't look it, Jodi Knowles was already a superb quilter. A large Sawtooth quilt of hers had sold for sixteen hundred dollars at the auction. In the short time since Nadia had opened the store, she'd sold two of Jodi's quilts, one online.

"I'm afraid I need to take back the quilt you have," she said, with no preamble.

Nadia didn't bother asking why. She only said, "Of course," and went for her step stool so she could carefully take down the quilt that had been hanging from a thin rod that ran through the fabric sleeve on the back. A star variation, the quilt had only been in the store for a couple of weeks.

She gently bundled it in tissue paper and put it in a bag before handing it over. "This is truly lovely. I feel sure you'll find a home for it," she said.

Jodi lifted eyebrows plucked and penciled in. "I wouldn't want it to disappear," she said coolly, and marched out.

The moment the door closed behind her, Hannah, who had hovered in the background, burst out, "A week ago, I heard her telling someone how wonderful you are!"

"How quickly we forget," Nadia muttered, before sighing. "Hannah…I need you to know I may not be able to keep you on full-time if business stays this slow. I hope it doesn't come to that, but you deserve a warning."

Her plump assistant, wearing a lilac dress and apron today along with the traditional, gauzy white *kapp*, shook her head. "Earning money isn't so important for me. I have three sisters home to help my *mamm*, and I love the quilts. I can come when you need me, even if you can't pay me."

Tears stung Nadia's eyes. "You don't think I stole that money, do you?"

"No!" Hannah took her hand and squeezed. "Trust in God," she said kindly. "He will be your strength."

A lump in her throat, Nadia nodded even though the advice was more easily given than practiced. It had been a very long time since she'd been able to lean on anyone, and her faith wasn't sturdy enough to sustain her.

Two women did appear for the class, one quiet and not wanting to meet Nadia's eyes, the other cheerful and apparently oblivious to the weekend's events. Showing them how to use patterns to cut out the curved pieces and then how to hand sew them together without ending up with puckers, Nadia was able to put her troubles from her mind for the hour.

Once the class ended, she let Hannah go home. For the last hour, not a soul came through the door. She went back to restoring order, and chose another quilt to display in place of Jodi's.

What if several other women pulled their quilts, too? Ellen Shaw, for example; Nadia had three—or was it four?—of hers right now.

Worrying didn't do much good if she couldn't fix any part of her problems, and, right this minute, Nadia couldn't think of a single proactive thing she could do. Except remove Jodi's quilt from the website, she reminded herself wryly.

Somehow, the what-will-be-will-be acceptance didn't work for her. The knot in her stomach didn't loosen.

Closing and locking up was a relief. As was the fact that Ben Slater hadn't reappeared since she'd told him to get out on Monday.

Since then, Nadia had contacted an attorney who practiced in a neighboring county. They had an appointment scheduled tomorrow. The woman had agreed that she shouldn't talk to the police on her own again.

Of course, paying her might become a problem soon.

Nadia made a face. One more thing to worry about.

She settled for a salad for dinner, and picked at that. She did update the website, which had been designed to be user-friendly, thank goodness.

She fought exhaustion until nine o'clock, which seemed like an acceptable hour to go to bed. She might even turn her lights out before old Mr. Orton down the street did. Well, so what?

Tonight, sleep came before she could hop onto the carousel of worries.

Startled awake, she identified the sound of glass splintering. And...a *thud*?

Nadia's heart pounded. She scrambled out of bed, going to the window to separate blinds and peer out at the dark alley. Nothing looked out of the usual, or moved.

After pulling on yoga pants, she hurried through the apartment to look out over the street. Except for streetlamps, she didn't see any lights. Only a few cars remained parked on this block at night. She waited, but nothing moved out there, either. Could the sounds have been part of a dream, or a nightmare?

Still, she went downstairs, moving as quietly as she could, unwedged the chair and nerved herself to unlock her apartment door. Before stepping out into the hall, she groped for the switch and flicked on the light. A scan reassured her that the back door was closed, as were the closet and restroom doors, just as she'd left them. Through the open arch, the shop was dark but for what light fell through the front window.

She didn't know why she was scared. The night was quiet. She couldn't even hear distant traffic, as she

sometimes could. With her feet bare, she eased into
the shop and flipped on those lights.

Immediately, she saw the big, splintered hole in the
large front window. With a cry of dismay, she started
forward. A jagged rock that had to be eight inches in
diameter had scored the wood floor and come to a stop
ten feet or so inside.

Movement just beyond the window made her jerk to
a stop. A dark figure reared beyond the glass, the arm
going back. Something shot through the hole, trailing sparks.

Nadia twisted and flung herself behind the case
holding the display of thread. Her arms came up to
protect her head as she hit the floor, seconds before a
boom rattled the building and deafened her.

FISTS CLENCHED AT his sides, grinding his teeth, Ben
stood on the sidewalk glaring through the shattered
glass into A Stitch in Time Quilts & Fabrics. Damage was easy to see—blackened fabric, a splintered
wood base—and the stench of smoke was acrid in his
nostrils.

Behind him, lights flashed atop an ambulance and
a police car. A raised voice inside said, "Ma'am? Can
you hear me?"

Nadia had been close enough to the cherry bomb
to be deafened. Furious that she'd been targeted, he
stalked inside.

To his frustration, she was surrounded, and looked
so shaken, so unguarded, he knew he had to leash his
anger and the fear that roared behind it.

She sat on the floor, legs outstretched, back against

the wall next to the arched opening into the hall beyond. Her hair was wild, her face bleached white. EMTs crouched to each side of her. One had fingers to her wrist and was presumably taking her pulse. The other used an otoscope to peer into her right ear. While Ben watched, the man and woman changed places so her other ear could be checked.

The minute he started forward, her gaze lifted to him. She didn't so much as blink, and he didn't think he did, either. He quit being aware of anyone else. When a place beside her opened, Ben dropped to his knees, able to see how shell-shocked she looked. Without even thinking about it, he took her hand, disturbed to discover that it once again felt icy.

"Nadia."

She kept staring at him, but didn't respond.

He wrenched his gaze from hers to look at the EMT holding the otoscope. Marty McClun. Ben knew him.

"How is she?"

"Her eardrums are intact, but her hearing is impacted. Shock may be disguising some injury, but she's refusing to be transported."

He made sure she was still focused on him. "Nadia, you need to go to the ER, get checked out."

She shook her head in mute stubbornness.

After a minute, Ben sank back on his heels. "All right. I'll drive her if she changes her mind."

The pair cleaned up and departed, leaving only the officer who'd been first responder, currently taking photos of the rock, window and damage.

"Let's get you upstairs," Ben said, rising to a crouch and grasping her elbow.

She hesitated, her gaze going to the shattered window. "I've already called someone to cover it with plywood," he said, feeling like he was shouting but wanting to be sure she heard him.

After a minute, Nadia nodded and let him boost her to her feet. She went ahead of him, keeping a hand on the rail, him poised to catch her if she sagged or faltered. He had to curl his fingers into fists again to keep from reaching for her.

Partway up, she stopped, head hanging, and rested. If they had faced another flight of stairs, he would have scooped her up in his arms whether she liked it or not and carried her. She drew a deep breath, grabbed the railing and plodded on. She kept going through the small living room into the kitchen and sank down at the table.

As if he'd been here a hundred times, he put on water to boil and took the box of tea bags out of the cupboard. Caffeine wasn't ideal in the middle of the night—but she needed a stimulant. After spooning sugar into the mug, he turned to find her watching him.

"Why are you here?" she asked, her own voice pitched louder than usual.

"Your neighbors called 911. Please tell me you'd have done the same once you had the chance. Or called me."

Her chin tipped up. "I told you I wouldn't. In my experience, calling the police doesn't do any good. And you didn't answer my question."

What did she mean by that? Hadn't he responded every time she needed him? But he shoved aside her dig.

"The night-duty sergeant let me know what happened."

He had a feeling his teeth were showing. "Nadia, this was an attack on *you*."

"You don't know that. It was...it was vandalism."

"Yeah?" He took a couple of steps closer, the better to loom over her. "Why were you in the shop at 3:00 a.m.?"

"I heard the rock come through the window."

"And where were you when you heard it?"

Wariness in her eyes, she said, "In bed. The window breaking woke me up."

"So you got up, put on pants—or were you sleeping in them?"

Lips pressed together, Nadia shook her head. She wasn't a stupid woman. She knew what he was getting at.

"You turned on lights, made your way downstairs, stepped into the shop."

She continued to meet his stare, but her shoulders hunched just a little, making him think of a turtle.

"How long did that take, Nadia?"

Her lips tightened, but finally she answered. "I don't know."

"Five minutes? Ten?" Behind him the teakettle rumbled. It would be screeching any second. He ignored it.

"Maybe."

Bending forward, Ben flattened his hands on the table so he could get in her face. "He *waited* for you, Nadia. He waited to toss that bomb in through the window until he saw you. *You* were the target."

She seemed mesmerized. So much so, she jerked when the teakettle screamed.

He'd have kept ignoring the thing, but Nadia's ears had already suffered an insult. With a growl, he shoved off from the table and went to the stove, filling her mug and turning off the burner. He brought the mug to the table, setting it down in front of her.

Nadia looked at her tea, even stirring with the spoon he'd left in it. But then she lifted her gaze again. "It was meant to scare me. I couldn't have been hurt that badly."

"You could have two shattered eardrums if you'd been a few feet closer," Ben said flatly. "What if it had landed right at your feet and then went off? Kids lose fingers or vision from firecrackers. This was a lot more powerful than a firecracker." He knew his voice was rising.

"Don't yell at me!"

He planted his hands on his hips and glowered.

"And why would I call you?" Her voice was almost soft now. "Give yourself a few hours, and you'll decide I threw the thing through my own front window. I could have, you know. I must have wanted the attention. Or maybe I'm trying to make you see me as a victim instead of the thief." She shook her head. "I didn't call you because I don't want you here. You need to go. My attorney told me not to talk to you again."

"Your attorney?" he repeated, incredulous.

Her look held pure dislike. "You should have told me I was your principal suspect. I was foolish enough to trust you."

He was close to exploding himself. This burn wasn't the fury that demanded violence; it was…hurt?

Not sure he trusted himself right now, he took a step back and summoned an invisible shield around himself. "If you're certain you don't need to go to emergency, I'll leave you now," he said impassively. "I'll make sure the window is covered before I go, and request drive-bys for the rest of the night. From now on, pull the blinds at closing."

Her lips parted. He didn't want to hear it, so he nodded and left.

A second officer had showed up and was hammering a large piece of plywood in place over the bottom two-thirds of the window. It looked awful, but Ben presumed she'd get the glass replaced tomorrow. He spoke to the two, who promised to drive by at no more than fifteen-minute intervals for the remainder of their shifts, street and alley.

And then he went home, grateful when Lucy didn't emerge from her bedroom. Talking was the last thing he wanted to do.

HEARING THE BELL on the door, Nadia tucked her needle through the fabric and dropped her thimble onto the quilt as she rose to her feet. Hannah had come in for a few hours this morning, but with the absence of business, Nadia had sent her home. Now she walked out of the back room to see a woman hovering just inside the door.

"Hi, can I help you?" Nadia asked.

The woman offered a shy smile. "Yes. I'm...well, visiting. I'd like to try quilting."

No more than midthirties, she was tall and model thin with ash-brown hair and eyes. Unlike with most beautiful women, nothing about her posture or clothes suggested she wanted to advertise. To the contrary.

Visiting. With sudden suspicion Nadia realized there was something a little familiar about this woman.

"You have family in town?" she asked, trying for casually friendly.

The newcomer wrinkled her nose. "I hoped you wouldn't notice."

"You're Chief Slater's sister."

"That would be me."

Nadia crossed her arms. "Are you here undercover?"

A smile lit her face. "Spying for him? No, he has no idea what I'm up to. What I said about quilting is true, but also… I guess I was curious. You have him tangled in knots, you know."

"*I* have him?" Nadia snorted. "Did he tell you I'm new in Byrum? He's pretty well destroyed any chance I had of making a life here. All he wants is to slap cuffs on me."

Which even she knew wasn't true; there was a definite spark between them, but he was doing his best to stamp it out. Nadia *hated* that he'd come rushing to her rescue again last night. She hated even more knowing that she had lied when she told him she didn't want him here. Because she'd ached to feel his arms around her, to let herself lean against him and draw strength from him.

The man who'd humiliated her and, by shredding any reputation she had left, was driving her to leave town. She gave her head an unconscious shake.

"That's…not really true," Slater's sister said. "He told me—" She grimaced. "In confidence. Shut up, Lucy. Besides, that's not why I'm here."

Nadia forced another smile. "As you obviously know, I'm Nadia Markovic. You're Lucy…?"

"Slater. Unmarried. So." She looked around, her expression yearning.

Nadia remembered feeling that way the first time she'd seen an antique quilt at a friend's house. A Grandmother's Flower Garden. She could still picture it, feel the texture when she had tentatively touched it. She and her mother had taken a class together, Nadia not admitting her enthusiasm to her friends. She remembered rolling her eyes and saying, "It'll make Mom happy." Her mother enjoyed the new hobby, but Nadia had fallen in love.

"Is there any chance you have a beginning class?" Lucy asked. "And, if not, can you steer me to any books that would get me started?"

Nadia hesitated. "As it happens, I have an ongoing class for people in the beginning to intermediate stages. I keep it small enough to allow me to help everyone with whatever problem arises. When students start new projects, I steer them to ones that will be satisfying, just a little challenging, but not so frustrating they quit."

"When is the class?" Lucy asked eagerly.

"Actually, this afternoon. It's Tuesdays and Thursdays at two, and I hold additional sessions on Saturday afternoons for anyone who wants to come, but mostly to accommodate people who work weekdays."

"Sign me up. In the meantime, will you help me choose a project and buy the fabric?"

"My favorite part." Leading her to the library of well-thumbed books in the back room, Nadia said, "You may get my undivided attention this afternoon. Class attendance has dropped way off. I've become a pariah."

"I'm sorry. I don't know what's wrong with people."

That sounded like the voice of experience. Nadia

looked at her sharply, but Lucy was focused on the books.

Nadia let her browse for a while, then sat with her to discuss patterns.

"I encourage beginners to start with a relatively simple pattern, which doesn't mean the result won't be gorgeous. A Nine Patch, for example, or even a Double Nine Patch." She found pictures, then showed Lucy examples of T-Block and Pinwheel quilts.

Lucy agreed bed-sized sounded overwhelming. She wanted to do a wall-hanging, crib-sized or smaller. Although admitting she loved the Ocean Waves, Bear's Paw and various star patterns, she decided on the Pinwheel for simplicity. Nadia left her alone to spend a happy hour among the fabrics before she finally asked for help with her final choices.

Nadia always found those choices to be revealing. Timidity or boldness came out, as did an artist's eye— or the complete lack of one. She had half expected Lucy Slater to choose soft colors, like Julie Baird did. Gentle or even bland colors went with Lucy's self-effacing manner and wrinkled tan linen pants and muddy-brown T-shirt.

She would have been wrong, though. Instead, Lucy seemed to instinctively understand she needed strong contrast and went with vivid colors on the dark end of the spectrum: a rich rose red, deep teal blue and navy against a pinkish-cream background fabric. Lucy bought several books, a hoop suitable for hand quilting smaller projects and everything else she needed.

"And I have just enough time to hustle back to Ben's house and wash and dry the fabric before the class starts." Beaming, Lucy departed with her bags, leaving Nadia in a whole lot better mood than she'd been.

She couldn't help wondering what Lucy's brother would think of her new hobby, though.

CHAPTER SEVEN

BEN HAD ANOTHER crap day in what seemed to be a stretch of them. For June, the weather was really hot, for starters. Sweating the way he was, he couldn't figure out how Amish men endured working out in the fields in the heat of the sun wearing long pants and hats. Straw hats, sure, in contrast to the black felt ones worn in colder months, but still. Their only concession to the heat was to roll up their shirtsleeves.

Driving out to talk to another couple who had attended the auction, Ben passed two men plowing under what must have been a spring crop of some kind, draft horses throwing all their weight into the harnesses, the men controlling the plows to dig deep into the rich soil. Neither even looked up at the passing vehicle.

Ben's morning had been spent canvassing Nadia's neighbors yet again in hopes someone had seen something last night. No surprise, they'd all been in bed, asleep. A couple had awakened when they heard breaking glass, just as she had, others the explosion. Three people had called 911.

He gritted his teeth. She'd rather be assaulted than call him. Hurt. Scared for her life. He hated knowing she felt that way, hated remembering her face as the search went on.

There had to be a way to get past her animosity, but

he didn't know what it was. And while he understood, he also remembered their first meeting and that flash of fear. She hadn't *expected* to be able to trust him. Why? In Colorado, the police had been the rescuers, not the accusers.

He shook his head. As long as she was a suspect, he had no business thinking about her the way he was.

He learned zilch from talking to the Wagners. The missus didn't see very well—used a white cane, in fact—and the mister had been bored, present only to please his wife who insisted on buying a quilt to help. They were distressed by the theft and had unhesitatingly replaced the check written that night. Neither had an opinion on who might have done such a thing.

Returning, he once again passed the gristmill, his eye caught by grass matted over time where cars had parked. A quick glint of metal in longer grass had his foot going to the brake, and, after checking the rearview mirror, he backed up.

A bicycle, laid on its side.

For no good reason, he decided to see who was here. A teenager? Could be meeting another one who lived within walking distance. The Amish didn't often use bicycles, but their teenagers sometimes did. Handy for when *Daad* was stingy with the horse-and-buggy privileges. Besides, not all farms in the immediate area were Amish owned.

Ben moved quietly, following a path that was more visible than the last time he'd been here. He kept just as wary an eye on the grass and vegetation to each side—he didn't like snakes *or* poison ivy.

As he approached the crumbling brick structure, he heard a rustling sound. He laid a hand on the butt of his gun as he took the last couple of steps to be able to see inside.

"Lyle?" he said in surprise.

The head of the historical society jumped and swung around. "Chief Slater? What are you doing here?"

"What are *you* doing here?" Ben countered. "Is that your bike by the road?"

"I ride for exercise." He lifted a plastic kitchen trash bag that appeared half-full. "I come now and again to clean up. I just can't stand to think of this place contaminated with beer cans and fast-food wrappers and what all."

Condoms presumably fell into the what-all category. Ben saw that Lyle had the common sense to be wearing heavy leather gardening gloves.

He hadn't had a bag to pick up trash the day Ben had run him down out here. So what *had* he been doing? Coveting?

"You do realize you're trespassing?"

Lyle snorted. "If Hershberger won't take care of a historic site on his land, I will. Would you really arrest me?"

No, not unless Aaron called with a complaint, which he wouldn't. And, heck, if all Lyle did when he came out here was clean up, he was doing the property owner a favor.

"I wonder if posting no trespassing signs would keep the teenagers away," Ben speculated.

"More like a few shotgun blasts over their heads," Lyle snapped. "I thought about setting some mouse-traps disguised by leaves. At least it might give a scare to anybody who *defiles* a site like this."

"It's not a church."

Hate burned in Lyle's brown eyes. "It's part of our history. It deserves respect, not—" he hoisted the garbage bag "—*this*."

After a few calming remarks, Ben left the guy to his self-appointed task. Walking to his car, he pondered the disturbing conversation. For a second there, Lyle Warren's eyes had burned with the light of a fanatic. Was it really all about the gristmill? Or was something else going on?

FRIDAY, NADIA TOOK advantage of Hannah's presence to go grocery shopping. Maybe if she hustled through the store during the late morning on a weekday, she could get her groceries without encountering anyone she knew.

She had forgotten the realities of living in a community the size of Byrum. She had no sooner pulled into the parking lot at the Hy-Vee than she spotted a regular customer of hers coming out with a laden grocery cart. Instead of continuing straight ahead, she turned quickly down the next row and parked. Then, head down, she hurried into the store, grabbed a cart and started with fresh produce.

Making her selections fast, Nadia had just added a container of strawberries to her cart when she saw trouble approaching. Allison Edgerton must have started on the other side of the store, because her cart was nearly full. Nadia tried to slink behind a display of bananas, but was too late.

Allison's expression froze. "I hear your little shop is still open."

Head up. "Yes, I have every hope that once the police arrest the culprit and recover the money, life will go back to normal."

"What a shame Chief Slater didn't find the money Monday," the older woman said disdainfully. "I trust he's checked your bank accounts, too."

"Why would you think for a minute that I kept that money?" Nadia asked in genuine puzzlement. "Was I rude to you when you came into A Stitch in Time? Did you see me cheat a customer?"

Allison looked back at her without a grain of embarrassment. "Who are *you* accusing? Julie? Karen? How many people knew where to find the money, Ms. Markovic? It can't be many. And I know *them*." Turning her head away, she pushed her cart forward, to all appearances having dismissed Nadia from her mind.

Nadia stayed where she was, glad she had the cart handle to hang on to. She felt shaky. She'd never enjoyed confrontation, but being berated in public was a whole new experience. And to think she'd fled Colorado Springs because people were being too nice to her!

"What a nasty piece of work," a woman said behind her. "You should have slammed your cart into hers. Or...no, tipped hers over. Oh, oops."

Laughing despite herself, Nadia turned to see who was approaching. The voice wasn't familiar, but...the face was, even though she had to search her memory to know why.

The young woman—late twenties or early thirties—gaped at her. "I know you. Why do I know you?"

"I'm...not sure. Colorado?"

"No, I've never been."

The platinum blonde hair didn't seem right with the face. Well, it obviously wasn't natural; her eyebrows were too dark, and she had brown eyes besides. Had her hair been a different color whenever they'd met? Almost immediately, Nadia's mind formed a different picture. Brown hair, shorter then. Not as much makeup, either. And she didn't *know* know her, it had just been one of those casual encounters.

"Trenton," she blurted. South of Byrum, Trenton attracted tourists drawn to Amish goods and culture. "I remember now. We shared a table at a café because it was so crowded, and got talking."

The other woman—oh, what was her name? Or had they not introduced themselves?—looked astonished. "You're right. But…what are you doing *here*?"

"I live here," Nadia said, "although, as you may have gathered, I'm not very popular. I don't know if you heard about the quilt auction—"

"Oh, no! That's *you*?"

"Yes. I own the quilt shop here in town. I bought it about six months ago. My name is Nadia Markovic."

The woman blinked. "I had no idea. You bought the building from me. It was my aunt who died."

"You're…" What was the name? "Corinne Bissett?"

"That's me." She grimaced. "Obviously, I'm not a sewer or quilter, much to Aunt Edith's disappointment. I work at the Harley-Davidson dealership."

"I'm surprised we haven't run into each other before this," Nadia said.

"*I'm* surprised we even recognized each other." For a second, she looked as if she wished they hadn't. Probably because of the rumors she'd heard. "That had to be six or eight months ago."

"More than that, actually. I'd been looking for the right location for a long time before I spotted the ad for your aunt's business. It was about a year ago when I flew out to look at Trenton and Jamestown and that general area."

Corinne didn't look as if she believed Nadia, but she gave a quick, dismissive shrug. "Well. I doubt we have the same friends, and we must not usually grocery shop at the same times. Still—I'm sorry about the mess you're in."

"I… Thank you."

She was talking to Corinne Bissett's back. She headed for the dairy aisle and was quickly out of sight.

How odd, Nadia thought. She had vaguely wondered if the old lady's niece lived here in Byrum. She remembered thinking that, if she did, Ms. Bissett would likely stop by to say hi. Well, if she'd had no interest in the fabric store and wasn't especially close to her aunt, she'd probably just wanted to sell quickly and take advantage of her inheritance, such as it was. With really short shorts, wedge sandals that made Nadia's feet hurt to look at and a skintight T-shirt, she was a contrast to Nadia in her flowing, gauzy skirt and far more modest knit shirt.

Starting slowly after Corinne, however, it struck Nadia that they did have something more in common than having shared a table for lunch in a crowded restaurant a year ago. Corinne would surely have been interviewed about her aunt's death, given that she was the heir. And Nadia would put money on it having been Ben Slater who'd interviewed her and probably done his best to scare her, too, in hopes she'd break down and confess all.

They really should have exchanged notes. Maybe

Corinne could have given her some tips, Nadia thought wryly.

Hearing two women talking behind her, she remembered her mission: grab enough food to last at least a week and get out of here as quick as possible, preferably without encountering anyone else she knew.

"Do you know many of the Amish?" Lucy asked over the dinner table that evening.

Ben knew she'd been out most of yesterday; he'd seen bulging shopping bags heaped on the floor in her bedroom. He had no idea what she'd done today. Given her question, he had to wonder if she'd been hitting every Amish-owned shop in town.

And wasn't that what all visitors to Byrum did? If not for the Amish, travelers wouldn't stop here longer than it took to fill a tank with gasoline or buy burgers and fries to eat on the road.

"I know some, but not well." He reached for a third biscuit. They tasted good, even if they were out of one of those little tubes that popped open. Lucy had wished aloud that she had some sourdough starter here. Ben wasn't feeling picky; he was just happy to walk in the door to a home-cooked meal. "The Amish are friendly but reserved," he continued. "Like I said before, their mandate is to remain apart from the world. That's not to say real friendships don't form between Amish and *Englischers*, but how deep those go, I'm not sure. There are quite a few Amish businesses within the city limits, but not many of them live here. So I deal with an occasional buggy/car collision and complaints about horse patties on the streets and the grooves the steel buggy wheels wear in asphalt, while the Amish refrain from calling on the police whenever possible." That still frustrated him. Six or eight months ago, a rash of burglaries in the downtown could have been stopped sooner if the Amish business owners had reported their losses instead of admitting to them long after the fact.

Having an idea, he said, "I'll invite the county sheriff and his wife over for dinner one of these evenings. I think you'd like his wife, Rebecca. Daniel is a lot more involved on the job with the Amish than I am, and both he and Rebecca have family among them."

"What a good idea." Lucy smiled at him while nudging the casserole dish in his direction.

Ben didn't really need seconds, but he helped himself anyway. When he and Lucy were teenagers, she hadn't been all that interested in cooking, but she'd learned somewhere along the way. He'd have assumed she'd developed the skill because she didn't want to leave her apartment more than she had to, but she hadn't hesitated about exploring since she had arrived to stay with him. At least, not during the daytimes. She hadn't asked about nightlife. Maybe she'd guessed it was close to nonexistent. Byrum did have a two-screen movie theater, the only one in the county, and of course there were restaurants. Otherwise, unless a special event was being held—say, square dancing or bingo at the Grange hall— the town shut down early except for the taverns and bars.

He had a sudden memory of the day he and his parents had left her at the dorm at the University of Pennsylvania for her freshman year. Tears in her beautiful eyes as they were saying goodbye, but her cheeks pink with excitement, and he could tell how conscious she was of some guys walking by in athletic shorts and sweat-soaked T-shirts. That Lucy was gone forever.

"You haven't told me what happened," he said, maybe too abruptly.

"What happ— Oh." Her expression dimmed.

Sorry he had raised the subject, Ben said, "We don't have to talk about it."

"No, it's okay. It really wasn't any big deal, just embarrassing." With her fork, she squished what was left of the casserole on her plate. "I went out with a guy a friend introduced me to."

He stared at her. "You went on a date."

Her eyes flashed to meet his, then lowered again. "You don't have to make it sound so unlikely. Like… like a robin hatching a chicken."

Ben smiled crookedly at the picture of a chick tumbling out of a robin's nest. Except then he realized how apt her analogy might be. Clearly, she hadn't been able to fly, either.

"I've been stagnating," Lucy said after a minute. "I was able to function at a certain level and hardly noticed when I quit trying for more. This guy was good-looking and he seemed nice, so I thought—" She hunched her shoulders, much as Nadia had done when uncomfortable. "Dinner was fine. He brought me home and walked me to my door. He, um, tried to kiss me—I freaked out—he fled."

"Okay," he said, since that was about what he had expected, "but I don't get how that precipitated a visit to me."

She'd quit playing with her food. He had a feeling she was wringing her hands beneath the table.

"I needed to push myself out of my comfort zone, but in a different way."

Lucy had gone on vacation a few times with their parents, but, from what Mom said, had clung to them.

"Is this the first time you've flown alone? Rented a car yourself?"

She nodded, looking hopeful. "That's something, isn't it?"

Ben smiled at her, this sister who'd secretly been his best friend as they were growing up. "It's something big." He hesitated. "Did it scare you when I went out in the middle of the night?"

"Not scared, exactly. I didn't sleep again until you got home."

"Would you rather I not wake you when I have to go out?"

Lucy shook her head vehemently. "No! If I woke up and found you gone—" She shuddered. "It's much better to know you're just doing your job."

There she went again, touching a raw nerve.

"It doesn't happen all that often," he told her. "Wednesday night, the sergeant wouldn't have called me if the vandalism didn't appear to be part of an ongoing investigation of mine. Normally, for anything short of a murder or kidnapping—" or rape "—I'd get the rundown the next morning. My two detectives aren't very experienced, so I'm taking lead on some crimes and using them as teaching opportunities."

Except, he hadn't been on this one. He'd been sucked in from the minute he met Nadia's eyes at the auction.

Why was it that every train of thought circled back to her?

HANNAH TOOK HER lunch at one o'clock to be sure she'd be back before Nadia started the afternoon class. This was the Saturday session technically for beginning to intermediate students, but really open to any student who needed some extra help.

Sitting on a stool behind the cash register in her empty store, she had the painful thought that eight days ago, at this exact time, she had been strolling from table to table during the quilt sale, watching for problems, laughing and talking with participants and buyers even as she felt a flicker of panic at knowing how little time they had to clear the ballroom before the night's auction began.

How much could change in one week.

She shivered, or maybe it was a shudder. She, of all people, knew how fast lives could change—and end. In bad moments, she still wondered whether either of Paige's boys might have lived if the police had acted sooner instead of letting hours pass while their father taunted the negotiator. She would never know about Colin, but Keenan…well, maybe doctors couldn't have saved him no matter what. Probably it was just as well she couldn't know exactly when they had died. Paige… *she* had been dead before she hit the floor.

The bell on the door tinkled, and Nadia returned to the present. Seeing who had walked in the door, she wasn't sure that was an improvement.

No matter how angry she was, Nadia couldn't help responding to everything about Ben Slater—his unruly dark hair, broad shoulders and lean hips, the long-legged stride that was always purposeful, his strong, shadowed jaw and sharp cheekbones. He looked good in the uniform that reminded her of who and what he was—a man very capable of violence, and one who likely closed his mind to the terrible consequences his decisions could have.

Too quickly, his intense, dark eyes captured her. She would swear those eyes hadn't left her face since he entered the store.

Instinct had her sliding off the stool. He still towered over her standing, but the disadvantage was less.

She raised her eyebrows. "I hope you're not here to arrest me. I have a class beginning in fifteen minutes."

Creases deepened on his forehead. "You know I'm not."

"How would I know that?" She held on to a disdainful expression even if her heart was racing.

He came to a stop, only the counter separating them. "I don't enjoy what I've had to do, Nadia."

"Then you should have gone into another line of work, shouldn't you?" she shot back.

"There are days I think so, too." Rueful, deep, velvety, his voice seemed designed to undercut her resistance.

"I don't understand you." Alarmed, she didn't understand why she'd said that. This was the man who was helping ruin her life. Did it matter what drove him?

Was that a flinch, or only a nerve or muscle twitching beneath his eye? "I don't know if you'd like me if you did," he said, his eyes darkening, if that was possible.

I am in such trouble, she thought. Because…she hadn't been able to say, or even think, *I already don't like you*. She almost sank back onto the stool, but somehow fortified herself. *No, no, no.* She could not let herself trust him. Not given his profession or his capability for violence. *Oh, and remember the latest reason?*

"You've gotten access to my bank accounts."

He just looked at her for a minute. "How do you know?"

"Yesterday, one of my admirers was being nasty and said something, so I called the bank. The manager admitted the police did have a warrant."

He looked angry. "Who told you?"

"You mean, at the bank?"

"No. The *admirer.* Nobody outside the department and the DA's office should have known about a warrant."

"Oh." He was right, except... "I think she actually said she hoped you were looking at my bank accounts."

"She?" He was implacable, and Nadia had no reason not to tell him.

"Allison Edgerton."

He grunted. "I hoped you'd never know."

"I'm sure you did hope I'd be stupid enough to wait a few weeks and then deposit the money," she agreed, sharp as the blade on her rotary cutter.

"Nadia, I don't believe you stole the money. I don't believe you have it cached away somewhere. But you were the last person who had it. You could have made up your story. I had to eliminate you. If you were in my shoes, wouldn't you have made the same decisions I have?"

She shook her head, and kept shaking it. "You could have handled all of this differently. What about this country's founding principle that says citizens are innocent until proved guilty?" Her voice caught. "You, and everyone else in this town, started with the belief that I'm guilty. Am I supposed to say I understand? I don't."

They stared at each other, and she had the startled awareness that she'd hurt him. No, she had to be imagining that. Why would he care what she thought of him?

Except…he did. He wouldn't keep coming back like this if he didn't. Unless he was trying to trick her into trusting him, of course. Only, she didn't quite believe that.

She lifted her chin. "You never did say why you're here."

Wait—she wasn't supposed to talk to him without her attorney at her side.

His laugh wasn't really a laugh. "I wanted to find out how you're doing. Whether your business is hanging in there, whether you're sleeping, eating." His mouth twisted. "I don't know about the business, but you're not sleeping well, are you? Or eating?"

Stiffening, Nadia said, "What a lovely compliment. And I thought I already knew how charming you can be."

He lifted a hand as if he was going to touch her, but aborted the gesture. "I don't like seeing bruises under your eyes."

She swallowed, her throat dry. "When I go to bed, I remember that locked doors weren't enough. Someone got all the way into my bedroom without my ever knowing it, could have been as close to me as you are right now. Call me sensitive, but that makes it a little hard now to settle down for a cozy night's sleep." And no, she wouldn't tell him she still had nightmares about those hours surrounded by the dead and dying.

Compassion and unexpected understanding altered the lines of his face. He opened his mouth to say something, but the bell on the door rang. Ben turned, even as Nadia forced herself to look past him.

His sister walked in, carrying her project stuffed in a tote. Only a few feet inside the door, she stopped dead when she saw Ben.

Nadia made the mistake of glancing at him just in time to see a flare of something intense—anger?—before he said with an unpleasant tinge of sarcasm, "Is there a little something you forgot to tell me about your activities this week?"

CHAPTER EIGHT

CLUTCHING THAT TOTE bag to her chest as if it was her baby, Lucy opened and closed her mouth a couple times.

Ben shook his head, all his protective instincts bristling. As if side by side, he saw Nadia, dazed and shocked, being worked over by the medics—and Lucy, naked, battered, bloody, sprawled on that bed. Never again.

"You need to stay away from here," he said in a hard voice. "I'll see you outside." Taking for granted that she'd obey, he turned to Nadia in time to catch her expression of shock. No, worse than that: she looked as if he'd just cut her to the bone. Horrified by his sudden understanding of how she must have taken his reaction to seeing his sister here, he said urgently, "Nadia..."

She backed away, her hands up as if to ward him off. "No. I don't want to hear it. By all means, be sure Lucy doesn't get contaminated by associating with me."

"That's not what—" She'd been so strong despite a trauma as horrific as the one Lucy had suffered. Would she understand that his sister was different, that she could be destroyed if she was even a bystander during an ugly incident?

But that bell was tinkling again, and Ben swung back to see another two women walking in, both carrying bags of their own. One of them greeted Lucy as if she knew her, and he realized Lucy had come here for the class—and that it wouldn't be her first. He also realized his sister hadn't gone outside when he asked.

She was forcing a smile for the benefit of the other women, giving him a second to glance over his shoulder. Nadia had retreated to the opening into the back room. She looked as if she wanted not to be here. As if she was trying to shrink into nothingness.

Ben took an involuntary step her way, but there was the bell again, and more voices, and Nadia wouldn't even meet his eyes.

Swearing silently, he went toward the door. "Lucy…"

Chattering, the others had streamed ahead toward Nadia and the back room.

"Don't even think about it," his sister snapped. "I want to learn to quilt, and Nadia is a good teacher. I *like* her."

"I like her, too. You know that. But a lot of people hate her right now, and if you're too close to her, you could get hurt."

"*My* decision."

He hadn't seen her angry and determined in a lot of years. Ben ought to be rejoicing. And it was true that an attack was unlikely in the middle of a business day. Which meant…he'd overreacted.

"You have no right to tell me what to do," she added, voice low but resolute. "Goodbye." And she walked right past him to join the other women.

He saw no alternative but to leave, knowing he'd screwed up again. Now the snapshot of Nadia's face replaced everything else, and he felt sick. If only he could explain why he'd been afraid for Lucy. Nadia would understand. She had to.

"Excuse me," a woman said.

Ben blinked, discovering that he'd come to a dead stop on the sidewalk, blocking the door. It was Hannah Yoder who waited politely to go by, the lenses of her glasses magnifying her blue eyes. She was as tidy as always. He glanced at the clunky black athletic shoes that didn't seem to go with a calf-length dress and stockings.

"Sorry, Hannah." He managed what he hoped was an apologetic smile. "I think I was *fernhoodled*. If that's the right word." So far as he understood it, *bewildered* fit within the meaning.

Hannah giggled. "*Ja*, it could be. You have a good day now, Chief Slater." She opened the shop door and, with a swish of her skirt, went inside.

He headed straight to his car parked a few storefronts down the block. Once behind the wheel, he sat frowning straight ahead, unable to shake the memory of how he'd hurt Nadia. A good start to redeeming himself would be finding out who'd stolen the money. Too bad he was flat out of ideas.

He had no witnesses, no strings to pull. If a local had taken the money, he or she might eventually brag to the wrong person about it, or spend it in a way that had neighbors wondering where the sudden wealth had come from. Otherwise… He didn't want to think about the *otherwise*, because it would mean another investigation going cold, another unsolved crime like Edith Jefferson's murder.

The usual uneasiness stirred when he reflected on the parallels. Same building in both cases, and both intruder had seemingly had a key. But Ben couldn't fit the two crimes together. The intent was different, and the victims had nothing in common except an interest in sewing and quilting. They'd never met; Mrs. Jefferson had been dead for over six months when Nadia moved here.

His attention snapped to his radio when voices crackled from it. A kid on a bike had been hit near the corner of Fourth and Oak. The officer pleading for an ambulance sounded frantic. Dread supplanting everything else, Ben pulled away from the curb and switched on the lights and siren to clear his way.

LUCY WHISPERED ANOTHER apology as she passed close to Nadia on her way around the table to an empty chair. Nadia managed a smile and a slight nod. Roiling with rage and hurt, she hadn't even been able to enjoy watching Ben's sister defy him. The very fact that he'd believed he could snap his fingers and his sister would jump to obey said a whole lot about him.

What it really did was reaffirm what she already knew about the man. To give him credit, he'd admitted there was reason she wouldn't like him. That he was the most attractive man she'd ever met, that her body felt tuned to his, that she had felt the gentleness in his touch, that sometimes she would swear she saw tenderness in his eyes…none of that could matter. Rats sometimes looked really good. Even monsters could. Paige's husband had been a handsome, athletic man who succeeded for a long time in hiding his sick, pathological anger and need to control from most people.

Nadia refused to let Ben ruin what was shaping up to be a great class. Six women had showed, the highest number this week. They were all enthusiastic, already oohing and aahing over each other's projects. Lucy was the newest, and those who hadn't attended the Thursday session gave rave reviews to her fabric choices.

"Are you planning to hand quilt?" Donna Adamski asked. "So far, that's my favorite part."

"Yes." Lucy beamed. "I bought a hoop. That seems the most practical for now."

Nadia let them talk for a few minutes, then encouraged them to get to work and asked if anyone had questions or problems. A couple of the women did. She helped them one at a time through the latest snag, and then focused a lot of her time on Lucy, the only real beginner. She'd made paper patterns and started cutting out triangles during Thursday's class. Today, she continued cutting out pieces and long strips for borders, after which Nadia talked her through sewing half-square triangles on one of the machines available for student use, then snipping off the corners of the triangles before pressing the squares flat.

My mother tried to teach me to sew, Lucy had confessed the day she first came into the store, *but I wasn't all that interested. I hope I remember at least some of it.*

It appeared she did, or else she caught on fast. Her excitement as she saw how the fabrics contrasted was contagious. Stories about initial disasters flew around the table, and the ready laughter felt like a balm to Nadia's wounds. This was what she'd imagined when she opened the store. Women helping other women. Supporting each other, learning. Friendships being stitched together as surely as were pieces of fabric.

Quilting had been her salvation after she got out of

the hospital. She could concentrate on it in a way she couldn't on anything else. She could imagine the quilt she was hand stitching keeping a descendent warm a hundred years in the future. She dreamed about helping others, like Lucy, find the same passion.

So enjoy it, she told herself. *Don't think about all the crap or the people you* thought *were becoming friends. Especially don't think about Lucy Slater's brother.*

A couple of times, she heard Hannah speaking to customers, and in between Hannah popped into the room to admire the progress students were making and offer small tips of her own.

When the session officially ended, Nadia told them to feel free to stay if they'd like to keep working. Three women did, including Lucy, who didn't have a sewing machine at Ben's house.

As glad as Nadia was now to hear murmurs of conversation and the whir of sewing machines in the back room, she kept a nervous eye on the door in case Ben decided to find out why his sister hadn't left when she was supposed to.

Lucy was still in back when a middle-aged couple wandered in, looking for quilts. The husband appeared indulgent but disinterested as his wife looked at every quilt for sale, asking eager questions and exclaiming with pleasure. He became absorbed in his smartphone. Every so often, she'd say, "What do you think, honey?" and he'd shake his head.

"You're the decorator, not me."

"He's actually color-blind," the woman whispered. "I do avoid red and certain shades of pink, because they look gray to him."

Which meant a goodly number of flowers must look gray. How odd that would be.

Nadia had hoped the woman was serious, and she proved to be when she chose two quilts, one full-size for a guest bedroom and a queen-size for their own room. The smaller of the two was a marvelous Texas Star quilt in soft shades, the queen-size an Irish Chain done in navy blue against a white background. When his wife showed him that one, the man blinked a few times.

"I thought quilts were all fussy."

"Using only two fabrics is actually quite common," Nadia said. Beaming, Hannah wrapped both while Nadia happily rang up the purchase. Having learned the couple was, appropriately enough, from Texas, she dropped a card in the bag, mentioning that most quilts in the shop were pictured on her website and available for purchase online.

Carrying her tote bag, Lucy appeared from the back room shortly after the couple left. She looked in surprise at Hannah and Nadia. "What happened?"

Nadia knew she was still grinning. "A *huge* sale." Her percent would stave off bankruptcy for a month. Or let her keep Hannah on longer.

Lucy's gaze went to the blank place on the wall. "The Star quilt!"

"Yes, and a second one from the bed." A lacy, white-painted iron bedstead held twenty quilts or more, rotated so that each had turns being on top. And now another could go on the wall instead.

Lucy waited until Hannah went to collect a couple of bolts of fabric from the cutting table to return them to their place to repeat her apology.

"Ben was a butthead," she concluded.

Suspecting she ought to demur, Nadia said, "Yes, he

was. But he's convinced I stole money raised for charity, so I guess it's no surprise he'd rather you didn't hang around with me."

"He didn't sound to me like he does think that," Lucy protested.

"He brought a CSI team in to search my building top to bottom on Monday." Her chest still tightened at the memory. "They went through my underwear drawer, turned over my sofa and chairs, poked through my medicine cabinet and lifted the toilet lid in case I'd taped the bag of money under there. Forgive me for thinking that denotes suspicion."

Lucy made a face. "He says he had to do it, if only for appearances."

"Appearances." Nadia had never laughed with so little humor. "He could have lowered the window blinds so passersby couldn't see what was going on. He didn't. If you'd been a customer here, how would that search *appear* to you?"

Lucy hesitated then admitted, "Not good."

"Except for your purchase, I've hardly sold a thing all week. The store is empty for hours on end. Most people who signed up for classes aren't attending. Today's was the best I've had, and that's probably because the women are mostly beginners who weren't involved in the auction. The couple who just bought two quilts were tourists. They didn't know they'd stepped into a den of iniquity."

"Aren't most of the quilts sold to tourists?"

"Yes, but I need the fabric store to make a profit, too. Quilt sales are occasional, not steady. And—" She shook her head, aware of Hannah now listening. "No, that's enough whining."

"Tell me." Lucy's expression was fierce.

Oh, what difference did it make? "I've had three quilt makers stop by to pick up ones they'd consigned for sale. They're all locals. If more follow their example and quit trusting me with their quilts, I'm done."

Hannah had been quietly listening. Now she said, "The *Leit* will keep bringing their quilts here. I haven't heard any bad talk about you."

Nadia smiled shakily at her, aware the Amish called themselves the *Leit*—the people. "That's good to hear. Speaking of… I won't be able to get the cash until Monday, but will you be able to drop it off at Emma Troyer's? And…maybe she has another quilt ready for sale?"

"*Ja*, for certain sure! So glad, she'll be."

Nadia smiled, hating the poison of bitterness she'd let leak out. "And I'll call Jennifer Bronske right now."

She told Lucy she was welcome to come in and use a sewing machine any time the room wasn't otherwise occupied, after which Ben's sister left. Nadia thought they could become friends if Lucy wasn't in town only temporarily…and if Ben wasn't so opposed to it.

Hannah turned the sign to Closed and locked the front door while Nadia dialed Jennifer's number. When Jennifer answered, Nadia said, "I hope I didn't call when you're in the middle of dinner preparations, but I wanted to let you know that your beautiful Texas Star quilt sold. I can mail a check to you or—"

"I prefer cash," the other woman said with noticeable coolness.

Because her checks were certain to bounce? Nadia choked back what she really wanted to say. She couldn't afford to burn bridges.

"That's fine." She managed what sounded to her

like a pleasant voice. "Obviously, I won't be able to get to the bank until Monday morning. If you want to come by and pick the money up, any time after I open would be fine."

"I'll be there." Then she was gone.

Would she bring another quilt to be sold? Doubtful. Nadia wanted to think she'd never accept it if Jennifer did offer another one, but as long as she was trying to stay in business here in Byrum she'd have to keep swallowing her pride. But, oh, she hated doing it.

Hannah suddenly said, "Jacob is here, I must go," and let herself out the front. Indeed, a horse and buggy had stopped at the curb. Jacob and his father, Roy Yoder, owned the cabinetmaking business down the block. Hannah had sometimes helped them in the showroom, which was why she'd immediately noticed when Nadia opened the fabric store again. She waved out the window and thought Jacob lifted a hand in return. He seemed like a good man, as did his father, who always had a twinkle in his eyes. Jacob had his own place, but his wife had died from a separated placenta during a third pregnancy, leaving him a widower with two young children now cared for by his mother and younger sisters during the day.

She had turned out the lights when she saw Ben passing the front window. A moment later, he knocked on the door. Nadia froze where she was, at the end of a row of fabric. He scanned the dim interior but apparently didn't see her. When he pulled out his phone and bent his head, she ducked, even though she felt foolish. Hide and seek.

Her phone, left beside the cash register, rang. If he could hear it, he'd know she was still downstairs somewhere. Did it matter? She couldn't take one more apology from him. Really, she should walk over, grab her phone and keep going without even turning her head to look at him.

Since that wasn't in her nature, Nadia stayed where she was until a peek told her he had given up.

Trudging upstairs, she tried to recapture her delight at how well the class had gone followed by the sale of two—count 'em, *two*—quilts, but couldn't quite pull off the trick. *Thank you, Ben and Jennifer.*

NADIA WASN'T ANSWERING her phone.

Thanks to his sister, Ben was currently leaning on a shovel in his front yard, filthy and wiping sweat off his brow. Lucy had decided to take on clearing a couple of flower beds, one in his front yard, one in back. Both were choked with weeds, but some stubborn roses and perennials were still hanging on and blooming, if sparsely. Instead of being able to take advantage of his day off to sit around reading in the air-conditioned house, he'd had to pretend enthusiasm to join her laboring out in the hot sun.

He'd insisted on doing the heavy digging on the bed in the front yard. All the while, he kept an eye on his phone, sitting on the railing so he didn't miss a call. He would have kept it close no matter what, of course, since he needed to be available to his officers 24/7. Them, he'd rather not hear from on a day off. What he had hoped for was a return call from Nadia once she calmed down and listened to his message.

Using the hem of his ratty T-shirt, he wiped sweat out of his eyes and spared a scowl in the general direction of the phone.

"Are you waiting to hear from someone?" his sister asked. Still on her knees holding a trowel in one of her gloved hands, she had paused to look at him.

"Your nose is pink," he said. "You know the sweat is washing off the suntan lotion."

She snorted. "You don't really think Nadia will call, do you? After you were such an ass?"

He turned the scowl on her. "I didn't mean what I said the way she took it."

"Really?" She tipped her head to scrutinize him over the top of her sunglasses. "You ordered me out of the store. Because your delicate, innocent sister needed to stay away." She pretended to ponder. "I think that was it."

"I didn't imply—"

"Sure you did." She looked distinctly unfriendly, considering he was her beloved brother. "You hit two targets with one shot. She's inappropriate company for me, and I'm too fragile to… I'm not sure. Resist the temptation if she tries to recruit me to join her in a criminal spree?"

He growled a word he didn't use around her—okay, he *did* think of her as somewhat fragile—and snapped, "I told you about the cherry bomb tossed through her window. You saying that wouldn't scare you?"

"No more than it would anyone else," Lucy said hotly. "I have…particular issues. That doesn't mean I'll faint if I happen to be around when someone is nasty to her." She paused. "Which is fortunate, given that *you* were downright vicious."

"I wasn't." The protest came automatically even though he still winced at the memory of Nadia's face when he said what he had.

His sister only stared unrevealingly at him through the lenses of those dark glasses, then bent her head and went back to work ripping out weeds and dropping them in the rusting bucket he had found in the shed that also held the temperamental lawn mower the former owner had left for his use. He might have been better employed mowing today than clearing a flower bed he would now feel compelled to keep weeded.

When his phone rang, Ben took his time stretching before he reached for it even though he doubted he was fooling Lucy. Nadia's name did not show on the screen. Instead, the caller was Danny Carroll, the officer he intended to promote as soon as he could make other shifts in the department.

"Danny?"

"Chief? I know you're off today—actually, I am, too—but I heard something I thought would interest you. If you're busy…"

"Doing yard work. Nothing I mind being interrupted."

The other officer chuckled. "I know what you mean. Well, this probably isn't anything big, but the Neeleys live about a block from me. I know Carol was involved with the auction committee, and Ron helped with setup. I guess some carpentry know-how was needed."

"I talked to her," Ben agreed.

"Well, my next-door neighbor mentioned that the Neeleys are going on a ten-day Alaskan cruise in July. And that Ron is talking about buying a boat. Something he can use for fishing and maybe even waterskiing. Last time I talked to him, he was complaining about how slow construction has been, and how he didn't like having his wife work but Carol was looking for a job to help out."

"Could she have found a good one?"

"She was talking about cashiering at a convenience store or at the Hy-Vee if she was real lucky. That's not the kind of work that pays for luxuries."

"No, it isn't," Ben agreed. He couldn't quite picture the woman he'd met conspiring to steal money raised for charity…but someone had. "I'll talk to Ron. I won't mention you."

"Thanks. We have a friendly neighborhood. You know how it is."

"I do." Ben thanked him and put his phone on the railing.

Naturally, Lucy had been eavesdropping and he had to explain to her. She encouraged him to shower and go talk to the man *now*. "You don't know how awful this has been for Nadia."

She was wrong; he had a good idea. Which motivated him to take one of the quickest showers on record and head out the door.

The Neeleys lived in a modest rambler. It was Carol who came to the door, obviously surprised to see him on her doorstep.

"Just thought I could catch your husband at home on a Sunday," Ben said easily. "Is he here?"

"You bet." A pleasantly rounded, middle-aged woman wearing a lot of pink, she led him into the living room, where two recliners faced the TV. When she called, "Ron, Chief Slater is here to see you," a man appeared from the kitchen. A good foot taller than his wife and rail thin, Ron Neeley was losing his hair.

Ben didn't see even a hint of wariness on either face. He took a seat at one end of the sofa and waited until both had perched on their respective recliners.

"I imagine Carol told you the kinds of questions I was asking," he began.

Shaking his head with apparent regret, Ron said, "I don't think I can help you at all. I put together some racks first thing that Friday morning, then came back to help dismantle the sales tables and set up for the auction. I didn't even stay for it. Carol drove herself so I didn't have to go back for her."

"I suppose you've heard all the talk."

It was Carol who answered. "Yes, but we've been distracted. In fact, we were away for the two weeks before the auction. I don't remember if I told you that. I felt guilty not being here to help, but it's been a crazy past few months. My mother passed away in May, so Ron and I have been going back and forth to Springfield ever since, clearing out her house. Ron kept it in good shape for her." She smiled at her husband. "It sold right away, thank goodness."

Ben said the conventional, "I'm sorry for your loss," and knew this visit was another dead end.

"Oh, I'll miss her, but we were starting to talk about nursing homes, and Mom would have hated that, so…"

They mentioned the Alaskan cruise and how excited they were. As soon as he reasonably could, Ben stood and said, "I don't see any need to bother you anymore on a Sunday. I'm getting a little desperate here, so I just wanted to make sure I didn't miss talking to anyone involved with the auction."

They both accompanied him to the door, Carol shaking her head over such wickedness but also telling him she worried about Nadia. "Such a hard worker, and with a kind word for everyone. I've been meaning to stop by the store to tell her I don't believe any of those people bad-mouthing her, but with so little time to quilt, I haven't needed to shop for fabric."

Her husband gave her a sidelong look. "As if you ever need to, with a closet stuffed full of fabric you haven't used."

Ben left them still amiably arguing about the issue. They were such nice people, he was ashamed to be disappointed that they hadn't turned out to be crooks.

Although it wouldn't hurt to do a little research, make sure he hadn't just been conned, he decided.

CHAPTER NINE

SUNDAY WAS COMPLETELY UNEVENTFUL. Nadia wished she could think of it as peaceful, but truthfully she felt more as if she was waiting for the other shoe to drop. She didn't once go downstairs. A couple times, she looked to be sure the chair was still wedged in place. If somebody broke into her shop or vandalized the exterior, they did it quietly.

Monday morning, dread crawled through her even before she opened her eyes. The days of being excited about her new business and the auction were gone.

Don't want to get up.

Maybe from now on she should keep the shop closed on Sundays *and* Mondays.

Something to think about, but right now the sign promised she'd be open, so she needed to get moving if she didn't want to alienate any of her remaining customers. Plus, she needed to dash to the bank for the money she owed Jennifer and still be back before ten.

Thinking about the bank during the five-block walk, Nadia became aggrieved anew that her financial information had been handed to the police. Okay, the bank manager might have been legally required to cooperate, but he could have called to let her know about the warrant. Wasn't she owed something as a customer? Byrum did have branches from two different banks, so she could move her money. Although, why bother, when the chance was so good that she wouldn't be staying?

As many buggies passed as cars. At least half the downtown businesses were either Amish owned or employed Amish workers. Small paddocks and sheds off the alleys were shared to shelter the horses during the day.

Barely over a week ago, Nadia would have enjoyed the walk. Today, she was grateful to see so few pedestrians this early in the morning.

Her business at the bank didn't take long. The teller divided the cash she needed between two envelopes, one for each of the quilters. Seeing increased foot traffic as soon as she stepped out of the bank, Nadia walked fast, purposefully, on the return trip.

When she came abreast of the Amish Custom Cabinet Shop, though, Jacob Yoder stepped out. "*Gute mariye.*"

Smiling politely, she said, "Good morning to you, too." Had he been watching so he could waylay her? They'd never had a real conversation before. It was possible, she decided, that he was concerned she'd have to let his sister go.

Solidly built and around her own age, Jacob wore a blue shirt with the customary black pants and suspenders. The straw hat shaded his face. His chestnut-colored beard signaled that he was—or, in his case, had been—married. Only unmarried Amish men shaved their jaws. It had taken Nadia a little while to get used to seeing bearded men with clean-shaven upper lips.

Jacob met her eyes, his sympathetic. "Hannah says business has been slow for you."

So she'd been right that his worry was for his sister. "Did she tell you what a good day Saturday was? Maybe I've turned the corner."

"*Ja*, I hope that is so." He glanced over his shoulder. "*Ach*, I think that is *Daad* yelling for me. I must go, but call for us anytime if you need help."

His kindness gave her a lump in her throat. Maybe he was thinking about her as well as Hannah. "Thank you. *Denke*," she ventured.

Jacob laughed. "So you speak *Deitsch*, do you?"

Nadia couldn't help laughing, too. "So far, some polite phrases. Oh—because of the name of my shop, Hannah did teach me to say, *En schtich in zeit is neine wart schpaeder naus.*"

A stitch in time saves nine.

Eyes twinkling, Jacob agreed she had needed to learn that much.

Her uplifted mood lasted about one minute. First, she saw Jennifer Bronske getting out of a car parked at the curb, and realized a second woman sat in the passenger seat. Then she saw an approaching police car, slowing to pull in behind Jennifer's black Mustang.

What's more, a man was walking fast toward her on the sidewalk. A stranger. She wanted to be relieved, but he didn't avert his gaze the way most passersby did. *Should* she know him?

Her thoughts jumped. Jennifer had to be well aware that the store didn't open until ten. Was she really so afraid she wouldn't get paid?

But Nadia forgot Jennifer now that she was close enough to see the burning intensity of the stranger's stare, trained on *her*. She stepped sideways toward the vacant storefront next to A Stitch in Time, giving the man plenty of room to go by.

But he didn't. Her heart thudded as he came straight to her. The cords in his neck stood out and his face was flushed an angry color. He stopped barely a foot from her, his hands balling into fists as his sides. And then he spit on her face.

BEN ERUPTED FROM his car in time to hear Nadia's assailant snarl, "*That's* what I think of you, lady."

He covered the distance in seconds. The two formed a frozen tableau when he reached them. Grabbing the creep's shoulder, Ben yanked him around. "You are under arrest for—" The words died in his mouth. He knew this guy. Not to meet, but he'd seen his face. One of the spring tornadoes had ripped a swath through his dairy farm, destroying his barn and taking the roof off his house. One of his kids had been killed. There'd been a lot of devastation this year, but only the one death.

The man just glared at him. Behind him, Nadia hadn't even lifted a hand to wipe off the spittle dripping down her cheek. She looked stricken. Meantime, Ben had heard brakes applied as a passing motorist stopped to watch the scene, and he was well aware Jennifer Bronske and some other woman had home-plate seats to the action.

Ben said evenly, "I'm aware of your troubles, Mr...?"

The man's Adam's apple bobbed. "Hixson. Leonard Hixson."

Ben nodded. "Mr. Hixson. I'm the chief of the Byrum police department. Whether you know it or not, you just committed the crime of battery on a woman who worked very hard to raise funds to help you among many others." He raised his voice slightly, wanting to be heard. "There is *no* evidence to support any belief that Ms. Markovic took the money. To the contrary. How are you going to feel when we arrest someone else?"

Hixson blinked a couple of times. The crazed fury in his eyes became confusion. "I didn't…"

"You did." Now Ben let his voice harden. "Spitting is considered battery as much as striking another person would be."

His mouth fell open. "But…"

Ben propelled him around to face Nadia, who had finally taken a tissue from her purse and was wiping her cheek.

"Ms. Markovic," Ben said formally, "this is Leonard Hixson. His farm suffered severe damage this spring from a twister. Worse, his son was killed."

Shock and pain transformed her face.

Ben continued, "He has good reason to be feeling a lot of anger, but there is no excuse for directing it at you this way. I'm very willing to arrest him if you want to press charges—"

As he'd expected, she was already shaking her head. "No. No, of course not." Tears stood out in her eyes. "I'm so sorry for what you went through, Mr. Hixson. I can only promise you that I didn't take that money."

Hixson's face crumpled. "Thank you. Thank you. I don't know what I was thinking. I have to go." He staggered as he turned away from her, his shock showing when he saw the growing audience. Then he bent his head and began walking. By the time he reached the corner, he had broken into a run.

Ben exhaled when he lost sight of Hixson. He took Nadia's arm and said quietly, "Let's get you inside."

"Yes, I—"

Cheeks crimson, she still held her chin high when she looked at Jennifer Bronske, who hadn't moved an inch since Ben arrived on the scene. If the woman had looked pleased, he'd have been tempted to arrest *her*, but he thought shock was what held her in place.

Nadia delved in her big handbag and pulled out what was obviously a bank envelope. She held it out to Jennifer. "As promised."

A flush spread on the other woman's face, too. She lifted a hand, hesitated and then took the envelope. "What happened... I'm sorry, I didn't mean..."

Nadia simply nodded and said, "Please excuse me." Her hand shook when she took her ring of keys from her bag.

Ben deftly removed them from her hand and unlocked the front door of the shop. While ushering Nadia inside, he didn't so much as look at Ms. Bronske or any of the several other people who had clustered on the street out of sheer nosiness. After relocking the door, he steered Nadia toward the archway that led into the hall. That she didn't once protest told him how raw she felt.

Once they were out of sight in the hall, he gave her a nudge. "Go wash your face."

"Oh." Her hand lifted toward her face but stopped short, as if she didn't want to touch it. "Yes."

With her in the bathroom and the door shut, Ben stalked from one end of the hall to the other. Had he done the right thing, not arresting Hixson? Would the guy have also hit Nadia, if Ben hadn't been there to intervene? And what was the deal with the bank envelope Nadia had handed over to Jennifer Bronske?

The rush of fear-fueled adrenaline still had him on

edge. That moment, when he'd realized a man was closing in on Nadia… If he hadn't been here, if he'd gotten a call she'd been seriously injured and was being transported to the hospital…

He couldn't think like this. He didn't know how his feelings for her had gotten so out of hand, but—

He spun around when he heard the bathroom door opening. Nadia emerged with her composure almost reassembled. Only her eyes betrayed the aftereffects of the ugly scene.

Without even thinking, he took the couple steps to reach her and pulled her into his arms. For a moment her body stayed rigid, but then her purse clunked to the floor and she wrapped her arms around him, too. She shuddered as she laid her head on his shoulder, and in back she grabbed handfuls of his shirt.

"It's okay," he murmured into her hair. "I was proud of you. You kept your dignity. He ended up ashamed the way he should be. This will pass. It will."

Yeah? Who was he trying to convince? But he knew. *Both of us, that's who.* Because if this didn't pass, she'd move away. No question. And he didn't want her going anywhere.

As boneless as she felt right now, only the knuckles digging into his back told him she wasn't truly relaxed. He fell silent as he became disturbingly aware of her body, pressed up to his.

She needed comfort, not him coming on to her. Especially not him. Except, she did trust him enough to let him hold her. That meant something, didn't it?

Finally she sighed and began to straighten away from him. One hand released his shirt, then the other.

The color in her cheeks hadn't subsided—or maybe it was new heat in her cheeks.

He wondered if she was aware that, after releasing him, she had placed one hand on his chest, her fingers spread. When those fingers flexed slightly, he almost groaned.

"Thank you." Nadia nibbled on her lower lip. "I'm still mad at you, but…I don't know what I'd have done without you." Her huff was almost a laugh. "Well, I suppose you were just doing your job."

"No." Not smart. He made himself elaborate anyway, be completely honest. "Yeah, I'd have intervened for anybody, but…I wouldn't have been so scared."

"Scared?" she whispered, searching his eyes.

"He could have had a weapon. No matter what, he was a lot bigger than you are. I didn't know if I could get to you in time."

Her hand moved in a circle, comforting—still unconsciously, he thought.

"But you did. And…I doubt he meant to hurt me."

"I hope not."

"This is why you didn't want Lucy near me."

"It is." What else could he say? "But I don't think she's as fragile as I believed her to be." He shook his head. "How could I have just let Hixson walk away? I should have asked if he just happened to see you, or came looking for you. Either way, he's an angry, depressed man."

Pain infusing her voice, she said, "Who might have been helped with some of the money I lost." Her hand falling to her side, Nadia started to step back.

Ben caught her before she was out of reach, his fingers sliding beneath the bundle of hair at her nape to hold her. "The money was stolen. You didn't lose it."

She stared back, not lowering her chin. "Unless I took it."

"You didn't." When he saw no softening on her face, Ben lost what grip he'd had on his self-control. The distance he'd had to keep, her anger, had been eating at the lining of his stomach and causing a chronic ache beneath his breastbone. He couldn't prevent himself from bending his head and kissing her.

NADIA HAD FELT too much in such a short period of time. Mad and frightened, grateful and yearning. Somehow, Ben's mouth covering hers was exactly what she needed.

With a whimper, she rose on tiptoe and flung her arms around his neck.

She'd wanted to hate him.

I can't.

He was turning her in a slow circle, as if this was a dance. Except…during one of those slow twirls, something bumped her side. His gun.

She froze.

Nadia put both hands on his chest and pushed.

Ben lifted his head. "Nadia?" he said hoarsely.

"I have to open my shop. You're parked right out in front. People will think…"

An indescribable sound tore from his throat, and his hands fell from her waist and hip. He backed up until he hit the wall.

"I didn't mean…"

"To kiss me?"

His gaze lowered to her mouth, then lifted to meet

hers again. "I've been wanting to kiss you since I set eyes on you."

At the auction. The reminder was painful, but needed. "I'm still…" Nadia hesitated.

"A suspect?" He shook his head. "Not in my eyes."

She retreated a couple steps, needing distance to regain her common sense. "How can you say that?"

"Easily…" He ran a hand over his face. "No. I won't push. You have a lot to deal with."

Yes, she did. But the kiss, him telling her he believed in her, changed something fundamental.

After this, it would hurt even more to have him turn on her.

What if a customer was peering in the front window wondering why the door was locked and the lights weren't on? "I need…" She gestured toward the archway, even as she couldn't seem to quite look away from his dark eyes.

"I know. I have to get to work, too." He didn't sound any more motivated than she felt. But after a minute, Ben grimaced. "I'll call later. I should talk to Bill Jarvis and find out if there isn't something that can be done to help the Hixson family."

Nadia nodded. "A lot of the people who paid with credit cards or by check have reimbursed us. That's nowhere near enough money, but…"

"Most people's losses were at least partially covered by insurance. I wonder if his weren't."

"It might not be that," she said. "Grief changes a person. But also, when I started working on the auction, I was told that some companies specifically exclude wind storm damage. It can come as a shock to people who didn't read the policies carefully."

Ben grunted his agreement. "Some of the folks who got hit had coverage on their houses but not the barns, tools, livestock. For a dairy farmer, that would put him out of business."

"Does he have other children?" She had to ask, even though she doubted it lessened the agony of losing a child. Ben's expression suggested he knew she was remembering Molly...and Molly's brothers.

"Two younger, if I remember right. The boy he lost was the oldest, out exploring with his dog, too far away to make it to the house. I know Hixson kept the door to their storm shelter open as long as he could."

Praying, she thought. He would have had to let himself believe the path of the tornado would miss his son, that he would come running after it had passed, calling for his mom and dad. They would have climbed out of the shelter, looking frantically in every direction, uncaring of barn or house. She imagined the desperate search—

"Nadia." Ben squeezed her shoulder. He waited until she focused on him. "It was a tragedy. You can't save every child."

"I already know that." How well she'd learned that lesson. She backed away. "I'm okay. I am," she repeated, when she saw that he remained unconvinced.

"All right." He gave her a quick, hard kiss. "I'll call later."

It surprised her that she could smile. "I might even answer."

His husky chuckle made it easier to see him leave, and to greet a woman who appeared minutes later.

She only bought two rolls of thread—but she hadn't

had to go somewhere else because A Stitch in Time was inexplicably closed.

BEN NEEDED A decent cup of coffee, which he wouldn't get at the station. Only after he had accepted the job and moved to Byrum had he discovered he couldn't get anything but an old-fashioned cup of coffee anywhere in Henness County. He'd bought an espresso machine and resigned himself, but six months later a drive-through coffee stand with a serious drink menu opened on what had formerly been a vacant lot two blocks off the main drag.

Today he bought a double espresso on ice that should hold him for a couple hours. After one long, cold drink, he drove the short distance to the police station and parked in his reserved slot, taking the cup in with him.

After letting dispatch know where he was, Ben settled down to work in his office on scheduling for August.

Boyd had put in for vacation—two weeks, which Ben had approved back in March. And, crap, Jose Garcia was getting married the first Saturday of August and then taking a honeymoon. Their absences overlapped by only a few days, but if anyone got sick—

His desk phone rang, the internal line. "Slater."

Sherry, the fount of gossip, said, "Chief, Jim Wilcox is here to see you."

The locksmith? If he'd suffered a loss of some kind, why wouldn't he have called 911?

"I'll be right out."

What few dealings Ben had had with Jim Wilcox, he'd liked him. Somewhere in his forties, the man had a way of sliding into the background. Just one of those unmemorable faces.

When Ben opened the door into the waiting room, Wilcox stood. He picked up a brown paper bag from the seat beside him and brought it along. They shook hands, and Ben ushered him into a small conference room.

Once they were seated, Ben said, "So what's this about?"

"Someone managed to shove this through the mail slot in the door of my shop." He pushed the bag across the table, looking glad to get rid of it.

Ben had never been in his store, but had seen ads. Wilcox made copies of keys and sold a variety of padlocks and dead bolts as well as safes for homes and businesses.

The brown paper sack in front of Ben was the kind just about every grocery store used when customers didn't want the plastic ones. This one was plain, lacking a store name or logo. It had been folded several times and the whole thing flattened. Ben opened it and looked inside. From long practice, he suppressed his jolt of surprise. He didn't reach in. In fact, he regretted handling the bag at all without having put on latex gloves first.

He met the locksmith's troubled brown eyes. "I assume you took a look to see what was in here."

"Sure, I thought it was for me. The first check I picked up was written for forty-seven hundred dollars. I know the woman who wrote it. I'm thinking this is some of what was stolen after that auction."

Ben tapped his fingers on the table as he thought. "Why you?" he finally asked.

"I don't know." Wilcox appeared less than happy. "A lot of folks in town know me."

"I wonder if your mail slot is deeper or wider than some."

The locksmith shook his head. "I don't know. I never paid any attention. My building is an old one. The mail slot is brass, an old-timer."

"Do you mind if I fingerprint it?"

"No, of course not."

"All right." Ben pushed back his chair. "Thanks, Jim. We'll see if we can get lucky and find someone who saw this being delivered."

Visibly relieved to have off-loaded a problem, Wilcox left, and Terry Uhrich came in response to Ben's summons.

He studied the bag without noticeable enthusiasm. "Well, paper absorbs oils so it's ideal for picking up fingerprints. But this one isn't crisp out of the store. Fact is, I'll probably find lots of them. I'll have to get yours and Jim Wilcox's for elimination. And that's just the beginning. Presumably a grocery clerk or bagger and at least one customer handled it. And people keep these around and reuse them. There could be an innocent reason for just about anybody leaving a print on it."

"And the guy who decided out of the goodness of his heart to give back the credit card slips and checks probably wore gloves."

"Unless he's never watched television or read a book or newspaper," Terry agreed.

"Or just got careless."

Terry shrugged. "It happens. Anything I lift from here would mostly be useful to match up once you have a suspect." Peering inside, he said, "I'll see what

I can do with a couple of the top and bottom slips and checks, too."

"Go for it," Ben said, and went straight to his office to call Nadia. She deserved to hear the news first.

CHAPTER TEN

NADIA HUNG UP the phone, her hand not quite steady. She didn't know what to make of Ben's news. Had somebody suffered from a guilty conscience? If so, not enough to return the cash—the irreplaceable part of what was stolen.

She'd be happier if the return of the credit card slips and checks cleared her of suspicion, but anyone who had already condemned her wouldn't have any trouble believing she had been the one to jam the sack through the locksmith's mail slot. It was logical to suppose that, under suspicion, she would have decided to get rid of the physical evidence.

The bell on the door let her know she had a customer, so she arranged a smile on her face and stepped around the counter. The smile immediately became natural.

"Katie-Ann!" Besides Hannah, Katie-Ann Chupp was the only Amish woman she considered a real friend. "And Ruth!"

Elderly and tiny, Ruth Graber was widely considered the finest quilter in the area. Nadia had been captivated from their first meeting by Ruth's bright eyes and mischievous smile.

Today, both women carried bundles in their arms.

Quilts, Nadia saw, and gave silent thanks. This was their way of expressing support.

"Do you have room to display more?" Katie-Ann asked, as if there was any doubt. "Mine is only crib-sized, but Ruth's is for a bed."

"For you two, I always have room." Nadia hurried forward to take the larger bundle from Ruth. The top of her head barely reached shoulder height on Nadia. "I'm excited to see what you've brought."

Their voices must have carried, because Hannah and Lucy emerged from the back room. Lucy had arrived shortly after the shop opened to use a sewing machine. Nadia introduced her.

"Learning to quilt?" Ruth surveyed Ben's sister and nodded with apparent satisfaction. "Smart, you are, coming to Nadia. A fine teacher she is."

Lucy beamed. "I think so, too. Do you mind if I peek at your work, since I'm here?"

Of course they didn't; quilters almost always welcomed newcomers. And although the Amish abhorred pride—they said someone was taken over by *hochmut*—the finest of craftsmen and women surely wouldn't strive for such perfection and grace without feeling gratification anyone else would call pride, or so Nadia suspected.

First, she spread Katie-Ann's crib quilt atop the pile on the bed. The Tumbling Blocks pattern used fabrics shading from the palest lemon in one corner through richer yellows and vibrant greens before flowing into blue at the opposite corner.

"Oh," Lucy breathed, reaching out to touch it reverently with her fingertips. "If I had a little boy..." Sadness crossed her face as she withdrew her hand.

Nadia filed away what she'd seen, wondering if Ben's sister was unable to have children or had lost a baby. Not the kind of thing she could ask.

And then they all sighed with pleasure as Nadia unrolled Ruth's Sunshine and Shadows quilt that truly seemed to capture sunlight contrasting with secret corners that were never quite illuminated. Yellow, gold and bronze, it glowed. The tiny, perfectly spaced stitches made it a masterpiece.

"I'll take pictures of this today for the website," Nadia said. "I predict it will sell by the end of the week. I think it might be the most beautiful quilt I've ever seen."

Ruth demurred, of course. *Ach*, she knew so many fine quilters! She did her best, she said, but her eyesight wasn't what it had been, which Nadia didn't believe for a minute. Not after seeing her stitches in this newest quilt.

She took Ruth's hand, small, calloused and arthritic, and Katie-Ann's, no softer but stronger, and said, "Thank you for bringing these. For…trusting me."

The wrinkles giving Ruth's face a crepe-paper-like texture deepened into crevasses. "*Was der schinner is letz?* Not trust you? Who would not?"

What in the world is wrong? she had asked. Hadn't any of the women told Ruth what was happening? In Nadia's experience, the Amish grapevine was lightning fast despite the fact that they didn't use telephones.

"You know about the stolen money?" she said.

"*Ja*, sure."

"Quite a few people think I took the money myself. They are no longer shopping in my store, and—" she made a face "—several women have taken their quilts back. I guess they're convinced I won't pay them."

Ruth's grip tightened until it almost hurt. "Moderns. A good shake, is what they all need! You are honest as the day is long. Any fool can see that."

"*Denke*," Nadia said shakily.

Ruth turned her fierceness on poor Katie-Ann. "Why did you not tell me?"

"You've had enough troubles—"

She snorted. "If I don't know, I can't talk sense into people. This must be set right."

"Chief Slater called a few minutes ago," Nadia said. "Um, he's Lucy's brother."

Hannah already knew, of course. The other two women stared at Lucy for a moment.

Nadia told them about the credit card slips and checks being returned via the mail slot on the locksmith's door. "I told him to take them to Julie Baird. There's enough distrust of me—I can't handle them. A lot of the people have already stopped payment at their banks or credit card companies. There are a few from people we were unable to contact, and those can cash."

"So more of the money can go to help people," Hannah said with satisfaction.

"Yes. But, no matter what, it isn't even half what we brought in. A third of the total, maybe? So many people paid with cash, and whoever took it didn't give that back."

Ruth gave a firm nod. "What I earn from this one—" she nodded at the Sunshine and Shadows quilt "—you will give that money in place of what was stolen."

Katie-Ann beamed. "*Ja*, you must do the same for mine. I will talk to other quilters."

Nadia's eyes stung. "You can tell them that I won't keep a commission if they're willing to donate their part, too."

"No, no." Ruth squeezed Nadia's hand and let it go. "You must keep your part. What will we do if you go out of business? What I offer is for you, too."

Katie-Ann nodded vigorously.

Nadia swiped at damp eyes. "You're making me cry."

"In a good way, I hope." Katie-Ann hugged her.

Laughing through her sniffles, she said, "Of course, in a good way! Thank you both. *Denke*."

Eventually Ruth and Katie-Ann went to the back room to see what Lucy was working on, and approved both her fabric choices and the care she was taking in cutting, sewing and ironing. So many beginners thought they could be slapdash, not realizing how the tiniest imperfection would cause problems down the line.

Nadia caught sight of a buggy stopping in front, the glossy brown horse calm even as a motorcycle roared past. "Is that your ride?" she asked.

Following her gaze, Katie-Ann exclaimed, "*Ach*, Elijah is here already."

"So soon?" Ruth chuckled. "Well, *blabbermauls*, we've been, ain't so?"

Hannah walked them out, and Nadia saw the three out on the sidewalk, their heads close together, and guessed they had switched to Pennsylvania Dutch. The better for Hannah to tell them hastily about this morning's events. Nadia touched her cheek, remembering how filthy she had felt, when a baby's spit wouldn't have bothered her at all.

Knowing she did have friends warmed her inside. The effect lingered even though by lunchtime her sole sale of the day was the two spools of thread.

BEN HAD KNOWN before he and his officers began canvassing people who worked up and down the street from Wilcox Lock and Key that the odds of finding a witness to the bag being poked through the mail slot were about one in a million. Few buildings here had upstairs apartments. With no restaurants or taverns, the street shut down at five o'clock. Yeah, there were streetlamps, but it wouldn't have taken a minute for somebody to pull up to the curb, hustle over to shove the sack through the slot then drive away.

Still, they'd had to try.

When he returned to the station after the fruitless quest, Terry reported finding fingerprints from eight different people on the bag, but none of those were also on the checks and credit card slips that had been on the bottom and top of the pile. Except for Wilcox's and Ben's, Terry ran the prints from the bags, but Ben's gut feeling was that this thief wasn't anyone who'd already be in the system. Not to say the individual hadn't stolen before, but nothing about this had been impulsive. Somehow, he or she had had a key. He—if it was a man—hadn't taken the opportunity to rape Nadia.

Not for the first time, Ben wished he'd followed her home and made sure she got inside safely. If so, he might have seen someone else watching.

Had the thief savored the irony of returning that envelope via Wilcox Lock and Key? Or was it an outright

taunt? *I have a key, didn't need a locksmith?* He gave
a passing thought to Lyle Warren, but odd as the man
was, Ben couldn't fit him into any believable scenario.

He forced himself to set aside the brooding in favor
of a few hours dedicated to the frustrating administrative stuff. He and the principal had a lengthy discussion about what presence the police would have at
the high school come fall semester. An officer who'd
done a lot of the safety talks at the elementary school
had taken a job elsewhere, so Ben now had to decide
who could replace him. He took a call from an irate
father who didn't want to believe his daughter had actually shoplifted.

Midafternoon, Ben checked in with Lucy. She mentioned having spent several hours at A Stitch in Time.
He asked her to hold dinner to give him time to stop
by and talk to Nadia before coming home. What he'd
have liked was to invite her to join them for dinner,
but he didn't dare, not yet. He had been told that the
city council had erupted in some hot debates before he
had been offered the job of police chief. He felt sure
he knew which councilmen—and every one of them
was male—hadn't wanted to hire a brash, know-it-all
Northerner. Ben had worked hard so far to do his job
effectively while not giving anyone ammunition to get
rid of him. However he felt about it, Nadia was still a
suspect in the eyes of too many influential members
of this community.

He slipped away early enough to park in front of
her building just as she was turning the sign to read
Closed. She waited, opening the door as he crossed
the sidewalk to her. He wanted to sweep her into his
arms and resume this morning's kiss, but restrained

himself. Nadia had had reservations about him from the first, even before the theft, and he needed to know why before he presumed too much.

She locked and said, "You do know everyone who sees your Explorer out front will wonder why you're here."

"It's not a police car. Why would anyone notice it?"

Nadia's look said, *Get real.*

"How do you know so much about small towns when you didn't grow up in one?" he grumbled.

"Being the subject of vitriolic gossip is a speed-learning experience," she said tersely. "Are you staying long enough to come upstairs?"

"Yes."

Without comment, she led the way, her reserve solidly in place. Maybe he *should* have kissed her the minute he walked in the door, regardless of who might have seen them.

"I made lemonade earlier," she said without looking at him as they entered the apartment. "Would you like a glass?"

"That sounds good. Thanks."

Another nod, and she disappeared into the kitchen. Not liking this uncertainty, Ben hovered in the small living room, listening to the sounds of her moving around. The cupboard door, the refrigerator, the clink of glasses. Soft but unmistakable. Would she really have slept through those kinds of sounds while an intruder searched her place?

Yeah, but if she'd turned lights on and off quickly on the way upstairs, an interested observer might rightly have assumed she hadn't stopped long enough along the way to hide the money. And what if the only light she turned on in the apartment was in her bedroom? The intruder could have started the search there. With a penlight, he could have seen the money box immediately.

When she returned with the lemonade, he sat on the sofa, her on the easy chair facing him.

"Walk me through what you did when you got home that night."

"What?" Shock showed on her face.

"You parked out in front and let yourself into the store. Did you turn on any lights downstairs?"

"The hall, just long enough for me to check that the back door was still locked. And then the ones above the stairs, of course."

The light in the hall would show as a glow through the store's front windows, for sure, and more faintly through the back window. The staircase lights probably couldn't be seen from outside at all, front or back.

Needing to pin her down, he said, "But not in the store."

She shook her head.

"Upstairs?"

Her eyes briefly became unfocused. "As I was going up, I thought about having a glass of wine. But I was so tired, I think I was weaving a little, so I went straight to the bedroom."

"No lights on the way."

She frowned at him. "What's this obsession with lights?"

He explained, and she said, "How will that help you figure out who he was?"

"It probably won't, but you've satisfied my curiosity. It kept bugging me. How could somebody search out here without waking you?"

"I was awfully tired—"

"I know, but I also think we all have a strong sense of self-preservation and an internal filter. We ignore a lot of noises when we sleep. But there are noises that *shouldn't* be there. A cupboard door closing, a footstep outside your bedroom door—"

Shivering, she carefully set her glass on the coffee table. "But…he or she must have come with the intention of searching thoroughly."

This was the part that still chilled him. "Yeah."

"If I *had* woken up…"

"Thankfully you didn't," he said roughly.

Nadia blinked a couple of times. "Yes." She was quiet for a minute. "You won't give up, will you?"

"No. I'm not good at quitting." He heard more heat in his voice than he'd intended to give away.

She searched his eyes and finally nodded. "Thank you." She cleared her voice. "I've said that a lot today."

When he asked, she told him about Katie-Ann Chupp and Ruth Graber's visit, and their kindness. There was awe in her voice when she mentioned Ruth's offer to donate the entire amount earned from her quilt sale—and Katie-Ann's immediate willingness to do the same.

"It's their way," Ben said simply, and Nadia nodded.

"So I'm discovering." She smiled at him. "Ruth's quilt is spectacular." Some less welcome thought had her smile dying. He'd swear she was challenging him when she added, "I'll bet Lucy will tell you about it."

Ah. He'd hinted, but they never had put that incident to rest. Unfortunately, he couldn't explain why he'd reacted the way he had without violating his sister's privacy. And the last thing he wanted to tell her was that he still wished Lucy would keep her distance until he made an arrest or the community uproar died down.

So all he said was, "She mentioned that she planned to use a sewing machine at your place."

"I can assure you that she left in good health."

"I am worried about her," he admitted, knowing he couldn't lie to her. "And no, it's not because I think you'd be a bad influence on her. It's her. And I can't tell you any more."

Nadia's chin lowered. "Today, she said something…" She rubbed her hands over the arms of the chair. "Katie-Ann's crib quilt made her sad. I wondered if she'd lost a child, or—"

Ben shook his head. "Not that." He knew how much Lucy wanted children, but in the normal course of events you needed a man for that. He'd be sorry if she decided the only way she'd ever have a baby was to go to a sperm bank, but he and—he felt sure—his parents would accept that. "I'll talk to her about it tonight. I stepped in it big-time, and she might take pity on me and let me tell you why I'm nervous about her being here if anything else like the cherry bomb happens."

Worry shadowed her eyes. "Don't push her too hard. I don't want her to be uncomfortable with me."

Not surprised that her first concern was Lucy, Ben nodded and decided to change the subject. Before he could, she said tentatively, "Do you have other siblings? Lucy hasn't said."

So she wanted to know more about him. Did that mean forgiveness was possible?

Ben shook his head. "Just the two of us. We're only

a year and a half apart in age. Two pregnancies so close together probably convinced Mom that enough was enough."

Nadia's chuckle lifted his mood another notch.

"Having two kids in diapers at the same time might have had something to do with that."

Ben laughed, too. "Yeah, that could be. I'm pretty sure I was an oops baby. At least an 'oops, not yet' baby." Intensely curious, he asked, "What about you?"

"Like you, I have only one sister, several years older than me. We were pretty good friends, even though Sonya always was bossy. After…you know, she wanted me to get over it. It was like she couldn't stand not being able to fix me." Her forehead crimped. "Her and Mom, both. They're…"

When she seemed to be searching for words, he suggested, "Overbearing?"

She hesitated. "I know they love me and want the best for me."

In other words, yes.

Unhappily aware that he should shove off and leave her to her dinner plans, he asked if she'd heard from Julie.

"No." She appeared unsurprised.

From his interviews with the volunteers, Ben knew that Nadia had been the driving force behind the fundraiser and had committed a daunting amount of time and energy. In contrast, Julie Baird mostly liked committees and having a reputation for charitable work without having to seriously apply herself. He had a few things he'd like to say to her but, given his position, never would.

"Did you talk to Bill Jarvis about Mr. Hixson?" she asked.

"I did. And you were right. Their coverage on the house excluded wind damage. He didn't have insurance at all on the barn, farm equipment or animals. Raising three kids, and having a relatively small operation like his, they had to be tight with their money. Bill says right now the Hixsons are living with the wife's sister and her family. He has the impression they're getting desperate. Leonard hasn't had any luck finding a job, but doesn't want to sell the land."

"Would anyone buy it, given the obvious tornado damage?"

"Maybe. Farmland usually does go, but without buildings? Anyway, what he'd get wouldn't support a family for long." He sighed. "The Hixsons are near the top of Bill's list, but there just isn't enough money to go around." Seeing Nadia's expression, he said, "Don't go there. The rest of the money you raised would have been welcome, but spread it around between two or three families, and it wouldn't get any of them back on their feet."

"No, but... It's too bad the farmers that were impacted didn't have Amish-style barn raisings."

"They'd have had to be able to afford the lumber. And what good is an empty barn?"

"Not all the cows were killed, were they?"

"Probably not, but he may have had to sell the herd. Anyway, dairy farming is mostly automated these days, even among the Amish. You need tanks to keep the milk cool and sterile, and I'm guessing that's just the beginning."

"It's not right!" she exclaimed in frustration. She'd

obviously forgiven Hixson and ached to help him, giving her a lot in common with the Amish women who had rallied around her.

Despite everything going so wrong with the auction into which she had poured so much energy, her generosity and compassion remained alive and well. Aware of a sharp twinge in the region of his heart, Ben smiled at her.

"No, it isn't right. But you did something extraordinary to try to help, and that's more than most people do." He needed to get out of here before he pushed for something she couldn't possibly be ready to give.

When he expressed his need to go and stood, Nadia rose, too. "You didn't find out anything about the checks and credit card slips being returned."

He shook his head. "I didn't expect to. Whoever he is, he used his head."

And why did he keep thinking of the thief as "he"? If someone involved with the auction took the money, "he" was more likely a "she."

Convenience, he decided. And reality was that he arrested way more men than he did women.

"Why do you suppose the person bothered?" Nadia asked.

"I don't know," he admitted. "Burning the pile would have been easy and less risky."

"Maybe he does feel guilty."

There she went again, holding on to faith that everyone had a heart. Given that she'd seen the darkest side of human nature, that was a miracle.

How would she classify the rage that kept a coal burning white-hot inside him? Would she believe it was justified? Protective? Or would she see a man like her friend's husband, ready to explode at the right provocation?

And are you so sure that doesn't describe you?

Yes. He was sure. But whether Nadia would agree was another story. He still hadn't forgotten the fear darkening her eyes when they met.

That's long past.

Ben wanted to think so, but he was careful to keep his kiss light and not demand more before he left.

CHAPTER ELEVEN

LUCY ARRIVED NOT ten minutes after Nadia opened A Stitch in Time the next morning. Her tote bag bulged, and this time she'd brought the large wooden hoop.

After greeting her, Nadia nodded at the tote. "Are you ready to start quilting?"

"Not quite, but all I have to do is add the borders and cut out the backing and batting. Well, and pin it. And… I don't need to mark it if I'm just planning to quilt straight lines, right?"

Nadia laughed. "No, you don't. Don't sound so nervous! Remember, if your first stitches are huge or crooked, you can pull them out. Besides, this is your first quilt. You can't improve if you don't start."

"I know." She scrunched up her nose. "I'm a perfectionist, which means I drive myself crazy."

"I understand that," Nadia admitted. "It bodes well for you as a quilter, though. The best are, you know."

Lucy looked thoughtful. "That makes sense. I've been studying the quilt in the frame in back. Hannah told me it's yours."

"It is." She hadn't touched it while she was so shaken after the auction, but in the past few days she'd had plenty of time to work on it. No annoying distractions like customers.

"The stitches are incredibly tiny and so even. Which says *you're* a perfectionist, too."

"I am, but part of it is just practice. I've done it so long, now I can quilt with my mind a million miles away, or while I'm carrying on a conversation, and my hand just knows what to do. I use a really small needle, and almost always pack twelve stitches on it."

"But you don't count."

She shook her head. "I don't need to anymore."

Lucy sighed. "I'm hoping you'll give me a quick lesson before I start that part."

Nadia smiled. "Of course I will. And no, we don't have to wait until the class this afternoon. If things stay quiet, I'll be glad to have something to do."

Lucy looked around. "Where's Hannah?"

"Not coming in until noon. Yesterday was so dead..." *Quiet.* That's what she meant.

In a different voice, low and almost timid, Lucy asked, "Do you have time to talk for a minute?"

Ben must have kept his promise, but now Nadia felt guilty. Did she really need to know the details of what his sister had suffered, instead of being willing to accept that he had reason to be extra protective of her?

"Of course I do," she said, "but...if this is because of Ben, you don't have to tell me anything, you know. I don't want you feeling coerced."

"No, I don't mind telling you. Really. I'd like to think we can be friends."

Nadia hugged her. "Me, too. Okay, let's sit in back."

She brought them both bottles of water from the dorm-sized fridge she had under the checkout counter, and sat at the work table where she could see into the store.

"I was raped," Lucy said.

"Oh, no." From their first meeting, Nadia had seen the same darkness in Lucy's eyes she saw in her own sometimes when she looked in the mirror. But by body language and her choice of clothing, Lucy carried it further. Whether consciously or not, she was trying to pass unnoticed, certainly by men.

"It happened the summer after my sophomore year. I didn't go home because I had a job showing prospective students around the campus and doing some filing and data entry for the admissions department. I was living in an off-campus apartment. Then…one night I woke up and he was ripping my clothes off. I tried to scream and he clamped a hand over my face." She stopped, swallowed, distress coming off her in waves. "He—"

Nadia took her hand and squeezed it. "You don't need to tell me. If…it helps to get it all out, I'll listen, but please don't relive it for my sake or your brother's."

Lucy held on to Nadia's hand as if desperate for the connection. Despite dry eyes, her devastation was easy to see. "Thank you. I'm sure you can imagine what happened. What woman hasn't known it could happen to her?"

A lump in her throat, Nadia nodded.

"The rape was…really brutal. When he was done, he hit me, over and over. He must have thought I was dead when he left. The irony was, he'd used a condom and worn those thin plastic gloves, but when he battered me, they must have ripped, because he left blood on me."

"So police had his DNA."

"Yes. I'm told that usually the state lab wouldn't have run it until the police had a suspect, but I was lucky enough to have a detective who kept up the pressure until he got the results even though he and the other investigators never identified the man. So the DNA is out there in case he commits another crime, but it's been sixteen years, and there's never been a hit." She smiled wryly. "Ben calls the detective at least once a year."

Of course he did. Nadia admired him for it.

"The rapist. How is it possible he hasn't done it again?" she said.

Lucy shook her head. "Maybe there was something about me—"

Nadia wouldn't even let her finish the sentence. "You know better than that."

Lucy tried to smile again, the result pathetic. "I do. What I really believe is that he's raped a lot of other women since. The gloves might not have ripped again. Or the condom. And the vast majority of rapes are never reported to police, you know."

Nadia had read that up to 90 percent of rape victims didn't go to the police. "If he injured any other women the way he did you, how could it *not* have been reported?"

"Maybe he didn't. Maybe he got home and freaked when he saw that the gloves had ripped and his knuckles bled. He'd been careful otherwise. He could have learned his lesson. And…I've read that a lot of identified rapists don't come across as frightening. They can be nice guys, really successful, well liked, even married and with children."

"And now you look at every man you meet and wonder," Nadia said slowly.

That same, twisty smile. "I do."

"Who found you? Did a neighbor hear, or...?"

"No, the next morning was Saturday and my parents and Ben decided to take me to breakfast. When I didn't answer my phone or the door, they let themselves in. Ben had a key because he slept on my couch sometimes."

"Oh, no," Nadia whispered again. Ben would have just finished his freshman year in college, which meant he was only nineteen. To see his sister like that... Of course he'd become a cop. Of course he was still intensely protective of her.

"I was lucky. If not for their surprise visit, I'd have lain there all weekend. Even if I hadn't showed up for work Monday morning, who knows if anyone would have come to my apartment to find out why?"

"You were still unconscious."

"Yes. Doctors called it a coma. It was Sunday before I regained consciousness. I had lots of broken bones, including my cheekbones." She touched her face lightly, seemingly without being aware she had. "I was in the hospital for two weeks. I didn't go back to school there, because I was afraid the rapist was someone I knew. How else would he have targeted me? I did eventually finish my degree, but I've lived with a lot of anxiety. I don't go out at night if I can help it, I check the locks about twenty times before I go to bed and I still wake up with a start, thinking I've heard something, at least every half an hour all night long." Her fingers bit into Nadia's. "Don't tell Ben that, please. He worries enough. Anyway, here with him, I've slept better than I have in forever."

"I won't. I promise. He's good at making a woman feel safe." Except, of course, when he suspected her of a crime, when he had the opposite effect. Nadia hesitated. "Did he tell you about what happened to me?"

"You mean, someone getting into your bedroom to take the money?"

"No. Before I moved here." When Lucy shook her head, Nadia described her own ordeal in more detail than when she'd told Ben. "I can't completely understand what you went through, but maybe better than most people. I still have nightmares. And I don't trust as readily."

"Yes." Tears welled in Lucy's brown eyes. "But I'm letting life pass me by, and I want to change that. Coming here was a first step." She tugged a corner of her pieced quilt top from the bag. "Maybe this is one, too."

"I hope so."

The bell over the door was followed by women's voices.

"Friend or foe?" Lucy murmured, even as she wiped away the tears.

Nadia was able to laugh. "Keep your fingers crossed for me."

SOMEHOW, SHE WASN'T surprised when her doorbell rang soon after she closed the store. A second later, her phone rang, too.

Ben.

"Hi," she said, answering. "Is that you downstairs?"

"Yeah. I should have called sooner. I just realized you might be nervous having to come down without knowing who's at the door."

She would have been, if she hadn't guessed Ben would stop by. All she said was, "I'll be right down." But, setting aside her phone, she almost wished she'd made an excuse. Or ignored call and doorbell alike. The intensity of her attraction to a man who reminded her of the worst moments of her life made her wary.

Although, she reflected on her way down, apparently not wary enough.

He still wore his uniform, which reminded her every time of all the good reasons she had to keep her distance from him.

Nadia opened the door anyway, but he didn't move.

"Don't look at me that way," he said roughly.

Not liking the way *he* was looking at *her*, she took a cautious step back. "What way?"

"As though…" He shook his head and walked in. "I remind you of someone, don't I?"

She blinked. "No."

"I scare you."

It was disconcerting to discover how easily those dark eyes read her.

"I just get…flashes."

His knotted jaw told her he wasn't happy about her admission.

"Do you have time to come upstairs?" she asked.

"Maybe that's not a good idea."

"I don't expect you to attack me."

After a moment, he nodded, following when she started up. Feeling strangely awkward once they reached her apartment, Nadia took refuge in politeness. "Can I get you something to drink? I haven't started on dinner yet, but…"

He accepted again, allowing her to flee to the kitchen. There, she took a few deep breaths and tried to figure out why she felt so vulnerable. The answer wasn't hard to find. Lucy's story, and then retelling her own, had opened doors she tried to keep shut.

Returning with two glasses and a pitcher of iced tea, she found Ben studying the framed photos atop a mahogany bookcase.

"Your family?"

"Yes." She set down the pitcher and glasses and joined him. "You must have seen these when you did the search."

"No. I was keeping an eye on the men, and on you. I didn't let myself get distracted."

"God forbid you let yourself be moved by anything like family photos."

Ben slanted a glance at her. "I don't blame you for being ticked, but would you really have wanted me getting that personal? Maybe asking about your family?"

Nadia looked away. "No." After a moment, she focused on the photo he held in his hand. "That's my sister with her husband and kids. She's a paralegal, he's an attorney. She stayed home for a few years, until the kids had both started school. He went out on his own recently, and now Sonya works with him."

"You don't look much alike."

"I took after Dad—really my grandmother on his side—while she took after Mom."

He studied her parents. "Yeah, I can see that. Does anyone else in your family quilt?"

"Mom. She talked me into taking a class with her. I was the one who got hooked. She pieces and machine quilts things like Christmas table runners. Me, I found a passion."

As if her choice of word had triggered something, he carefully set the photo down in the same place it had been, then turned to face her. "Why aren't you married, too?"

She remembered him asking about previous relationships as part of his investigation. "I just...haven't met the right man." Or should she have said, *I hadn't met the right man*? On a wave of shock, she thought, *No, no*. She was attracted to him, sure; sometimes she even liked him. But that wasn't...whatever she'd been thinking.

His eyes narrowed, telling her he'd seen her perturbation. No more than that, she hoped.

Retreating to her favorite chair, she poured iced tea and waited until he'd taken a seat, too, before saying, "What about you? I assume you're not married."

His dark eyebrows rose. "Are you trying to insult me?"

"Maybe?"

He shook his head, but one corner of his mouth lifted enough to tell her he'd suppressed a smile.

"Never been married. I've had relationships, but I think I was too driven by the job to give enough to satisfy any woman."

Nadia noted his verb tense, just as she had hers earlier. "Something changed."

His "What makes you say that?" didn't come across as relaxed as he'd probably meant it.

"You left your big-city job and moved here." She held his gaze in a kind of challenge. "I told you why I did."

Ben took a long swallow of tea and then grimaced, looking at it. "Like a little sugar, do you?"

"Yep."

He sighed and set down the glass. "Lucy told you what happened to her."

Nadia nodded. "And that you'd found her. I assume that's why you went into law enforcement."

"I will never forget what she looked like." Roughened by rage, his voice was even deeper. "Her face a bloody mess..." He swallowed. "That guy destroyed her, physically and emotionally. Lucy could be bossy when we were growing up, but she was also my best friend. Seeing the change in her just about killed me. She was alive, but the light had been snuffed out. She was always shy, but not timid, not afraid of experiencing everything she could. Her standing up to me that day in your store was the first time I'd seen her show any spirit since the rape."

"That's a good thing, isn't it?"

"Yeah. It worries me, too, though. If she were attacked again..." He shook his head, as if he was trying to block even the idea. "The possibility scares me. Could she come back from that?"

"I don't know," Nadia said softly. "But what kind of life does she have if she never takes any kind of risk?"

A nerve twitched in his cheek. "You're right, but I don't have to like it when she does."

"I'd feel the same." She sat quiet for a minute. "Maybe it would be better if she *didn't*—"

Ben was already shaking his head. "As she reminds me, she's an adult. I'm seeing the Lucy I remember, Nadia." Astonishment and what might be joy made him look younger, probably more like the boy he'd been before he found his sister battered and barely alive. "This quilting thing has given her something she needs. You're responsible for that."

Nadia shook her head. "She came to me because she wanted to learn." Nadia prayed that quilting would give Lucy both satisfaction and the knowledge that she was creating something that would outlast her. What could be more healing than that?

"She wanted to learn, huh?" His crooked grin was ridiculously attractive. "I think she was just making an excuse to take a look at you. Me and my big mouth."

Nadia knew she was gaping. "What did you *say*?"

His grin widened. "Not going to tell you."

"What? Then you shouldn't have hinted." She shrugged. "I'll just ask Lucy. She'll tell me."

"Not a chance. She's always on my side."

"Like you're on hers."

His expression softened. "I guess so."

"You're trying to distract me, aren't you? This whole thing started with me asking why you threw over big-city law enforcement in favor of Byrum."

"You don't have to say it that way. You chose to move here, too."

"This wouldn't have happened if I'd picked any other town." She could tell he didn't like that. Because they wouldn't have met if she'd bought that fabric store in Willow Springs in the Ozarks, or in any of the other states where she'd searched real estate?

"Your business was doing well. It will do well again."

That remained to be seen, but she only nodded.

"I didn't choose Byrum," he said abruptly. "I wanted to make a change to small-town policing. I interviewed for several jobs that were open. This one felt right." He moved his shoulders as if uncomfortable. "I've always had a special rage for rapists. No mystery why."

She nodded.

"Even though my last promotion had me spending a lot of time behind a desk, I'd taken lead in hunting down a man who we were pretty sure had raped at least half a dozen women. He was developing his style as he went, getting off on hurting them. The last one died."

Nadia listened in horror, Ben's near-monotone delivery raising the hair on her arms.

"He screwed up with her, though. A neighbor, an older man who doesn't sleep very well, had seen this guy parking and then walking away down the sidewalk shortly after midnight. It bothered him, because this was a residential neighborhood. Most people had garages, which left plenty of street parking. Why leave his car there if he wasn't going to one of the houses on the block? The guy shrugged it off, but he was woken up a couple hours later by a car engine starting. Same car. He didn't even know why, but he wrote down the license number. When he saw the flashing police lights, he called 911 and told us what he'd seen. Turned out, the car belonged to a woman who had reported it stolen the evening before. Middle of the night, we went to talk to her. Funny thing, I'd been to that same apartment complex several times. Investigating the rapes, a name kept coming up. This time, thanks to the witness, we were able to move fast, catching him arriving back at his apartment. Later, we found out he'd ditched the car a mile away and hoofed it. His hair was wet, like he'd just washed it or dunked his head. He didn't want to explain. He was carrying a duffel bag. I asked him to open it, and he ran."

Nadia rubbed her arms, unable to take her eyes off his face. It was expressionless, but he couldn't do anything about his eyes. They were turbulent, betraying everything he'd felt.

"We'd come straight from seeing that woman's body. It looked too much like—" For the first time in this speech, his voice broke, but he recovered quickly. "I wanted to kill him." He paused. "I think I would have if one of my men hadn't stopped me."

The unemotional tone and the words didn't go together. Nadia grappled with what he'd said. She'd always known his capacity for violence. Maybe...maybe *this* was what she'd sensed, the first time she set eyes on him.

Even while wearing a badge, he would have freed his rage and killed a man instead of taking him in.

Nadia had such mixed feelings about his confession, she couldn't figure out what to say. *Why weren't you arrested?* Well, that was easy—nobody, including him, had told his superiors that he had lost control. *I'm shocked?* She was, but...something else lurked beneath.

The silence must have stretched too long, because he stirred. "Now you know you were right to be afraid of me."

"No." Wait. No? "What you felt, what you almost did," she began slowly, "was because you're human. If you'd gone through with attacking him, you would have violated your own beliefs." She had to think this through even as she talked. "But he was vile. And he'd reenacted your worst nightmare."

Ben stared at her, not even blinking.

"And would you really have done it? Hit him, maybe, but to keep on until he was dead? When you hadn't even seen yet what he had in that duffel?" Nadia found herself shaking her head. "I don't believe it."

"I told you."

"How many times in your life have you really lost control?" A thought darted into her head: even making love with a woman, would he?

He still hadn't blinked. "Twice," he said hoarsely. "The first time was after we found Lucy and got her to the hospital. Once I was home, alone in my bedroom, I lost it. I threw things, punched holes in the walls, broke my hand. Sobbed."

"That doesn't really count, you know."

"Why?"

"Because you waited. Even as a teenager, you had the self-control to know you needed to be alone before you vented everything you felt. How many hours did you hold it in? Eight? Ten? More?"

Ben shuddered and closed his eyes. She wanted to think he was seeing the past in a new light, but he could as well be angry that she presumed to know him better than he knew himself.

She blurted, "I wished—"

When she didn't finish, he opened eyes now red-rimmed. "What did you wish, Nadia?"

Despite the rasp in his voice, he sounded gentle, the way she remembered him being so many other times.

"The police in Colorado Springs. The cops who just stood around outside the house. For *hours*. The crisis negotiator." She'd hated him most of all, the burn worse than the pain from her wound. "He was calm and deliberate and sympathetic. And I know that's what he is supposed to do! But Damon refused to let any of us talk on the phone. Why did they give him a hundred chances? Why didn't they *understand*?" She was crying, yelling, and didn't care.

Ben moved fast, kneeling in front of her and spreading his hands on her thighs. "That none of you were capable of coming to the phone? That you were suffering, waiting?"

"That our lives were in their hands," she whispered. "Trickling through their fingers, and they never got mad at what he'd done. Why didn't they care more about *us* than they did *him*?"

"You do know they thought they were protecting you by bringing him down slowly, don't you?"

Face wet, eyes blurry, Nadia nodded. In her head she did. But not in her heart.

"You and Molly held out."

"But Keenan didn't."

He rocked back. "Another of the kids was alive?"

"Yes. I don't know exactly when he died, but if they'd mounted an assault in the first hour, he might have survived. Their job wasn't to pacify a monster, it was to rescue *us*. I was so angry." She balled one hand into a fist and pressed it to her stomach. "I still am. That's why—"

"You reacted the way you did to me. Oh, honey." In a single motion, he got to his feet and scooped her up, then sat in the chair with her in his lap.

And she cried. Hot, angry tears, sad tears, tears that stung. She pounded his chest with a fist, hearing his murmur, "That's it. Hit me all you want." In the end, exhaustion brought emptiness that might even be peace.

Ben kept holding her.

CHAPTER TWELVE

DAYS LATER, NADIA still hadn't come to terms with her breakdown. How could she not have known how much she'd been keeping penned up inside? Struggling with grief, that was one thing, but anger corrosive enough to eat through the walls… That was different.

Too much like what Ben had gone through, after finding his sister?

And why did it disturb her so much to discover they had this in common?

She had managed mostly to avoid him since Tuesday evening. Lucy had been here almost every day, but Nadia hadn't seen any questions in her eyes. There'd been no searching looks, or pity. Which meant Ben hadn't told her about their talk. He must have come up with some excuse for being later than Lucy had likely expected him that evening, but whatever it was couldn't have borne any resemblance to the truth.

See, I told her I'd tried to kill a man, which led to Nadia confessing that she wished the police back home had killed the guy who shot her. She told me a little boy died when he didn't have to, and that made me so furious, she sobbed and punched me.

No, Lucy would not be looking at her the same way if she'd heard that story.

Hannah and Lucy had left a few minutes ago to have

lunch together. Even though Nadia had declined their offer to bring her a sandwich, she half expected them to return with one of the fabulous—and fattening—Amish goodies. A slice of shoofly pie, maybe, or perhaps a butter cookie.

Two browsers thanked her and departed without making any purchase. She had to hope they'd be back. A few real shoppers *had* come and gone. Not enough to justify paying Hannah for eight hours, but this was Saturday, usually the busiest day.

Now the bell tinkled and another woman walked in. Ellen Shaw, a quilter who lived right here in Byrum. She'd become a good customer and Nadia had sold half a dozen of her crib- or wall-hanging-sized quilts. In fact, just yesterday she had called Ellen to let her know one of the small ones she had on consignment had sold.

Nadia smiled and took a few steps to meet the stocky woman who at a guess was in her early sixties. "Oh, I'm glad you came by. I can give you cash or a check, whichever you'd prefer. The young woman who bought your quilt was so excited. She didn't show yet, but said she's almost four months pregnant."

Any of the Amish women would have expressed pleasure that the work of their hands had found a *gut* home. The right home.

But Ellen only nodded, her expression cool. "Cash would be handy. And I'd like to take back my remaining quilts, Nadia."

Nadia went still. "I would regret losing you as a friend and customer."

"I kept waiting for you to do the right thing. Since apparently that isn't going to happen, I can't continue to support your business."

Stung, she still kept it together. Maybe she had developed an emotional callus, if such a thing was possible. "I loved the place I was making for myself here. I offered to work on the auction out of a desire to help other people. How can you believe I would steal the money we raised?"

"If somebody had really broken into your place, I have to believe the police would have made an arrest by now."

She knew arguing was hopeless, but had to try. If she could convince one person... "Whoever it is had a key."

Ellen raised her eyebrows. "And who might that be?"

"I don't know. Mrs. Jefferson might have handed out keys to any number of people. How would I know?"

"All thieves, of course."

"You might recall that one of those people killed her."

Ellen took a step back. "That was never proved. She might have fallen."

"Chief Slater seems certain."

"If someone did push her, he hasn't managed to arrest *that* person, either, has he?"

The spiteful tone told Nadia she was wasting time and hope. "Excuse me. I need to get the ladder to take down your quilt."

Neither spoke while Nadia carefully lifted a queen-size Lady of the Lake quilt from the hooks, climbed down and folded it and two smaller quilts before putting them into bags. At the end, she opened the cash register and carefully counted out bills. She also brought out the forms she had every quilter sign, setting the terms of their agreement, noted the sale and money she was giving Ellen and asked her to sign all four forms.

She should have insisted Jennifer Bronske count the cash she'd been given and sign, too.

Ellen's signatures were closer to slashes than the more rounded handwriting she'd used when she brought these quilts in.

Nadia said, "You do beautiful work. I hope you have luck selling these."

"Thank you," Ellen said stiffly, dropping the cash into her purse before she gathered up the bags and walked out.

Watching her go, Nadia felt all-too-familiar humiliation, anger and dread. Whatever Ben believed to the contrary, she couldn't see how bouncing back from this was possible.

SUNDAY MORNING, BEN and Lucy attended church services.

He had drifted away from organized religion after he left home. College life was new and exciting, and there were better things to do on Sundays. The faith he had taken for granted as a boy probably lingered—until the attack on Lucy. Ben was too angry to worship Him. Later, nothing he encountered on the job led him back to that faith. He saw too much brutality and hate, too many senseless deaths.

But it had become clear to him shortly after moving to Byrum that he was expected to choose a church and show his face every Sunday morning unless he was desperately needed elsewhere. Amish, Baptist, Methodist or Seventh Day Adventist, the people in Henness

County were believers, and they'd look askance at a police chief who wasn't.

He wouldn't have blamed Lucy if she hadn't wanted to join him, but the first Saturday of her visit, she'd asked him what time they needed to leave for church in the morning. This week, she seemed to take it for granted they would go.

After the service, he suggested they go out for brunch. Instead of eating in Byrum, he drove to Hadburg, the next-largest town in the county. He knew the food was good at the Amish-owned Hadburg Café, and he hoped to pass unrecognized.

The minute they walked in, he saw Henness County Sheriff Daniel Byler and his wife, Rebecca, alone in a booth. He'd learned the previous week that they were in San Francisco, where Rebecca was testifying in court at the trial of one of the men who had tried to kill her last year.

Now he paused beside their booth. "Bet it's a relief to be home."

Strain briefly showed on Rebecca's fine-boned face. "I pray they won't need me again."

Daniel and he clasped hands, and Ben made introductions.

"Please join us," Rebecca urged, so Daniel switched sides to sit beside his wife, and Lucy and Ben slid into the booth across from them.

In no time, Rebecca and Lucy were chatting like old friends, while Daniel and Ben caught each other up on their jobs—including the theft of the proceeds from the auction.

Rebecca, a beautiful blonde, jumped right in once that subject came up. "Just yesterday, *Grossmammi* told me all about it," she said. "She's outraged that so many people are convinced the owner of the shop kept the money."

Ben glanced at his sister. "Rebecca's grandmother is Ruth Graber, who you met."

"Oh, she's sweet and fierce both!" When Rebecca laughed, Lucy said, "You're so lucky to have her. And the quilt she brought in for sale is exquisite. Even Nadia said it was the most beautiful one she'd ever seen."

"She is talented. And I think quilting has been a lifeline to her since my grandfather died last fall. She really believes he's with God and she'll join him when her time comes, but she seemed lost without him. Making a quilt for our wedding gave her a purpose." Rebecca frowned. "She won't admit any possibility Nadia would have done such a hateful thing."

Daniel raised his eyebrows at Ben.

"It's been ugly," he said. "I'm getting the feeling people rushed to blame her so they didn't have to look around and wonder who might have taken the money. Better to see horns and forked tail on the outsider than imagine them on your next-door neighbor or your cousin."

Lucy jumped in to tell the other couple about the quilters who no longer trusted Nadia to sell their work, or who insisted on a cash payment instead of a check. Lucy puffed out a breath of frustration. "Because, of course, she's not trustworthy."

"According to Ruth, the Amish all trust her," Daniel put in. "I asked my mother to be sure it isn't just Ruth, but *Mamm* said the same."

Lucy explained why Nadia's store was in trouble anyway. Amish women might offer enough quilts for her to sell, but most didn't purchase their fabric from her. And Nadia didn't want them to, not when it would take business away from the fabric store in Hadburg.

Rebecca looked as fired up as Lucy was. "*Gross-mammi* said some man actually *spit* on her?"

Ben explained Hixson's story without naming him, and told them how quickly Nadia had come around to wanting to help the man and his family.

He'd been aware of a couple in the booth behind him, a good reason to have kept his voice low and avoid using names. It was why he'd cut Lucy off when she'd started to say who'd just pulled her quilts from A Stitch in Time.

But he'd no sooner finished than he became aware that the woman behind him had slid off her seat to plant herself in front of their table.

This was why he'd wanted to get out of town.

"Chief Slater." She nodded at him, then frowned at Daniel. "You're Sheriff Byler, aren't you?"

Daniel agreed he was. Ben saw that he wasn't the only one whose instant reaction was wariness.

She switched her gaze to Ben. "I don't usually eavesdrop, but I couldn't help hearing. I was already mad enough about what Nadia has gone through, but now I realize how complacent I've been. I donated a quilt to the auction, convinced I'd done my part, but none of us have done enough."

A man behind her said, "Colleen, maybe you shouldn't bother these folks while they're eating."

Ben shook his head. "We don't mind." And he didn't, not once she'd said her piece. He hoped he spoke for the rest. "You look familiar…"

"Oh, I should have introduced myself, shouldn't I? I'm Colleen Hoefling, and this is my husband, Rob."

Lucy leaned forward. "Nadia pointed out one of your quilts in her shop. It's gorgeous."

"Thank you. That's kind of you. Are you a quilter?"

"Only a beginner. I'm taking a class—" His sister shook her head. "Never mind that. Do you have an idea about how we can raise more money?"

"No, but there must be a way."

"And if you manage to help one family, what about the others?" Ben felt obliged to insert.

"Even one family is a start." This Colleen sounded as stubborn as Nadia could be.

"Ruth Graber and Katie-Ann Chupp have offered to donate the money they would otherwise earn when quilts sell to the aid organization," Lucy put in.

"That's a lovely, generous idea," Colleen said decisively, "and I'll do the same. But it's not enough."

Rebecca leaned forward. "What about doing something online?"

Colleen's face lit. "Crowdfunding, right?"

"Yes," Lucy crowed. "Ooh, that's a great idea!"

Daniel grinned at Ben, who shook his head bemusedly. The women were off and running…and he knew darn well Nadia would be right with them.

Which was probably one reason he was falling in love with her, he thought ruefully, without feeling any surprise at using a word as new to him as the term *crowdfunding* probably would be to the Amish.

Of course, the Amish lived the concept, it occurred to him. Only the technology was new.

He tuned back in to find the women had already agreed on a meeting to make plans. They'd aim for

Tuesday evening. Colleen had offered to host it and would ask friends to join them. Lucy promised to invite Nadia.

"I know Sondra Vance, the staff photographer at the *Henness Herald*, took hundreds of photos of the damage done by this spring's tornadoes," Ben contributed. "She was all but chasing the things. I'll bet she'd let you use any you want for an online appeal."

Rebecca said thoughtfully, "I remember the ones in the paper. They were really powerful. People picking through the ruins of their homes, animals injured, this horrible swath of destruction."

Colleen nodded. "That one of dairy cows lining up to be milked in front of a flattened barn really got to me."

Fired up, the three exchanged phone numbers and email addresses. Colleen's husband grinned over his shoulder at the other two men as he and she left. Apparently, her instinctive urge to jump in with both feet had come as no surprise to him.

The rest of them finished eating, paid and walked out together. Daniel dropped back to join Ben. "I thought you said your sister is just here for a visit."

Gaze on the back of Lucy's head, Ben said, "Something tells me it's going to be an extended visit." Months instead of weeks. Or…forever? Watching as the two women hugged in parting, Ben wondered what Lucy really did have in mind.

NADIA JOINED IN the laughter as the Amish women teased each other. She had been flattered to be invited to this quilting bee—or would the Amish say it was a frolic? In fact, she was the only *Englischer* among them, but the eight women had gone out of their way to make her feel welcome.

Katie-Ann's youngest daughter was due to have her first baby two weeks from now. Every time she had tried to stand up today to help in the kitchen, a chorus of voices ordered her to rest.

When Nadia arrived, two frames had been set up in the living room. The group had separated to hand quilt two crib-sized bedcoverings for the new *boppli*, as the Amish said.

As they worked, there had been much teasing about which group would finish first. Susan Byler, who had introduced herself as the county sheriff's mother, had only chuckled and said, "Fast is not always best."

Their hostess, Katie-Ann, had only quilted intermittently. She was occupied with feeding such a crowd, which included her husband, two sons and a teenage grandson who had also appeared midday for a meal, taking over the kitchen while the women ate outside, in the shade of a large, spreading maple tree.

As the chattering women prepared to depart, Nadia stopped to look closely at both quilts, needing only the binding to be finished. With so many hands wielding needles, she would have expected more variation in stitches, but these were astonishingly uniform.

When she remarked on it, Katie-Ann said comfortably, "*Ach*, we have done this so many times! The finest quilters make their stitches just a little longer, and those who are not so skilled do their very best."

Nadia had quilted the way she always did, and wondered now if she hadn't been steered to a group of women with similar expertise to hers.

"These both came out beautifully," Nadia said. Mary

King, Katie-Ann's daughter, hadn't had an ultrasound and therefore didn't know whether she was having a boy or girl, so both quilts used fabrics and colors that would work for either gender.

"You will stay to eat, *ja*?" Katie-Ann asked. "Driving in the dark in a car is not so bad, ain't so?"

Of course the other women would prefer to be home before dark, given that they were driving buggies. Yes, the local Amish all had battery-operated lights on their buggies, but they weren't as bright as her car headlights. And at the speed a horse-drawn buggy was overtaken by a speeding car, the lights could be seen too late.

Katie-Ann's menfolk were currently harnessing the women's horses and bringing one buggy after another around front. A few of the quilters had come in pairs; one had walked, although Susan Byler insisted she would drive her home. Others must have miles to go.

"No, I don't mind driving in the dark," Nadia said, "but you don't need company for another meal."

"The more people at the table, the happier I am," Katie-Ann assured her. "I have talked about you before. I think Elijah is glad to get to know you."

In a quiet way, Katie-Ann's husband had seemed curious, so Nadia agreed with no more argument even though after the bounteous offerings at midday, she wasn't hungry at all. Katie-Ann allowed her to set the table and pour drinks. Once they sat down, the crowd was nearly as large around the table as it had been for lunch. Mary was staying in her childhood bedroom for a few days since her husband, part of a carpentry crew, was away on a job. One of Katie-Ann's daughters-in-law joined them with her three children, the oldest of which, a girl, hurried to help her grandmother with the meal although she couldn't be more than eight or nine years old. The adults spoke English except when murmuring to the two younger children.

Elijah told Nadia he was sorry about all the foolishness over the money. "Ashamed, they will all be, when the truth comes out."

"If it does," she said wryly.

"You must have faith," he said, and she knew he meant it literally.

Her smile and nod seemed to satisfy him. "*Gut, gut,*" he declared, before applying himself again to his meal.

Despite her hostess's protests, Nadia insisted on helping clear the table after dinner and dried dishes while the others put away food. A cheerful woman who might have been a younger version of her mother, Mary was once again urged to "Rest."

"I can help—"

"No, no, sit," her sister-in-law told her sternly.

Nadia caught her rolling her eyes, and the two of them laughed.

Katie-Ann walked her out to her car. Bats darted against a deep purple sky. The wide doors on the barn stood open and the yellow light of lanterns showed inside, as the men had excused themselves from the table to feed animals. Without even a hint of a breeze to stir the leaves on the trees, the silence was uncanny.

There'd been no way she could turn down the leftovers Katie-Ann pressed on her. After setting the heavy basket on the passenger seat, Nadia closed the car door. She winced at the noise.

"It's so quiet." Instinctively, she kept her voice soft.

"*Ja*, we don't have so many cars down this road, and

the closest *Englischers* are Don and Gale Amundson, on the corner by the stop sign. Nice people they are, but we're glad not to have their outside lights right next door, or the sound of their television and the music their fifteen-year-old son plays so loud."

"I've never lived in the country. Even in a town as small as Byrum."

"Small, is it?" Katie-Ann chuckled. "To me it seems so busy. Cars and stoplights and people rushing in and out of stores."

"I can see that." Nadia gave her a quick hug. "This was a wonderful day. Thank you for inviting me. I'm excited to hear when Mary has her baby."

"You are *wilkom* anytime." This time, Katie-Ann initiated the hug. "Elijah is right. People are acting crazy. They will come to their senses."

Nadia's smile was more forced, but she said, "I hope you're right. Good night, Katie-Ann."

By the time she drove away, the murky light had deepened toward full night. As she turned onto the paved road, her headlights picked out a small animal racing across in front of her. A rabbit, she thought, but as fast as it moved, she couldn't be sure.

Just for now, she didn't let herself think about her problems. She had made up her mind last week to close the store on Mondays, and updated the sign and her website to reflect the change. Taking today off had been a relief. Plus, she loved quilting with other women who felt the same, and the sense of achievement was heartwarming. The friendliness and generosity with which she'd been met gave her a lift, too.

Full night had fallen by the time she turned into the alley behind her building. The only light was one above

a door at the far end. Mr. Orton must have already gone
to bed, since no glow shone from his apartment window. She'd have left her own back light on if she'd expected to stay as late as she had, but really it wasn't far
to the door once she parked in her usual spot out of the
way of the garbage truck that would lumber down the
alley Wednesday morning to empty the Dumpsters. It
wasn't as if she hadn't returned after dark before, especially in the late winter and early spring, when days
were shorter. Besides, she wasn't carrying anything of
value this time, she thought wryly.

Getting out of her car and locking, Nadia wondered
whether the thief had waited out here that night, expecting to be able to knock her down, maybe, and grab the
money box without entering the building at all.

She hurried to the back door, keys in her hand. With
touch alone, she fumbled a little getting the key in the
lock. She hadn't yet turned it when she heard an odd
noise behind her. Metallic? Nadia turned to look even
as her brain supplied the answer. A dog or raccoon or
even a person had bumped the Dumpster. The metal
had rebounded with a small clang.

Something moved between her car and the big bin.
She had no chance to react before a shot rang out and
almost simultaneously something pinged off her metal
door.

A bullet.

With a gasp, she whirled, hunched low and turned
the key. *Bang. Bang.* Time slowed, and the air felt thick
and hard to move through. Her shoulder burned and
she couldn't seem to lift her left hand. Too far away,

voices called out. She pulled the door open, only her grip on the knob holding her up.

And then she fell forward through the opening, into darkness.

CHAPTER THIRTEEN

"Ben?"

If Nadia's name hadn't come up when he answered the phone, he wouldn't have recognized her voice in the single, shaky word.

"Nadia?"

"I know I said I'd never call you again, but…I think I need you."

He lunged forward in his recliner, stabbing a button on the remote to turn off the television. Lucy was calling something from his home office, where she had been researching crowdfunding on her laptop, but he was focused entirely on the phone.

"Tell me what's wrong."

"Somebody tried to shoot me."

His heart lurched.

"I guess somebody *did* shoot me." Nadia sounded vaguely surprised, which told him she was in shock. "Again."

"Where are you?" he asked urgently. "Are you safe?"

"I feel kind of strange. I think I'm going to be sick." A clunk told him she'd dropped the phone.

He moved fast, grabbing his gun from a side table and his keys from the small dish where he dropped them whenever he got home.

Lucy had come out into the hall, alarm on her face.

"I have to go," he said. "Lock up behind me."

Using lights and siren, Ben drove faster than he should have. On the way, he called dispatch, to be told units were already en route. Either she'd called 911, or neighbors had. With traffic scant, he made it downtown in less than four minutes and swerved into the alley.

A police car blocked the far end. He braked where he was, left headlights on to illuminate the stretch right behind her store and ran.

A uniformed officer standing in the door opening turned at the sound of running footsteps.

"Chief. I was just going to call you."

"Nadia did."

Officer Ackley held up a hand. "Wait. You better not come in this way. There's blood on the door and concrete pad. I unlocked the front for the paramedics."

Ben wanted to swear viciously, but managed to hold back. Dennis Ackley was right to stop him from contaminating the scene. And at least Nadia was already receiving care.

"Nadia?" he asked anyway.

"Awake and talking."

All Ben wanted was to get to Nadia, but he had to do his job. Story of his life.

"Have you searched out here?"

"Only to shine a flashlight behind the Dumpsters and the parked cars, but I didn't see anybody. They must have taken off."

"Okay. I'll find out what happened from Nadia. When backup gets here, I want the alley taped off."

"Yes, sir."

Ben ran the way he'd come, turned off the headlights but left on the flashing lights, and then on foot circled to the front door of her building.

A few people clustered on the sidewalk to stare, even though all they could see was the ambulance parked at the curb. From their nightclothes, he guessed them to be apartment dwellers on this block. Lights shone in several apartments above stores.

Ackley waited for him just inside. "The EMTs are with her."

Ben kept going.

Until he was well down the hall, he couldn't see much but the broad back of a man crouched, looking down at someone. A turn of the head allowed Ben to identify Marty McClun.

Marty glanced up at his approach. "Déjà vu."

From that moment, all Ben saw was Nadia, lying on the floor, eyes closed, blood staining her shoulder and arm. The same woman paired with McClun last time was using scissors to cut away Nadia's shirt.

McClun got out of Ben's way.

He crouched beside her and took her good hand. "Hey."

Her lashes fluttered and her eyes opened. "You came."

"You called."

Her mouth curved just a little. "So much for vows."

"Yeah." His voice had been scraped over asphalt. "You hanging in there?"

"Uh-huh."

"We gave her something for pain," Marty said behind him.

No wonder she seemed to have trouble focusing on his face. Ben squeezed her hand. "Can you tell me what happened?"

"I got shot." She sounded both perplexed and indignant.

"Yeah, I can see that." A woman who didn't hold a high-risk job had been shot twice now. How could that be?

The EMT was wiping away blood to give her a better look at the wound. She pressed a thick gauze pad to it. Marty sidled around to help her ease Nadia onto her side so they could clean up her back, too.

"Exit wound?" Ben asked.

Marty nodded. "Looks like. Saw a nick in the wallboard. Bet you find the bullet there."

It had punched through her and into the wall. Ben bet on a hunting rifle. Seemed everyone in these parts owned one or more. Kids around here learned to shoot and hunt before they were old enough to get behind the wheel of a car. Many of the families depended on the meat to supplement their incomes.

Nadia's eyes had started to drift closed again, but he went to his knees and bent forward to lock gazes with her. "Talk to me. Why were you going out back?"

She shook her head. "Not. Coming home. Parked. Wished I'd left an outside light on."

"Did you park in the same place as always?"

"Uh-huh."

He wormed the story out of her. There wasn't much to it. If she hadn't heard something—she thought the shooter bumped the Dumpster—there wouldn't have been any warning at all. As it was, she'd managed to make herself a smaller target, the first and maybe a second shot missing her. She was pretty sure there'd been at least three and possibly four shots fired. They ought to be able to find bullets that had ricocheted off the door or brick wall in the alley. If the shooter was cool enough, he might have picked up the shells before fleeing.

When he asked Nadia if she had heard footsteps, she mumbled, "Uh-uh. Hit my head."

McClun made an exclamation and began exploring her head. When Nadia winced, he said, "Yep. You have a goose egg, all right."

"When you hit your head, was the door still open?"

"I think so. I sort of fell inside. There wasn't anybody here when I woke up. I called you." She frowned. "You weren't here first."

Door open, Nadia unconscious, completely vulnerable. The realization felt like a gut punch to Ben. He couldn't forget she'd been shot before, and lay waiting for medical assistance for hours, unable to so much as twitch or whimper without drawing the attention of the man who'd believed she and the little girl she protected were dead.

Not relevant, he told himself. *Think about tonight.*

Something had scared away the shooter. A passing car? The neighbors' voices? He could get some of the sequence from Ackley as first responder.

"You didn't call 911?"

"Uh-uh."

"Then someone else did. Gunshots have a way of grabbing attention."

"Good thing," the female EMT said. "Brought us here quick." Her eyes met Ben's. "We're ready to transport."

"Okay." He gently placed Nadia's hand on her stomach, then let himself cup her cheek. "I need to get things started here, then I'll follow you to the hospital, okay?" He had an idea. "I'll call Lucy. Unless there's someone you'd rather have with you?"

"No, but if she's in bed—"

He skated his thumb over her lips. "No, she heard me talking to you."

"'Kay." Her eyes closed, her dark lashes forming fans above her too pale cheeks.

Ben made himself release her, stand and step back. She groaned as she was rolled again to allow a stretcher to be slid beneath her. McClun raced off to bring a gurney, and Ben retreated to the shop, where he called Lucy.

He told her Nadia had been shot and was on her way to the hospital. "I know you don't like to go out at night—"

"You have to stay to search for whoever shot her, don't you?"

The shooter was long gone, but he would have left traces of his presence. Those were what Ben would be looking for.

Not necessarily a *he*, he reminded himself. Plenty of women hunted, too, and had equal expertise with a rifle.

"We'll block off the alley until daylight so we can get a better look," he said, "but yes. I want to find the bullets and where the shooter set up."

"I'll go to the hospital. She should have someone with her," his sister said sturdily.

"Thanks." He had to clear his throat. "I'll see you when I get there."

Time to shut down the emotions and focus on the details that would tell him how and why this crime had been committed.

NADIA AWAKENED TO a sharp, throbbing pain in her shoulder and a headache that made her reluctant to open her eyes or move a single muscle.

But the antiseptic smell and the sounds of far-off beeps told her she wasn't home.

She slitted her eyes open enough to see gray light seeping between the slats of window blinds. And she saw something else: a man sprawled in a chair right beside the bed. Ben, slouched low, asleep.

The hospital—yes, she did remember that, but it was Lucy who had been with her, asking questions, smoothing hair back from her forehead, reminding her how to use the pump that supplied the painkiller through an IV.

Not that she'd needed the lesson, given her previous hospital stay. The first time she'd had a GSW. Never having been a fan of murder mysteries or thrillers, she had had to ask a cop interviewing her what that meant after he used the acronym. He'd appeared a little embarrassed and said, "Gunshot wound."

How unlucky was she to have a second GSW in her life?

She really hurt, and she was procrastinating. Nadia opened her eyes the rest of the way and groped for the button. To find it, she had to turn her head, which made her gasp.

When she pressed the button, relief spread through her.

"You're awake." Ben, but his voice a rasp.

"I woke you." Very, very carefully, she rolled her head on the pillow. "I'm sorry."

"Don't be. I've dozed on and off."

Exhaustion or something else carved lines in his

face she was sure hadn't been there. Furrows in his forehead, others between his nose and mouth. Dark stubble covered his jaw and throat. His hair stuck out every which way. He wore a gray T-shirt and worn, faded jeans instead of his usual uniform. Even tired and disheveled, he was attractive.

Oh, heavens, what did *her* hair look like? The throbbing inside her skull didn't let her cling to the worry. "Wasn't Lucy here?" she asked, puzzled.

"Yeah. I sent her home when I arrived."

"Oh." Nadia thought about that. "It was dark. Wasn't she scared to go out?"

"Maybe, but she did it anyway. And no, don't even start feeling guilty. She offered, and she did it. I walked her to her car, and I'm betting she had left on every light inside and outside the house. She texted to let me know she'd made it, safe and sound."

"Okay."

He moved from the chair to sit beside her on the bed. His hand lifted to her face, his fingertips gentle and somehow knowing. He stroked her forehead and applied just the right amount of pressure to her temples. His touch felt so good, Nadia moaned.

"How do you feel?" he asked.

"I've been better." She searched his face. If anyone would have answers, it was Ben. "Somebody shot me."

He smiled crookedly. "Yep."

"I could have been killed."

The smile disappeared, leaving him grim. "I'm guessing that was the idea. This wasn't meant to scare you in hopes you'd sell out and move. Your death wouldn't bring the money back. It's hard to figure what anyone had to gain."

Reluctantly, she said, "Leonard Hixson?"

"A county sheriff's deputy drove out to where Hixson and his family are staying with the wife's relatives. He was there. He and the brother-in-law had watched the same Cardinal game I had on when you called me. Both their wives were home, half a dozen kids. They couldn't have all been lying when they said he'd been there all day and evening. The deputy told me he said, *After what I did, I can see why she'd think—* And then he got all choked up. His wife fired up and said Leonard would never do anything like that."

"Oh." She relaxed. "I'm glad."

"Someone else in the same boat he is could be holding a grudge, though. We'll need to take a look at other people who lost everything and are still waiting for help."

The fingers softly caressing her face went away. She would have protested, except that suddenly his large, warm hand had slid between her neck and the pillow, and now he was kneading aching muscles. Her mind hazed with pleasure, making it hard to think. But what he'd said...

"If it was a million dollars, I could sort of see it. But the seventy-eight thousand dollars that's still missing wouldn't go very far. Is it really enough to make someone kill?"

Ben shook his head, but she didn't see the same disbelief she felt on his face. Bleak knowledge infused his voice. "A punk will kill a convenience store clerk for twenty-five bucks. Abusive men have beaten their wives to death because dinner wasn't ready. Normal people, no. These farmers who lost everything could see you as a scapegoat, though. A symbol. From their point of view, they've been screwed over by everyone, from insurance companies to FEMA and every aid organization that hasn't done anything for them. But you, you're an individual, easy to find, a convenient focus for hate." His expression altered at whatever he saw on her face. "I'm sorry. I was thinking out loud, and I shouldn't have been. What I said—that's unlikely. You know that, don't you?"

It was as if some small insect had stung her all over. Her skin prickled, burned. She found the bed controls, and raised the head of it. Ben's hand dropped away from her.

The focus for hate. Me.

"Who else could it be?"

They looked at each other, his conflict showing. She could almost, but not quite, see all the things he didn't want to say there on his face. There was only the two of them, existing in a bubble.

"I don't know," Ben admitted finally. "I can't help wondering whether this really has anything to do with the auction or the money."

Breathing became a struggle. "You mean, someone *else* hates me?"

He frowned at her. "I want you to come home with me. You shouldn't be alone."

She ached to agree, but knew she shouldn't. "I have a dead bolt lock at the foot of the stairs," she argued. "There's no other access to my apartment."

"Someone could shoot through a window."

She tried to hide her flinch. "I'll keep the curtains and blinds drawn."

Frustration thinned his lips. "You *want* to be alone?"

"You can't be the investigator if I'm living with you. Right?"

"I could explain—"

"And what if my being there endangers your sister?"

"Crap!" he said explosively. Clearly, he hadn't thought of that, and Lucy came first. He ran a hand over his face. "I'll think of something else."

Right. He thought he could unload her on one of his officers? She could imagine it—awkward conversation, trying to sleep in a guest room while she listened for any sound outside the window, or even in the hall. With the new locks and the sturdy chair braced under the doorknob, getting to her in her aerie wouldn't be easy.

What about a fire? She'd be trapped.

With a sort of fatalism, she knew she wouldn't feel safe anywhere. She might as well toss and turn in her own bed as anyplace.

"The doctor might not even release you today," Ben said. And wouldn't, if he had anything to say about it, Nadia suspected.

"I'll be fine with pain meds." She hesitated. "Hannah will show up. She has a key. Can you make sure someone lets her know what happened?"

"Of course I will. No reason she can't tend the shop until you're back, is there?"

"I suppose not." Of course there wasn't. Hannah could teach this afternoon's class as well as she could. With business so slow, Nadia knew she wasn't needed at all, a thought that left her feeling hollow. Or maybe that came from facing the harsh truth that some faceless, unknown person wanted her dead. "Did you find anything last night?"

"Bullets. They're thirty-five caliber, common as

dirt. Both we found last night are in bad shape." His teeth could be heard grinding. "One bounced off the metal door. The other is the one that went through your shoulder. We were able to dig it out of the wall."

"Common?" she said uncertainly.

"It's a caliber used for hunting everything from coyotes to deer. Works in the most popular rifles, like the Remington 700. I'm hoping in daylight we can find a casing, because there could be a fingerprint. Looks like the shooter picked them up, but in better light I'm hoping we spot one he or she missed. Both you and your neighbors think there were four shots taken, so we'll be looking for a less damaged bullet, too, with rifling that could be matched to a particular weapon."

Nadia latched on to one word. "She?"

"Women hunt, too," Ben said simply. "Didn't it cross your mind that the attacker might be a woman?"

Well, yes, it had. But her, she'd never so much as picked up a gun of any kind. Neither her parents nor brother-in-law owned one. The men she'd been involved with in the past were hikers, skiers or mountain climbers, not hunters. Until she met Ben, the closest she'd ever come to a gun was looking down the barrel of the ugly black pistol Paige's husband had used in his rampage. No wonder she'd been startled when she felt the hard bulk of the grip of Ben's holstered gun when he kissed her. In fact, it should have been more of a mood-killer than it was, considering how literally gun-shy she was.

Without any advance warning, the overhead light came on and a woman in purple scrubs appeared at the foot of the bed. She pushed back the curtains and smiled approvingly. "Good morning! My name is

Nancy Jones. I'll be your nurse today. Time for me to take your temp and check your blood pressure so you're ready for breakfast. The carts will be here in no time. If you need to get up…" She looked inquiring.

"Yes." And, oh, she didn't look forward to the trek.

Of course, Ben took the nurse's arrival as his cue to leave. He made Nadia promise to let him know what the doctor had to say, and insisted he'd pick her up if she was released.

Once he disappeared around the curtain, she couldn't hear his departing footsteps any more than she'd heard the nurse's approach. He was just gone. She became more aware of her pain…and that he would be scouring the alley for the most minute of evidence that might identify the person who had come so close to killing her.

THE DAY WAS as maddening as Ben had expected it to be. Of all crime scenes, he thought he hated alleys the most. At best, they were filthy. At worst…well, he didn't have to worry about that in Byrum. There wasn't a lot of homelessness in a town this size, and garbage service was reliable. Since taking the job here, he had yet to go Dumpster diving. Today, he'd have volunteered, if Terry Uhrich thought there was any chance the shooter had tossed something in.

He didn't. "Sounds like there would have been a window of only a few minutes when Ms. Markovic was unconscious and wouldn't have heard the clang of someone lifting that metal lid and letting it fall," he said, contemplating the bin. "We'll take a quick look, but I don't believe this assailant was stupid enough to dump shell casings or anything else right behind her building."

Another officer was currently fingerprinting the trunk, back fenders and bumper of Nadia's car. The shooter had almost had to be standing or crouching in the four feet or so between the rear of her car and the side of the Dumpster. Terry himself was presently flat on his belly, peering beneath the garbage bin.

Ben's phone rang, and he turned away. It was Nadia letting him know the doctor wanted to keep her one more night. She grumbled about missing the meeting to plan a fund-raising strategy for the Hixson family's benefit. Even so, Ben couldn't decide if she sounded genuinely unhappy about being stuck in the hospital, or relieved. He knew which he was. The hospital administrator had agreed to have a security guard patrol her hall today, until Ben was able to return. He wouldn't have been able to drop her off at her apartment and head home to a good meal and his own bed. She might not like it, but no matter where she stayed tonight, he intended to be there, too. She'd find it harder to ban him from her hospital room than from her apartment.

He kept the call brief, and had just ended it when Terry murmured, "Will you look at this?" before he began wriggling backward, holding up tweezers he'd used to grip something. Sunlight lit the thing on fire.

Ben stepped forward. "What the—"

"Earring."

Terry dropped it in a small brown paper evidence bag, but held it open so they could both study it.

"Is it a real diamond, do you think?" Ben asked. If so, that had been a pricey set of earrings, because this was noticeably bigger than the one-carat diamond studs his dad had bought for his mom for Christmas a few years back. Two carats, at least?

It was a simple post earring, the stone set in silver or white gold, or even in platinum. No back, of course.

"Don't know," Terry said, "but it looks like it could be."

"There's no surface that would hold a fingerprint."

"No, but the post would have DNA, if we get that far. When I'm done here, I'll take this by Larson's." The town's one and only fine jeweler.

"If it's a diamond, somebody had to miss this," Ben said thoughtfully.

"Oh, yeah. If we're lucky, Larson will recognize it and still have a record of sales. I don't think it's been here long. No dirt even under the prongs. Let me see if I can find the back. You might look under the car."

It wasn't there, but Ben located it a few minutes later, in a weedy area of cracked pavement running along the windowless, cinder block back of an abandoned building that had once been a mattress manufacturer. The woman could have taken a couple steps before it fell. Or it could have been kicked away. Terry could be mistaken about how long the earring had lain there.

He had picked up some hairs with his tweezers, too, but this *was* an alley. The proprietors in buildings all down the block brought their garbage either here or to the Dumpster near the other end. People probably cut through here. The garbage collectors might get out of their trucks on occasion. Ben would have bet one long, dark hair was Nadia's.

They didn't find a single rifle shell. Of course, they lifted multiple fingerprints from the back of Nadia's car and the side of the Dumpster. In the case of the Dumpster, *years* worth of them.

And Terry did finally lift the lid and hoist himself

in, but he didn't stay long. "Almost everything in here is bagged, neat as can be. Nothing dropped on top."

Canvassing didn't tell them anything, either. None of the people who'd heard the gunshots had been able to see the alley. Mr. Orton, who could have looked out a window, had slept through the whole thing. Apparently, even a siren didn't wake him.

Neither the neighbors nor anybody else within a radius of several blocks had seen anyone on foot in the dark, far less someone carrying a rifle. Nobody had particularly noticed a car engine starting, or driving away, but why would they have? They didn't remember hearing Nadia driving into the alley and parking, either.

The diamond—if it was a diamond—was the only significant find.

Having noticed Nadia's ears were pierced, he called to ask if she'd lost an earring.

"Not that I've noticed," she said immediately. "I pretty much wear plain yellow-gold balls. I can't remember the last time I took them out."

In the city, Ben wouldn't have leaped to assume a woman had lost it. Men wore post earrings, too. But not here. Anyway, aside from the fabric store and the barbershop, most of the businesses on the block were Amish owned and had Amish employees. "Prettying themselves" up with jewelry wasn't their way.

He went home, showered, shaved and changed into his uniform, ate lunch with Lucy, then went into the station to work on the myriad administrative tasks always waiting for him. Terry called to say that their diamond was indeed real, and the jeweler agreed with his estimation of two carats and said it had excellent clarity. A rough valuation lay in the five- to ten-thousand-dollar range. Unfortunately, it had not been purchased at Larson's.

Ben checked, but no one had reported it missing or stolen to the police. Shaking his head, he tried to imagine a woman wearing her best diamond earrings to an attempted assassination.

And if they belonged to the shooter, it seemed to rule out the farmers who might have been enraged thinking Nadia had kept money intended to help them rebuild. Wouldn't anyone have sold earrings that valuable, if they'd owned them in the first place?

What he found himself thinking uncomfortably about were some of those auction volunteers he'd interviewed in the first round. Julie Baird, Karen Llewellyn, Jennifer Bronske and a few others. Women likely to wear diamonds.

What he couldn't understand was why any of them would hate or fear Nadia enough to want her dead.

CHAPTER FOURTEEN

NADIA HAD MADE the front page of the *Henness Herald*.

When Ben appeared at the breakfast table, Lucy had said, "You need to read *that*." Loathing filled her voice

A snippet about the late-evening shooting in the business district had appeared in yesterday's paper. Today's article expanded on it. By the time Ben reached the second paragraph, his blood pressure was soaring.

Anonymous sources identified Nadia Markovic as the victim. Markovic was previously named as a suspect in the theft of over $100,000 raised during a community-wide charitable event to benefit victims needing help to rebuild after tornado damage.

Previously named? Presumably an anonymous source for that statement, too, since in fact the police department had not named *any* persons of interest.

The article continued with more details about the shooting, including a mention that Markovic remained in the hospital, recovering from her wound. There was a suggestion that the "widespread anger Markovic stirred in the wake of the charity event" left investigators flummoxed as to where to begin seeking this perpetrator. Police had declined to comment, as did the Amish co-chair of the quilt auction and sale, put on with such hopeful intentions.

Declined? Ben hadn't been asked for a comment, and no one in his department would have done anything but refer a call from the newspaper editor to him.

With a growl, Ben turned to the next-to-last page, where editorials, political cartoons and letters to the editor appeared. The editorial had to do with a noise ordinance the city council was considering. But the two letters to the editor concerned Nadia and her "alleged" theft of the money, and were both vicious and small-minded. He'd have liked to call them actionable, but all the right qualifiers had been inserted, and he'd be willing to bet the editor and principal reporter of the newspaper had taken care of that. Nice way to make his point without *his* name being appended.

Ben had clashed with Dave Rutledge before, but this time he'd gone too far. As angry as Ben was that Rutledge had made clear how inept he thought "investigators"— read Ben—were, it was the slaps at Nadia that enraged him.

The front-page article wasn't news; it was a thinly disguised editorial. And Ben was going to force a retraction. He'd be stopping by to chat with the two authors of the letters to the editor, too. Their nastiness made them prime suspects in Monday night's attack on Nadia, as far as he was concerned. He might even "name" them as such. Let Rutledge publish that.

"Does Nadia subscribe?" he asked.

"I think so." Lucy sounded as shaken as she was angry. "She's being released this morning, right? I'll go by and ask Hannah to get rid of this morning's paper before Nadia can see it."

The article and, even worse, the letters to the editor were another slap to cement her certainty that she couldn't stay in Byrum.

Didn't these fools realize that only the Amish were keeping this town alive at all? That the vacant space next door to her store where a florist had gone out of business, that the abandoned building behind hers where a small manufacturer had probably once employed twenty people or more, were only a few of the empty commercial buildings and storefronts in Byrum? Nadia was the first outsider in a long time to open a business in Byrum—replacing one that had been closed—and make it thrive. A business that offered products locals needed, and drew tourists as well.

Her success might have inspired someone else to try. But it would seem the good citizens of Byrum and Henness County in general would rather suffer a continued economic decline than welcome anyone they hadn't known their entire lives.

Right this minute, he despised the people he had sworn to serve and protect. Ben didn't much like the feeling.

"Much as I hate knowing how this crap will make her feel, I think we need to let Nadia see this," he said. "Sooner or later, someone will mention it. She wouldn't appreciate being unprepared."

"But…"

"Nadia is strong," he said quietly. "You'll see."

Not looking at him, Lucy nodded and pushed away from the table. "I wish I could say that about myself."

"I wasn't comparing you."

"I know you weren't. I was comparing myself."

A moment later, he heard her footsteps on the stairs.

"I CAN SIT behind the cash register and ring up sales," Nadia told Hannah in the late morning Wednesday, "if you'll take over the class this afternoon." Fortunately, this was their block of the month class. Not that canceling would be the end of the world, she thought. At best, two or three of the registrants might show up.

Hands planted on her hips, expression stern, Hannah looked like a mother taking on a recalcitrant teenager. "You should lie down."

"I've been lying down for two days. I'll go crazy if I have to stare at another ceiling." Accepting her determination to spend at least a little time in the shop, Ben had taken her medication and hospital paperwork up to her apartment.

She hadn't admitted to him that she felt a teeny bit light-headed every time she stood up. With her left arm in a sling at the doctor's insistence, she wouldn't be able to heft bolts of fabric onto the cutting table, either. But, by heavens, she could sit here. Probably she should use her time to look at mail, catch up on her newspapers, but she wasn't ready for a dose of reality on top of the pain pills. Bills could wait.

And, if any customers materialized, she could operate the cash register.

Hannah threw up her hands. "*Ja*, fine. *Ach*, you are as muleheaded as Jacob."

Nadia laughed. It hurt—but it felt good, too.

"Someone is here," Hannah said, looking past her.

The tension in her voice had Nadia swiveling on her stool. An extra-long van had pulled up right in front. It seemed to be crammed full of people. An attack squad? Protesters?

Well, attack squad was probably out, since the passengers seemed to all be women, some young enough to spring out of the van, the middle-aged and elderly passengers taking more care. They streamed toward her door.

Nadia braced herself.

The first through the door swept the store with an avid look. The second, middle-aged, wore a hot-pink T-shirt that said, "Old quilters never die. They just go to pieces."

She grinned at Hannah and Nadia, both of whom were probably gaping. "We're a little overwhelming, aren't we? We're all quilters from Kansas City. Every six months or so, we hire a van and take two days to travel from one fabric store to another. You weren't here the last time we came to this part of the state."

In Colorado, Nadia had belonged to a group like this. They were all hungry to find that one special fabric or a color and pattern perfect for a quilt in the planning. No two stores carried the same stock. Nadia made a point of searching out new and unusual lines.

"We've only been open six months. Welcome!"

The women spread throughout the store with gasps and cries of delight. Several others, she saw in passing, also wore T-shirts with slogans. The most apropos was one that said, "Ever hear about the quilter that had too much fabric? Me neither." She counted—it felt like more, but there were nine women in the group.

They exclaimed over quilts on display, but most plunged right in between rows of fabric. In no time, they were heaping bolts of fabric on the cutting table, where Hannah worked nonstop with the rotary cutter.

"Oh, I'm not sure there's five yards left on this bolt,"

she'd say. "Let's see." Then, "*Ja, ja! Chust* enough." Her accent seemed to be thickening with the excitement.

A minute later. "Three yards of each? I will *chust* pile them here, see?"

Nadia directed several of the women to her displays of fat quarters and fat eighths—small pieces perfect for accents. She bundled many that went together.

The crowd stayed for almost two hours, and spent an astronomical amount of money, sweeping out at last with bags bulging with fabric, thread and a few quilting books.

"This is a fabulous store," one woman assured her, while another said, "We'll be back!"

The women piled into the van. As it pulled away from the curb, waving hands could be seen.

Neither Hannah nor Nadia moved for a minute. Then they looked at each other and laughed.

"I think I need to lie down now!" Hannah declared.

"Oh, my. It was like two weeks' worth of customers all in two hours."

"The blade on the cutter was getting dull."

"It felt like a whirlwind."

Hannah giggled. "*Ja!* That one woman—did you see her? She bought thirty yards, and some fat quarters, too."

If gloating was prideful, Hannah didn't remark on it. Unfortunately, the anesthetic properties of all that excitement wore off with the speed of a birthday balloon losing its helium, and Nadia realized if she didn't take a pain pill and lie down, she'd be flat on her face any minute.

Hannah shooed her upstairs, where she ate a couple soda crackers in hopes they'd protect her stomach, swallowed a pill and lay down very carefully on her side in bed. She couldn't decide if her shoulder or her head hurt the worst. But thank goodness she'd been stubborn! Hannah couldn't have coped on her own, not with so many eager shoppers at the same time.

A smile curved Nadia's mouth as her eyelids grew heavy. But it wasn't the numbers she'd rung up on the cash register she was thinking about as sleep sucked her in. No, she pictured Ben in the chair beside her bed the past two nights. Every time she started awake, he seemed to know and would sooth her back to sleep with gentle touches and the deep velvet of his voice.

She hadn't overcome her fears where he was concerned, and she winced away from the memory of the humiliating search and the scary and hurtful knowledge that he believed she had stolen the money. But... the Ben who hadn't left her side all night, who had held her hand and kept her safe, he was hard to resist.

When she woke up two hours later, heart pounding from a dream that slid away from her while leaving a weight of dread, she moved stiffly to the kitchen where she ate cottage cheese and a peach, then went downstairs.

Somebody tried to kill me.

And that was why Ben had stayed at her side. Not out of passionate devotion, but because he was determined to keep her alive.

She nodded at the women just arriving for the class session, puzzled when their gazes touched on her sling and slid away. Neither asked how she'd been hurt. Because they already knew?

Lips pressing together, she marched to the hallway where her mailbox was located. Mail and newspapers went in from the street side; she unlocked a small door to retrieve what had been delivered.

The handful of envelopes probably did contain bills; she didn't really look at them. It was the two newspapers she hadn't yet seen she set on the counter beside the cash register. The Downtown Shooting headline caught her eye immediately.

Within seconds, nausea hit.

Markovic was previously named as a suspect in the theft of over $100,000 raised during a community-wide charitable event to benefit victims needing help to rebuild after tornado damage.

Still absorbing the other veiled allegations, she read the rest of the newspaper mechanically, not really taking any of it in.

But she did take in the vitriolic content of the letters to the editor. Oh, yes. She did.

AFTER CONTEMPLATING THE surprisingly full parking lot, Ben walked into the Harley-Davidson store on the outskirts of Byrum. The place was busier than Hy-Vee, the only large grocery store in town. He scanned the store as he did any space when he entered it, his eye catching on a cluster of guys in their late teens or early twenties ogling a bike, chrome and black leather and a powerful engine, not to mention a price way out of their means. Dreaming was a lot of fun, though, and it appeared the salesman was being indulgent.

He recognized the woman he'd come to see, working behind the counter. Her hair wasn't the same color it had been, but he knew her, all right. She was tied up right now, apparently helping a pair of women make a decision on... He couldn't tell from this distance. Coffee mugs? Maybe. Another customer was hanging back waiting for her attention.

It was logical that the store offered replacement parts and accessories for the motorcycles, as he'd have expected, and, okay, riding pants and chaps, helmets, boots and bandannas. But regular clothes? Men's and women's departments both carried shirts, jeans, caps, distinguished by the Harley name or logo. There was even luggage. When he finally approached the glass counter, he saw the coffee mugs, along with barware, clocks, sunglasses and heated gloves. No, not just gloves—heated vests, jacket liners and pants, too. Seemed like cheating to him.

"Chief Slater." The platinum blonde behind the counter said. "Did you find something that interests you?"

"Afraid not," he said easily. "I was passing by, thought I'd stop by to check in with you."

"With me?" Alarm flickered in her eyes, but he didn't get excited; most people got worried when he came looking for them. "Have you found out something about Aunt Edith?"

"Afraid not. Although I've been in and out of her place a lot these past few weeks, as you probably know."

"There does seem to have been some excitement there." She gave a quirky smile. "I kind of pay attention, since I owned the building for a little while."

Thirty years old in March, Corinne Bissett must have been a lot prettier before she started looking hard. He guessed she smoked, which had an aging effect. Or maybe it was just the heavy makeup, the too obvious cleavage and the white-blond hair contrasting with darker roots. Ben's gaze flicked to her hand—no wedding or engagement ring. She did have pierced ears, along with probably 90 percent of the other women her age, today wearing something dangly.

"Seems odd, doesn't it? Your aunt getting killed, and then the woman who bought the building having so much trouble."

Just as she always had, she argued, "I still can't believe anyone pushed Aunt Edith. Why would they? She was a nice old lady. She'd lived there forever and ever. Everybody *liked* my aunt."

That was true enough, although a few times Ms. Bissett had slipped a little, revealing the sharpness and irritation she had felt for Mrs. Jefferson. That in itself wouldn't have been enough to make him suspect her of her aunt's murder. The young often had reason to find the elderly exasperating. Corinne probably hadn't expected to be stuck with the responsibility of an aging aunt. But she was the only remaining family—and she was Edith Jefferson's heir.

She'd had an alibi. He'd verified her airline tickets and the hotel room in New York City, where she and a couple girlfriends had met up to sample big-city life. He'd had to rule her out, even though she was the only person who seemed to benefit from Mrs. Jefferson's death. That, and he'd seen right through her pretense at grief.

"You know why we're certain she didn't just fall." He kept his response mild, although she'd *seen* the spot dented in the wall by her aunt's head. Common sense said Edith Jefferson couldn't fly. Still, denial was a normal human failing.

Ben didn't like coincidences, though, and the idea of two intruders in the same building, albeit a year apart, both seemingly having keys to let themselves in, nagged at him. She was one of only two people who'd admitted to having a key, and the other one was a dear friend of Mrs. Jefferson's, also in her seventies. Ms. Bissett could have kept a key. There'd been nothing to stop her from making as many copies as she wanted before she signed the papers selling the building.

All of that would bother him even more if Ms. Bissett had any interest in quilts or had showed her face that day at the Brevitt House.

He had solved other crimes this way, though. He didn't let people drop from his radar. A cop stopping by to see them now and again tended to make people edgy. Especially people with guilty consciences. Edgy enough, sometimes, to do something stupid.

Corinne was tough, though. He could tell she didn't like having him here, but she stayed calm.

Ben settled himself comfortably against the counter. "So, were you able to buy a house once the inheritance came through?" He didn't add, *What about a really nice pair of diamond earrings?* He couldn't imagine she'd admit that, not if she'd happened to lose one in the alley behind Nadia's building.

Her chin rose as if he'd made an accusation. "Yes, I did. I was really tired of always having to share to cut costs." Only then she wrinkled her nose. "Sometimes I'm sorry, though. I didn't think about having to mow my own lawn."

Ben laughed despite himself. "I have to admit, I don't love mowing."

She grinned. "Can't call the landlord to whine if the shower starts dripping or the furnace craps out, either."

"But you can call a repairman without waiting days to hear from your landlord first."

With them both laughing now, he left it at that. His only goal had been to remind her that he had his eye on her, and he'd accomplished that.

"I WANT TO sue them all," Nadia snapped. "Starting with that creep—" her gaze strayed to the newspaper on the table "—Rutledge. He was sweet as shoofly pie when he came to interview me about the store opening. I've never talked to the man again!" She slapped the paper. "He doesn't know me *at all*, but he despises me?"

"No." Ben almost told her to sit down, but knew better. Wounded or not, she needed to vent some of her anger and pain. "He wants to make people talk. Sell papers and advertising. I doubt he cares about you one way or another."

She stopped to look at him. "You don't sound as if you like him, either."

"I don't. And the feeling is mutual. Whatever the crime, if we haven't made an arrest by the time the paper goes to print, he gets in a few jabs. He's all but accused me of police brutality, or condoning it in one of my men, but he always stops just short of setting himself up for a lawsuit. If we bring someone in for questioning and determine they had nothing to do with the crime, we've sullied the reputation of a fine citizen of this community." He didn't even try to hide his bitterness. "Not *we*—it's the police chief 'some members of the community now believe was mistakenly imported from New Jersey by the city council, who may be questioning their own decision with this latest outrage.'"

Nadia pulled out a chair and sat across her kitchen table from him. "That sounds like a quote."

"It burned itself into my memory."

"So I'm not the first person he's insulted."

"No, and you won't be the last. Hey, didn't you notice a jab or two aimed at me in that article?"

"You mean the part about you being flummoxed?"

"Yeah." He rubbed a hand over his jaw. "I shouldn't let the jackass get to me."

Her distress appeared to have eased. Because misery loves company?

"Police brutality?"

Figures she'd home in on that.

"On top of all his other sins, he's a bigot. If someone with a smartphone catches one of my officers wrestling with a black or Latino suspect who has resisted arrest, you won't see a mention in the *Herald*. Make it a seemingly upstanding white citizen—even if, really, he's brewing meth in his spare bedroom—and Rutledge jumps right on it." He was getting angry all over again, and probably grinding his molars to dust.

"Figures." Nadia sniffed.

"We'll make him grovel once we arrest the person who really stole the money."

"That would be nice." She went quiet for a moment. "But what are the odds after all this time?"

Not good, but Ben wasn't going to admit as much.

"The whole thing's a puzzler," he did say. "Right now, I'm more worried about who ambushed you."

"You don't believe it's the same person?"

"It's not logical." He probably sounded as frustrated

as he felt. "He got away with the money. How can you be a threat to him?"

"Because I know something I don't know I know." She made an awful face. "That didn't come out so well. But you know—"

Laughing despite the topic, he said, "I do know what you mean. And, yeah, I guess that's possible."

"What if he's afraid I saw him?"

"If you had, why wouldn't we long since have arrested him?" Ben countered.

Nadia lifted a shoulder to concede his point. "Well, what if someone wants to take over my store? Or just buy my building?"

Why *would* somebody be desperate to take over the building? And if they did…it had been for sale not that long ago. So maybe owning it wasn't what mattered— it was having free access. A chance to retrieve something left here? Or to search for something that had been hidden?

Terry Uhrich's crew had done a pretty thorough search already, he reminded himself, albeit they hadn't pried up floorboards or blasted holes in the walls.

Frowning, Ben said, "Far as I know, there's never been so much as a rumor that Mrs. Jefferson might have stashed anything valuable here."

"Who owned the building before her?"

"No idea. I do know she ran that fabric store for something like forty years."

Troubled eyes met Ben's. "But somebody murdered her. And now, somebody tried to kill me, too. What could we have in common?"

The fabric store. A love of quilts. And the building, which wasn't anything special. The very similar one next door was vacant, available for sale or lease.

But he also could not believe Mrs. Jefferson's death and the shooting weren't connected somehow.

Right now, he just shook his head.

CHAPTER FIFTEEN

SHE SHOULDN'T HAVE let Ben win the argument, Nadia thought, unsettled to have a man lounging on her sofa as comfortably as if he lived here. The worst part was that his insistence on staying sharpened her fear. She couldn't push it back, even for a few minutes at a time.

She worried about Lucy, too. How would she sleep tonight, with her brother not home? She had been so determined not to let Ben know that she was sleeping better than she had in years because he made her feel safe.

All of the above was true, but Nadia wasn't into self-deceit. The real reason his presence disturbed her was because of the attraction between them. She had to make an effort not to stare. Okay, not to stare too *obviously*. It was really, really hard *not* to look.

He'd taken off his shoes earlier, removed his belt and slung it over a chair back and stripped off his uniform shirt to reveal a plain white T-shirt beneath. His holstered handgun he'd set on the end table within reach of the sofa he had taken over. After asking whether she minded, he stacked his feet on the coffee table and took possession of the remote control. To all appearances, he was absorbed in a baseball game while Nadia pretended to read. With the volume low, the commentators' voices and occasional crack of a bat connecting with a ball were background noises she could ignore.

As she stole another look at him, he stretched, flexing all those muscles, and then clasped his hands behind his head. His intensity and restlessness, the way his dark eyes bored into hers, usually kept her from being able to absorb details, like the dusting of dark hair on his tanned forearms or the shape of his ears or the tendons in his strong neck. He had broad palms and long fingers, she had noticed, with a few hairs curling on the backs of those fingers. But given how heavy his beard growth was, she'd have expected his arms to be hairier. And she could make out the definition of powerful chest muscles, so surely if he'd had a lot of chest hair, she would have been able to see that, too. He had distinct stubble by evening; once, he'd run his hand over his jaw, and Nadia had heard the rasping sound. It would be scratchy, wouldn't it, if he kissed her…

That was the moment when she realized he was watching her, too, his eyes even darker than usual.

"I don't suppose you'd like to join me," Ben said, voice husky. He lowered a hand to pat the cushion beside him. "We could cuddle."

Nadia gave her head a panicky shake. She was too vulnerable right now. If he held her, if he kissed her… She was too uncertain about him to let that happen.

"Nadia. I won't ask for more than you're ready for."

He'd read her mind. She cleared her throat to be sure she sounded at least seminormal. "I know."

"Do I still scare you?"

Her "No-o" didn't sound as decisive as she meant it to. His eyes narrowed.

"Is it because I lost it with a suspect? Are you going to make me sorry I told you?"

"No! It's not that. I think… I trust you more because

you did tell me. I'm not a very violent person, but after Lucy told me what she went through, I understand how you felt. You might be her little brother, but I'll bet you always felt protective of her, didn't you?"

He stayed quiet for a minute, scanning her face. Then, as if accepting that she intended to keep her distance, he clasped his hands behind his head again. "I guess I did. The age difference wasn't much, and I was bigger and stronger than her by the time I was four or five."

"I'll bet that annoyed her."

A smile tweaked his lips. "You'd win that bet. My size advantage kept her from getting too bossy." Lines deepened on his forehead even as the smile disappeared. She was confident in her own way, but uncomfortable with new people or in crowds. She didn't know how to deal with it if a guy came on too strong.

Gaze intense, he said. "When she told me she wanted to come down here for a visit, I wondered—" His lips compressed.

"You wondered what?"

"She talked about the Amish. What a peaceful people they are. She sounded so…wistful."

The way he said that, Nadia wondered if he'd ever used that word before.

"You know she'd be accepted among them only if her conversion was genuine, don't you? That is what you're worried about, right?"

"I guess so. Not that it would be so bad. It's her motives I don't like. Are the Amish in general more peaceful than the rest of us? Sure. Becoming Amish wouldn't come with a guarantee, though. They struggle, like everyone else. And plenty of crimes are committed against them." He lowered his hands and let his head fall back. "It's probably all in my imagination anyway. Except for this quilting thing, I haven't seen any sign—"

"She's gone to lunch several times with Hannah and Jacob," Nadia blurted.

He stared at her. "Jacob?"

"Hannah's brother." Oh, why had she opened her big mouth? She felt as if she'd betrayed Lucy. "He and their dad have the custom cabinet shop on my block."

"I've seen him," Ben said slowly, his eyebrows drawn together. "He has a beard. Doesn't that mean he's married?"

"Or was married. An Amish man doesn't shave his beard off even if his wife dies. Jacob is a widower."

He groaned. "Has Lucy said anything to you about it?"

"I'm not sure I'd tell you if she had, but...no. It just seemed friendly to me, except, well, *I've* never had lunch with him. Although," she added in fairness, "that's probably because Hannah is usually covering for me when I take a lunch break, and vice versa." She shook her head. "I can't imagine. If Jacob is thinking of remarrying, he wouldn't even look at a woman outside the faith."

"But she might look at him."

Nadia shook her head again, now that she'd had a minute to think about it. "I don't believe it. She hasn't been...secretive, or, I don't know, blushing or too eager."

"I hope you're right." Ben gazed at the television, but not as if he really saw it. "Let me use your bathroom, and then I think you should go to bed."

The change of subject was so abrupt, she guessed he wanted to be alone.

"Okay." He had the right idea. She could be tempted so easily. Besides, the idea of stretching out in bed brought on a wave of exhaustion.

She brushed her teeth, washed her face and braided her hair, then took a pillow and blanket from the linen closet for him.

When Ben saw the blanket in her arms, he said, "You do know it's probably ninety degrees up here."

"Well…just in case." If he stripped down to shorts, he might feel cool before morning.

If she got up early and came out here…

His hand grazed hers as he accepted the armful of bedding. Their eyes met, and she knew she was blushing. Was he remembering how little she wore to bed the night the money was stolen?

She rushed into speech. "I'll turn on my air conditioner. If I leave the bedroom door open, it ought to help a little out here, too."

"Thank you." He dropped pillow and blanket on the sofa and rose to his feet. "Did you take another pain pill?"

"They're in the kitchen. I will on the way to bed."

"Sleep tight." Ben's voice was low and husky, as tangible as a touch. Except he touched her, too, running his knuckles softly over her cheek. "Nothing will get by me."

"I know." She tried to smile, felt her lips tremble. "I didn't thank you for staying with me in the hospital."

Both of them were talking quietly now, as if they were trying not to wake someone else, only that wasn't it at all. It was more as if… She didn't know, just that she wanted to step forward and wrap her arms around his waist, let herself lay her head on his shoulder. But if she did that, she would want more, and so would he, and she needed to trust him absolutely before she let that *more* happen.

Ben's hand dropped to his side and she backed away, not wanting to tear her gaze from his. His tender expression warmed her deep inside. When she bumped into the other end table and had to grab the lamp to keep it from falling, Nadia knew her cheeks had heated again.

She turned and fled to the kitchen, and then to her bedroom.

However good it felt to lie down, she heard every quiet movement he made, even with the air conditioner rattling. Not until the last light went out did she close her eyes and relax toward sleep. She prayed Lucy wasn't lying rigidly awake because Ben was here instead of in his own house.

Tonight, he was protecting her.

BEN KNEW THAT stopping by to have a few words with the two creeps who'd written those letters to the editor was not wise for a police chief who had enemies on the city council. His internal debate lasted a whole thirty seconds or so. He wouldn't let his anger show, but they needed to know that vilifying an innocent woman wasn't acceptable.

The easiest to track down, Kyle Crandall owned a well-drilling and service business. Ben had never met him, but hadn't liked what he'd heard. Crandall was evidently a hard man to work for. Even with jobs scarce around here, employees tended not to stay long.

A white van ahead of him on the street turned into the parking lot in front of the business. Pulling in next to it, Ben saw Crandall Pump & Well Service emblazoned on the side. The solid, middle-aged man who got out wore a blue shirt with what Ben guessed was the business name embroidered on the pocket. Instead of continuing on in, he waited until Ben reached him.

"I'm Crandall," he said tersely. "What can I do for you?"

"Chief Slater." Ben held out a hand, reluctantly accepted for a quick shake. "I read your letter to the editor in yesterday's paper."

Crandall's expression and voice hardened. "And?"

"You seemed so certain of Ms. Markovic's guilt, I hoped you could share what you know with me," Ben said. "Since apparently you've uncovered something we haven't."

Angry color tinted leathery skin. "I didn't say anything that everybody else isn't, too. I just had the guts to speak out."

"Have you ever met Ms. Markovic?"

Crandall snorted. "You mean, when I was buying some flowery material to sew a new apron?"

"That's a no, then?"

"No, I haven't. Doesn't mean I haven't heard enough," he snapped.

"Care to name your sources?"

"No, I don't."

"In other words," Ben said, as if just reaching a surprising conclusion, "you accused her of a felony offense based on common gossip."

The color deepened. "In my experience, that many people aren't wrong."

"That so? What about Nazi Germany? McCarthy-ism?" *Wasting my breath*, he thought. He shook his head, losing patience. "I'm here to tell you that investigators, myself included, looked hard at her and are confident that Ms. Markovic was a victim, not a suspect in that crime. Maybe you should have called the department before you jumped to your conclusion."

Neither the bull-like stance nor the glare altered. *I'm making an enemy here*, Ben knew, and didn't care.

He dropped all pretense of friendliness. "You're aware that someone laid in wait for Ms. Markovic Monday evening and shot her."

Crandall was smart enough to look a little wary. "I read about it in the *Herald*."

"I need to ask you where you were Monday evening."

"*What?* You're accusing *me*?"

Ben let his eyebrows rise. "Accusing? Of course not. But the opinion you expressed in print of Ms. Markovic was…extreme. I'd go so far as to call it hateful. I've been a police officer for a long time, Mr. Crandall. Coincidences make me itchy. You had to have turned in that letter to the editor at the latest on Tuesday. Maybe you wrote it over the weekend, or on Monday. Monday night, someone tried to kill her. The attack had nothing to do with the theft…unless the man who attempted murder was riled into doing so by violent outrage. Which you felt."

Oh, yeah, the guy was vibrating with outrage right this minute. Didn't much like having the tables turned on him.

"Expressing an opinion is not a crime in this country, last I heard."

"No, it is not. Unless that same person took his outrage a step further."

"You can't pin this on me!"

Ben had long since learned how to sound unemotional but inflexible. "Mr. Crandall, all I'm asking is
for your whereabouts at the time in question."

His glare felt like standing too close to a bonfire.
"I was home, of course! With my wife. Feel free to
ask her."

"I may do that." Ben inclined his head. "You have
a good day, Mr. Crandall. I would advise you to check
your facts in the future before you express an opinion
publicly again."

He heard sputtering behind him as he walked back
to his car and got in. Ben didn't look at the jackass
again as he backed out and drove away.

Number two: Jay Bradshaw, long-haul trucker.

"YOU ASKED HIM *THAT*?" Nadia looked at Ben in shock.

"You heard me." He took a bite out of his burger,
almost enjoying the attention they were drawing.

The Cozy Home Café was the classic diner—rotating
stools lining a long counter, booths with padded, red
vinyl-covered benches along three walls and tables
filling the remaining space. Ben ate lunch here often,
considering it an excellent place to shake hands and
exchange a few words with citizens of his town. Keep
his finger on the pulse. The good food was a bonus.

Today, he'd decided to make a statement. His hand
had rested lightly on Nadia's back as they walked in.
Fortunately, the corner booth had been empty, allowing
him to see the entire restaurant including the entrance.

This being the busiest time of day, he was really hoping Dave Rutledge decided to have lunch here today.

Nadia was still sputtering. "But…you can't really think either of those men shot me."

He shrugged. "Why not? They both expressed rage at your very existence. Could be one of them is just unhinged enough to decide to do something about that."

Shivering, she cast a surreptitious peek at the other diners. "You're scaring me."

Ben reached across the table for her hand, enclosing cold fingers in his. "I'm sorry. No, I really don't think either of them is anything but an intolerant, loud-mouth know-it-all with anger management problems. I decided to shake them a little bit, that's all."

"Did it work?"

His grin probably wasn't very nice. "Oh, yeah. Especially Bradshaw. He didn't have even a wife for an alibi. I left him quaking."

The set of Nadia's mouth became prim. "What if one of them complains about you?"

"I say I had to look at the two of them as suspects given their open dislike of you."

"You shouldn't have done it." A smile bloomed. "But thank you."

Ben laughed, then nodded at her plate. "Eat."

She picked up her BLT, then sneaked another look around. "Is everyone staring because of all the talk about me?"

"Nope, they're staring at us. Because the big, bad police chief appears to be romantically involved with that woman they read about in the newspaper."

Nadia made an inarticulate sound and dropped her

sandwich. "I shouldn't have come! You could be putting your job at risk."

"Nadia." He held her gaze. "You are *not* a suspect. Repeat after me. Not a suspect. I have every right to be romantically involved with the beautiful businesswoman who was just the subject of an assault. In fact, I *am* romantically involved with her." He paused. "Or so I'd like to think."

They stared at each other. No cop should let this happen, but he lost all awareness of the people around them. Only she mattered. What if she said—

"Yes." Her smile and those glorious eyes both reflected her tangled feelings, but she hadn't said no. "Any man willing to sleep in a chair for two nights running and then on a sofa at least two feet too short for him so that he can protect a woman almost has to have romantic feelings for her, doesn't he?"

He could feel his heartbeat in a way he usually didn't. "Well, he'd do it for his sister or mother, but not any other woman. But she has something to say about it, too, you know."

This time, she answered with a tremulous smile. "She... *I* may be a little nervous, but you make me feel things I haven't in a long time. Or—" Nadia shook her head, deciding not to finish.

Or ever? Was that what had nearly slipped out? He hoped so. Because she was a first for him, too.

A cheerful voice intruded. "You need a refill, Chief?" Their waitress poised a coffeepot over his cup.

And he hadn't even seen her coming.

"Thanks," he said.

The waitress smiled at Nadia. "You need anything else, hon?"

"I'm good, thanks."

Once she moved on, Nadia wrinkled her nose a[t] him. "I think we ought to talk about something else."

Ben grimaced. "I think so, too." He'd intended t[o] make a statement by taking her out to lunch, but no[t] the kind of statement he would if he kissed her pas[s]ionately in front of half the town.

He didn't want to discuss his investigation—eithe[r] of them—here and now, either. He had other stuf[f] going on at work, too, of course, but couldn't take th[e] chance of being overheard. Family, he decided. Tha[t] was something two people who'd gone out togethe[r] could talk about.

"Your parents know what's going on?" he asked.

"More or less." Nadia didn't look thrilled with th[e] topic. "The money part, and I did say some peopl[e] seem to think I must have stolen it. I haven't told the[m] about the shooting yet."

"You think they'd be on the first flight out here i[f] they knew."

"Yes, and what could they do? What if they got caug[ht] in the crossfire?" She made another face. "Literally."

"This isn't good timing for a visit," Ben agreed. "P[ut] them off if you can."

"I will. If nothing else happens, I might not have t[o] tell them about the shooting."

He gave her a quizzical look. "Do you ever plan t[o] go clothes shopping with your mother again? Swim[m]ming with anyone in your family?"

She had refused to wear the sling today, but hel[d] her arm carefully to her side and wasn't using her le[ft] hand even to pick up a drink.

"Oh," she said after a minute. "Well, crud."

Ben laughed, if softly. Apparently Nadia hadn't given much thought to the recent scar. She was something new to him: a beautiful woman who didn't seem to waste a lot of thought on her appearance. She kept makeup to a minimum, wore pretty clothes that weren't obviously trendy and never posed or paid attention to whether people were looking at her or not. Except right now, of course, when every single person in the place had definitely noticed her.

Speaking of... "Incoming," he murmured. He didn't know the woman, which meant he hadn't interviewed her post auction. Didn't mean she wasn't a former customer who'd turned her back on Nadia.

But Nadia's face relaxed and she smiled. "Audrey. Have you gotten started on that Pine Tree quilt?"

"I managed to get the pieces cut out, and then my daughter's appendix burst. I have the kids daytimes. Not complaining, but...how do young mothers ever manage to get a thing done?"

Laughing, Nadia said, "You should know. You had three of your own."

The plump woman didn't look old enough to have grandkids. Her laugh merry, she said, "Too many years ago! I don't remember."

They chatted for another minute, her friendliness extending to Ben, before she excused herself. She'd left her husband waiting by the door, although he'd found someone to talk to, too. Audrey concluded with, "Glad to see you out and about."

"I hope your daughter recovers quickly."

The happy chuckle trailed behind the woman.

"A customer," Ben said.

"Yes, and really nice. I inherited her from Mrs. Jefferson, so to speak, but Audrey tells me I have a better selection."

"Dessert?" Ben asked. "The pies are really good."

"I'd better not, but go ahead." Her lips curved. " might steal a bite or two from you."

Grinning, he lifted a hand to summon the waitress.

Hearing Nadia's ringtone sobered him for no good reason.

She had to twist in her seat to delve into her purse with her right hand. After taking out the phone, she lifted her gaze to Ben, letting him see her apprehension. "It's the shop phone. Hannah *hates* making calls."

Then she answered with a "Hannah?"

Eavesdropping, Ben could make out only enough to know that her Amish assistant was agitated. She spoke unusually fluent English, reflecting her exposure to *Englischers* first at her father's business and now at Nadia's. At the moment, her accent had deteriorated, and he caught a few German words thrown in amongst the English.

"Yes, I'm with Ben. I'll come back right away. You shouldn't have to deal with this. Why don't you lock the door and turn the sign to Closed?"

The waitress was bearing down on them. He said quietly, "Just the check, please."

Nadia dropped her phone in her purse. Her face was as close to expressionless as she could make it but he knew her well enough to see the turbulence in her eyes. "I have to go."

"I gathered. Let me pay the bill."

"I could walk—"

"Don't be ridiculous."

He waited until he'd paid and escorted Nadia out to the car before he asked what was wrong.

"A demonstration is being staged in front of my shop." Bitterness edged her voice. "Hannah says they have signs. And it would appear a TV station has sent a reporter and cameraman. They tried to come into the shop, but she shooed them out."

"Amish don't want to be photographed. Anyone local would know that."

"But news must come first." Her clutch on the seat belt revealed white knuckles. "This will never end."

Rage had swept him first, but now he felt sick. How could he let her go?

He braked at the corner, where they could see the scene in front of her shop. Unbelievably enough, eight or nine people blocked the sidewalk, each carrying a sign. And sure enough, there was a TV camera.

The icing on the cake was seeing Rutledge scribbling in a notebook as he talked to one of the demonstrators.

CHAPTER SIXTEEN

BEN BRAKED BEFORE turning the corner. No one among the demonstrators had yet noticed his approaching SUV. "I want to commit mass murder," he said grimly.

"You could accidentally swerve onto the sidewalk." Nadia had never said anything so awful in her life, but she was too mad to care.

"I can't tell you how tempted I am." He rolled his shoulders. "I'll park in back."

"I'll look cowardly."

"Unless Hannah told them, they can't know whether you're there or not. Once you have a chance to think about what to say, you can step out front long enough to make a dignified statement. If we go in the front, you'll be mobbed. I don't want to take that risk."

The alley proved to be empty, no scout for the opposition posted there to yell when he spotted her. Even so, she hurried to the back door, surprised when Ben managed to lock his SUV and get there as fast as she did.

They slipped in, stopping at the far end of the hall where they could see through the store to one of the large front windows. Hannah came to them, her face pink with dismay, her *kapp* askew with one tie dangling down her back, one down her ample front.

"That Allison Edgerton is there. After you were

so nice to her! And Jodi Knowles! *Ach*, understand them, I do not!"

Chest so tight, she didn't know how to take a breath, Nadia still managed to pat Hannah's arm. "I'm lucky to have you."

Ben kept his hand on Nadia's lower back. "Are any customers trapped here in the store?" he asked.

"Only Lucy. Staying out of sight in back, but upset."

Seeing Ben's dark face tighten, Nadia added another layer of dread onto everything she already felt. This was what he'd feared when he tried to order his sister to stay away. How could he help but blame her?

Not my first worry.

"Can you see who else is out front?" she asked.

"Allison's husband is with her," Ben said. "Son of a—" He swallowed the rest with a glance at Hannah. "I'm surprised they were willing to go so far. Edgerton raises harness horses. He's got to know the Amish support you. This can't be good for his business."

"I'm not." Nadia craned her neck to see past him. "Did I tell you she confronted me in the grocery store?"

"No." His jaw muscles bulged. "It's mostly women out there."

Nadia recognized several more, women who had shopped here and showed off their quilts to her and volunteered to work at the auction. They had to feel betrayed by her to do something like this, but she was shaken again by such ready condemnation.

"Your father and Jacob were out on the sidewalk, looking to see what's going on," Ben commented.

Riveted on the action, Nadia hadn't noticed them.

Nodding, Hannah said, "*Daad* called, worried, uh-huh. I think he sent Jacob to tell other people."

What, and start a counterdemonstration?

What if the two sides came to blows? Wouldn't that be a spectacle for the five o'clock news? But no—the Amish believed in turning the other cheek. Any blows would be one-sided.

Ben turned his broad back to the scene outside, his gaze on her penetrating. "You saw that Rutledge is out there."

"Jerk."

A smile flickered in his eyes, as if he found her puny insult to be funny. She might have said worse if not for Hannah. She'd never done a lot of swearing, and she restrained even that much out of deference for Hannah and her other Amish friends and customers.

She took a deep breath. "What should I say?"

The three of them hastily came up with a brief statement. Nadia closed her eyes, ran through it a couple of times in her head and nodded.

"I need to get it over with." She tried to convince herself they'd go away once she'd spoken and then thought, *Yeah, right*. They'd apologize and slink away? Only if the real thief was caught would any of these people concede they had been wrong, and maybe not even then. And, considering the weeks that had gone by since the money was stolen, Nadia knew it was unrealistic for her to hold on to any hope that would happen.

"There's *Daad* and Jacob," Hannah said suddenly. "And Amos, too. He works with them."

Nadia peeked again, to find herself looking at the backs of the three Amish men. They had arrayed themselves in front of the store, facing the protesters.

"Oh, no," she exclaimed. "They'll be on television!"

She dashed forward, aware that Ben was sticking close to her. When she flung open the door, she saw that more Amish were hurrying down the street. Men and women both.

The distinctive clip-clop of hooves and whir of steel tire rims on pavement had her looking the other way. A black buggy approached, and another came around the corner behind it.

Were they coming to defend her, even though doing so would place them in a position so uncomfortable to people of their faith? Tears burned the backs of her eyes, but Nadia refused to let them give her away. She stopped where she was, a couple of feet outside the door, Ben a solid presence at her back.

The small group of protesters drew into a tighter clump, their heads turning uneasily. The basilisk stares of the two Yoder men as well as their employee were enough to give anyone the willies. All three stood with their feet planted apart, their arms crossed, the brims of their hats shading their faces. And now they were joined by several other men, who ranged themselves with their backs to the window and wall on the other side of her doorway. A wall of defenders, she thought in astonishment.

The women…they hurried forward, calling, "Nadia, *was der schinner is letz*?" What in the world is wrong? "What is this crazy thing happening?"

A stout, middle-aged woman who had been at the quilting frolic on Monday tucked her arm through Nadia's while the others encircled her. Only a couple of them even looked familiar.

The first buggy stopped at the curb, the horse snorting as if in disgust. The second one advanced as if the driver was blind to the television cameraman, who had positioned himself in the street. He had to scramble back, and was suddenly cut off from the scene in front of the store.

More people were rushing down the street now, some Amish, some not. And two more buggies had appeared. Word must have spread like wildfire.

Likely, they were here for Hannah and her family; most had never set foot inside her store. But they had been told of an injustice, and came. Nadia hoped their bishops wouldn't disapprove.

The cameraman reappeared around the front of the horse that had cut him off, scuttling as if he expected to be trampled or bitten. Too bad the harness horses were too well trained to do any such thing, Nadia thought vengefully.

Ben bent his head, his warm breath tickling her ear. "They're off balance. Do it."

She squared her shoulders and raised her voice. "Excuse me! I have something to say."

The Amish women who had been exclaiming to each other fell silent. And, oh—she did know many of the latest arrivals, other merchants from a several-block radius, two customers who must have been shopping or eating at the café.

She focused on the protesters, looking from face to face, reading the signs they held.

DON'T SUPPORT A THIEF!

BOYCOTT THIS STORE!

HER KIND ISN'T WANTED IN BYRUM.

The last bothered her the most. It was carried by a woman who had taken one of the first classes Nadia offered, and had been delighted by the start she'd made on a quilt that would be far more complex than she had ever attempted before.

Not acknowledging by word or glance the reporters or camera, Nadia said, "I loved this town when I came, when I opened A Stitch in Time. People were so welcoming. I had never lived anyplace where so many of the women shared my love of fabric arts and quilting in particular. I was unbelievably moved that so many of you gave generously of your time and skill to raise money for neighbors, even for strangers, who are so desperately in need." She was quiet for a minute, holding gazes, seeing the angry color in people's cheeks, the defiance in their eyes. At least they were listening. Traffic two blocks away could be heard; the jingle as a horse shook his head could be heard, the silence was so complete.

"That evening was one of the happiest of my life. The most satisfying. I would *never* have stolen that money." She had to swallow before she could get another word out. Ben's hand on her back helped. She let herself lean into it, just a little. She had intended to keep her statement shorter, but now she was talking to these people, saying everything that had been eating at her. "I wanted to build a life here in Byrum. To make friends, help quilters sell their extraordinary work to a wider market, to someday know I belonged. I have been stunned at how quickly people I thought I knew turned against me." Once again, she looked from face to face. Some would no longer meet her eyes. "I don't even understand it. Because I was the last person known to have the auction proceeds, the police had to look at me. I understood—" *lie, lie* "—and allowed a search of my building and car so that they could rule me out as quickly as possible. Chief Slater has made it clear that he does not consider me a suspect in the disappearance of the money." Her vision had become blurry, and she realized in panic that she was crying. But she had to finish.

"I have never in my life committed a crime. I have never shoplifted, or shorted a customer on change or cut a fabric length a little short. I keep promises. This—" she gestured at the signs and the people who held them "—hurts. I didn't do anything to deserve this. I hope…" She had to breathe for a moment, summon the will to finish. "I hope you'll search your hearts before you attack another person the way you have me."

With that, she turned and hurried inside, ignoring shouted questions. And applause. To her astonishment, many of the bystanders were clapping, for her. Was the camera panning the crowd? She felt sure Mr. Rutledge would say as little about her supporters in tomorrow morning's article as he thought he could get away with.

Nadia kept going, holding her head high but wanting only to reach the back room, to be out of sight. Behind her, she heard Ben's deep, firm voice saying, "I'd like to make a statement as well."

TWENTY MINUTES LATER, having also answered questions, he found Nadia in the back room sitting beside Lucy. The two women held hands, their eyes red and puffy and their faces splotchy. Hannah and several of the other Amish women hovered. All looked at him when he walked into the room.

"They've cleared out," he said. "Or should I say, they've run for their rat holes."

Nadia shook her head. "They'll hate me even more. I should have been more diplomatic. I could have said I understood why they were angry—"

He cut her off with a "No. There's nothing understandable about their race to judgment. You hadn't given a one of them any reason to think you'd do something that crummy. To the contrary."

Her bloodshot eyes didn't waver. "I hadn't given *you* any reason to think I'd do something like that, either."

The sting silenced Ben for a moment. "I thought we'd gotten past that. I didn't know you."

"I…" Nadia averted her gaze, then met his again. "I'm sorry. That just…came out."

Very aware of their audience, he nodded. Inside… he was shaken to realize that she might have forgiven him on the surface, but still harbor anger. *You really thought it was that easy?* he asked himself.

"To get back to the point, understanding was the last thing you had any reason to offer. Puzzlement, hurt, those will get better results."

Nadia gave a forlorn sniff and looked around. "Having so many people come running to the rescue helps more than anything I said."

Ben smiled at the group still here. "You're right."

"I just wish there hadn't been cameras here."

One of the women said, "You don't need to worry about us! *Gott* will understand. We don't have the televisions, so we won't see our faces there."

Hannah's father, who had unexpectedly followed Ben in, spoke up. "They know we ask them not to take their pictures of us. We cannot let cameras scare us from helping our friends."

Nadia burst into tears. With so many women to fuss over her, Ben kept his distance. Roy Yoder chuckled.

"Nadia must become used to having friends, ain't so? I think Ruth Graber would have hit me over the head with an iron skillet if I had done nothing today."

Ben found himself smiling, too. "If she could have reached as high as your head."

Roy's laugh became heartier. "*Ja, ja!* Ruth is only so high." He held a hand at belt level. "But me, I would have bent over for her."

"Fierce, is she?"

"I would say so. She and Katie-Ann Chupp, they say Nadia is a good woman who tries to do right by people. None of us want her to close her store and move away."

"No," Ben said huskily. "None of us do."

He would have liked to stay, but knew there might be fallout in his town he would have to deal with. He exchanged a quiet word with his sister, bent to kiss Nadia's cheek and whispered, "You did good," and then went out the back.

One of Ben's least favorite city council members, Maurice Abbott, called not an hour after he reached his office.

"I understand you held a press conference to answer questions about an ongoing investigation," he said sharply.

"A press conference? No, I didn't. Did I answer questions when they were raised? Yes."

"Was that wise? How can you publicly proclaim Ms. Markovic isn't a suspect in the crime when you haven't identified anyone who *is*? Did this unknown person really waltz into a locked building, go straight to the money and vanish without a sound or a clue left behind? Or do you think it's a ghost?"

Ben would have smiled at the sarcasm if he liked Abbott better. "I feel confident in saying Ms. Markovic was the victim and is not a suspect," he said. And how many times would he have to repeat that? "As for the waltzing, she had not replaced the locks from the former owner. You may recall that Mrs. Jefferson was murdered by an individual who very likely had a key."

Abbott grumbled about him leaping to call a mere fall down the stairs murder. He explained again about the laws of gravity, about force and trajectory. This repetition was really beginning to annoy Ben. He also reminded the city councilman that the medical examiner had felt the severity of fractures suggested an accelerated fall. "Now, a gymnast with a springboard might have managed to hit the wall where she did, but you tell me how an elderly woman taking a tumble did."

Abbott didn't have a comeback, but complained that Ben shouldn't have made a statement without discussing it with the city council.

"It's part of the job," he said, forcing himself to sound a lot more patient than he felt. "That job is to enforce the law and provide justice when possible. Impartiality is essential, as is my ability to act for the good for the citizens of this city rather than for individual city council members." He was tempted to ask what he'd recommend if a member of the city government were to break a law, but refrained.

Maurice went away, but Ben didn't kid himself that the guy was satisfied.

He hadn't realized that a police chief had to be a politician, but the calls kept coming. In addition, a car versus buggy accident was reported, the car driven by a fourteen-year-old joyriding with three friends. The buggy was damaged but horse and driver were unscathed. None of the kids had been wearing seat belts, however. All were carried in screaming ambulances to the hospital. One was currently listed in critical condition, another in serious condition.

Ben wasn't able to get away, so at five o'clock he went downstairs to turn on the only television in the station, kept on a rolling cart in the bull pen.

The demonstration in front of A Stitch in Time and the surprising counterdemonstration led by peace-loving and reserved Amish was at the top of the hour. It began with a recap of the theft, followed by a couple of harsh comments given by Allison Edgerton and a woman identified as Sandy Houser. But the arrival of not just Amish, but also store customers and other merchants was televised, and well-edited clips from Nadia's statement were aired. An angry reaction from another woman following the statement was kept brief, and the segment concluded with Colleen Hoefling, whom he hadn't seen arrive, stoutly defending Nadia.

Ben thought the station had been fair, and noticed that the cameraman had done his best to show the Amish slightly unfocused only in the background or in profile.

He called Nadia, who said, "Yes, I watched it. It wasn't as bad as I expected. Am I wrong in thinking the reporter came down on my side?"

"No, I think she did. Rutledge, now…"

She huffed. "I used to deceive myself that journalists tried for fair and accurate."

Ben laughed. "I suspect some—most—do. Unfortunately, Rutledge owns the *Henness Herald*, which gives him complete freedom to indulge his every nasty bias and desire to increase circulation by stirring the pot whenever he can."

"Do you know, I ran a weekly advertisement in his paper? Never again."

"Not many options," he pointed out.

"I'll go with the weekly. And I can do handouts, post on bulletin boards. Anything but the *Herald*. Maybe I should talk to other merchants, try to start a rebellion."

Ben laughed, imagining Rutledge's reaction.

Hearing her temper and determination let him release some tension. She didn't sound like someone planning to close her store tomorrow morning. Ben hoped she had paid attention to the proportion today of demonstrators versus supporters. While many of the supporters wouldn't be customers of hers, the small group of women waving those signs wouldn't be any big loss to her business, either.

Well aware she'd lost a lot of other customers who hadn't turned out today, Ben grimaced. Not only customers—Nadia had lost her sense of security, probably hard-won after the hideous shooting she had survived in Colorado. To have someone break into her place? To be shot again? It was a wonder she hadn't already upped and gone.

Having people turn against her would have stolen her assurance as well. Would she ever be able to trust the same way again?

Ben's inbox was still piled high, he hadn't answered all his emails, he ought to check on how the injured kids at the hospital were doing—but what he wanted was to go home. Lucy intended to invite Nadia home with her for dinner, at least.

So, to hell with it. This was Saturday. He was entitled to time off, and for once, he would be selfish. He had been trying to make himself delegate more anyway; his first two years here, he had concentrated on training, and maybe it was time to believe his efforts had been effective.

He powered down his computer, verified that he had his cell phone and started for the door. Of course, that was the moment his desk phone rang. If it was an outside call—

Of course, it wasn't. If one of his officers or the dispatcher needed him, he had no choice but to answer.

"Chief?" It was Denise Small, the evening dispatcher. "Jim Wilcox is here to see you."

Surprised, he asked, "Did he say what he wants?"

"No, sir. He looks upset, though."

"Okay, I'll be right down."

Strange, Ben thought, leaving his office. For Wilcox to show up at the station twice in as many weeks...

Ben's feet quit moving. Did Jim Wilcox ever *keep* a key to a lock he installed for someone? He had a solid reputation, so that seemed unlikely, but it would be easy for him to do. And what if canvassing hadn't turned up a witness to the packet of credit card slips being shoved through the Wilcox Lock and Key mail slot because nobody *had* shoved it through?

What if he'd had it all along?

Don't jump to conclusions, Ben ordered himself. Why would Wilcox be here now if he'd committed a crime of that magnitude? The last thing he'd want would be to draw attention to himself.

Ben almost had himself talked out of his suspicion when he stepped into the waiting room and saw the man's face—and the brown paper sack with handles on the seat beside him.

CHAPTER SEVENTEEN

WITHOUT SAYING A WORD, Jim stood, picked up the sack and followed Ben into the same room they had used the last time. He set the sack on the table and dropped into a nearby chair.

Then he made a raw sound and buried his face in his hands.

Ben lifted the gray metal box from the bag, discovering it had some heft. The latch should have required a key, but sprang open with a touch. Inside, bills of every denomination were neatly piled in the slots sized for them on a tray. When he lifted the tray, he found rolls of coins in the bottom, ready to go to the bank, as well as the hundred-dollar bills, rubber-banded.

Exultant for Nadia's sake but regretful, too, Ben sat and waited until Wilcox wiped his cheeks with his forearm and lifted his head.

"I'm sorry. So sorry I—" He choked and shook his head.

"Is the money all here?"

"Yes. I needed it real bad, but…I couldn't do it. I kept thinking we won't need it because things will turn around, and even though I knew that wouldn't happen, I still—" His Adam's apple bobbed. "I've never done anything like this before. It's not me."

Ben had seen torment before, but not for this reason. He couldn't afford to sympathize, however, not yet. "Why did you take it?"

The story poured out. Jim's nine-year-old daughter Maddie had leukemia. "People have been real nice." His face contorted. "Only nobody knew that business has been down, and they didn't think about what it meant when Pam had to quit her job because Maddie is in and out of the hospital and needs one of us with her. We... I dropped our health insurance almost two years ago. Stupid when you have kids, but we just weren't making it. And then Maddie got sick, and I borrowed everything I could, but we're about to lose our house and probably the business. I don't know if they'll keep treating her if I can't pay for it."

Instinctively revolting against the possibility that local hospital administrators could be that inhumane, Ben said, "I can't imagine." Except he read about things like that happening all the time.

Wilcox shrugged hopelessly. "Maybe, but what if the chemo doesn't work and she needs a bone marrow transplant?" Despair made his voice thin. "What then?"

Ben shook his head, understanding on a level he didn't want to. Working as a new patrol officer, he'd had to arrest homeless people for shoplifting even though he knew hunger made them desperate. Sometimes, he could manage to justify what he was required to do, but there were occasions when he couldn't. When children were involved, he helped as much as he could personally afford, quietly and asking not to be credited. But he could never do enough. The problems were too big for a single man on a cop's income.

This one certainly was.

Now, he made himself push ahead, asking how long

in advance Jim had planned the heist, how he'd known Nadia had the money.

Maybe a week in advance, he'd started thinking about it, Jim admitted. Not really believing he would do something like that, but imagining what he could do with all that money.

"Pam went over for an hour or so to watch the auction. She came home talking about how much those quilts were selling for." Alarm flashed across his face. "She doesn't have any part in this! You wouldn't—"

Lock up a sick girl's mother *and* father? No, he wouldn't. Even if the evidence came to suggest that Pam had conspired with her husband, Ben would do his best to suppress it. That, he could do.

"Does she know about this?"

Once again, Jim's face crumpled and he shook his head. He kept his gaze fixed on the table.

"You have to know we never would have suspected you. Why did you change your mind and return the money?"

Voice thick with tears and emotion, the locksmith said, "I felt so bad every time I even looked at it. I had it stashed out in the garage, where Pam wouldn't find it. I, uh, went to the bank and got the rolls to hold the coins."

Ben nodded. He had guessed that volunteer cashiers at the auction hadn't had time to do anything but drop coins into the metal box.

"I'd heard talk, and I read the newspaper article Wednesday. It was all eating at me. Then today, I turned on the news. I saw what happened at Ms. Markovic's place. The ugly things said." He raised pain-filled eyes to Ben. "I should have brought it back the minute I realized she was being blamed." He swallowed, his Adam's apple prominent. "No, I shouldn't have even thought about taking it. Will you tell her how sorry I am?"

"I will." Ben squeezed the back of his neck. It was to Wilcox's credit that, after watching the news, he hadn't hesitated. He had come straight to the station. "Jim, you knew she was home when you went in to her apartment."

Wilcox stared uncomprehendingly at him.

"You got lucky that she'd set the money box down in plain sight. You must have expected to have to search. Open cupboards, drawers. She could have put it in her closet." He paused. "You planned in advance. You must have realized there was a possibility Ms. Markovic would wake up while you were there in her apartment. What did you intend to do if that happened?"

"You think I'd have…?" The chair scraped as the man half stood. "I'd have run away! I wouldn't hurt anybody!"

"You might not have wanted to. But she could have switched on her bedside lamp and *seen* you. Recognized you."

Sinking into his seat, Wilcox just shook his head and kept shaking it. "I would never," he mumbled. "Never."

Was he a sucker to believe the guy? Ben asked himself.

He let another pause develop before he asked, "Jim, how did you come to have a key?"

"To the box? I didn't, but they're not hard to…" Comprehension dawned. "The building, you mean."

"Yes."

"Edith Jefferson asked me to keep one. She didn't like the idea of having a hideout key. Like she said, where would she put it? Tape it under a Dumpster? She wanted to know there was someone she could call."

"Her niece had one, too, I understand."

"Yes, but…Mrs. Jefferson said she didn't want to get thrown into a nursing home just because she had an absentminded moment. I told her it's not that easy to get someone committed, and she said she knew that, she just didn't want that niece of hers rolling her eyes."

"You ever done anything like that before? I mean, keeping a copy of the key?"

He looked puzzled. "Sure, I have half a dozen on hooks at my shop. I'm careful with 'em. They're color-coded, not labeled with names or anything like that. They're all older folks worrying about the same thing."

"Did you ever think about letting yourself into any of those homes?"

For an instant, Jim looked offended before he sagged. "No. I wouldn't. They're…people I know."

Ben made his voice hard. "And you didn't know Ms. Markovic."

Shame stark on his face, he said, "It's not that. I convinced myself that money was raised for people who had been wiped out, and that my family qualified. And I know that's no excuse. You don't have to tell me. I've just been so scared. Felt so hopeless."

"Did you ever use Mrs. Jefferson's key before?"

"You mean, did she ever lose hers? No." He almost smiled. "I reminded her once that I had a copy, and she had forgotten."

"Whoever killed her seems to have had a key, Jim."

His face froze. "I would never… You can't think…?" He stiffened, but the starch didn't last long. Speaking dully, he said, "I guess I can't blame you."

Ben sighed. No, he didn't believe Jim Wilcox had murdered Mrs. Jefferson. This was a man under horrendous stress who had just returned the money he had stolen because he was too honest to use it, and too decent to see an innocent woman blamed for his crime.

And no, he wouldn't have hurt that same woman so he could make a clean getaway.

Finally, Ben said, "I can't let this go, Jim." If Wilcox had brought it back the next day, before the crime became so public... Water under the bridge. "If I don't lock you up right now, can I trust you not to leave town?"

Appearing bewildered, Wilcox bobbed his head. "I wouldn't leave Pam and the kids. Except... I guess I'll have to when—" A sheen in his eyes, he made Ben think of an animal waiting for slaughter.

"I think we can keep you from going to jail," Ben said gently. "That you brought the money back makes all the difference." He drew a breath, hating what he had to say. "Jim, you are under arrest."

THE SIGHT OF Ben always startled Nadia in a way she didn't understand. She'd never reacted to a man like this, been so conscious of how he moved, every flex of his muscles, the sharpness of his cheekbones and the brooding depths of his eyes. Her heart took the little jump that she expected, but when he walked into his own kitchen, she saw something on his face that had the beat continuing hard and fast.

"Ben?"

"I have the money," he said. "It was returned by the man who took it."

"Returned?" She could hardly comprehend it. "All of it?"

"I haven't counted yet. He says it's all there."

Lucy, too, had turned from the stove to gape at him. He nodded past her. "Something is boiling over."

"Oh!" Lucy spun back and lifted a pan lid before adjusting the burner heat. "Dinner will be ready in about five minutes. I put the noodles in when I heard your car."

"Okay." His gaze hadn't left Nadia. "Let me go change out of my uniform and I'll tell you all about it."

"Wait! Who?"

"I'd rather tell you the whole story at once."

What could she do but nod? He left the kitchen and his footsteps sounded on the stairs, slow, heavy.

Nadia didn't move, staring at the empty doorway he had gone through. "Did he really say he has the money?"

Lucy hugged her. "He did."

"I'm stunned."

"I can hardly *wait* to see all those people eat humble pie."

"Some of them won't, you know. They'll just… avoid me. Or even insist Ben isn't telling everything he knows. That I *had* to be involved."

"They've been awful to you. They deserve some comeuppance."

Nadia gave herself a shake. "Let me finish making the salad."

Ben returned just as Lucy dumped the noodles into the strainer. Seeing him in worn jeans that hugged long thigh muscles, a faded blue T-shirt and athletic shoes,

Nadia stopped in the middle of the kitchen with the salad bowl in her hands, unable to look away from him.

She told herself not to be an idiot. He had left the room. Now he was back. Only…she liked him even better when he was less official. Although *liked* might not be quite the right word.

His mouth quirking, he took the bowl out of her hands and carried it to the dining room table himself.

Nadia rolled her eyes at herself and went to the refrigerator for the dressing.

The minute they sat down, Ben began serving himself with noodles and Stroganoff. He reached for the bowl of green beans, but went still.

"It was Jim Wilcox."

"Jim…" Nadia knew her mouth had fallen open. "The *locksmith*?"

"Yeah."

"But…" She floundered. "He was so nice. Except…" It was like building with Lego blocks. Pieces snapped into place. "He brought back the checks and credit card slips, too. And…he told me he'd replaced the locks for Mrs. Jefferson." Indignation rose. "He kept a key?"

"I think he is nice." Ben repeated what Wilcox had told him. "He asked me to tell you how sorry he is."

Her shoulders slumped. "He's another Leonard Hixson."

"Yes."

Ben finished dishing up then began to eat, but obviously kept an eye on her. Lucy urged her to eat, too, and Nadia did, although she didn't really taste anything that went in her mouth.

She couldn't seem to wrap her mind around this alternate reality. The thief wasn't a monster, he was a kind, anxious man with a gravely ill child. Instead of taking lascivious notice of her scantily clad body, he had probably averted his eyes, horrified to have to enter her bedroom.

In fact, she remembered his distress when they discussed the theft, him saying he hoped she hadn't been hurt or frightened. He had even said he was sorry— which she now realized hadn't been sympathy; it was an apology.

"How did he know I had the money?" she asked at last.

"He hid in front and saw you come out with the box."

"I couldn't have been more obvious if I'd tried, could I?"

"I'm afraid not." Ben's expression was sympathetic, but also cautious, as if he half expected her to melt down.

Still stunned, Nadia grappled with the idea of Jim Wilcox violating his deepest values to steal the money, but unable in the end to use any of it. And confessing to the police chief, rather than thinking of a way to return the money anonymously.

"You can't arrest him" was what came out of her mouth.

"I already did." Deep furrows carved Ben's forehead. "He committed a crime. Whatever his motivations, what he did was wrong. He left *you* hanging out to dry."

Lucy stirred beside her, making Nadia aware how quiet she'd been.

"Don't I have the right to choose not to press charges?" she asked.

"Not for something like this." There was no give in Ben's voice. "Sorry."

"But—"

"The money he took wasn't yours. He stole from a lot of people. Including the folks the money was intended for."

"Like Leonard Hixson," she said slowly.

"Exactly."

"He'll go to prison."

Ben shook his head. "I doubt it, considering he returned what he took. I'll push for him to get community service, some supervision. He's not going to be a repeat offender."

Nadia wanted to feel relief, but Ben's expression didn't let her.

"No matter how easy the judge is on him, Jim likely will lose his livelihood. A man convicted of stealing? And using a key he kept to a lock he'd installed? He says Mrs. Jefferson asked him to hold on to it, but she's not here to call him a liar. Who will trust him again?"

Nadia pressed a hand to her chest, trying to quell a deep-down ache. She reminded herself that this was the man responsible for everything rotten that had happened to her since the morning after the auction…but she still felt sorry for him.

"He could get something for it if he sells the business. And…he and his family could move." Like she had known she would have to do.

Ben couldn't have read her mind, but he said, "A felony on his record will follow along wherever he goes."

"You're making all the arguments I should be!"

"That's because I don't like what I had to do." Anger infused his voice. "But how could I justify not arresting him to other people who did something stupid and impulsive and faced trial because of it?"

Nadia absorbed that. "The hospital wouldn't really stop treatment, would they?"

He sighed. "I doubt they can, but are they obligated to provide a treatment beyond what they're already doing? I don't know. No matter what, Jim's daughter is old enough to see what taking care of her has done to her family. That will be hard to live with."

"You couldn't have claimed the money was found on the police station doorstep?"

"It's too late, Nadia. I booked him." He gusted out another sigh. "I thought about it, but two things stopped me. I doubt I'd have gotten away with it. The dispatcher saw him come in carrying something. Other people might have seen him going into the police station or sitting in the waiting room." The full force of all that intensity was zeroed in on her.

She nodded.

His expression hardened. "And doing that wouldn't remove the shadow over you, Nadia. In fact, it might convince our local citizenry that you surrendered the money because of their pressure. Can't you see the Edgertons feeling smug because *they* got results?"

Of course, he was right, and that would really grate. Nadia sat silent, coming to terms with those consequences. Even so... "I could have moved away. Business has bounced back some, but not enough. I may still have to move."

"No," Ben said, implacable.

At the same moment his sister cried, "No! You can't do that!"

Nadia reached for this new friend's hand and squeezed.

"If…if I'd been given the choice, I'd have done that rather than see his life ruined."

"Fortunately—" and Ben sounded grim "—the choice wasn't yours."

Was she relieved? She couldn't help it. Ben had a lot to do with that. To move and know she'd likely never see him again? Never find out whether this tension and yearning would take them anywhere important? But she pictured Jim Wilcox's kind, friendly face, and imagined him sitting beside his daughter's hospital bed, holding her hand.

"I understand why you had to arrest him, but I wish there was something we could do to help."

Lucy sat up straighter. "Maybe there is."

Her brother groaned.

She turned a narrowed-eye look on him. "We're really excited about our crowdfunding plan. Nadia has been out of the loop because of her hospital stay, but the photos that woman at the *Herald* produced are awesome. Colleen has a friend who is designing the appeal. There's no saying we couldn't do one for the Wilcoxes, too."

"Put pictures of his sick kid out there? Talk about how he was driven to steal money to pay for her treatment?"

"No!"

"Ben's right," Nadia interjected. "Putting their story out there could be insensitive. Do we label him as the man who can't take care of his family, and then couldn't even go through with the crime he committed for them?"

"So we let him crash and burn?" Lucy fired back.

Very aware of Ben watching their exchange, Nadia said, "All I'm saying is, we need to think about this."

Then they both looked at him. "What will happen next?" Nadia asked hesitantly.

He talked about the next steps and his belief that a plea bargain would prevent a trial and lead to minimal consequences beyond the fact that everyone in the community would know what he had done. "We need that for your sake."

Nadia's stomach was tied in knots, but she could only nod. If Ben had tried to cover up Jim Wilcox's role, he could well have lost his job. He'd said enough about the city council members who didn't like him to make her feel sure they would have seized the opportunity. And…he was thinking about *her*. Protecting *her*. She couldn't forget his vehement reaction to the suggestion she might still have to sell out and move.

So she met those espresso dark eyes and said, "Thank you. And now I should be getting home."

His expression darkened. "You could stay."

"I didn't bring a change of clothes, or a toothbrush, or… Besides, I bet you don't have an extra bed, do you?"

"You can have mine. I'll bunk down on the couch."

She shook her head. "That's silly when I have a perfectly good bed of my own not fifteen minutes away. Lucy said you'd drive me."

He wasn't happy about it, but he gave in. Lucy declined Nadia's offer to help clear the table and load the dishwasher, electing to stay behind. Nadia and she hugged, Lucy whispering, "Maybe we can talk to the others about how we can help him," before she stepped back.

With daylight lingering Nadia was able to look

around as Ben drove. She felt odd—as if she was see-ing the town anew.

Byrum wasn't a beautiful town, but it had a solid, settled feel. She liked that a mall hadn't torn the heart out of downtown, that small businesses dominated. Despite some fast-food restaurants on the outskirts, the old-fashioned diners thrived. People knew what to expect from each other. For the Wilcoxes, that was probably a source of comfort.

Until things went very wrong. In her case, she had been a logical culprit because residents *hadn't* known her forever and ever. That hurt, especially when she thought back to her rosy belief going into the auction that she'd made so many friends, that maybe she would be more than the newcomer now.

Would they all turn on Jim Wilcox now? Drive him out of business because he'd proved himself untrust-worthy, even though his returning the money proved that he *could* be trusted? Or would they rally around, because they really did know him and cared?

They were halfway to her apartment when Ben said, "Don't move away."

Startled by his demand, coming out of the blue—or had he been having similar thoughts?—Nadia turned to look at him. He kept his gaze on the road ahead, al-though she had no doubt he was aware of her scrutiny.

"I don't know. I can't think right now."

He was quiet for a good minute. Then, steering his SUV into her alley, he said, "Okay. We'll put off that discussion. Unless you're trying to think of a way to tell me it's not my business."

Without knowing it, she'd made this decision.

"I'm not." She grasped his hand then made herself let it go so he could park.

He ordered her to stay put and did a look around before permitting her to cross the open alley to the back door of her building.

"It's still light out here," she protested.

"Sun still up or not, it's evening, which means the alley is deserted."

That not only silenced her, she took an uneasy glance to each side before unlocking the door. Somehow, Nadia wasn't surprised when he followed her in. Still, she said, "Isn't Lucy expecting—"

Ben backed her into a wall, cupped her face in his big hands and kissed her.

CHAPTER EIGHTEEN

HE'D ALL BUT knocked her into a wall. His hands were shaking.

Out of control.

Nadia hadn't given any signal suggesting she was ready for more, but the certainty in her voice when she talked about moving away had slammed into him like a hammer blow. And knowing she would have sacrificed the dream that had brought her to Byrum for the sake of a sick little girl and her family—yeah, that hit him hard, too. She could still *care* about a man who had sneaked into her home to steal the money she'd worked so hard to raise, who had let her take the blame.

Any doubts Ben had had that he was in love with her had been erased tonight during dinner.

With a groan that rumbled up from his chest, he tore his mouth from hers and gulped for air, then rested his forehead against hers.

Taking a deep breath, Ben made himself lift his head and look at her. Really look. What he saw was stunning vulnerability.

"I'm sorry," he whispered.

A tiny smile curved her lips. "I think I'm insulted."

"I'm not sorry I kissed you. Just…that I was pushing."

One hand hadn't made it up to his neck. She flattened it now on his chest, then began slow circles.

"I'm not sorry you kissed me, either," Nadia murmured. "I'm sorry you stopped."

THE TENDERNESS IN Ben's touch, in his eyes, settled Nadia's nerves. This wasn't wrong, or too soon, or any of the things she'd been fearing. He wouldn't turn on her again. She believed that. There'd been so many times already when he had stood at her back, a hand resting on her as if to say, *I'm here.* She had no doubt he'd been staring down her opponents at the same time. And while she might never get over her reaction to the sight of a gun, she knew Ben would never use the one he carried for anything but the right reasons.

All her doubts evaporated.

She skimmed her fingertips over his rough jaw, then down his neck, corded with tension.

Nadia splayed her hands on that chest. "You have the most beautiful body," she whispered.

"Not like yours."

He kissed her as if starved for her, as if he'd never get enough.

The hot Missouri sun had nothing on his blistering gaze.

SHE MUST HAVE been drowsing, but Nadia roused when Ben got up and went to the living room. Voice low, he talked briefly to someone. Lucy, of course. Who would now know he was spending the night in Nadia's bed.

When she awakened the next time, sunlight poured in. The temperature was already rising in the room. Not that she and Ben had ever pulled a cover over themselves. He was still sound asleep.

Nadia didn't move for a long time, savoring the beat of his heart beneath her hand, the curve of his shoulder providing a pillow for her head, the utter relaxation on a face too often taut and guarded. But temptation beckoned, and she let her hand stray. Not more than a minute passed before his dark lashes lifted and a smile tugged at his mouth.

"You're an early bird," he said in a voice roughened by sleep.

"I don't actually think it's early." She hadn't looked at the clock yet, but the angle of the sun suggested they had slept in. And why not? It was Sunday. She'd hardly have to see a soul until Tuesday morning, by which time everyone in Henness County who followed the news or belonged to a gossip network would know who had taken the money and why—and that it had been returned. That *she* hadn't had anything to do with it. She let herself feel giddy, uncomplicated relief, if only for right now.

But finally he sighed. "It may be Sunday, but I have things I need to do."

They took turns showering. To shave, Ben used a small, plastic razor she offered, muttering a curse or two as he nicked himself. Both dressed; Nadia scrambled eggs while he made toast and poured the coffee.

Once they were finished, she asked what he could accomplish on a Sunday.

"Count the money and be sure it really is all there. Let the prosecuting attorney know. Give the mayor a heads-up. Prepare a statement, although I may not issue until Monday. Depends on how successful I am talking to people today."

"Will you let me know about the money? And... then you'll be making a statement?"

Ben's face softened and he reached across the table for her hand. "I will. If you don't object, once we count the money, I'll put it back in a locker until tomorrow."

Nadia shuddered. No, she didn't want it here in her apartment ever again.

"I'll return it to you tomorrow morning," Ben added.

That made her twitch. "Maybe it would be better if you took it right to the aid organization."

"You're not opening on Mondays anymore, are you? Once I confirm the money is all there, you can give the good news to Bill Jarvis and have him meet us tomorrow morning at whatever bank they're using."

"Yes." She relaxed. Except... "Should we wait until you've made the statement?"

"Maybe." He frowned. "That might be better. I don't want a garbled story getting out."

With a lingering kiss and caution to be careful, Ben took off.

Now alone, Nadia wished she wasn't, that she, too, had somewhere she needed to be. Instead... What *was* she going to do today, besides wonder how her detractors would react to the news?

Quilt, she decided. She wasn't far from done with the one in the frame downstairs. She might even finish it today.

She did work, but also found herself glancing at the clock with absurd regularity, frustrated by how slowly the minute hand moved. A tiny jerk forward now and again wasn't nearly enough.

When her phone rang after a seeming eternity, sh pounced on it. "Ben?"

"Are you home? If so, do you mind if I come by?"

"Yes. Hurry!"

His chuckle warmed her.

When he pulled up in front, Nadia unlocked th door and had it open by the time he crossed the park ing lot. He had driven his own SUV, but wore a cris blue uniform with badge.

"You went home and changed," she said in surpris

"I didn't think I should wear jeans and a T-shirt th spent the night on the floor when I met with His Hono Besides, I rarely appear at the station in civvies."

Nadia took a deep breath. "Was the money a there?"

"Every penny, plus a few."

"What?"

"Someone miscounted. You have an extra eleve dollars and sixty-seven cents. We counted twice."

"Come on in back. I've been quilting."

She resumed her seat, but didn't reach for her thim ble or needle. She just waited as he pulled up a chai

"Those weren't easy conversations," Ben said. "Bo the mayor and the prosecuting attorney have know Jim for years."

She only nodded.

"Neither had heard about Jim's daughter, though Ben continued. "He tripped over his pride. If he'd bee more open about what was happening, I'm guessing th community would have come together for the famil They were both more sympathetic than I am to Jim f not coming forward sooner. *And* planning the theft we in advance. Impulse, that's easier to forgive."

"He did bring the money back."

Ben's mouth twisted. "That's unusual—I'll give ou that."

"Do you think the prosecutor will go easy on him?"

"No question. I called Jim, told him he needs to ind an attorney, and he said he already has. His wife ushed him. So I'll be out of this soon. Bob and I sat own together and roughed out a statement."

Bob? Oh. The mayor. Bob Finzel. She'd seen his ame in the paper often enough.

"I'll announce that an arrest has been made because he man who took it deeply regrets his actions and re- urned every penny. I have to name him." Ben's regret olored his voice. "I'll say that we can't condone his riminal behavior, but do feel he redeemed himself n bringing back the money and is unlikely to offend gain. That Ms. Markovic, whose reputation has suf- ered from unwarranted suspicion and accusation, is elieved to have her name cleared but wouldn't have ressed charges if given a choice. She's deeply con- erned for Mr. Wilcox's daughter, undergoing treat- ment for childhood leukemia." He paused. "I'll delete hat part if you'd prefer."

"No, I like it."

"And in conclusion—" he deepened his voice and ave her a wry grin "—we're very pleased to be able to and over the money to the aid organization for which t was intended, etcetera, etcetera."

"So…it's over, for everyone but Jim and his family." he felt oddly numb.

"Yeah."

"If only he were Amish."

Ben grunted. "Hospital bills would be paid, church

members would be sitting with his daughter, babysitting his son, providing meals so his wife didn't have to cook, and he'd never have fallen behind on his mortgage."

Nadia frowned, thinking. "He must have a church."

"Yeah, and I'm sure a collection will be taken up for his family, but the total will be a drop in the bucket. In a community this size, people would have to dig deep in their pockets to cover the kind of medical bill showing up in his mailbox. A lot of those people will be thinking about how tight their budgets are and how *they're* still paying for insurance, so why didn't he?"

Maybe no jail time wasn't that big a favor, Nadia realized, depressed. It was like throwing a drowning man a life ring with no attached rope. He might not go under right away, but nobody would pull him in, either.

"Can I tell people now?"

Ben glanced at his watch. "The press conference is scheduled for one o'clock. So yes, I don't see any reason you can't contact anyone you please." He raised his eyebrows. "Say, Allison Edgerton, or Julie Baird."

"Neither of them deserves a minute of my time. I was mostly thinking of Colleen, and then I can drive out to see Hannah and—oh, shoot—it's Sunday. Is it church Sunday?"

He frowned. "I've lost track."

Nadia touched his hand. "Thank you. For caring about me and still doing your best for him."

"Even cops can be decent human beings, you know."

He didn't sound offended, but she jumped to her feet and kissed him anyway. "I know," she said softly. "I even know the negotiator and SWAT officers in Colorado Springs thought they were doing the right thing. I shouldn't blame them."

When she straightened, he grabbed her hands. "We have to make hard decisions too often," he said, eyes intent. "It's not always about whether to shoot or not. In law enforcement, the most minor actions or inactions can have deadly consequences."

Was that a warning? Maybe it was one she needed to hear, if they were to be involved. She couldn't let her own experiences color her reaction when he told her about something that happened. Or when some small-minded or embittered person did.

"I need to go." He grimaced as he got to his feet. "Gotta do my favorite part of the job."

"Come on," she teased. "Most people love to see themselves on television."

Ben grunted his opinion of that. "You going to stay here?"

"I think so. I don't want to intrude even if the Amish don't have church today. But I will call Colleen and some of the other women who have been so nice."

He tugged her into his arms. "You need to do some prep, too. The minute I step away from the podium, your phone will start ringing, so prepare a short statement of your own, then stick to it."

"Oh, no."

He grinned. "Oh, yes. News outlets will all want a comment from you."

She made a face. "Do I have to talk to Dave Rutledge?"

Ben chuckled and kissed her cheek. "Console yourself that he's having to eat his words. Be *extra* sweet."

"Oh, fun."

"And be careful." All trace of his amusement was gone. "Don't open the door to anyone but a good friend. I'd rather you don't drive out to the Yoders or anywhere else, not yet. We still don't know what was behind the shooting."

"If it had to do with the money—"

"You'd be safe after word gets out."

She searched his face. "But you don't think I will be."

"No. Spitting on you, that's one thing. Being willing to kill, that's different."

Her stomach took a big swoop, or maybe it was her heart. This morning's giddy relief? Premature.

Somebody wants to kill me.

And she couldn't afford to forget that.

CHAPTER NINETEEN

PROVING THE EFFECTIVENESS of the Amish grapevine, Hannah dashed into the shop Tuesday morning and exclaimed, "I am so glad for you! You must be relieved, *ja*?"

Nadia looked up from the fabric bolt she was returning to a row. "You already know?" Then she laughed. "Of course you do. And yes, I'm relieved. But also... sad."

Hannah nodded. "Mr. Wilcox has done work for many of us, too. So kind, he is. People are always saying he doesn't ask enough money, not when he has to drive so far out into the country."

"He put my new locks in, too." Nadia hesitated. "And the locks for Mrs. Jefferson, of course. You know he kept a key? That's how he got in to take the money."

"It's true, he brought it all back?"

"And a few extra dollars. Either a cashier miscounted, or somebody made a small, last minute donation at the auction. Ben—Chief Slater—and I met Bill Jarvis yesterday at the bank. The money is safely deposited, and he can start distributing it."

"*Gut.* Good. But sad, too. To think of his little girl so sick."

"Yes. Ben thinks no one will trust him again, after he stole, so I don't know what he and his family will do."

"That should not be," Hannah insisted.

"No." Nadia told her what Ben said, about Jim'
pride keeping him from letting people know he neede
help. "He and his wife were having trouble keeping u
with bills, so he quit paying for medical insurance."

"I hear all the time that people pay for insuranc
but it doesn't always take care of them."

"That's true, but mostly for people who didn't rea
carefully what the insurance would pay out for an
what it wouldn't. Like all those farmers, who though
their homeowners' insurance would rebuild thei
houses, but their policies didn't cover tornado dam
age." Nadia went to the front door and flipped the sig
to Open. "It will be interesting to see who stops b
today." She wouldn't be surprised if nobody who ha
shunned her ever offered an apology. Doing so woul
be awkward, uncomfortable on both sides. Avoidin
her would be easier.

And truthfully, Nadia hadn't decided how she'd re
spond to anyone who *did* apologize. If she were Amish
of course, that wouldn't even be a question. Forgivenes
would come naturally, intrinsic to her faith.

So—if she admired their willingness to offer gen
uine forgiveness without hesitation, shouldn't she d
the same? Or was holding on to anger more satisfying

She was a teeny bit disturbed to discover she wasn
sure, which meant she wasn't as good a person as she'
like to think she was.

The bell on the door tinkled, and she braced hersel
Don't make me have to decide now.

Jennifer Bronske walked in.

Nadia glanced at Hannah, who smiled gently at he

as if it hadn't occurred to her that Nadia's response to people like Jennifer would be anything but generous.

Of course, Jennifer might have no intention of apologizing.

Nadia managed a pleasant smile. "Jennifer." Oh, how she wanted to say, *What a surprise to see you.* But snide was not the way to regain friends and customers.

Jennifer came directly to her, stopping on the other side of the counter. "I know how inadequate this is, but I'm here to tell you how sorry I am that I jumped to conclusions. I owe you that much."

Nadia's anger quivered and dissolved. She shook her head. "You don't owe me anything. You felt betrayed. I understood that. I won't deny that it hurt to have so many women I'd started to believe might be friends decide I had to be guilty. But there are plenty of con artists out there, and I could have been one of them. You really hadn't known me long." She smiled weakly. "At least you didn't join the demonstration out front."

Usually composed, Jennifer flushed with hot color. She held herself stiffly. "After that man spit on you and you handed me the money from the quilt, I saw your expression. I…think I knew then. I almost said I was sorry, but…" Her one-shouldered shrug spoke of hesitation and doubts.

"I appreciate you saying this." Nadia tried to project sincerity. "I know it's hard to do. As far as I'm concerned, the whole episode is forgotten." From somewhere inside, she found the ability to offer a warm smile. "I'll hope to see you in here again. In fact, I'd love it if you'd consider teaching a class on appliqué techniques sometime. I don't know anyone who does it better. You may have noticed that the idea of doing teeny, tiny leaves or cherries on a tree, or, heaven forbid, a bird's beak gives me hives."

Jennifer actually laughed. "I had noticed. Not many people seem to enjoy that kind of finicky handwork. If you think there are enough to fill a class, I'd be glad to teach one."

"Excellent! I'm putting together a schedule for August. Or if you have a vacation planned, we could do it in September."

"Either would be fine. Just give me a call when you have dates that might work. Now, if you'll excuse me." She gave Hannah a vague smile, Nadia a still embarrassed one, and left.

The moment the door closed behind her, Nadia sighed. "I really had to bite my tongue."

"Forgiveness is never easy." Seeing Nadia's expression, Hannah chuckled. "No, not even for us! We get mad, too, you know. I have had to pretend once or twice." The humor in her eyes suggested that was an understatement. "But I know I *should* forgive," she went on, "so I say the right words, and one day I know I mean them."

"That makes me feel a little better." Nadia wrinkled her nose. "Jennifer was a good one to start with, because she didn't do or say anything that bad."

"Not like that Allison."

"Julie Baird, too," Nadia admitted. "She didn't say anything terrible, either, but we'd spent a lot of time together planning the auction. And yet, the very second I told her about the money disappearing, I could tell she blamed me. She didn't even hesitate. That really stung. I don't think I'd have lasted if it hadn't been for people like you and Katie-Ann and Ruth and Colleen."

In the course of the day, three other women came into the store to apologize. Having already accepted one graciously gave Nadia a template for responding to more apologies. Ellen Shaw's was her favorite. She marched in looking militant to say, "You were so dignified that day, and I was such a bitch." Nadia wouldn't have guessed the word was in Ellen's vocabulary. Ellen even had the guts to ask if she could bring quilts again for Nadia to sell. Of course, Nadia agreed. Aside from appreciating the apology, there was the old saying about not cutting off your nose to spite your face.

The smile was cracking by the time Ben arrived to take her to his house for dinner again.

He kissed her softly. "The worst is over."

"Maybe."

Neither of them talked about the other threat she still faced, the one that had her scared to carry a bag of trash out to the Dumpster or drive alone anywhere. How long could she go on this way? What if two weeks from now, a month from now, nothing else had happened? The shot might have been fired by someone mad about the auction money…or the person who hated her might be really patient.

Nadia always came back to the *why*. Had she done something offensive? Seen something she shouldn't have? But what? Thinking about it made her head ache.

Midafternoon Wednesday, Colleen burst in, excited because within twenty-four hours of the crowdfunding appeal going up, donations had begun pouring in. "It's amazing!" she crowed. "Two separate people gave five thousand dollars each! I don't know how fast the response tails off, but if it lasts even for a week or two, we might be able to give the Hixsons a good start on rebuilding."

"Would it be possible to organize a community barn raising?" Nadia asked. "Well, and house raising, too? Not having to pay contractors would save a bunch."

Hannah's face lit. "I'll talk to *Daad* and Jacob. If they agree, we can go to the bishop and ask for the members of our church district to join in. I think that not so many *Englischers* know *how* to build a barn. They might need our help."

Colleen hugged her. "They will, because you're right. But I'll bet a lot of the other farmers within a several-county radius would come, too. They may need the same help someday."

"And then we could post photos of what the donations have accomplished, along with an appeal for another family who lost their home, too," Nadia suggested.

Ben stopped by in the middle of their excited plotting, shook his head and said, "I guess I don't need to worry about you being alone here," and left.

Just seeing him, even for a few minutes at a time, lifted her spirits.

BEN DIDN'T LIKE his constant awareness of the danger to Nadia. Back at the station, he propped his feet on his desk. His phone momentarily silent, he brooded. When would the next strike come?

Living here, he'd seen tornadoes from a distance. This felt too much like that. He imagined one approaching, the sky a sickening yellowish green, the dark, spinning monster's path unpredictable. Worse, he put himself in Leonard Hixson's head, when he bellowed his son's name over and over, finally realizing the boy wouldn't make it to shelter. Closing and latching that door, listening to the roar, offering up house, barn, anything the monster wanted, if only it would pass by the terrified kid and his dog.

Ben rubbed both hands over his face. Every time his phone rang lately, he expected the caller to be either Nadia or a first responder, letting him know she'd been attacked again. If she died…

He couldn't let himself think that way. She was being careful, not being stupid enough to be rebellious. Unless she was slipping out when he was unaware, she hadn't yet stepped out of her building alone. She should be safe there. Daytimes, the risk of being seen and recognized would be too great for a gunman to, say, walk right into the fabric store and gun her down. The streets were busy, A Stitch in Time surrounded by other businesses.

Breaking in at night…that would be harder, but not impossible. It wouldn't happen quietly, though. The chair she was still bracing beneath the doorknob at the foot of the stairs was low-tech, but it would be a surprise to an intruder, and probably a noisy one. She'd have time to call for help, maybe blockade herself in the bedroom.

In the next days, he took to stopping by her store often, making his visits at unpredictable intervals, even on days when they planned to get together for dinner. That was just about every night. Lucy usually cooked. Either he'd pick Nadia up, or he and Lucy would bring the meal to her place. Those times, he didn't even get a serious good-night kiss, but he liked to see the growing friendship between the two women. They both needed the connection. What he didn't like was leaving Nadia alone. So far, she had stubbornly refused to stay at his house, either putting him out of his bed or sleeping with him across the hall from his sister's room.

This morning, Lucy had displayed her finished quilt for him. These past weeks, he'd become enough of a connoisseur to see that the stitches weren't as tiny as Nadia was putting in the quilt in the frame at the back of her shop, or on some of the quilts displayed on the walls there, but they weren't far off. Lucy pointed out her mistakes, then told him she intended to start another one right away. Not bed-sized yet, but her third quilt would be. The firm way she said that was just another sign of her growing confidence.

She hadn't said a word about when she intended to leave, and that made him uneasy. Just yesterday, he had asked Nadia if she'd seen Lucy with Jacob Yoder again.

Her hesitation was answer enough.

He had growled, *That's what I thought.*

She had been cutting out fabric at the time, but the rotary cutter went still. Nadia didn't look at him. *You'd rather she wasn't hanging out here so much, wouldn't you?*

His *Don't be ridiculous* was probably too brusque, and not 100 percent honest. What if somebody came after Nadia again, and Lucy was injured, too? Or instead? Or was so traumatized, all the progress she'd made was erased?

But he had to believe that Nadia was safer when somebody was with her. Alone, that was when she became vulnerable.

Identifying the would-be killer was the only way to ensure her safety. His investigation into the shooting had gone dead in the water, which made him more than a little unhappy. All he had to go on was a dyed blond hair that might or might not be from the shooter, and a whopping big diamond that logic said could have lain there beneath the Dumpster for days and had nothing to do with the assailant. Ben just didn't believe it. Given the value of the earring, it didn't make sense that the woman who'd lost it wouldn't be searching. Plus, wasn't an alley an unlikely place to have an earring happen to fall off? Nobody who lived or worked on the block had claimed it. The alley didn't see much foot traffic. Why would it, when the nearby street had wide sidewalks, crosswalks and attractive shop windows?

Now, a woman crouched in the narrow space between Dumpster and car bumper, sighting in the dark down the barrel of a rifle, shooting, maybe losing her balance when she scrambled away…*she* could have jarred the earring loose with the butt of the rifle or even her shoulder.

Women were less likely than men to use a gun even when they did kill. That said, plenty of women around here were as handy with a hunting rifle as their husbands, brothers and fathers were.

He grumbled under his breath. This was getting him nowhere. He'd grill Nadia again this evening. Somewhere in her head was the answer. Sooner or later, he'd ask the right question.

"I SAW A Square-in-Square pattern that I really liked," Lucy said, taking the rinsed casserole dish from Nadia and drying it. "I love the idea of using colors in new ways, but this time I want to leave open blocks so I can experiment with fancier hand quilting."

"That sounds like a good idea, but I can't picture the pattern." Nadia let the water drain from the sink and dried her hands. "Was it in one of my books?"

"Uh-huh. I think I can put my hands right on it."

"Why don't we go look for it right now?" With her hip, Nadia nudged Ben, who hadn't seemed crushed when his offer to help clean up had been rebuffed. "Unless your brother is itching to get home."

Sitting at the table, he looked up from his phone. "No hurry." His gaze drifted over her in a way that warmed her skin as it went. The impact when his eyes met hers had her wishing this was one of the evenings when he drove her home and stayed for a couple of hours—or all night. "Shades drawn down there?" he asked.

Dose of reality, thank you. "Yes, I let down the ones in front every day when I close now. And I never raise the blinds in the back room." The alley view wouldn't exactly enhance the colorful, feminine world she had created in her store.

"Okay." He smiled at his sister. "I'll stay here, if you'll forgive me for not coming along to share my opinion."

She kissed his cheek. "I think I can live without it. Do you remember what you said when I showed you the fabrics I chose for the first quilt?"

He was smart enough to look wary. "Ah...no."

"Direct quote—'Those don't really go together, do they?'"

Nadia laughed. "Remind me never to consult him."

Downstairs, Lucy began in front by browsing the books for sale, some displayed face out, some spine out. "I know it was a hardback. Country something…" Her face cleared. "Wait, it might have been in back."

Nadia had a good selection of books available for sale, but she kept the larger library in the back room, available for customers and students to browse or even borrow. She could think of at least a couple of books with *country* in the title that were out here, however, so she scanned for them as Lucy turned on the light in the back room and started for the shelves.

The explosive *crack* of a gunshot and the sound of shattering glass came at the same time.

"Lucy!" Nadia screamed.

Furniture scraped on the floor, as if Lucy had stumbled against it. Then came the thud of a falling body. Within seconds, Ben thundered down the stairs.

Nadia bent low and started into the back room.

Crack.

Something splintered behind her even as she fell to her hands and knees. She crawled toward Lucy, who lay unmoving on the floor, an overturned chair half on top of her.

THE FIRST GUNSHOT acted like a starter's pistol. Ben tore down the stairs and sprinted for the back door, even though he desperately wanted to go to Nadia and Lucy. But Lucy and he had come separately, him straight from work, and since he'd parked in front, the shooter might not know he was here at all.

He'd have given a lot to be wearing a vest, but turned the dead bolt and flung open the door anyway. He went through fast, gun in his hand, leaping to the side off the concrete pad.

"Police! Put your weapon down. Now!"

A scrape of gravel, a metallic clatter and running footsteps.

He wouldn't shoot somebody in the back. But if that had been a rifle, and he thought it was, he had the advantage now. He sprinted after the dark figure.

THIS WAS WORSE than being shot herself. It felt like a nightmare, as if the monster who still haunted her dreams was pacing just out of sight and would appear any moment to make sure none of them had moved, that they were really dead.

No, no, no. This was different. *He* was dead and hadn't come back. *It's Lucy. No children. No staring eyes.*

But it shouldn't be Lucy. *I was the target*, she thought, even as she carefully rolled the other woman enough to see the bloody front of her shirt. Bone white, Lucy's face had a familiar slackness to it, a lock of hair hanging over her open mouth. She looked dead.

No, she was breathing. *Not dead.*

Having heard Ben go out the back door and start yelling, Nadia strained to hear more. *Don't let him be shot, too, please, not him. I can't bear it.* She tore open Lucy's shirt, finding a wound high on her shoulder.

Then she sank back on her heels. Why was Lucy unconscious? Shock? No, smoothing back her hair, Nadia saw more blood. A bullet graze? But looking around, she spotted the smear of blood on the edge of the table, which along with the chair had been pushed askew. Lucy had hit it as she went down, knocked herself unconscious.

Another gunshot rang out from the alley, farther away, and Nadia's heart skipped a beat. Ben!

ALMOST TO THE CORNER, the dark figure slowed enough to swing the rifle around and take a shot. It went wild, of course. Ben used the chance to gain ground. His longer legs ate up the distance.

He launched himself and they crashed down, skidding on gravel and pavement. The minute he gripped one wrist, he knew this was a woman. She fought wildly, with wiry strength, bucking and screaming, but she'd come down atop her rifle, and Ben used his weight and greater size to keep her flat.

He managed to holster his gun with one hand. But he didn't carry cuffs. He hoped somebody had called 911, because he'd left his phone on the table upstairs.

He tried not to think about Nadia or Lucy.

At last he got his hand on the woman's other arm. He yanked both behind her and pushed himself up, one knee planted on her back. "Fighting won't get you anywhere," he growled. "You are under arrest."

Distant siren.

The streetlight was adequate for him to see that she wore a black hooded sweatshirt. The back of his hand had brushed her breast during the struggle, verifying that he was holding a woman captive, not a small man or teenager. The *why* was still a mystery—but his gut told him that once he could free a hand to yank off the hood, he'd see bleached-blond hair.

He recited her Miranda rights even as he prayed she hadn't succeeded in killing either of the women he loved.

CHAPTER TWENTY

"CORINNE BISSETT." SITTING IN a small waiting room at the hospital, Nadia gaped at Ben, who had just joined her. "But…that's the woman I bought the building from."

"Mrs. Jefferson's heir," he agreed. He had a secure hold on her hand, which he needed. His fear for her and Lucy had settled to a simmer, but whatever his eyes told him, he needed the contact to help him believe Nadia, at least, was safe. Unhurt.

Lucy had been taken right into surgery, but she had regained consciousness by the time the ambulance reached the hospital. That helped when he called his parents to tell them their already fragile daughter had been shot. They were catching a red-eye to Saint Louis and would be here by morning. He wasn't thrilled, but understood.

"I have to see her myself," his mother had declared, anxiety threading her voice.

Now he and Nadia were waiting while the surgeon dug out the bullet.

Her expression held only perplexity. "That doesn't make any sense."

"I have to believe it has something to do with her aunt's death." The theft hadn't, as it turned out, but these attempts on Nadia's life…no other possibility made sense.

Nadia's forehead stayed crinkled. "But…I never even met her when I was buying the building. And that was months after the murder."

"Did she ever stop by to say hello?" he asked.

Nadia shook her head, but her expression changed. "Actually, I did finally meet her by chance…oh, not that long ago. I told you, didn't I?"

"No." He could all but hear the *ping*. "When?"

Her forehead crinkled. "I think it was the week after the auction. I mentioned Allison Edgerton cornering me at the store, right?" When he nodded, she said, "Apparently Corinne was right behind me and overheard. She commiserated and—" Her voice slowed. "Well, I recognized her."

"From?"

"She and I had met, oh, months before I even considered Byrum. I'd flown to Missouri to check out half a dozen possible towns. In a couple places, fabric stores were up for sale, and in the others—" She shook her head. "It doesn't matter. That day at the grocery store, it took me a minute to recognize her, because her hair wasn't blond the first time I saw her, but then it came to me. We were in Trenton. This café was really full, and she was nice enough to tell me I could sit at her table. We chatted while we ate, just, 'oh, are you a tourist' kind of stuff. You know."

But they'd talked long enough for Nadia to recognize Corinne…how much later?

"When was this?" he asked.

"It was over a year ago."

She had confirmed what his intuition was telling

him. Corinne's alibi for her aunt's death had always bothered him. A woman who, from all reports, rarely traveled, just happening to visit the Big Apple the weekend her aunt was murdered. But her friends had insisted she was with them, and the airline had confirmed her flights.

Seeing his expression, Nadia said, "I kept a, well, sort of a diary. Notes about possibilities I spotted online, my trips to scout them out—that kind of thing. I'd have to look at it to tell you exactly when I was in Trenton."

Had Corinne *driven* back and forth from New York? Or, now that he knew where to look, would he be able to prove she'd taken a bus or train to get home for a day or two? Trenton made a nice stopover—just far enough away from Byrum, she'd be unlikely to run into anyone she knew, but also an easy drive. Into town, push aunt down the stairs, confirm she was dead, out of town.

"You think…?" Nadia said.

"I do think."

"So…if we hadn't happened to meet in the store that day…"

Ben shook his head. "You'd have met another time. This isn't that big a town. She had a shock running into you and finding out that, of all people in the world, *you* were the one who bought her aunt's building and business. But I imagine it was the theft that sent her into panic mode. I was investigating you, asking a lot of questions. I'd made it plain I wouldn't give up on her aunt's death. Because you bought that building, there was a connection. She had to know that if you mentioned her even in passing, I'd jump on it."

"That's it, then." Nadia sounded numb now. "She

tried to kill me, an almost complete stranger, on the chance that I might blow her alibi."

"I'm afraid so."

Misery apparent, Nadia pulled back a little, even tugging at her hand, but he didn't let go.

"I'm sorry. I mean, about Lucy. You were right. She *should* have stayed away from me."

This was probably the strangest of times for him to feel a smile forming, but he couldn't seem to stop it. "You know what she said to me, when they were wheeling her from the ER to surgery?"

Eyes big and luminous, Nadia shook her head. She'd hung back when he walked beside his sister down the hall to the elevator. Ignoring the orderly pushing the bed, Lucy had grabbed his hand. Her eyes had been doing whirligigs—Ben guessed they'd already given her a painkiller—but she had still managed to project fierce determination.

"Lucy told me not to dare blame you. She also said—" his voice thickened "—that she was glad you hadn't gotten shot again."

He didn't tell Nadia that the last thing his sister had mumbled was, "Only fair to spread it around."

"I still feel—"

"Don't." Ben pulled until she was leaning against him, her head resting on his chest. With the wooden arm of the chair denting his ribs and probably hers, too, the embrace wouldn't last long. But he had to hold her. He'd have lifted her onto his lap if the chance of someone walking in on them hadn't been so good.

Nadia said something he didn't catch. He rubbed his cheek against her already disordered hair. "What?"

"She's the best friend I've made here. I wish she didn't have to go home."

That let him ease his grip. He nuzzled her temple. "I kind of doubt she has any intention of leaving Byrum."

Nadia lifted her head. "But you don't want her to stay."

"I'd love to have her live here. My fear is that the Amish were the draw for her, and that she might make some decisions for the wrong reasons."

"I really don't think…"

"I don't, either." He smiled at her. "Quit worrying."

Her eyes shimmered, and for a moment he was afraid she'd cry, but instead she said, "It wouldn't be the end of the world if she and Jacob hooked up, would it?"

Ben laughed. "Do you think that's how he'd put it? *Hey, babe, wanna hook up?*"

Nadia giggled—just as Ben heard a soft footfall. The graying surgeon in his green scrubs, face mask pushed below his chin, stepped into the small room.

"Lucy is in recovery," he said briskly. "We had no difficulty getting the bullet out, and the damage is less than we feared. I'll be surprised if she isn't ready to go home tomorrow, the next day at the latest. Oh—I saved the bullet for you."

The bullets from Nadia's shooting were already in the evidence room. Ben had no doubt that they would match up with the Marlin Model 336 hunting rifle Corinne had carried. The shell casings she hadn't had a chance to pick up tonight might well have her fingerprints on them, too.

"Thanks," he said huskily. "When can we see her?"

"I'd suggest tomorrow morning. Sleep is what she needs."

Ben hesitated, but finally nodded. He felt drained himself. "You have my number."

"Yes." The surgeon nodded at both of them and strode away.

After a moment, Nadia said, "I'm glad we didn't have the same surgeon. He'd be really wondering about us right now."

Ben's chuckle left him feeling loose. "He'd figure it was all in the family."

Her eyes widened in what he was afraid was shock. Did that mean she wasn't ready for what he had in mind?

As they walked out to the car, he called his parents, getting his father this time, who in his usual way received the good news with a long silence. Call over, Ben said to Nadia, "I asked for your window to be boarded up—"

"Déjà vu," she muttered.

His mouth quirked. "—but I'd like it if you'd come home with me tonight."

"Yes. Please." And Nadia tucked her hand in his.

Emotion swelled in him, complex, painful and good. Since he'd started his freshman year in college, an eighteen-year-old boy who didn't yet know his big sister would be brutally raped a year later, he wouldn't have used the word *happy* to describe himself. *Happy*, he discovered now, was no longer the same, simplistic concept…but it was powerful.

NADIA SHOWERED IMMEDIATELY, frantic to wash the blood off. The sharp scent made her want to gag. Ben had promised to find her something to wear. Toweling herself dry, she discovered his idea of *something* was one of his T-shirts. Period.

She emerged from the bathroom to find him waiting in the hall, leaning against the wall. The sight of him in nothing but low-slung sweatpants made her cramp with longing.

Ben made a rough sound in his throat and straightened. Nadia walked right into his arms, her head against his shoulder.

"When I heard that gunshot…" His voice broke. "I was so scared. Not knowing which of you had been shot, how bad you were hurt—"

"If you hadn't gone after her, we still wouldn't know who and why. I'd still be in danger."

"I know." His arms tightened. "But it killed me to leave you two to cope on your own."

Eyes burning, Nadia nodded. She thought she knew what he was telling her, but believing, that was something else. He wasn't the kind of man she had ever imagined herself loving, and especially not after her terrible exposure to violence. But there had been something between them from the beginning. The search of her shop and apartment would have been humiliating under any circumstances. She'd have been angry. But the hurt that seemed to tear her open…that had been because it was *Ben* who suspected her, *Ben* who was callous enough not to care what he was putting her through.

She had believed she could never forgive him.

And yet, here they were.

He let out a long, ragged breath. Nadia lifted her head to meet his eyes.

A muscle twitched in his cheek. "You know I'm in love with you." Just like that, he had bared himself.

The uncertainty Nadia saw on his face shook her. Still, she heard herself saying, "We haven't known each other that long," but knew perfectly well that she was pushing back against herself as much as him. Even so, she laid an open hand on his scratchy jaw.

"That's true." As always, those dark eyes saw deep, increasing her unsettling sense of vulnerability. "When we met at the auction, you flipped a switch in me," he said huskily. "But I could see I scared you, so I tried to convince myself to give you some time before I stopped by at your store." He mocked himself with a twisted smile. "I might have lasted a whole week."

"You're so intense." She wasn't sure how else to explain her reaction. "I looked at you and *knew* you were fully capable of exploding into violence." Eyes stinging again, she pressed a kiss to his throat. "The next morning, you made me feel safe instead."

He lifted one hand to massage her nape.

"Until I blew it," he murmured.

"Yes." But her thoughts blurred.

"I had to investigate you."

"I know." She squirmed.

"Nadia. Will you look at me?"

She went completely still for an instant, then tipped up her chin.

"If you decide not to stay in Byrum, I won't, either." His jaw tightened. "No, I don't plan to turn into a stalker. But...I want to be with you."

Struck speechless, Nadia gaped at him.

His eyes burned. "I need to know how you feel about me. And I mean it. Anywhere you want to go."

Some chances in life, you had to take.

"I want to stay. At least…to see how it goes. And if the atmosphere stays too ugly for me to feel at home, I hope we'll make a decision together about where we should go." She took a deep breath for courage, even as his expression changed. "I love you, too."

For what had to be ten seconds, he only stared at her, as if he really had thought she might reject him, or say, *Hey, you're moving too fast.* The next thing she knew, he swept her up and carried her into his bedroom.

"I WISH PEOPLE would quit apologizing!" Nadia exclaimed two weeks later. "It's horribly awkward, and I'm afraid they're ending up so embarrassed they'll slink around avoiding me forevermore."

Ben laughed at both the sentiment and her choice of words. "You don't feel even a *little* secret pleasure when they're groveling?"

She tried to frown at him, but the effort wasn't convincing. Finally she sighed. "Okay, sometimes."

Lucy appeared from the kitchen with a basket of cookies from the Hadburg Café. She'd gone earlier today to scope out the shopping in a smaller town, she had told them. If she'd explained what stores she'd visited or what she'd bought, Ben had tuned her out. The cookies were a bonus, though. "Julie Baird," she said now, taking her seat.

"No." He looked at Nadia. "Really?"

"Really." She made a face. "She even did it graciously."

Lucy rolled her eyes. "Because in her egocentricity she had no doubt you'd accept even more graciously and all would be forgiven and forgotten."

Ben reached for a cookie. Oatmeal raisin. "Kills the idea of *forevermore*."

She made a face. "Unfortunately."

"She told us how much she admired the online campaign for the Hixsons and other people." Which had, to date, brought in over ninety thousand dollars and was still going strong. Lucy gave a small, feminine snort. "She was sure she could help."

"What did you say?" Ben asked Nadia.

"I told her that I'm not really involved in the effort—" which she wasn't, since Colleen, Lucy and Rebecca Byler had run with it "—but that I'd let Colleen know she was interested in case they ever felt they needed more input."

"A polite 'thanks, but no thanks.'" He took a big bite of cookie.

"She couldn't hide her surprise." Lucy's smile brimmed with satisfaction. "With luck, she won't be back."

"I don't think she was ever really interested in quilting." Nadia took a cookie, too. "What she does enjoy is being in charge. She'll find some other cause."

Ben said, "I saw Jim Wilcox today when I stopped by the hospital to check on the motorcyclist who hit the overpass embankment."

Both women nodded. In a town this size, everyone would hear about a serious accident within a matter of hours, even if they never turned on a television or radio.

"How was he?" Lucy asked. "The guy on the motorcycle, not Jim."

"Hasn't regained consciousness. Doctor is still hopeful, though."

His sister nodded.

"Jim and I crossed paths in the parking lot. He was

stunned. Maybe this isn't news to you two, but Bishop Josiah and Roy Yoder—" He stopped. "Did you know he's a minister along with running the cabinet-making business?"

Nadia nodded as Lucy said, "Hannah has said so."

"Anyway, they sat Jim down and said they have agreed among themselves to take care of the hospital and doctor bills for his little girl, just as they would for a member of their faith. He has dealt fairly with them, the bishop said, and should not have to face such a burden alone."

"Oh, thank goodness." Tears shimmered in Nadia's eyes. "Hannah said her father agreed to talk to the others, but I hadn't heard what they'd decided. That has to be a staggering amount of money!"

Ben grimaced in agreement. "Jim was surprised to find they had a good idea of how much it would amount to. I reminded him that the Amish undergo extensive surgeries and medical procedures, too. They're not naive. After telling me, Jim, ah, broke down and cried, and I'm guessing it wasn't for the first time."

"His own church members are pitching in, too," Lucy contributed. "Colleen attends the same church. They're taking meals to the family, and have raised over ten thousand dollars so far to help with bills. Maybe now he can use that money for the mortgage or whatever else he's behind on."

Ben chased the last of the cookie with coffee. "His problems aren't over, but he has a chance now."

"Him and the Hixsons." Nadia used her napkin to dab at her eyes. "I don't know why I keep crying. It's just…"

When she failed to come up with an explanation

he filled it in for her. "Happy endings get to you." For that instant, he'd almost forgotten his sister was in the room. It was Nadia he saw, with her perplexity and joy.

Her face lit. "Yes!"

There *were* happy endings all around them. People were too often small-minded, selfish, even mean. But he was learning that they were also capable of coming together, of forgiveness and sacrifice, which made him feel better about staying on in Byrum.

The barn raising at Leonard Hixson's place was scheduled for next Friday and Saturday. Unless something came up at work, Ben intended to help at least one of the two days. He knew both Lucy and Nadia were involved in planning and preparing meals to feed the volunteers, in the way of the Amish who used work "frolics" as a social gathering, too.

The Hixsons had already moved back to their property, thanks to the donation of an old manufactured home. They planned to stay in it for the time being, and use the donated funds to buy the equipment dairy farming required.

The decision had been made to get the Hixsons back on their feet before moving on to raising money for another family. Their loss was the greatest. Some of the other victims had received insurance payouts, and a number of organizations were contributing to the rebuilding.

While Ben's parents were here, they'd driven out to survey the tornado damage. Before leaving three days ago, his dad told them he had kicked in ten thousand dollars to the Hixson dairy farm fund.

"So, I have an announcement," Lucy said suddenly.

The other two looked at her.

"I got a job. I'm going to be working for Hannah's dad, in the cabinet shop. They've gotten busier and busier, and want someone to take over billing, answering phones, greeting people who come in. After Hannah went to work for Nadia, they thought they could do without her, but they're having trouble keeping up."

Ben was careful to hide his conflicted feelings about a job that would have her working closely with an unmarried Amish man she already counted as a friend. She'd have every right to slap him down if he so much as mentioned his concern, however. She was definitely an adult.

And, he reminded himself, happier than she'd been in a lot of years.

Nadia beat him with her congratulations, but he added his.

"I had an idea." It was Nadia his sister was now looking at. "I wondered if you'd rent your apartment to me."

Now *that* was a great idea.

She blinked a couple of times, then turned her gaze on him. "Ben?"

Why did she sound as if she wasn't sure what he wanted?

He took her hand in his. He paused. This wasn't the usual way to do this, but why not? "I want us to start planning a wedding."

The tiny gasp from his sister was easily ignored. He stayed focused on Nadia, who had gone completely still. She might not even be breathing, but she searched his face with those haunting eyes.

After a moment, she gave a small nod, as if she'd seen everything she needed to. "Yes." Her smile felt like the sunrise, glorious and hopeful. "I love you."

"I love you, too," he said, voice scratchy. Didn't matter how many times he told her that. Every time, his rib cage constricted his breathing.

Then Nadia smiled at Lucy. "I would love to have you in the apartment."

His sister's delight tightened the squeeze around Ben's chest.

He wouldn't cry, but happy endings got to him, too. Something about himself he'd never known.

Not minding Lucy's presence, he pulled Nadia from her chair and kissed her.

* * * * *

We hope you enjoyed
these two stories.

Look for more great

Amish reads in the

HARLEQUIN

section of the

WALMART

book department!

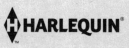

Save $1.00

on the purchase of any
Love Inspired®,
Love Inspired® Suspense or
Love Inspired® Historical book.

Redeemable at Participating Walmart Outlets.

---- ✂ --

Save $1.00

on the purchase of any Love Inspired®, Love Inspired® Suspense
or Love Inspired® Historical book.

Coupon valid until September 30, 2017.
Redeemable at Participating Walmart Outlets. Limit one coupon per customer.

52614822

65373 00076 2 (8100)0 12279

nd ™ are trademarks owned and used by the trademark owner and/or its licensee.

2017 Harlequin Enterprises Limited

LIINC1COUP0617

Will a pretend courtship fend off matchmaking mother
or will it lead to true love?

Read on for a sneak preview of
THEIR PRETEND AMISH COURTSHIP,
the next book in **Patricia Davids**'s
heartwarming series, **AMISH BACHELORS**.

"Noah, where are you? I need to speak to you."

Working near the back of his father's barn, Noah
Bowman dropped the hoof of his buggy horse Willy, took
the last nail out of his mouth and stood upright to stare
over his horse's back. Fannie Erb, his neighbor's younger
daughter, came hurrying down the wide center aisle
checking each stall as she passed. Her white *kapp* hung
off the back of her head dangling by a single bobby pin.
Her curly red hair was still in a bun, but it was windblown
and lopsided. No doubt, it would be completely undone
before she got home. Fannie was always in a rush.

"What's up, *karotte oben*?" He picked up his horse's
hoof again, positioned it between his knees and drove in
the last nail of the new shoe.

Fannie stopped outside the stall gate and fisted her
hands on her hips. "You know I hate being called a carrot
top."

"Sorry." Noah grinned.

He wasn't sorry a bit. He liked the way her unusual
olet eyes darkened and flashed when she was annoyed.
nnoying Fannie had been one of his favorite pastimes
hen they were schoolchildren.

Framed as she was in a rectangle of light cast by the
rly-morning sun shining through the open top of a
utch door, dust motes danced around Fannie's head like
eflies drawn to the fire in her hair. The summer sun had
xpanded the freckles on her upturned nose and given her
in a healthy glow, but Fannie didn't tan the way most
omen did. Her skin always looked cool and creamy. As
ual, she was wearing blue jeans and riding boots under
r plain green dress and black apron.

"What you need, Fannie? Did your hot temper spark
fire and you want me to put it out?" He chuckled at his
vn wit. He along with his four brothers were volunteer
embers of the local fire department.

"This isn't a joke, Noah. I need to get engaged, and
iickly. Will you help me?"

Don't miss
THEIR PRETEND AMISH COURTSHIP
by Patricia Davids, available June 2017 wherever
Love Inspired® books and ebooks are sold.

www.LoveInspired.com

Save $1.00

on the purchase of any
Love Inspired®,
Love Inspired® Suspense or
Love Inspired® Historical book.

Redeemable at Participating Walmart Outlet

Save $1.00

on the purchase of any Love Inspired®, Love Inspired® Suspense or Love Inspired® Historical book.

Coupon valid until September 30, 2017.
Redeemable at Participating Walmart Outlets. Limit one coupon per customer.

52614822

5 65373 00076 2   (8100)0 12279